"A fun and sexy romp! Kit Brennan's heroine, Lola Montez, is irresistible—even more so because she's historically-based. *Whip Smart* is a wonderful debut. Brennan really knows how to tell a story. I can't wait for the sequel."

—Gywn Cready, RITA award-winning author of
Timeless Desire: An Outlander Love Story

whip smart

Lola Montez Conquers the Spaniards

kit brennan

This is a work of fiction. All characters and events portrayed in this novel are either fictitious or are used fictitiously.

WHIP SMART: LOLA MONTEZ CONQUERS THE SPANIARDS
Astor + Blue Editions LLC

Copyright © 2012 by Kit Brennan

All rights reserved, including the right to reproduce this book or portions thereof, in any form under the International and Pan-American Copyright Conventions. Published in the United States by:

Astor + Blue Editions, LLC
New York, NY 10003
www.astotandblue.com

Publisher's Cataloging-In-Publication Data

BRENNAN, KIT WHIP SMART: LOLA MONTEZ CONQUERS THE SPANIARDS—1st ed.

ISBN: 978-1-938231-47-6 (paperback)
ISBN: 978-1-938231-46-9 (epdf)
ISBN: 978-1-938231-45-2 (epub)

1. Women's Historical Romance—Fiction 2. Fiction 3. Inspired by Life of Eliza Gilbert; aka Lola Montez—Fiction 4. High Adventure, High Romance—Fiction 5. Sex and Flirtation—Fiction 6. Danger and Romantic History (19th Century England, France and Spain) I. Title

Book Design: Bookmasters
Jacket Cover Design: Danielle Fiorella

For Andrew—always.
And for Punch.
In loving memory of my beautiful mother, Beth B. Watters Morley.

FOREWORD

Lola Montez blazed like a fiery meteor shower throughout a decade and a half in the middle of the Victoria era, and because she was unquenchable in a time when women were not allowed to be so, her reputation turned notorious. Her adventures were remarkable; the places she traveled and the people she met (and loved, and fought) were legendary.

This novel is based on the truth and peppered with lies—much like the real Lola's own life. Although a number of excellent biographies deal with the facts and put straight many of the fictions about this extraordinary woman, none of them have been able to unearth exactly what she did during the trip she made to Spain in the summer of 1842, before her splashy arrival in London in the spring of 1843. When she left for Madrid, she was Eliza Gilbert; upon her return, she was someone brand new. What happened to her during those months in hot, rebellious Spain?

My version of events explores this alluring gap of time—and the exquisite bravado of a twenty-two-year-old beauty caught up in dangerous political undercurrents and intrigues.

The Début—1843

"Tell us in your own words." The small, elegantly dressed man speaks.

The Cockney pulls up a chair and seats himself after a quick glance at the other man. Obviously the dandy is the one in charge.

"This evening was a very important night for me, gentlemen," I begin carefully. "You have no idea how dangerous this intruder is. In my country, he is a murderer!"

"We agree there is danger." The miniscule man's accent is a mystery to me. It is not English, nor Irish, nor Scottish. It is Continental—but from where? Not Spanish or Italian . . . not German. It worries me.

"Are you from the police?" I ask, my chin high, about to take offence—or at least to seem so.

"We're askin' the questions," the big Cockney purrs, leaning closer and giving me a head-to-toe lick with his eyes.

My usual bravado has been given a jolt, and I realize that I'm frightened, which makes me more so. There was shocking manhandling and a stumbling drag through the streets, into the mouth of a building, and down hallways; both the Cockney and I are still puffing from the struggle. And now this room reveals nothing. I have no idea where they've taken me; it could be anywhere. The paneling on the walls of the room is solid, a dark burnished wood, and the hangings are rich brocade. But here are only two chairs and a lumpy settee, and one candelabra with three tapers burning, nothing else. Not a soul in the world knows that I'm here.

"Right from the top of the evening, if you would, madam."

"Señora," I correct the small European. No response, not a flicker. "My friend, the Earl of Malmesbury—a member of Parliament, as I'm sure you know—was in attendance tonight." I want them to understand I have friends in high places, even if that friend . . . Don't think it, don't let it show. Their faces remain impassive. Well, I can play at that as well as any man, I think, as a jolt of fury fizzes through my veins and prickles out to the ends of my fingers. They wouldn't expect a lash and a sting! I long to deliver it. But, of course, this sort of behavior is always my downfall.

Calm, Lola, give nothing away.

What to tell them? Images from the evening jostle for attention: Well-dressed people in the street outside, descending from carriages, smoking cheroots. Inside, a turmoil of men shifting scenery, the sound of singers warming up in their underground lair. The stage doorman's whispered caution—policemen had been around, asking questions; there'd been another murder.

Then, waiting in the wings, an eye to the peekhole: Every seat taken, the royalty box full! Check the backstage mirror in its ornate frame—tight black velvet bodice, dark red and violet skirt, soft red shoes. I look remarkable! Stagehands scurry to bring in my backdrop, set up the folding screen, then away into the wings left and right. The first bars of music—my cue to wrap myself in the black lace mantilla, take a firm hold of the castanets. The stage manager signaling, the curtain rising. I step out into the lights.

That moment of connection! Then something else takes over. The performance itself is a blur of absorption, with the earl yelling support and his friends joining in. My signature dance, my own creation: *El Oleano*. The story is simple. I enter, a young girl in a meadow enjoying the sunshine, picking the flowers. But there's a large spider's nest down stage left. I don't see the nest, and I step upon it—thousands of little spiders have just been born. They climb my skirts; they're everywhere! Sudden whirling, twirling energy—get them out!—and then I turn. I see it in my mind's eye: the enormous parent spider! I leap towards it, and oh the stamping and crushing that ensues! A rivulet of sweat runs from my temple to land on my breast. Hair flying, sheer animal pleasure surging through me; in the dance I am transformed into sheer movement—no past or future, just these delicious sensations.

The curtain descends with a thud; on the other side, the syncopated, muffled sound of approval, like the beginnings of a rain storm, slow at first and then enormous; the theatre swept with round after round of applause. They love me, I think, I can scarcely believe it! The curtain rises and, thanks to the earl, flowers are landing upon the stage. The audience is requesting an encore—it's a triumphant début, in London, in England! At Her Majesty's Theatre, before royalty and nobility! And then . . .

I gasp, suddenly confused. The spell is broken.

"Madam?" the small man pounces with the word.

Spit it out, Lola, then brave it out.

"My performance was perfection. Then out of nowhere, that devil began to scream his vile lies."

The Cockney enjoys repeating them for me. "'She's a hoax, a fraud. How can anyone be fooled?' Ain't that what 'e said?"

The memory makes me cover my eyes and shiver from head to foot—the shape of a man moving swiftly along a row of seats, causing others to cry out as he pushes past with that high, angry voice.

"He then claimed, 'That's not Lola Montez,'" the European adds. "'Her name is Eliza Gilbert, formerly known as Mrs. James, as many of you men know. She's a fraud and an adulteress.' I believe those were the exact words."

I stare at him in horror.

"Tell us wha' you did then." The Cockney grins, clambering to his feet. "I love this part."

Again with my fear comes a spurt of anger. Don't you toy with Lola Montez. Don't dare bully me, you turds!

"I did what any professional would have done," I say. "The orchestra leader was looking up at me, astonished, so I waved at him to go on."

Yes, he raised his baton, my music began again, and I stepped behind the folding screen. To catch my breath, to ask myself, who is this *bastardo* trying to ruin my triumph? The hysterical voice began yelling again, and suddenly I recognized it! Before I knew what I was doing, I'd bent down and ripped off my shoes, reached to my thighs to unclip my garters, yanked the stockings from my legs, and stepped out again from behind the screen. In my head was an explosion of hot, red light, the flame of realization: I may know your obscene secrets, you fiend, the ones you hissed into my brain, but I also know exactly what you fear! So I danced again, I danced *El Oleano* barefoot and barelegged! I danced that *araña repulsivo* right out of the theatre! I leapt and stamped, naked legs flashing. Ladies were screaming and trying to get out of their seats; husbands covered their ladies' eyes while peering, bulgy-eyed, themselves. There was such a hubbub I could barely hear the music, but as the hideous shape slithered out the auditorium doors, I was inspired by a wild jubilation. Flinging my skirts back and forth in flamenco style, I shook my hips and my castanets, dancing towards the edge of the stage until the orchestra leader's eyes protruded in alarm, thinking I was about to drop upon him. Arching my back, I ripped the mantilla from my head and shook my tresses loose to cascade over my shoulders in a dark mass. The curtain fell, just missing me, the orchestra came to an abrupt, wheezy halt, and my encore was over.

I clear my throat, about to speak proudly of my victory, but in that very second the reality of the fiend's reappearance strikes: My God, I understand. He's found me out and come to kill me! And then, in horror: Are these the devil's henchmen? Give nothing away!

The Cockney, who's been pacing, reaches down to clamp my dirty bare left foot in a frightening grip. "I've never seen a woman dancin' with bare legs and flashin' 'er skirts—thought I'd died and ended in 'eaven!" He is laughing.

"Be silent," the other admonishes, turning back to me. "Tell me, madam, what do the words of the intruder—"

"The madman!" I pant. "The hound from hell!"

"—what do his words mean? Before leaving the theatre, he said you are wanted as a spy and that the Spanish government will pay handsomely—dead or alive." The three final words rip again through my vitals.

I yank my foot from the Cockney's grasp. The vile man is now jiggling a knife he's pulled from somewhere. "Yer luvly performance and yer luvly bare legs," he coos, "they're very distractin', but we need to know more." The yellow glimpse of his incisors is not encouraging.

Jesus, Mary, and Joseph, I'm shuddering like a dish of jellied eels. "What in God's name do you want of me?" The hair is rising on the back of my neck as another dreadful thought strikes: *Are* they toying with me; warming me up and then—?

"The truth," the Cockney is saying, "even the bits you don' unnerstan'."

The dapper one rises swiftly and moves towards me. I cry out and lunge away, but he pins me back into the chair.

"Calm down, we haven't hurt you. What did he mean by 'spy'? And why do they want you 'dead or alive'?"

"I don't know who 'they' are!" I cry. "It's only the madman who wants me dead! It's such a terrifying story, you would never believe it!"

He lets go of me, sits again, then steeples his fingers and waits, motionless. The Cockney begins pacing around behind my back, which makes my scalp prickle again.

"I cannot place you, madam," the dandy muses. "What we saw tonight is not the dance of a dignified widow."

"You're wrong! It is the dance of a heartbroken *Spanish* widow, the devastated survivor of her hero's tragic death!" Saying this, the shock of everything that has happened in the past six months cascades in upon me—and nearer still, the assassination and treachery, which is so appalling that I don't know how to bear it. My fearless rebel! My mask of bravery is slipping, and a sob bursts from me.

He watches silently as I struggle to bring myself under control. Then, "You're a performer, that is very clear."

Liar—you dog! My heart is beating like a sledgehammer and will surely break. I can barely hear the man's soft, measured voice above my agitated thoughts.

"You see, young lady, and this is very important: We think you know something you don't know that you know. And we're concerned for your health. For your . . . life. Do you understand?"

The Cockney smacks his lips. "Almost relives it, she does, tears an' all."

"Mmm . . . There's a thought." The dandy comes to some decision. "Doña Lola, listen to me carefully. Take your mind back to the beginning of your 'terrifying story', to how it started. Think through everything that's happened. We know what we're looking for; you don't."

The Cockney's breath is hot up against my neck. "Give it to us, very pretty. Jus' like you."

"Here's what's going to happen, Lola Montez, or whoever you are," the elegant one says with finality. "We're going to leave you here to calm yourself. You won't be able to escape, so don't bother trying. Put it all straight in your head. Every detail. And in the morning, you will tell it to us, sedately, with no histrionics."

"Yer life depends on it," adds his genial chum.

"How can I know what to tell you if I don't know who you are?" I quaver, trying to remain strong, the brave Spanish widow. "Are you from the government? The military? The . . . the church?" I manage to get this out, but just barely.

The small man's eyes go hooded, and the Cockney sucks his teeth. I am cold all over.

"How do I know I can trust you?" I persist.

"We don't know that we can trust you," the European says. "Think it through. We'll leave you now."

And they do.

I have no idea whose side they are on.

The minute they're gone and their footsteps can no longer be heard, I leap to my feet and dart around the room, checking everything—the paneling, behind the wall hangings, the floor boards. The door is locked fast, as they said it would be. There are no windows. Everything is stale and dusty, as if the air hasn't been disturbed for a very long time. Why oh why did I return to ghastly old England? I hate the place, it's always been bad luck! I could kick myself, so I kick the paneling, hard and repeatedly. I should have gone to America, I curse. The land of liberty, assertiveness, and impulsiveness! A country of free men, where women shoot pistols while riding astride. If I ever get out of this, I swear I will get to America, leave this detestable land of boiled milk and blood pudding once and for all, and never look back!

I collapse onto the settee, holding my head. My body's exhausted from the night's dancing and from the fear. I'm also suddenly hungrier than I can remember—and I've been through some hungry times in recent months.

There are three candles burning, but no others that I can see. With misgiving, but resolve, I blow two of the candles out. Then I sit again. I fear the coming dark almost as much as the men's return.

How can I tell them everything? There is so much I cannot tell, under any circumstances. When there's so much to conceal, I'm afraid to say anything, afraid I'll be caught in my lies.

But no. That's the reasoning of a frightened little girl. Everything that has come before has led me to this, to the new life I've created for myself. I put my hands to my hot cheeks, considering my options. And my resolve begins to rise again: After all, there's no going back. That story is dead; this one's alive. I have a quick mind and a certain wit. I'm young, I'm strong. Like a cat, thrown from a four-story building, I can twist and turn and land on my legs. That's my luck and my talent; it's what I'm good at.

My lost year in Spain . . . Can I bear to remember?

I let the shadows from the flickering candle paint the scene, searching, selecting, giving myself courage as my lover might: It's a game of chance, and I must shuffle the cards.

It Began in London

I'd arrived back in London from Scotland in the middle of May, just one year ago, in desperate need of money and no longer able to turn to my long-suffering stepfather. Yes, at twenty-two, I'd burned that bridge beyond a doubt; my mother never wished to hear from me again. What was open to a young woman of my reduced means? Not very much that was appealing: Governess? Hideous. Lady's companion? Perish the thought. I'd heard rumors of women on the continent who spent their lives pleasing men, but didn't fancy it. What if the man was not to your liking? I'd just escaped from that exact torment and wasn't eager to put my neck in the rope again any time soon. The person I was most keen to emulate, and quickly, was the famous Madame Vestris, though the theatre was not my world and I didn't know exactly how to go about becoming part of that milieu. But I wanted it. Needed it.

I took myself to George Lennox's lodgings as soon as I'd found rooms for myself. George had been a revelation in bed after Thomas, my erstwhile husband. I'd thought George and I were made for each other. I'd thought we had a future. Of course he'd never told his wealthy parents about me, nor anyone else in his life that mattered. Just his theatre friends and club mates, the jolly riffraff he collected.

He was at home—this time, alone. And very surprised to see me.

"Don't worry, George, I'm not here for you," I said, swanning into his drawing room and flinging my reticule down on the chair upon which I'd found him bouncing the fat, white ass of a third-rate actress named Angel six months before. "I need a favour."

"Do you know your heel of a husband has sued me?" George retorted. "He's filed papers suing me for 'criminal conversation' with his wife—that is, with you."

I had to laugh at the legal euphemism.

"Well, he's suing me for divorce," I said. "When's your court date?"

"Middle of September."

"Mine is earlier. I don't think I'll be here."

"For God's sake, Rosie."

"I'm serious—and don't call me that."

"Where've you been, anyway?"

"Mouldering in Scotland with my damned relatives, no thanks to you," I snapped. "I need the name of the very best teacher in London, George. Acting teacher. And don't you dare laugh."

It was all so hard to believe, standing there looking at him, that day of my return. The man I'd loved to distraction. I'd wasted my stepfather's present of a nest egg on him; George always seemed to be short when it came time to pay a bill. It had all ended when, planning his twentieth birthday celebration, I'd been tripping around for presents and edibles. I was close to his lodgings and needed a rest before our big night, so I'd stopped there. He was at his club—or so I thought. For a moment I didn't recognize the sounds coming from behind his door. My brain didn't take it in. I used the key, the door swung wide, and there at the end of the corridor was the coarse, slatternly actress George had taken me to meet one night after a musical play: Angel. Stark naked but for her boots, straddling a similarly naked George. My parcels tumbled to the floor, and before I knew what I was doing I'd grabbed up George's riding whip from his hall table, rushed towards them flourishing it, and walloped the blowsy slut across the shoulders several times. She fell backwards howling as George wrenched the whip from my hand. Angel scrabbled crab-like across the parquet towards her crumpled, abominable clothing.

"You filthy, lying cad!" I'd screamed at him, and then advanced on the tart. "Put your clothes on and get out of my house!"

George grabbed my arm in a viselike grip. "Not your house, Rosie. Mine. I didn't expect you. Leave her alone."

I'd twisted away and grabbed up the whip again, but quick as a flash he'd held the end. We wrestled wordlessly, glaring into each other's eyes, 'til it snapped. Then I spat at him. And he—the rat, the louse—stood there, naked, his member still half stiff with unfinished business, my spit trickling from his cheek onto its tip, while Angel moaned away in the corner. Oh, I could have killed him. I could have died. I wish I had, one or either. And then he gutted me.

"Go away, Rosie," he'd said.

Just seeing him again, still handsome and still rich, I needed to hurt someone! Scream!

"Acting lessons, let me think . . ." He was musing away, stroking his sideburns, and I longed to give one a mighty yank. "Miss Fanny Kelly might do. She set herself up with her own theatre and school last year."

"Fanny Kelly?"

"Drury Lane, acted with Kean. Decades ago now."

I longed to give him another cut with a riding crop; his new one lay on the hall table. "Thank you for nothing." I retrieved my reticule and swirled past.

"You're a fine piece of horseflesh, Rosana. Keep your looks and you'll go far."

"And you're a provincial little stink-brain. Say hello to Mama."

Damnable man! Could all this peril and international skullduggery really have begun with that one suggestion for an acting teacher?

That balmy May, I knew that I had become a ravishing young woman. (I like to believe I still am, but after all I've been through . . . I won't think about that now.) My best features are my thick and lustrous blue-black hair, eyes that sparkle like sapphires, high, pert breasts, and the smallest of waists. I have an instep like no other—an asset for dancing—so arched that it appears almost tortured, though of course it is not. My legs are long, strong and shapely from years of riding and running about as a young savage in India—chasing monkeys up into the trees, riding my hairy pony at breakneck pace across the rifle range. My fingers are slim and elegant, my lips naturally full and dark crimson (particularly when I bite them). For these and other reasons, I had realized I must strike while the iron was hot, let nothing stop me from climbing as high as I could in as short a time as possible. But what was I wishing to climb towards? I wasn't too sure about that. I fancied fame, but wasn't sure why. I wished to be known for something, to excel at something, but I didn't know what. I yearned for love, but I was head shy, thanks to that cad George, though horses and men (for the most part) were high on my list of pleasures. I was a simple creature, I admit that, why not?

Miss Fanny Kelly's school was situated in Soho, on Dean Street. I strolled past and was lucky enough to spot the woman herself getting out of her carriage. She was showily dressed, obviously a woman of the arts, possessing confidence and gusto. A little given to fat, but not too much considering her age.

I booked an appointment for the following morning and dressed myself in my best turnout and bonnet. Miss Kelly saw me in her office, a commodious room on the second floor. She came swiftly to the point: "A guinea per hour is the fee." I couldn't help but gasp, but recovered by turning it into a delicate sneeze. "God bless you. Now stand."

I did so, and she went on, "Walk away from me, let me see you." I stalked rather self-consciously to the window, then wasn't sure what she wanted next. "Mmpf. Turn around—gracefully!" I suppose I hadn't.

"Now, take up the fan on the windowsill there. If I ask you to show anger, for example, while using the fan, how would you do so?" I snapped it open and fanned myself vigorously. "Oh dear. And jealousy?" I did so again, but with slightly less force. She was beginning to confuse me. "Put that down. Show me your best curtsy." I did, and she looked very severe.

"Now I would like to hear you recite. Use these lines," she snapped, and passed me a sheet of paper on which was written one of the Shakespeare sonnets.

I cleared my throat. "Shall I compare thee—"

"Oh, stop." She wasn't even looking at me. I was beginning to feel anger for real. "Try to modulate your voice—and separate your words. Go ahead."

And the grueling interrogation went on in this manner. Finally, Miss Kelly pulled a delicate pocket watch from inside her bodice and studied its face. "Your voice is . . . tiny. No potential for amplification whatsoever apparent. Your movements are jerky, unrefined. Yet I think you have something, some quality, which I cannot put my finger on. I will take you, twice a week, for two months. After that, we shall see." She held out her hand. "One guinea, then."

Now I had another difficult problem, thanks to Miss Kelly's exorbitant fee. I could no longer luxuriate (or equivocate) with scruples. This required a game plan—and the strategy of a marshal in the field.

I took myself to the dining room of one of the very finest hotels and asked to be seated at a prominent table. Then I busied myself with the contents of my reticule. A brace of gentlemen approached, one at a time, but were startled off by something or other. Then a man—smelling strongly of lavender—slid his well-dressed bottom onto the seat beside mine. "Excuse me, miss," he cooed, "but are you here on your own?"

This was so exactly what I had imagined might be said that I almost burst out laughing. I looked up and recognized a gentleman I'd seen several times before at the theatre; he had a kind face, a high colour, and a wicked light in his eyes. I admit I was extremely nervous when I answered, "I am here alone, yes. To my chagrin."

"Not any longer," said he, and leaned towards me. "Allow me to introduce myself. I am Lord James Howard Harris, 3rd Earl of Malmesbury. You may call me Howard."

"And I am Eliza Rosana Gilbert."

"Delightful."

He was a member of the House of Commons and a generous, happy peer. He'd only recently become both of those things: His wife had convinced him to cease his travels abroad and come home to "do something useful." Then his father died shortly thereafter. I liked him immediately because of his well-travelled outlook, his love of foreign ways and foreign foods. He was in the first flush of middle age and very pleased with himself. He ordered us a splendid meal, and I ate every scrap. I watched him devour his sweet and felt again the first tingles of anxiety as he licked his fingers clean, apologizing for his appetite.

"Not at all, I find it appealing in a man," I said.

"Will you find this appealing, I hope?" he replied. "I have a room on the fifth floor. Will you follow me there in, say, five minutes?"

Now I must make the leap, I thought. But what could I do? The die was cast. The waiters had already been observing me archly throughout the course of the meal. No time for a sudden burst of shyness now; it was too late for that, surely. But how to go about it? My heart was skipping around in my chest in trepidation. The marshal marshaled her forces. "I cannot think what you mean, sir. I am not one of those women."

"No, no, of course not. Forgive me for implying . . . The truth is, I happen to have a sweet necklace—mostly diamonds—that I have been visualizing all evening clasped around your little neck, to set off and enhance your many charms. May I please, Miss Eliza Rosana . . . ? Present it to you with my compliments?"

Probably a gift he'd purchased for his wife, to be presented upon his return to the country at the end of the week. Never mind, he could buy her another.

"I would be charmed to see it."

"Room five hundred and ten."

Ignoring the muted insinuations of the waiters, who spoke to each other behind their hands as I waited the five minutes, I was surprised to find myself so apprehensive. I'd never been to bed with a man so much older. I didn't know what to expect. Would I have to do all the work? Would it be embarrassing? What would his appearance be, naked? Outside his door, I hemmed and hawed; perhaps anticipating this, the earl opened the door before I even knocked and ushered me in. Then, we just looked at each other. A funny grin came over his face, and he stepped closer. "You are so very lovely, my dear," he said, and then he kissed me sweetly and deeply. His lips felt like those of a younger man, and soon I could hear that his breathing was accelerating like that of a much younger man. For my part, I felt shy, which was surprising—but also I was now intrigued. What would it be like?

"Eliza Rosana, may I make your intimate acquaintance?" he asked me.

That made me laugh, which felt good.

"I take that as a yes?" And he kissed me again, before turning me around and helping to unlace me. At every step of the unlacing, he murmured his admiration and kissed each new piece of me. It was really quite endearing. As I stepped out of my dress, like Aphrodite upon her clamshell, he stood still as a statue, drinking me in.

And then things sped up. Although rather stout, Howard could fling his clothes off with remarkable alacrity, and he took such noisy enjoyment in all the various remaining stages of necktie loosening, breeches unraveling, boot unscrambling, and so on that he had me laughing long before he lay me back on the bed. I find laughter a wonderful tonic in the bedchamber, and luckily he did too. It had been such a long time since I'd been with a man (all of the six lonely months I'd endured in Edinburgh) that I was soon energetically enthusiastic. Never mind the pretense of modesty, and real skittishness, that I'd begun with. I enjoyed the honesty of his protruding tummy, like that of a two-year-old playing in his washtub. Howard was a man well past the point of holding back because of some self-imposed vanity. He let himself be exactly who he was, running my dark hair through his hands and burying his nose in the scented locks, tickling my skin with the tips of his fingers, letting loose a yelp of joy when he experienced his pleasure, then holding me in his arms for a little sleep afterward, which he seemed to need and treasure. I found it all interesting and different; I was aroused, certainly, but not in the feverish way that George had incited. I wasn't called upon to race to a swift conclusion, as such—and so, in the contradictory way of these things, I enjoyed a lovely pleasure of my own, which reduced my jitters marvelously. And I adored the necklace, which he introduced with a flourish once we awoke from our nap. He asked me to sit up—I was still stark naked—and he reached to the bedside table, opening a velvet box. My first diamonds! He laid them carefully against my skin and did up the clasp. They were very cold, and then all at once as warm as my blood. I fell in love then and there; I never wanted to take them off. It turned out he had earrings to match, and before the end of that first evening I had them as well.

The next six weeks were busy. My trial date was set for August; Thomas was actually going through with the divorce. I could hardly credit it and was saddened when I considered that he really must have hated me. The earl remained obsessively discreet, so most of our subsequent meetings took place in my lodgings. He'd have large baskets of food and drink sent over beforehand; he would arrive after dark, trailing the night air and his sense of boyish pleasure in being bad.

And my days were full of Miss Kelly's bossiness. I'd had no idea that trying to become an actress was going to be such hard and tedious work. The lessons took place in her large, airy workroom, high above the street, with plenty of windows and a lovely smooth wooden floor. She was always carefully dressed, and so was I—as well as I could manage, that is. Some of my dresses were terribly out of date, since India has always been interminably behind the times when it comes to fashion, and my stepfather's Scottish relatives had done little to mitigate this situation on my behalf. This was an ongoing embarrassment to me, and several times I caught Miss Kelly looking me up and down with a Londoner's disdain.

Her favourite teaching tool was the work of Congreve, particularly *The Way of the World*. She was greatly enamoured of the fan.

"The women duel, too, Miss Gilbert, but verbally. Feel the thrust and parry of the words, and the literal pointing up—often with the fan—of the wit."

When I thought of fighting a duel, however, my body couldn't help but tense and long to physically rush about. "No!" she would cry. "Ladylike, ladylike! Far too much physicality."

"But what the character wants is aggressive!"

"Not for the women; that is not how they operate. Formality on the surface, hostility well hidden. Have you seen the Spanish women with their fans?" She snapped hers in my face. "All fan gestures to men have sensual implications, and the slower the movement the more intense the implication. Do you follow me?"

"Oh yes." My fan caressed the imaginary arm of a grandee, moving lower, and ending with a mischievous flick.

At this, she gave me quite the look. Perhaps it was this little indiscretion, this braggadocio, on my part that gave her the dastardly idea in the first place. The woman would do anything for money.

"Where were you raised?"

"Many places," I told her. "India."

"Aha. That odd, displeasing lilting—it is barbaric, stop it at once." She looked me up and down in a calculated manner. "Where else have you lived?"

Still hoping to impress, silly me, I lied, "Oh, Paris. *C'est joli!*" I'd been accustomed to fabricating, teasing provincial young girls during the many dreary years I'd lived at the Ladies' Boarding Academy in Bath, lonely and bored with my real life. At age twelve I'd declared I would go by Rosana because it had a Continental zing, and had severely exasperated the Misses Aldridge by refusing to answer any longer to Eliza.

"Spain?" Miss Kelly prodded.

"*Sí.* Seville for a summer, and of course Madrid." Pure invention.

"Then how can you be so dense about the power of the fan? Other than carnal, which you seem to understand all too well."

In the middle of the second month, Miss Kelly finally allowed me to play a scene, with herself as my partner. For reasons unknown to me, she had invited a strange little man with dyed jet-black hair and an appearance of being shriveled by the sun. She didn't bother to introduce us, just had him sit off to the side while we went at it, and being observed by this fellow, who contorted himself into excited shapes and squiggles (in turn grabbing his hair, covering his eyes while peeking through his fingers, then corkscrewing his legs around one another)—well, I failed the scene utterly.

"You cannot seem to grasp the first rule of the theatre, Miss Gilbert!" an exasperated Miss Kelly cried, flinging down her pages. "You do not actually *feel* this, you *portray* it! God in Heaven!"

"But I wish . . . I want . . ."

"Wishing and wanting will not bring it to you, girl. I give up, you are not an actress."

"But I must be something!" I began to tremble, horrified to have come so far and have spent so much only to be told I was terrible.

"You possess an impressive self-importance, this is true," the termagant continued. "A strong will. And an abnormally restless body. Perhaps you are a dancer. Although, since you have no training there, that is likely also an avenue that is closed to you. What do you think, Mr. Hernandez?"

The dark little gnome leapt to his feet and pointed one toe. "*Maravilloso*. I think she will do, Miss Kelly. She is *exactamente* what we—that is, *I*—am looking for."

"Good. Then I'll leave you." And without further ado, other than to take my guinea from me, my teacher swept off.

I was at a loss. Here I was, sweaty from effort, left to deal with this stranger who thought I would do. Do what?

"Do you speak Spanish, Miss Gilbert?" His thick accent drew out every vowel in a greasy manner, especially when he spoke my name.

"That is not one of my languages, I regret to say, monsieur."

"But you do speak languages?"

I wondered where this was leading. "Of course. French, impeccably. Latin, German. Hindi, including several dialects."

"I am a dancing master, Miss Gilbert. I teach the dances of my country, of *España*. Do you know the dances to which I am referring?"

I had a vague idea. Spain had been in the news a great deal during the past decade, with the so-called Carlist Wars and England's dithering attempts to support Spain's Queen Regent, who'd been ruling the country until her young daughter, Isabel, came of age. All I'd gathered at that point was that an upstart younger brother of the recently dead king believed *he* should be king, not the girl, because of some ancient law or other. The country had taken sides and civil war had ensued. I didn't understand the politics; it seemed horribly convoluted—still does, God knows.

"Do you teach the stamping step? I'm sorry, but I don't know the name."

"All of that," he answered eagerly. "Boleros, and cachuchas, fandangos. Refined versions, for the English palate. Not quite so . . . scandalous?" Why was he leering in that dreadful manner? "You have a mysterious past, Miss Gilbert," he continued. "There is something that you are running from?"

He was almost hissing the words now, his smooth accent making it all the more sinister. How did he know?

"And—may I say—you have the acquaintance of a particular aristocrat, a gentleman who has been more than kind to you in your hours of need?"

The little shit had been spying on me! I could think of no other explanation. He pointed his toes again, one after the other, with a mincing hop in between.

"I am like the English raven, Miss Gilbert. I keep my eyes open, and I fly very swiftly to deliver the news."

I really didn't like the sound of this. And Miss Kelly had effectively handed me over to this tiny dago, wiping her hands of me in an instant.

"Mr. Hernandez, I do not think that I am interested in your proposal."

"Miss Gilbert, I think that you must be. I shall teach you everything I know about the cachucha and flamenco, and in return you will meet a man who will introduce you to your destiny." He spoke in such an odd, affected way, and God knows his words were to prove both prophetic and dangerous. "What do you have to lose?"

I should have said "Everything" and run away as swiftly as I could. But I didn't. Truthfully, I didn't know what else to do, since my lessons in acting had ended so abruptly. And he'd made me the slightest bit curious—always a weakness. "Very well," I agreed with a haughty sniff. "I shall come to one lesson, and then I'll decide."

"*¡Maravilloso! ¡Buena fortuna!*"

✢ ✢ ✢

By this time it was late July, and my trial date was approaching steadily. I could have cried with exasperation at the money and time lost with Miss Kelly. Instead I sat down to enumerate my skills and talents, and the earl helped me lengthen this list when he arrived with a lovely set of peridot earbobs.

"Maybe this is what I am, in my natural state—a dancer." I was sitting up in bed, naked, eating a currant bun, wearing the earbobs and trying out the idea. My lovely earl had set me up in a tiny apartment near the theatre district and had spared no expenses on the softness of the mattress. Was I a kept woman? I tried not to think about that.

All things Spanish had become quite à la mode because of the recent Carlist skirmishes, and I certainly approved when the earl presented me with a long-fringed shawl and a cunning pair of fashionable shoes. I went to my first dancing lesson wearing them proudly. Hernandez made me take both off at once. I was given an old, dingy pair with steel heels, which clicked alarmingly when I walked. He also had a flounced skirt that he made me wear instead of my own, and we spent a good deal of this first lesson swinging those flounces just so. This turned out to be part of the stamping step, as I had called it—an integral element of flamenco. To my surprise, I enjoyed the whole thing a great deal because he encouraged me to rush around in circles, or click my heels up and down in an increasing rhythm and work up a passion, to not hold back and be ladylike. By the end of the session, I was using the fan liberally, not as a gesture but as a cooling agent, and I had begun to answer Hernandez's excited exclamations with a few of my own. "¡*Fabulosa!*" he'd squeak, and "¡*Deliciosa!*" I'd gasp back.

Several lessons and two weeks later, Hernandez seemed to have something on his mind. We proceeded as usual for the first thirty minutes, rushing around the front room in his second-floor apartment (which had been cleared of furniture, the better to teach his pupils in, I assumed). Then he asked me to take a *café solo* with him. We sat looking out his window at the street below while a diminutive young woman served us the thick, black coffee. "Your daughter?" I asked, once she had left us. "Wife," he corrected sternly. I still didn't like him very much, so I did not feel too humiliated by my blunder.

"Miss Gilbert," he finally said, "I have something to tell you which you may find of great interest." My mind raced: A theatre manager had heard of me already and was hoping to sign me? A person unknown had died and left me a huge sum of cash? Hernandez corkscrewed his legs and then unscrewed them immediately. "I have now heard from my superior in France, and, as I guessed, he is very concerned to see you face-to-face. He is a generous man; he will pay for your expenses to France, where he will tell you what he wishes you to do."

"Your superior? Wants me in France? Whatever for?"

"You are a very promising student of the Spanish dances, Miss Gilbert. You have the fire and the light in your eyes. I think you could be very successful, *sí*?"

This sounded exciting, and though I didn't quite trust him, I was intrigued.

"I also do not think you have much money." He placed his little wrinkled hand on mine. "My superior will—how do I say—*sponsor* your travel to Paris. He is not interested in you as a woman, let me assure you. Or . . . not only as a woman. As an associate."

How curious. How devilish. What on earth could he mean?

He went on to tell me that if the meeting were successful, this man would cover my further expenses to Spain, where I would live and study the language, the dances, and the customs, for as long as I wished to be there. "Or," he concluded, "to put it another way—for as long as you *need* to be absent from England." He thrust out his foot in its soft small shoe, examining the instep as he said, "Especially with August almost upon us. At His Majesty's Court of Arches?"

He knew about my divorce date! He knew when and where it would take place! This was terrible! Did he also know how fervently I longed to skip out, ignore it, run away? "I *really* have no idea what you are talking about, Monsieur Hernandez. Good day to you!" As I clattered down the steep flight of stairs to the street, still in his dingy steel-heeled shoes, my heart was greatly distressed. I looked up at the window and he twinkled his fingers in a secretive wave. I flew straight home, sending word to the earl at the House of Commons, where I knew he was in session: "Please come immediately. Dastardly plot. ERG."

When Howard Harris of Malmesbury arrived, I had worked myself into a lather. I hadn't told the earl about the impending divorce, but he certainly could see that I was shaken. He took a deep breath, retrieved an ice bucket with champagne and two glasses, and attempted to winkle from me the worst of it.

"You know I lived in India when I was a little girl?" Despite my agitation, I needed to tread carefully. I couldn't afford to lose the earl's good opinion. "Then my mother sent me back here, out of her way, to a school in Bath. At any rate, when I was sixteen, she arrived to return me to India to marry an old judge or something."

I didn't mention the unsavory details: her breaking the news of my impending future with the crustaceous judge, and the way I threw a fit. Furniture flying, vases smashed, screams and recriminations. I would have done anything to escape the hideous trap I could feel closing around me. My mother's new shipboard acquaintance, who kept hanging about—a certain Lieutenant Thomas James, home from India on convalescent leave—had begun escorting me to my academy and then back at the end of the day. True, he'd seemed initially keen on my married but flirtatious mama, but, well, what can one expect? I was sixteen, she was thirty. When he finally suggested, stammeringly, that we elope, I was ecstatic and said yes with a squeal of delight and the first deep-throated kiss I had ever attempted. It seemed to do the trick.

"I married Lieutenant Thomas James, instead," I told the earl. "It wasn't a rational thing to have done, and I soon regretted it."

"You didn't love him?"

"I didn't know what love was. We were cruel to each other—he drank too much and then slept like a boa constrictor. Oh, it was terrible." Quite a lot of champagne was spilled over the bed linens at this point, as Howard Harris tried to comfort me and I tried to pick and choose carefully the things I would admit to and the things I wouldn't dare reveal.

"Finally, after we'd arrived in India, married, and they could see for themselves, my mother and stepfather realized that the match was a disaster and if they didn't help me I would be forced to do something even more drastic. My stepfather, Major Craigie, gave me a bank draft for one thousand pounds to help me get established, and he and Thomas sent me back to England, to be met by Craigie's sister and taken to their parents in Edinburgh." Instead, cue the cad George, I thought to myself, but of course didn't say.

"My dear girl. What you have been through." I arrested the earl's roving hand at this point and tucked it away safely in his lap.

"The point is, you see . . ." I faltered. "I did not go with Aunt Catherine. I stayed in London. I ran through my funds—which is a disease very common to the purses of ladies who have never been taught the value of money—"

"And this is where I found you?"

I nodded plaintively. "Perhaps Thomas has met someone else," I sniffled, "but I am appalled at the idea of standing up in front of a judge, of being called a . . . Well, I don't know what. In public! I'm so ashamed—" And I wept stormily.

Certainly divorce is considered a dreadful blot, particularly for a woman. But ashamed? That was not quite true. Perhaps it's my upbringing—boarding schools, distant, uninterested mother, who knows—but it seemed so unfair that a stranger could pronounce judgment on me. Why should I have to stand up and be scolded by some ill-humoured, antique fart in a long wig? None of his business. Pooh on them all.

The earl's eyebrows were creased with concern. "And your dancing teacher . . . has found this out?"

"He wants me to go to France, meet some old duffer for some reason I don't understand, and then go on to Spain. They want me to do a few things for them, which sounds nefarious. He says they will pay all my expenses. But why?"

We mulled this over until Howard Harris became too distracted to be of much further use. When we were quiet again, and over another glass of the now-flat champagne, he said, "I know a fair amount about Spain's recent upheavals, Liza. You must be very careful, should you decide to go. The Spanish are devious and love nothing better than intrigue and revenge. The Neapolitans are the same. Years ago while in Naples I met Spain's then-future Queen Regent, María Cristina. She's still deeply loved in some circles. Do you know much about all of this?"

"Only the minimum."

His eyes were twinkling. "Cristina was tall, fair, and blue-eyed, and had stayed single until she was twenty-three because she was waiting for a suitor who would make her a queen. But she'd caused her father no end of worry since, like all Bourbons, she was highly coquettish. I was told, in fact, that some of her admirers had found themselves in jail for having too openly admired this royal tease."

The twinkle made me think he'd been one of those warned away.

"I happened to be there just as the announcement of the impending marriage to King Ferdinand of Spain was being arranged. I was introduced to her, and she truly was bewitching!"

I gave him a smack and he kissed me.

"Now, now. I was presented to her at court, and instead of casting down her eyes, she stared at me boldly, then took hold of one of the buttons on my uniform, to see, as she said, the inscription on it. Her mother, the queen, indignantly called to her to come along, but not before that tug had registered on a lower part of my anatomy and Cristina—the minx—knew it." That lower part began to rise again, just in memory. She must truly have registered in Malmesbury's imagination to cause such an elevation again so soon.

"The marriage took place, which was a great blow to the upstart brother Carlos's supporters. Cristina immediately became pregnant."

"What does this have to do with Señor Hernandez's offer?"

Malmesbury laughed and pulled me under the covers. He whispered into my ear, "You're not a political animal, are you, Liza? Cristina's baby was a girl. A few months later she was pregnant again—another girl. Then the king died suddenly of a violent bout of apoplexy, and the stage was set for chaos."

At this point, we indulged again in a little chaos of our own and emerged ravenous. I brought some comestibles back to the thoroughly destroyed bed and while we ate, the earl mused, "The war is over now, everything is tranquil. Before you turn this opportunity down, Liza, consider all of the amazing things you'd see and hear in Spain. You might have a chance to meet royalty—perhaps even some of the people I've just described. Royalty doesn't have to obey rules as you and I do. It makes them both interesting and dangerous."

I imagined this was true. I liked the rich. (I didn't know many of the obnoxious prats at the time.)

He threw a plum into his mouth and chewed its flesh hungrily. "What about this, then, sweetheart? What if I were to match the money offered by this mysterious stranger in France? Your court date will still proceed, even if you're not there to make an appearance. Unless of course you're planning to object to the charge?"

"Oh, no. I am not." From this I knew he suspected adultery was the incriminating factor. Did he think less of me for it?

"Well then." Juice was all over his chin, but this seemed no hindrance to his enthusiasm. "You're excited about your Spanish dancing lessons, and this way you'll be able to drink in the sights and sounds of Spain for yourself, firsthand. I admit I would be extremely interested to hear how the people, and the lovely Cristina, are faring. You could curtsy, eye her as boldly as she eyes you, and give her warm greetings from the 3rd Earl of Malmesbury. It would be fun." (Is that what he thought? How wrong can one be?) He hunkered further down in the bedclothes, lacing his hands behind his head. "As for you, Liza, my bank draft, carried somewhere securely, will buy you the right, at any time, to quit the country and return home, should anything go amiss. You'll be safe."

And with those words, a summer jaunt to impertinent Spain—at someone else's expense—suddenly seemed like the most glorious of adventures. The divorce could leak its way through the courts like cod liver oil through one's system, nasty going down but quietly effective: one husband, purged. Neither Thomas nor I would likely be allowed to marry again—as if I would. That didn't worry me in the least. No, I would learn Spanish dances, and then come back lithe as a panther, ready to take London by storm.

A sobering thought hit me. "But what if I—? Should I decide to stay the course—?"

"You may keep the money, in that case, and spend it on something beautiful. Yourself."

Bliss! I thanked the earl in the ways he liked best, and he even spent the night, he was that exhausted.

The next few days were a flurry of activity as I met with Señor Hernandez, obtained information for my travelling plans, and managed to convince Howard Harris to equip me with a few (crucial) new garments (two large trunks and several hat boxes full). There were day dresses and a gown for the evening, in the latest colours and fabrics: one demure dove grey, one a vibrant summer sky blue, one I wasn't too keen about but that the earl liked in a soft pink with lots of frills and furbelows (which he certainly helped me rumple, the first time I tried it on for him). And my favourite of all, in a gaily patterned tartan above with stripes below, cunningly cut to emphasize my shape. Well, I needed to make a good impression when I met the mysterious "superior" in Paris. According to Hernandez, this man was named Juan de Grimaldi, an influential person who had the ears of Spanish royalty as well as the French. He was also a former theatrical impresario. The stars were aligning, I whispered to myself. I was moving on, seeing the world again, on my own and with full independence!

And though travel requires an enormous duration of time that many people consider to be lost from one's real, striving life, I knew that, in the space between what is expected of you when leaving at one end and before arriving at the other, there can be enormous change, both within and without. You can emerge an almost completely different person.

Two previous voyages have taught me that, most distinctly. On the way back to my beloved India after marrying Thomas, I was no longer an innocent young girl, grateful to be married at any price to escape the fate my mother had decreed. Aboard the ship, Thomas had grown moody, and then one night he'd struck me. Not hard, but it had shocked us both, and I'd realized things could get ugly. Problems in the bedroom had quickly become chronic, the main one being that he had a very tight foreskin, and whenever he put it up me, it hurt him. The injustice of blaming me for this inconvenience never seemed to occur to him. We spent so much time coaxing his small, inflamed member that I began to lose all interest in the business. I came to understand that runaway matches, like runaway horses, are almost sure to end in a smash-up.

However! My next travel adventure was quite heavenly. That time, my stepfather and now-estranged husband were saving their honours and mine. Looking over the side as Thomas finally descended the gangway and I saw the top of his head for the last time, I'd felt my heart rise and the air grow light around me.

That's when I discovered that time out of time can be glorious. I was free again, I could breathe; a whole voyage stretched ahead between me and my return to the Scottish relatives. The winds were hot, and I loosened my stays, shedding at least two layers of undergarments. As we drew in to Madras, I was idly observing those coming aboard when my pulse quickened at the sight of a long-legged young man with wavy blond hair. That evening at dinner, I learned that his name was George Lennox (bounder!). He was both the aide-de-camp of Lord Elphinstone and the nephew of the Duke of Richmond, and I've always been a fool for a title. Things had quickly gotten out of hand as far as my shipboard reputation was concerned, but I was in the throes of newly discovered passion and couldn't have cared a fig.

George would sometimes come to my cabin, and I would sometimes go to his. The place didn't matter, it was what began to happen inside that did. I discovered magical sensations vastly superior to those I'd been able to conjure myself during lonely spells. I howled like a banshee the first time I experienced the great sublimation, until George, laughing, put his hand over my mouth and hushed me. George's body was beautifully smooth and his sandy beard very thick, so that even by noon his cheeks had a reddish shadow. And his member, well! I'd never before known one that had been cut, and soon it seemed to me an eminently superior ritual. He would hold himself unabashedly and fondly, looking down along his body, and when I asked, he told me that his family had always done it. I asked if it had hurt, but he said he had no idea, it was done when he was a baby and he was sure he wasn't the worse for it, "so come here, cherub." It never caused him any discomfort, compared with poor, sore Thomas who moaned and writhed in pain even as he sought pleasure. George allowed me to know a man, truly, for the first time; to know what was pleasing to him and to discover what pleased me when I was with him. He told me I was beautiful beyond belief in the most secretive folds and byways, as he made me warble like a nightingale—and sometimes like a raven. Oh, cad, I'd loved you obscenely!

Blast and damn. How did that blackguard get back into my head? Because, I suppose, at the start of this whole thing—poised for Paris, the earl's bank draft secreted in the hem of my favourite new striped-tartan gown in case of emergencies—I found myself eager to travel again and easily talked into it. I'd asked very few questions! When I think of that now . . . Was I really so trusting? Or gullible, perhaps? The earl did seem awfully keen for me to travel. Well, I could sense my liaison with him was coming to an end. He had rather neglected his duties at the house, and his wife, he reported, had also complained about the size of the bills that he seemed to be running up, now that he was living in London during the week. Fine, I'd thought, no regrets. He'd cheered me up, set me going again, and that was a wonderful gift in itself. The bitterness of George's betrayal was behind me, my appetite for men had returned, and life and love beckoned once more. So yes, at that heady juncture, I suppose I decided to congratulate myself on my adventurous spirit and my undeniable talent for leaping off cliffs without a boring backwards glance. Nothing, I thought, could hurt me, because this time, I would betray before being betrayed.

Perfect for what they had in mind, had I but known it.

And on to Paris

Señor Hernandez had given me the name of an hotel not far from the Paris coaching station. Exhausted from the journey (days and days in coaches, jostling through the countryside), I collapsed and slept the sleep of the just, with my hatboxes still perched on the bed. I barely even registered the angelic little room and its amenities, nor the bouquet of fresh flowers that someone had placed on the side table. Outside the window, Paris rolled along in its nighttime delirium, and I didn't hear it. In the morning, waking to the sounds of the street, I discovered a message had been pushed under the door. It said, "Dear Miss Gilbert, I will be waiting for you at eight o'clock, in the dining room. Please come prepared to spend the day away from this establishment. Very sincerely, Juan de Grimaldi."

Heavens! I was in Paris (Paris!), it was already nine in the morning, and he'd been there an hour! I was thrown into a frenzy, attempting to pull out and straighten my finest day dress, which had become fatally wrinkled in transit. And the matching hat? Where was it? Which box? Oh, why hadn't I spent the evening arranging my new possessions? I'd certainly obsessed over them during those hectic days in London, imagining what the "superior" would think of the gorgeous, sleek creature who met his admiring eyes. Oh, I was a ninny!

A mere fifteen minutes later, dressed in my favourite half-striped, half-tartan day dress and with my cheeks pinched severely for colour, I was scanning the dining room for an impatient-looking man seated alone. The only single male was at the window and never looked up. My eye caught a flamboyant couple beside him—the woman was leaning towards her companion, and as I watched, she pointed me out with a purple-gloved finger. The man nodded, wiped his lips, and rose. My heart leapt into my throat as I smiled and went towards them. This was not what I had expected: Certainly this imposing woman would see that my hair, under the superficial sheen of a quick brushing, was still tangled and heavy with sleep. Damn and damn again. Had I pinched my cheeks sufficiently? I hoped I looked the part, whatever the "part" was supposed to be.

The man stopped a pace or two from me, bowed his head, and clicked his heels. Then he gestured for me to go past, ushering me towards the woman with his hand at my back. "*Mi querida*," he murmured to her softly, continuing in English, "I believe this is young Miss Gilbert. Let us make her supremely welcome." His voice was deep and mellifluous and made me feel a little less apprehensive. The woman did not get up but held out her gloved hand, fingers drooping. Surely she didn't mean for me to kiss it? I gave her purple fingers a little shake. She pulled them back.

"Sit, my dear, here," he said. "We have been eager to meet you, haven't we, darling?"

The woman said nothing. I sat and he followed, pinning me warmly in place between them. "I trust you had a pleasant night?"

"Oh yes, thank you, sir. I mean, Señor Grimaldi?"

"That is I. Allow me to introduce my wife, the famous Doña Concepción Rodríguez."

Famous? Oh dear, why hadn't Hernandez told me? Now I'd look an imbecile as well as untidy.

"I am most pleased to make your acquaintance, madam—I mean—"

"You have not heard of me?" She looked me up and down with disdain, her accent thick and evocative. Unlike Señor Hernandez, the sound of this woman's Spanish-flavoured English was exotically sensual, and I determined then and there to study it with fervour.

Physically, Juan de Grimaldi was powerful and intimidating; Corsican by blood, he'd been a lieutenant in the French National Guard under Napoleon, and following the emperor's defeat, when King Louis XVIII decided to send a massive army of one hundred thousand men across the Pyrenees to help restore Ferdinand VII to his Spanish throne, Grimaldi had volunteered, then stayed in Spain. When I met him, he was about forty-five years of age. He'd been running Madrid's two principal theatres, the Cruz and the Príncipe, for over a decade. His wife, Concepción, had been a young company actress at the Cruz. Married to Grimaldi, she'd held the title of *prima dama* for a dozen years or more. At the end of the recent war, after Grimaldi fled back to France from Spain, she'd had to support herself and their numerous children, then pack them all up in order to join him in Paris.

Hernandez had told me all this. At the time of our meeting, Señora Rodríguez was about forty and beginning to look it; I had the impression that she was terribly tired and terribly jealous. To go to breakfast (and to meet her husband's new female associate, if that's what I was, which I still found hard to believe), she had donned a crimson overskirt with orange taffeta underskirt, a crimson jacket with revealing details, and a cunning purple and orange hat with cascading black mantilla. There were gold jewels on every finger and at her ears. The ensemble took my breath away. I felt outmoded in the extreme in my new (and perfectly splendid) tartan dress, with my peridot earbobs.

They had already eaten—magnificently, if all of the empty plates and cups served as witnesses. "Please, Miss Gilbert, order whatever you wish," Grimaldi said, placing a sinewy hand upon mine.

"We will be pleased to watch," his wife added, and smiled.

I knew then that I wouldn't be able to eat a thing, and said, "If you please, I am ready to accompany you now. I have no appetite, having dined quite late, I assure you."

"Very well. We may speak in French, by the way? My wife will be more at ease, if so."

"*Oui, bien sûr.*"

He flipped his hand in the air and a waiter appeared as if by magic. All heads in the restaurant turned, and all mouths hung open as we promenaded past, Concepción's perfume wafting across their nostrils as her voice wafted past their ears: "We *must* stop at the *chocolaterie*, Juan, on the way."

Although I had told them I was not hungry, that was a lie. I was ravenous, my stomach growling angrily, and of course Concepción knew it. In their fiacre, as we bowled along the city streets, I ate a number of divine chocolates, which only made me feel worse. Grimaldi began to question me while his wife listened, her head to one side, eyes raking the view out the window. "You are, I understand, a married woman?"

"To my regret, yes."

"And part of your reason for undertaking this journey is to sidestep a court appearance?"

"Obviously Señor Hernandez has given you all the details, monsieur."

He patted my hand reassuringly, and then took his wife's. "Extremely unfortunate, isn't it, darling? Think of being saddled with an uncongenial husband."

"Too detestable," she agreed, with a toss of her head.

He turned his eyes back to mine. "Then, Miss Gilbert, you know the terms of our agreement. Yet there is much you do not know."

"Yes, including what I am to do for you in return. It has cost me many sleepless nights, I assure you." This was very true.

"All within your capability. Now that we've seen you, we know this for certain." His eyes caressed me briefly. "You are as stunning as Hernandez reported." I was thrilled by this, but he went on. "It will require nerve and quick reflexes. A certain amount of bravery."

This sounded a bit worrisome, though I tried not to let it show.

"And that is why I am taking you to the shooting gallery for a lesson. Discover what your natural aim is, and your tolerance." The fiacre, at this point, turned off the main street and up a circular drive, approaching an opulent stone house surrounded by manicured gardens with meticulously trimmed hedge ornaments. We drew up to the front door and the driver leapt down.

"Behave yourself, Juan," Concepción murmured, holding her hand out of the cab door. She descended with grace and a flourish of underskirts, as well as a complete lack of acknowledgment of the driver who had assisted her. Over a shoulder as she was moving away, she called, "I shall expect you for drinks at the usual time. Do not be late."

"*Mi querida.*"

The horses were again whipped up, and we headed back into the heart of the city. As soon as she was no longer with us, I felt immediately more at ease, and interestingly, so did Grimaldi. He let his head rest against the upholstered cushion, while his fingers played in the breeze out the window.

"Let me set the record straight. We are not aristocrats, Miss Gilbert. May I call you Eliza?"

"I prefer Rosana."

"Rosana, then. We are not aristocrats, though my wife occasionally likes to behave as if she is." He smiled indulgently and smacked his lips. "However, we count among our closest friends several members of royal families, both French and Spanish, as well as brothers of the cloth, some of whom are extremely close to God. We fight on their behalf, as we hope you will consent to do."

I murmured something that sounded encouraging.

"Though the civil war has nominally ended," he continued, "there is still great uneasiness. It could flare up again at any moment. The Spanish northerners are wildly patriotic about Don Carlos, the pretender for the throne. The northerners are fearsome *bandidos*, with mountainous terrain in which they can hide a thousand men at a moment's notice. We are on the side of the queens, naturally—the regent Cristina, and her young daughter and future queen, Isabel."

"I see."

"Cristina is in exile—in fact, she is here in Paris, due to unfortunate circumstances beyond her control. She will explain this herself when you meet her."

The legendary Cristina, I realized. The earl will be thrilled! Wait 'til he hears, I thought, he'll be tickled pink in more than one place!

"We understood, from Señor Hernandez, that you wish to learn traditional dances."

"Oh yes," I said, perking up even more.

"You wish to enter the world of the dance, as your profession?"

"More than anything. Or maybe an actress, I haven't decided."

"I will be able to help you with both. I have enormous influence upon *le monde du théâtre* in Madrid. They listen to me still. And, I suspect, always."

I couldn't believe this! Upon meeting me, the powerful Señor Juan de Grimaldi knew that *I* was exactly what he'd been looking for! I stole a glance at his profile. He had closed his eyes and a little smile twitched at the corners of his mouth. He certainly thought highly of himself—as did his wife. Perhaps this was a Spanish trait? Far more interesting than our British reticence and false politeness, our wretched habit of apologizing for everything and nothing. Something to emulate; I vowed to begin immediately.

"What will you have me do, monsieur?"

"Call me Juan, please, Rosana. First-name basis for adventurous undertakings."

His hand was on mine. How had that happened?

"In Madrid, you will be given an acting role in the revival of my play, *La pata de cabra*. I trust you have heard of it?"

"Not yet, but I long to." Take that, Fanny Kelly!

"As a member of the company, you will be in a better position to carry out the tasks, not onerous, but crucial to the Spanish cause, that will be assigned to you." He lifted my hand to his lips and kissed it, wetly, with apparent sincerity. "Dancing will follow, fear not, dear accomplice. I would never allow you to come to real harm."

"I am glad to hear it." Why must he speak about nasty things like harm when I was about to take the stage by storm in my first professional acting role!

At this point, we came to an abrupt halt. We disembarked, Grimaldi flung instructions at the driver, and we entered a monolithic, gloomy building that turned out to be the shooting gallery.

"First we must turn you into a crack shot, Mademoiselle Rosana. Follow me."

Now, although quite giddy with nerves and hunger, I was also realizing that I had unexpectedly entered a swashbuckling adventure and that I was going to be allowed, even encouraged, for the first time in my life to behave with the energy, fervour, and spark that has always animated me. Although women are trained from infancy to believe themselves the weaker sex, I have always had difficulty accepting this dogma. And now here I was in Paris, and here was this distinguished, powerful man, looking to *me* to help solve an international crisis. How had this happened? I felt like pinching myself with sudden joy, sure that I could rise to the occasion! If I needed good aim and a steady hand in order to do so, so be it, and gladly!

Grimaldi took me up a huge but shabby marble staircase and into a long room with targets on the far wall. We were quite alone. He placed a leather-bound book on a table and then opened it up: Inside the book lay two tiny, perfect pistols, each just over six inches long, with all the accoutrements. "I have spared no expense on these: finest of their kind. They call them muff guns in English because they can be hidden inside of a ladies' muff." He handed me one of the beautiful things. "Relatively small," he continued, ".41 caliber, weighs about two pounds." It was light, but felt so potent in the hand! "Listen carefully. It is a cap and ball pistol, or percussion. Here's how you load it." Taking the other pistol from the faux book, he showed me. A measured charge of black powder was poured down the upright barrel, then a wad was used to tamp it down, then a ball of lead forced down onto the wad. "Now it's loaded, but won't fire," he told me. "So to fire, you cock the hammer and place this small percussion cap on the nipple. Without the cap, no bang. With the cap—" He turned swiftly, fired, and hit the target in the exact centre. I jumped up and down and clapped my hands, I was so impressed.

And then I tried. It is embarrassing to remember how truly wretched I was. However, we all must learn, and on that day I began my true apprenticeship. After some mishandled loadings and a couple of hapless, wild firings, he got behind me and placed his arms on either side of my own, holding the pistol along with me, helping steady my aim. Not surprisingly, I suppose, this led to a number of little intimacies that I knew without his telling me that Concepción must not hear about, and which were, in fact, simply part of the introductory process. Pinching and tickling—why do they love to pinch, as if testing the flesh for edibility? A few wet-lipped smacks—they mean nothing by it, it's just a test of their power, as natural to them as breathing. Men will be men, and for the most part, I have always been happy that they are, particularly when they have something tremendous to impart to me.

As the shooting gallery began to fill with other *gentilshomme*s, coming from their clubs for a jot of diversion, I found myself again the recipient of admiring male attention. I was quite a novelty—the first woman, they claimed, to have dared enter their gallery. When the ribaldry and jostling began to accelerate, Grimaldi called a halt to our practice for the day. I was hot and exhausted and he, grumpy.

At that precise moment, I felt what I assumed to be a large buzzing insect zoom past my left ear. A second later, a little "thwok" sounded at the back wall. Several of the jocular gents cried out, some running to my side and others to examine the wall—where they discovered a fresh hole in the paneling with a bullet lodged in it. Exclamations and cries of alarm! Wait, I thought, disbelieving: Could that have been meant for me? Grimaldi, his face a threatening mask, had begun to pull me away when a tall, thin, dark-complexioned man with an enormous black mustache entered the gallery, having raced up the stairs three at a time and being all of a sweat.

"Señor, *por favor*," the man panted, bowing low with one hand on his heart and then, straightening, letting forth a violent stream of incoherent Spanish, complete with melodramatic gestures and breast beating.

"Buffoon," Grimaldi growled, and then he shoved the man violently. "¡*Imbécil!*" He grabbed the pistol from my nerveless hand and pointed it at the swarthy one in a threatening manner. "Get out of my sight!" The fellow turned on his heel and dashed from the room at breakneck speed.

"Juan," I said, tugging at his arm, "was that—?"

"A mistake," he told me, not very comfortingly, then loudly to the gentlemen who were clustered around, "One of you, and you know who you are, has been murderously careless. I shall be reporting this incident to the gallery's manager."

The men retorted: "You cannot believe . . . We would never . . . ! Only at the targets!"

"And she was your target!" Grimaldi roared. My stomach lurched. *Merde*!

Juan chaperoned me away as the men were reaching for me, declaring their innocence. We clattered down the stairs, their voices following, Juan's grip on my arm very hard. The fiacre—how did his driver know?—galloped up from somewhere and drew in to the curb in reckless haste. My patron yanked at the door, bundled me inside, looked up and down the street with suspicious, harried eyes, hauled himself aboard, and clashed the door shut. We were soon galloping headlong.

"Señor Grimaldi," I said sternly, rocking to and fro with the motion of the vehicle, "I need you to explain to me exactly what is going on. Are you going to tell me that I am already in danger?"

"No no, certainly not. That was my confederate. He watches out for us at all times. An accident; those Parisian fools, their aim is notoriously flamboyant."

My hungry, traumatized belly did an acidic flip-flop, and I sat back in my seat. How appalling, I thought: He's not telling me everything that the other gabbled to him. I've been shot at; I know it!

Looking forwards to the safety of my hotel room, I was surprised when I began to recognize landmarks we had passed on our way to the gallery, and even more surprised when the fiacre turned and headed up the laneway towards Grimaldi's mansion. "I have taken the liberty of relocating you for the remainder of your stay in Paris," Juan said coolly. "You will find all of your gewgaws arranged to your satisfaction."

Welcomed inside by an officious manservant, I was led to the bedchamber that was to be mine. My trunks and hatboxes had been unpacked and the contents sat or hung in well-ordered ranks. The room was opulently appointed in cream and blue fabrics, very French. I bobbed around, staring and becoming indignant. Who had handled my possessions—including my underthings? Had my removal from the hotel been decided from the beginning? A second chill note of apprehension seized me as I remembered the extreme chaos of my belongings, flung about the hotel room during my frantic search for a matching outfit early that morning. Since then, I'd been almost murdered (had I, really?) and everything I possessed had been handled and scrutinized, by one or several unknown persons. I sat upon the bed and stared at nothing.

After some minutes (and a good deal of disbelief), a knock at the door brought me the news that I was expected downstairs in the drawing room for drinks. Very well, I thought. I would need to maintain all the poise and sangfroid I could muster until I learned just who and what to fear and how to avoid same. I told myself that I could work these things out. I wanted so much to believe in my adventure, my new chances, and (recklessly, perhaps) I'd decided that my visit to Spain would be the making of me; the silky sibilance of the language matched the persona I was beginning to imagine for myself, and also the fiery temperament. In short, I vowed that if the Grimaldis were planning to use me, well, I would use them too.

Ensconced in the drawing room with a fine sherry, I turned to Juan, my chin held high. "May I ask—who am I to be in your play?"

I saw Concepción's nostrils flare before she took a small sip from her glass. Her husband answered, "A very important—no, crucial—role."

"Do I have a great many lines?" I tried not to flap or spill my sherry, but the very thought of my first role on stage was making me long to dash about. "Perhaps I could begin learning them now."

"No, no, *cariña*, you don't want to grow stale. Trust me with this. All in good time." And with that I had to be content.

※ ※ ※

Concepción began her work with me the very next morning. She was to teach me Spanish, as quickly and thoroughly as possible in a short period of time. I surmised she had done this before, teaching their five children the language of her blood now that they were no longer in Spain. Four of the children were still quite little and came trooping in and out of the library where she and I worked. Odilia was ten and an independent creature; Leopoldina, at seven, and Cecilia at six, were sweet and needy, and at first I shared my lessons with them. Their son, Josep, was only two and was the apple of his parents' eyes.

Their oldest daughter was named Clotilde; she was a short but precocious sixteen, aggressively interested in young men. She was standoffish with me at first, but when she heard I came from London she wanted to know all about "those odd, pale people with the long faces and bad teeth." Her father was indulgent of Clotilde, petting her and providing whatever she desired. Concepción treated their firstborn almost as an equal, and certainly as a rival for her husband's affection. Those two females were in the throes of mutual jealousy the whole time I stayed with them. It was quite exhausting.

I remained, day and night, under either Grimaldi's or his wife's supervision. And I was worked like a fiend. Luckily, I was very good and getting better daily—my shooting was improving by leaps and bounds, and my Spanish as well. Grimaldi usually arranged it so that we would have the shooting gallery to ourselves, though sometimes I caught a glimpse of the dark-skinned Spanish fellow looking severe on the staircase. A bodyguard, I told myself, and tried to relax. He was obviously paid to look out for me, *ergo* I was safe.

I rejoiced when, one day in the third week, Juan announced that I would be accompanying them to the theatre that night—the Comédie Française, no less, where a play by Alexandre Dumas was enjoying a revival. The only bits of Paris I had seen were the hotel (for such a short time), the gallery, and the Grimaldi mansion. I was hungry to see the real Paris at last.

"You have heard of Monsieur Dumas, of course?"

"Of course," I said (though I hadn't).

"We will meet him in the café afterward," Juan told me. "Be careful of his roving hands, Rosana." He was a fine one to talk.

The play was called *Mademoiselle de Belle-Isle*. It was rather silly but fun, though I was more taken by the opulence of the theatre itself and spent much of the evening looking down from our box at the composition of the audience. Beneath us were the less fortunate rabble, who had to sit below the stage and look up at the actors. Surrounding that lower level were three tiers of magnificent private boxes, where all of the privileged sat, and conversed, and went in and out of one another's loges with much laughter and merriment. Directly across from us was the box of Monsieur Dumas, a large, rolling thunder of a man, laughing immoderately at his own jokes. At his side sat a rotund little woman, a slight melancholic-seeming young man, and a young pretty woman dressed in very bright colours. "Wife, son, and courtesan of the moment," Concepción whispered behind her fan. "The son is besotted. It will end badly, no doubt." How interesting, I thought, and all out in the open! Clotilde, who was leaning forwards to hear every word on stage, hissed at her mother, "Be quiet!" All heads down below turned to look up. Concepción waved her fan regally; the heads returned to the action.

After curtain call, and leaving a short interval for the milling stream of audience members to disperse, Grimaldi led his cortege backstage. This was what I really longed to see—the actors, in their own skins—and I could barely contain my excitement. Clotilde, I think, was disgusted by my *naïveté*: She had grown up around these people, and for her it was merely the usual end to a theatrical evening. Concepción, I noticed, seemed tense as we moved through the entrails of the building. I wondered whether she missed the thrill of performing. Grimaldi looked angry. And then, there we were in the corridor of the dressing rooms. There was the unmistakable smell of greasepaint, of still-warm costumes and wigs—and here came the actors. The Grimaldi adults' response was fascinating: All of a sudden, their faces changed. They became animated, congratulating everyone, warmly and individually, clasping hands, murmuring endearments. Just moments before, they had appeared so unhappy and resentful.

At this point, Dumas and his coterie arrived; back-thumping hugs, cheek kisses, and jovial shouts of triumph resounded. The rest of the actors emerged from their rooms, shorn of wigs, white powder, and hoopskirts—they seemed tiny now, with their newly scrubbed faces.

"To the café!" Dumas shouted. "On me!" Grimaldi added, "Second round's on me," and the company cheered. It didn't take long for the corridor to empty; everyone moved to the stage door and off into the night.

"Rosana," Juan reassured me, as we followed, "I did not introduce you just then, as actors cannot take in much information so soon after coming away from applause. All they can absorb at that point is flattery or mutual admiration: 'Did I show well?' 'They loved me tonight, didn't they?' And so on. After a drink, their euphoria will begin to modulate into something approaching reality; then we shall introduce the dark beauty in our midst." Clotilde snorted derisively, and her father bestowed a kiss upon her head. "They already know *this* dark beauty. It is our guest's turn tonight."

"She's no guest. She's—"

"Hush."

By the time we arrived at the Café de Paris, most of the actors had flung off their coats and settled around tables, all in one unwieldy throng.

Alexandre Dumas was on his feet, waving money around, handing it over as the drinks arrived. The writer was immense in girth and stature, as well as in self-regard; a self-made man, you could see he would not let anyone forget it. Grimaldi managed to attract the attention of the nearest waiter as we squeezed ourselves in to the midst of the laughing group, while Dumas bellowed, "I have never refused money to anybody, except my creditors!" I was in a fever of exhilaration. To be in Paris, at the pinnacle of the society I so longed to join—surely it couldn't be too far out of reach now, not with Juan's patronage and my own active enterprise. I was almost there!

"In France," Dumas was announcing to the table at large, "some little obscure bauble that sells no copies is considered brilliant! Success is ignored—no, *hated*—by the Académie Française. They may regard you as an amusing fellow but you are not respected." Someone remonstrated, but he shot them down: "No, no, I tell you! Bores enjoy priority!"

"For heaven's sake, sit down now," said the small round woman, tugging aggressively on the writer's lapel.

Concepción leaned towards me to whisper, "The fat lady is Ida Ferrier. They married two years ago, and already they have had more lovers between them than you can believe. His son hates her with a passion."

Grimaldi added, out of the corner of his mouth, "She was a reasonably good actress, and she used to be slim, almost thin." When Concepción made a disparaging sound, he took her hand. "As Hugo says, my dear, 'There is a skeleton in every woman.' Though speaking for myself, I prefer that skeleton to be well covered."

"Not *that* well covered, I hope," she snarled.

"You have a point, beloved."

Dumas was looking around for something else to say as Grimaldi rose to his feet, glass in hand. "Esteemed company, congratulations again on your current success! May it continue apace!" Everyone cheered, and drank. "While I have your attention," Juan went on, "allow me to introduce—"

"Another of your agents?" someone called. "You're in too deep, Juan!"

"—my protégée, from England, Miss Eliza Rosana Gilbert." And he gestured me to my feet. Greetings were murmured, while a number of the men applauded and called, "*Belle femme!*" I heard surprised whispers, "A woman. This one's a woman!"

Ida Ferrier called, in a shrill voice, "Always before they have been men, Juan, and not very savory-looking men; men that would as soon stab you in the back, I'd have thought. Mutineers and bandits, with long waxed mustaches and glass eyes and scars." The group was nodding, and she turned to me, "What is it that he will have you do, *jeune fille*?"

Alexandre Dumas wiped his scarlet lips and for the first time gave me the benefit of his full attention. At that moment, that very second, I sensed he was a dangerous man, in usual and unusual ways.

"Mademoiselle Gilbert," he murmured, raising his glass. Everyone drank again as his small eyes appraised me, then, without taking a breath, "But I was saying earlier—for theatres to make money, the dancers must wear tights . . . which split! And in the *split* you can tell the sheep from the goats, the talented from the *obviously* talentless." His eyes on me were malignant; I felt as if I was falling from a great height and clutched at the table. "No, no, God's truth," he continued, well pleased that he'd seen his insult to a new young girl hit home, and he carried on with his rude joke about theatre managers and dancers' tights.

I sat down, slowly. Clotilde was smiling spitefully at my shattered countenance. I was only another young female with hopeful ambitions; such creatures are perennial and need no encouragement. If one falls by the wayside, three more are sure to follow. Across the table, the odious writer took pause to lick and suck noisily at an enormous cigar. Did anyone else see the blush that rose up from my chest to suffuse my cheeks? It was a fierce blush signaling anger rather than shame. As he got his repulsive cigar lit and put his thick tongue away, the café noise and smoke retreated from my consciousness. He had reminded me, viscerally, of another powerful, conceited man I'd known, another with whom I had experienced immediate and mutual antipathy. That man's name? Sir Jasper Nicolls.

My blood boils as I remember. And when my blood boils, I make enemies for life.

Banished from India at age eight, I lived with my stepfather's parents in Scotland, then was sent to Durham, England, to my stepfather's older sister, Mrs. Catherine Rae. Aunt Catherine and Uncle Herbert longed for children but had none; she found me difficult to manage, although she tried very hard. When my stepfather was promoted again, no doubt wishing to free his sister from thrall to his young charge, he arranged (from India) for my next move. I was to be 'put to school' under the aegis of the eminent Major General Sir Jasper Nicolls. There were eight school-age daughters in his household, and perhaps he agreed because arranging the education of one more would hardly cause a ripple. So, in September 1832, my step-aunt and I took the coach from Durham to Reading, in Berkshire. Once again I was being passed from one stranger to another like a sack of unwanted clothing. It's painful to recall how much I hated this, how inferior it made me feel. Like many a lonely girl, I'd convinced myself that I was an exotic princess in captivity and that one day I would escape and wreak my vengeance. My zest, my originality, would not be stifled. I swore it! I was better than that. I was better than any of them! I suppose I was not in any mood to confront my new reality when we finally arrived.

The major general was home from India, on leave, when I was delivered. A stiff military man, very high on his horse about punctuality, obedience, and silence. I barely recall his wife, a headache-ridden, exhausted soul who kept to the upper floors. My fate was in Sir Nicolls's hands, and I'd soon learned how to read what fate had in store for me: His library, on the main floor, was dark and forbidding but I would often creep across the carpet when he was not there, open the desk drawer, and read his diary. Very early on he wrote that he believed "the Gilbert girl" would "come to no good." I remember running into him one night when he'd caught me almost in the act: I'd managed to close the drawer and skip out from behind his desk, but there he was, an imposing red-faced mountain, looking down at me with distaste. I'd scampered away then, but I secretly spit into his teacup the next morning. That's how it was. And as we'd begun, so we'd unfortunately continued.

I was sent to the Misses Aldridge's in Bath, two spinster sisters who ran a boarding school. Five of the Nicolls girls were also there. At first I'd believed I was meant to feel like one of the Nicolls family—we spent time together, we did each other's hair—but then, at the first holiday, I'd waited with them at the front door, bags packed, full of excitement and anxiety to see fresh scenes, encounter new people. Their father had written that he was sending the family to Paris for several months—Paris! I was thirteen by then and hungry for life to begin. When the carriage drew up, there was intense consternation from the driver and footman, then a consultation with the Nicolls girls. Edith, the eldest, had to whisper into my ear that she was so very sorry, I had not been invited. I'd pulled my hand away from hers as if I had been stung. I pulled my glove off, flung it down, and stamped away inside, leaving my bags upon the front steps.

From that moment, I remade myself as far as life in the school was concerned. I no longer answered to my hated pet name of Betty; my name henceforth became Rosana. When the Nicolls girls returned, I had perfected my new image. I no longer knew them. I consoled myself, in my loneliness and pride, by pushing away the only people who attempted to care. I dressed in as close to an Indian fashion as I could arrange; I spoke to myself often in Hindi and expressed a hatred for all things English. And it was at this time that I began to lie. Or rather, I began to fabricate, to embroider. When other girls returned from various home visits or travels, I too would tell of my travels to faraway places. In my mind, I went to Paris: I met the French king and he couldn't resist kissing my hand. I danced with several courtiers; Versailles held no further interest for me. I'd received an invitation to the court of a Spanish grandee but had to refuse because I was in the middle of fittings for the most splendid velvet and satin gown and . . . I could go on for hours, and frequently did. No one dared contradict me. I was a spirited fighter and had perfected a blistering pinch-twist combination that could do swift damage.

Then misfortune befell me. One of the Misses Aldridge wrote to Sir Jasper Nicolls, asking him to remove me from the school (for a reason I cannot bear to think about). Back in Reading, I'd cowered before him. He called me "wretch Gilbert!" and said he had written to Craigie in the most strenuous terms. I was to live in one room at the top of the house. I was to receive meals but tell no one else that I was there, and I was to let no one see me in my shameful condition. Ultimately, I was to comply with whatever decision was put forth by my stepfather.

Oh, I cannot think of this. Not now.

Eventually, I was returned to the Aldridge School. The evening before I departed his house for the last time, Sir Jasper summoned me to the library to say, "We see no sign from you, Betty, that you will amount to anything but trouble. But what can one expect? I likened your mother, the first moment I laid eyes upon her, to a tortoise that buries her eggs lightly in the sand and leaves them to sun and to chance. You are the same."

"I am not!"

"Silence! Sooner or later, you will be reclaimed, although the goods are certainly damaged."

I am shaking now, the memory of it is so real. I had so little knowledge of the world, of men, of the ways in which smaller creatures have always been and always will be buffeted between opposing forces before being consumed by the most powerful in a great, voracious crunching of tiny bones. Though these men publicly profess to love and honour the "weaker sex"—Nicolls with his daughters, Dumas with his mistresses—they do not behave as if they do, obsessed as they are with belittling, deriding, and sneering at our minds, our bodies, and our dreams. So, yes, in the Café de Paris, as I stole another glance at Alexandre Dumas, with his shrewd piggy eyes, proclaiming in his loud voice, I again felt small, unimportant, and vehemently, immoderately angry.

⁂

The morning after the Parisian theatre excursion, I woke with an awful headache and its accompanying dread: An attack was imminent. Since contracting it during the rainy season the year I'd returned to India, bouts of malaria periodically knocked me flat. It began as it always does, with abdominal pain and sore muscles, swiftly followed by fever, dizziness, the chills, and sweats. I begged the Grimaldis to procure me quinine before the thing took hold, managing to ask between gusts of vomiting, white as a sheet, teeth chattering like castanets.

By the third day I was sitting up in bed and taking some soup, which the petite servant Francine had brought up. I was so hungry that I was groaning, spooning it in as quickly as possible, and biting greedily into a freshly baked roll slathered with butter. Suddenly, Grimaldi burst through the door. He shooed Francine away: "Out, out of here! Go!" He was carrying a parcel under his arm, containing a box, and he slammed it down upon the table at the end of the bed. Then he returned to the door and locked it. This alarmed me greatly. He had never locked a door with me in the room, alone. The expression on his face alarmed me even more.

"You are better today? Your strength is returning?" He strode to the window and impatiently yanked the curtain aside to stare down into the street. "We must capitalize upon what you have learned and send you hence. Your wit and bravado must make up for whatever skill may still be lacking, since it appears we have no time to waste."

What could have happened? He let the curtain fall again and turned to look at me. "Forgive me, Rosana. I see I must go back several steps, and then you must come forwards with me as swiftly as possible, or all may be lost. You agree?"

What could I say? "Very well."

He took the tray with soup and bread and placed it on the side table, then retrieved the mysterious box. "You don't feel faint anymore? You are quite strong?"

Well, that was pushing it, but the restlessness in his eyes did not allow me to gainsay him, so I nodded.

He brought the box over and placed it on my lap. "Look inside."

Opening the flaps, I saw wood shavings and ripped pieces of paper. "Underneath," came the directive. Pushing the material aside, I tried to feel for the object he must wish me to see but he cried, "Wait!" He reached, himself, to pull a wad of the shavings away, and then . . . At first I thought I was looking at a pair of large toadstools or field mushrooms of some kind. I peered and again put out my hand. Just as I was about to lift one of the objects, I finally understood what I was seeing. It seems impossible to recognize such things out of their usual context, they simply will not fall into place in one's mind because it seems so unlikely to see them lying in a box. They were a pair of large, filthy, human ears.

"Oh my God!" I gasped and recoiled, banging my head hard on the headboard.

"*Cochons*! Murderers." He sat down upon the bed, setting the box to one side. I was sure the soup was about to make a reappearance, but I closed my eyes and held up my hand to stop him from continuing while I struggled for control. He waited, and after some moments, I was able to open my eyes again. My thoughts in turmoil, I said, "What does it mean?"

"It means . . ." He took a deep breath and raised his eyebrows, then frowned mightily. "It means, without doubt, that Tristany is dead."

"And who . . . ?"

"He is—he was—your predecessor."

"What do you mean, predecessor?"

"What it usually means, *querida*. The one who went before you."

"Oh my *God*!" I cried again, this time more loudly and with even greater anxiety. I pulled my legs in under me and rose up on the mattress, exclaiming, "Is this why you haven't—? Because all along, you knew—! That it was dangerous, full of bandits and terror and, and death!" I was on my feet now, flailing about. "And I'm just dispensable, just a stupid girl from another country and no one knows that I'm here, no one important, and so you think you can just—! But that's not true! My member of Parliament knows, the 3rd Earl of Malmesbury *knows* that I'm here and he'll send a dragoon—no, a *platoon* of dragoons!—to come and fetch me home as *soon* as he realizes that I'm—That I . . ." There was a logistical problem with this line of thought, but I couldn't, at that precise moment, think what it might be.

"Are you finished?"

"No!" I cried, but then unfortunately I fell down again due to the softness and unsteadiness of the mattress. The box hurtled to the floor and the ears spilled forth, their severed edges illuminated in the sunshine from the window. My teeth began to chatter again as I crawled back in under the covers, pulling them up to my trembling chin.

"Rosana, listen to me," Grimaldi said. "This will not happen to you, not if you listen very carefully to what I am about to tell you."

"Oh my *God*."

"There are many plots in the Spanish court, although it is our fortune that Cristina is here in Paris. Her daughters, however, are not.

They remain in Madrid, under the protection of the prime minister, General Espartero."

"But . . . the ears?"

"I am coming to that. The princesses, Isabel and Luisa Fernanda, are twelve and ten. Isabel will be queen as soon as she comes of age; heads of state and conspirators are already lining up the list of possible suitors for her hand. The Bourbon women mature quickly, so this happy event is expected in the very near future, for as soon as the girl is capable of being a mother, she is certainly capable of being queen and a wife. Hence Cristina's anxiety—she wishes to return to Spain, to live once again in the court of her reigning daughter. But there are difficulties, not only in the undoubtedly tricky area of potential consorts. There is a new tutor."

"For the girls? Why is that difficult?"

"He is on the other side. It is abominable to be so far away, to hear only rumors! And now this!" He poked moodily at an ear with the tip of his shoe, and I tried not to gorge.

"Who was he?" I asked. I feared the answer.

Grimaldi looked at me with a faraway expression, then sat heavily upon the bed. "The best of my agents. They are Tristany's, of this I am sure. There is a mole, small but distinctive, inside the left pinna as it leads to the ear canal. He used to laugh and say it was his mole, his own personal spy, and it made him invincible."

"How terrible."

"Nothing else arrived in the package, which means he was tortured, and in all likelihood it was a long, miserable dying. Spanish vengeance is not something to take lightly, Rosana."

How had the room become so tiny and cramped?

"The war has been obscene for its atrocities. We thought nothing could be worse than the war of independence, after Napoleon, but . . . Memories are long. Terrible old men; terrible young men. Murdering women and children, exacting vengeance—one kills the other's mother in broad daylight by firing squad, the other kills the first's son with extreme savagery in retaliation. Unstoppable. Unspeakable." His face looked grey. "Just three years ago, all of Catalonia was under the sway of the count of España and his reign of terror. He was only stopped by being outwitted; a junta invited him to a council meeting, overpowered him, and took him prisoner. Then, with the junta's knowledge, he was strangled and his body was thrown into the river with a stone tied to it. Good riddance. But others leap up where one has gone down: General Maroto in Estella killed his fellow generals after inviting them to take chocolate with him. Maroto has now surrendered and sworn loyalty to the Cristinos, but who can believe him? Who would trust him? Turncoats for expedience. It is dangerous, the new prominence that has been given to—been seized by—Spain's military leaders. No good will come of it."

I had never seen Grimaldi look so old; the skin around his eyes was pouchy, and his cheeks were hollow.

"Tristany was a friend?" I put my hand on his arm. I'm not sure he even felt it.

"The son of a friend, yes. A fine, brave, aristocratic family. What will I tell his father? Yet, he must already know."

"But what did Tristany do to warrant such . . . ?" What I needed to know was, what did Grimaldi *make* him do that would prompt such retaliation?

"We must start." He stood quickly and shook his head, as if freeing it of horrible visions. "We have come too far for you to be deflected, Rosana. No one would hurt a young foreign woman; no one would dare." I didn't know about that, not if the stories he'd just related were true. Grimaldi picked up a clump of the sawdust and with that as shield replaced the ears in the box. "Get dressed. Cristina has summoned us and we must not keep her waiting. Everything is accelerating; everything must happen now. No, before now: yesterday!" He strode to the door, opened it and called for Concepción, and then returned to the window, clasped his hands behind his back and glared out.

He wasn't going to leave me alone to dress. This was also new, and frightened me a bit. I swung my feet out of the bed to stand, still dizzy from the illness.

His wife entered on the run, closed the door behind her and locked it again.

"Never mind the underthings, make haste," she snapped, rifling through my dresses and pulling out the soft pink one with all the frills and furbelows dancing down the front of it. I felt it made me look babyish, but maybe that's what they wanted, to emphasize my youth for the meeting with royalty. Certainly Concepción had no intention of letting me choose another one. She yanked the laces until I was gasping. As I twisted my hair up, securing it with a comb, she dug through the wardrobe and lobbed a pair of shoes out, one at a time, hitting me sharply on the ankle, twice. My reflection in the wardrobe mirror looked like hell, but why should that have surprised me? Wracked with malaria, gagging at lopped ears?

"Ready."

"Sit down, Rosana."

I did. He pulled up another chair as Concepción hovered sternly behind him. "Time to tell you exactly what is necessary."

"A few days ago, I would have rejoiced," I said, "but now—"

"Be quiet and listen. You are, in your heart, a reckless and bold young woman. I have recognized this from the look in your eye when you hit a target. Even I, far too old for you, can elicit a sensual response—don't bother to refute it. I envy the man you genuinely care for, if what I have experienced is only a small substitute. Either that or I pity him, since your blatant physicality seems to know no checks and balances."

"Oh! That is a lie! That is rude!" I was shocked; this was not the kind of *tête-à-tête* I had expected. I tried to rise, but Grimaldi placed an iron grip upon my thigh as Concepción gave a little puff of contempt.

"It is time to earn your keep after all of this cosseting," he went on. "I know you are not remotely a lady—"

"Oh!" I cried, and then "Aaah!" as his grip crushed my leg. I would have a bad bruise there, if I knew anything.

"—not remotely. I know this. Señor Hernandez is remarkably thorough. Thanks to Miss Kelly, he was able to ascertain your financial assets, such as they are. Or perhaps I should say as they were—that they were tied up with a certain member of Parliament. Hernandez dug and pried and knows your entire previous history." A cold shudder ran through me as I prayed, Not *all* of it, surely? "Your court date was one fact, and it led us to consider you: Evidence of at least one man—a husband—with whom you have had sexual relations. The MP is another. Well and good. The señor's searches took him straight to, according to the records of the chancery courts, one George Lennox, a third. Much better."

This was dreadful.

"And then the señor turned up something even *more* interesting. He pursued all names mentioned in any way in your trial papers: A certain Mrs. Catherine Rae, in Durham, and her husband, Mr. Herbert Rae, came to his attention. Hernandez travelled to Durham; he looked up the address. He watched them. Interestingly, the married couple was quite old; they were in their mid-fifties at least. Why is that *interesante*? Because—and this made the señor's mustachio quiver—they had a seven-year-old daughter. Very curious. Not many English people, with no previous offspring, will attempt such a dangerous feat. But perhaps, he thought, perhaps they were lucky, or different. Or the recipients of a baby in another manner. It happens. It happens, especially, within families. What was the connection? He did his research: The woman is the sister of your stepfather, Major Craigie in India. Close and closer. The señor studied the little girl. He contrived to meet her in a park; he returned her ball when it rolled too quickly away from her hoop. He saw a resemblance."

"*Verosímil.*" Concepción nodded emphatically and began pacing.

This couldn't be happening, I thought. The one thing I had promised . . . And not Aunt Catherine, but myself. For the sake of—

"It was the hair and the dark blue eyes that confirmed it."

And then it was as if I was falling backwards, back into a terrible time: I was again at the Misses Aldridges', during one of the long, dreary holiday periods. I was fourteen and the only girl remaining in the house. Most of the teachers had also gone; I ate with the cook and the servant. Not that this was a hardship, as I liked them very much, and the young maid was often the admirer of my wickedest pranks. That particular Christmas, she had a cousin arrive from London and had brought him over to eat with us one evening. I wish she hadn't. He was the very sort of handsome brand-new fellow (cheeks still raw from first shaves) that I would look at sideways on Sundays when the group of us young misses were allowed to walk, crocodile, from the school to the church and back again. Did I know how to speak to the rougher sex? Of course not; I'd had no practice. Did I know what they wanted? No. Did I know what *I* wanted? Not at all. Just a restlessness, a coal burning somewhere inside. I never knew his name, I didn't even want to. It wasn't about a connection that would go on into the future, it was about clothing and flesh and lips and yearning. There were so many layers to what I wore! Eventually we found a way. I helped him with nimble fingers, and the strangeness and shocking immediacy of that burning heat thrust deep inside me was an awakener—I woke up! I smelled India: the searing sun, the flowers, vivid colours, flavours that made you sweat rather than gag. No more oatmeal, no more interminable cups of tepid tea. Give me this! Give me more! I cried out, I laughed, grabbing at the boy's buttocks, and before we knew it, we were off again.

Of course, it was a terrible mistake. Of course the gods of irony were up there, waiting. It was all too repeatable. My mother, fourteen when she'd had me, had passed on her insultingly easy fecundity. At first I didn't know what was happening. I began to eat like a horse—all the girls remarked upon it—but then shortly thereafter I also began to throw it back up. I cried a lot, and I'd been a girl who would never cry, never show fear or dependency, ever. The elder Miss Aldridge was a canny woman and it did not take her long to understand what had happened. One day the maid was in fits of tears, and then disappeared, dismissed. To my horror, Miss Aldridge called me in to her office to inform me that she'd written to Sir Jasper Nicolls.

At the Nicholls's, confined to the upper floor, I was terrified as I grew larger. Eventually, of course, I figured it out, thanks to the servants who tried to be kind. I felt so ashamed to realize I was like my mother, that I was repeating her history—but with no military husband's good name to protect me or the child I was carrying. And as usual, I had no idea what to expect would happen afterwards. I only believed it would not be nice. The baby was born, once the normal course of such an event had picked me up and swept me into it, in about one hour, and this shamed me as well. I was fifteen by then. The baby, a little girl, was given to a wet-nurse who lived elsewhere, and I waited, breasts leaking, alert to the patriarch's towering rage two floors below.

The mails, of course, travel at the same rate as passengers, so it was not until several months after I had given birth that my stepfather's reply arrived. There was a package for Sir Jasper, with apologies and instructions. Craigie sent me a separate letter, and it made me weep. He explained that he loved me very much, that he had decided upon a course of action that he hoped would satisfy all concerned, and that he had decided not to tell my mother of my predicament and its consequences. He hoped I would approve. And I did. I did not wish her to know anything about me, not if it would put me in her debt. Oh, he knew me well, and I have often wondered why. Not only the little girl I had been for the few years I lived with them, but also the changing creature I was at that time. He put himself into my position, and into my mind as he had known it and as he imagined it. He is a sterling man.

Aunt Catherine arrived; she was to take my baby. Uncle Herbert came with her, and together they did their best to stand up to Sir Jasper. It was eventually arranged: The baby was handed over and they departed. Before they did so, Catherine found me and hugged me hard. She told me the little girl would be adored and cared for as their own forevermore. She urged me to have no worries for the infant's welfare, that she would be first and foremost in their hearts, always. Uncle Herbert, ever silent, nodded and pulled his whiskers, looking anywhere except at me. Aunt Catherine asked permission to call my baby Emma. What could I say? I hadn't seen the baby since the day she was born. I'd barely seen her then, and I didn't see her on the day my step-relatives took her. Catherine kissed me and whispered, "Never tell a soul, dear. This way is best."

I was returned to the school. For months, while my breasts continued to leak and I hid the evidence as well as could be, my spirits were in the dankest, coldest cellar. I believed that the baby was better off without me. I didn't even know how to miss her. I sat in the pews of the church in Bath and for the first time, really listened to the words. Virtually all of them were designed to punish and contain God's handiwork, particularly the women. I believe some young souls encounter despair at an early age and spend the rest of their lives trying to escape it. And in my experience, that despair is as often caused by religion as by human wrongdoing. Those words, in that church, filled me with fear, then loathing—and finally, rebellion. I suppose, if I have one particular attribute of which I am most proud, it would be this spirit: which moves me to action, which goads me into facing it out, whatever *it* might be. God knows I have many black marks to my name, but this restless, questing soul of mine has saved my life. I am not saying I was sorry for myself—far from it. I was angry, that was what it was, and I wanted answers. I wanted choices. And I'd begun to understand that if I wanted those things I would have to learn how to take them.

"Señor Hernandez did not *do* anything to her?" I cried. "Tell me he didn't do anything!"

"She is safe in the home of her surrogate parents," Grimaldi said. "But. We know everything now, everything we need in order to ensure that you cooperate fully on your mission to Spain."

This was not an outcome I had remotely anticipated. Little Emma, seven years of age, a pawn of these determined, tempestuous Europeans? It was too terrible. Travelling through Durham to Portsmouth with Thomas, and from thence to India, I had held Emma for all of ten minutes; she'd been three and wriggled as much as I had when I had been held at that age. Her hair was dark as a crow's wing, her eyes a deep sea blue. It had frightened me how much she looked like me, but no one else had seemed to notice, certainly not Thomas. I dreamt about her for many nights after that visit, trying to imagine what life would be like if she were mine. I couldn't do it. I didn't really want to, certainly not in that time and place, and not with that man. But I have made a promise, to myself and to her, that if I can ever help her in her later life, I will. Although I have only seen my birth child twice, only held her once, I truly love her. Where she is, that is my centre and always will be.

Knee to knee with Juan de Grimaldi, a savagery ran through me: You cannot, you will not, use her this way! Nobody will! I swear it!

"I was always prepared to do what you ask, Señor Grimaldi. You did not need to blackmail me."

He pursed his lips. "We have found, in the past, that it is a necessary greasing of the wheels, when the wheels get cold and begin to balk, as they always do at some point in the journey."

After this threat, Grimaldi became even more edgy and abrupt. The task I was to perform concerned the princesses' tutor. I was to get close to the princesses, to have them see and admire me. That was why I was to appear in *La pata de cabra*. The infantas would come to the theatre; I was to get myself invited to the palace. Once there, I was to meet the tutor who never let the little girls out of his sight. I needed to make him do so.

"But—?" My mind still was protecting Emma, and the instructions confused me.

"Can you *still* not see what service you are to render to the crown?" scolded Concepción.

"I am trying." Their eyes were burning holes in my head.

"Seduce the man!" she screeched, as Grimaldi put his hand upon her arm.

"We know that you have a talent for it," he added, "so don't waste our time with cries of outrage. There are other agents in Madrid; you will meet them and be given instructions for the next plan of action after you have accomplished the first. In your case, the less you know the better."

I didn't like the sound of that at all. "But what good will seducing this tutor do for your cause?"

"He will be discredited, of course, and then dismissed," Grimaldi answered. "Prime Minister Espartero has put an extremist politician in place as tutor in order to display the righteousness and purity of his government, to show how well they are looking after the interests of the soon-to-be queen. This will prove the tutor is not pure."

"Suppose I do what you ask." They had cornered me and betrayed my trust. I was right to demand answers. "What will happen to me, afterwards? Will I be blamed?"

"She is worried about her reputation, Juan?" Concepción sneered, and then to me, "You should have thought about that after your first transgression. Not now, after your—what is it, Juan? Her fifth? Her eighteenth?"

"*Querida, por favor . . .*" Juan took his wife's hand and led her to the door. She allowed herself to be ushered out, with one last baleful look at me to smarten me up.

Grimaldi turned and smiled. It was an empty smile that never reached his eyes. "Now then, Rosana. You see why we need a woman of your talents? Of your beauty? Of your undoubted amorousness?"

At that moment, I finally recognized his charismatic energy for what it really was: the exercise of power. He had me and he knew it.

My voice was small as I whispered, "I'm afraid for my ears."

"I'm afraid for them too. Let me see." He reached out, pulled a strand of fallen hair away from the side of my face. His hand smelled strongly of tobacco. I had been alone with him many times outside of that room, his arms about my waist and my laughter pealing around the empty heights of the shooting gallery. But our silly harmless intimacies had always had a playfulness about them. That was all gone. He leaned towards me and whispered, directly into my left ear, "You will not be allowed to go back, Rosana. Forwards is the only direction you can take. Your ears are not Tristany's. They are well attached to your head, and your head to your shoulders. I know you are the one to help us return our beloved country to its rightful ruler. If not, I have a smaller box. A decorative box that will just hold two other, tiny ears, and a lock of her dark black hair. Do you understand me?"

A knock at the door made me leap to my feet, heart thundering. Grimaldi growled, "¿Quién es?"

"Padre de la Vega," a male voice rejoined.

"Ah, good," Grimaldi said, and opened the door. There stood an enormously tall and thin priest, holding a large silver crucifix in his hands and wearing a long, black robe. His cheeks were covered with a well-trimmed black beard, his hair tonsured. His eyes glittered as he flicked them quickly around the room, coming to rest upon me in my gaudy pink furbelows. They flicked up my length and then down, then very slowly up again, only to dart away and stare past me out the window.

Grimaldi's smile was again a hollow one as he said, "Your travelling companion. You will be safe with him."

※ ※ ※

Tucked into the Grimaldi's finest carriage, we trotted along, heading out of Paris, on our way to Reuil-Malmaison to meet with the famed former-regent, Cristina. Inside the vehicle: the Spanish theatre couple, myself, and the dark piratical bodyguard from the shooting gallery, who said not a word but gazed malevolently out of the window the whole time, his hand yanking at his waxed mustache, his body redolent of sweat and garlic. I was woozy from a new dose of quinine, and for the first time I noticed that this man had a glass eye. It was incredibly distracting: The iris did not follow his facial movements, so at times it would be staring straight at me while the real eye contemplated the passing scene—or perhaps it was the other way around. It made me feel naked and vulnerable, as if that eye knew all my innermost weaknesses and fears. I could barely drag my attention away, though the rest of him lounged and lurked there like a malignity.

Concepción prepared me for the visitation by airing the essential gossip. Although officially Cristina was the royal widow of Ferdinand VII, in practice she had been with a man named Augustín Fernando Muñoz for nine years: She'd "found her destiny" with a guardsman. Early on the two had married in secret, though in the eyes of the world he was just her lover. If she had publicly acknowledged her new marriage while in Spain, Cristina would have had to give up her title as queen regent and that was something she had not wished to do. It had probably cost her the affection and advice of her elder sister, the Infanta Luisa Carlota, who'd been furious at Cristina's remarrying beneath her. However, Muñoz was a good man (so said Concepción). The couple had recently purchased a magnificent country house called the Chateau de Malmaison, where they lived with their own set of children. "Exile sounds rather pleasant," I remarked. Concepción smacked me with her fan and responded tartly, "No one asked your opinion."

We arrived. "Keep your wits about you and your impertinent comments to yourself." Admonitions, surreptitious smacking of me, and straightening of gowns.

Cristina—or María Cristina of Bourbon-Two Sicilies, to give her full, long-winded title—was indeed a beautiful woman, as my earl had claimed. I bowed low and for a long time, as Concepción had schooled me, and the tall, still fair, and still blue-eyed royal personage seemed to approve. We walked the grounds first so Cristina could take the air; she was about seven months pregnant. She gestured me up to stroll beside her, which annoyed Concepción enormously, as I could tell from the indignant splutters erupting behind us. These noises ceased when a large, handsome fellow came sauntering towards us.

"This is our new little spy, my darling. Isn't she precious?" Cristina called to her guardsman, fluttering her lashes.

"Certainly."

"She's leaving for Madrid *muy pronto*. Do you think the girls will like her?"

"Yes I do."

"And they will trust her to help them? Keep them safe from Arguëlles?"

"Indeed."

"That settles it. You always know best."

If this was his role—to agree with whatever she said and sire a load of children—I thought it couldn't be too onerous. He was wearing the jewels Concepción had told me about: the late king's scarfpin and several of his gigantic rings. I eyed Muñoz slyly, then looked away quickly because I caught him doing the same to me.

"Enough! I am puffed!" Her Majesty announced, looping her arm through mine. "Let us go inside." As we sashayed across the crushed golden stones, I wondered if I should give her warm greetings from my lust-addled earl. Would it be appropriate?

"Your Majesty," I hesitated, "I know someone who wishes you only the best, and who asked me—if I was lucky enough to meet you—to be remembered to you."

"Oh goody," she trilled. "I love admirers. Who is it?"

"James Howard Harris. In Naples? He is now 3rd Earl of Malmesbury and a member of Parliament."

"Hmm." She frowned as she thought.

"It was quite long ago, the year your engagement to the king was announced. There was a certain . . . button? Which he recalls particularly."

I loved the light that came into her eyes; as she remembered, they seemed to suddenly glow from within like sun through ice. "That funny, short man. With his elaborate buttons. And his trousers!" Her laugh was infectious as she leaned upon me, whispering conspiratorially, "My mother had turned around because I was lingering to talk with him, and all she could see was the mighty bump. She was so scandalized that I got a fit of the giggles, not even halfway around the room full of people to meet, and I had to leave, drink three glasses of water, and lie down. All

I could think about the rest of that afternoon was imagining what had happened to the poor man's bump!"

Malmesbury would have been so happy to know that golden Cristina remembered his adulation and had thought so long and hard about his bump!

Indoors, we sat in a remarkable room filled with flowers, art, and musical instruments. With my head still buzzing from the quinine, I imagined I mightn't have been the soul of discretion in bringing up the earl and his button, but he seemed to have done me a favour—royal Cristina and I had sparked. I was sure I would need all the friends in high places that I could get.

"My dear señora," Cristina cooed, turning to Concepción, "I remember how well you enjoy spending time with our children. Would you be so kind?" She put her jewelled hand upon her paramour's arm. "*Encanto*, perhaps you could escort her?"

This unexpected plan of action did not suit Doña Rodríguez, I could tell, but she swallowed her chagrin and stepped out with Muñoz.

"Now then, Juan," Cristina said, glancing at her highly buffed fingernails, "explain to me the puzzling reply you sent back this morning. I wish for immediate action, and know the time is ripe. That fine agent we met with last year, he has sent back astonishing reports!"

"Ah, Your Majesty," Juan demurred. "That is the thing. There will be no further reports from that quarter."

"Why ever not? I haven't given him leave to desert me."

"He is dead."

"*Diablo*. I see . . . And you're sure of this?"

"Terribly sure."

Without missing a beat, she turned her penetrating gaze upon me. "This one has agreed to everything?"

Juan gave me an admonitory glance, then answered, "Yes, Your Majesty."

"And she understands the political climate?"

"As much as she needs to, Your Majesty," Grimaldi answered.

"Not really, Highness," I interjected, "I am ready to get started though of course somewhat nervous—" I was babbling, then got hold of myself—"but I know next to nothing about the people involved, nor how a court functions, nor—"

Grimaldi looked at the carpet and frowned, his lips tightening further as Cristina patted my hand and said, "I agree with your concern to know more, little spy. You must anticipate the personalities you will encounter. Men always forget that because it does not interest them. So." She settled herself, index finger to her lip for a moment to think, then began. "The prime minister, General Baldomero Espartero, is a cunning man as well as an excellent soldier. During the war, he was not involved in politics; he was my finest commander. His tactical moves were full of luck and bravado, which he would quickly follow up with force. Fundamentally though, Espartero is a *progresisto* and I did not realize this in time. I made him head of the government, but in that I was wrong. Spain needs to be liberalized, yes—and I have certainly done my share to promote such a state—but I am a *moderada*. Espartero goes too far too fast."

"Your Majesty—" Juan interjected.

"Let me finish this, dear Señor Grimaldi," she said, "I shall try to be brief," and she turned her pale eyes back to me. "Six years ago my worst troubles began. That is when the sergeants—the military—rose against me, storming my palace at La Granja one night, drunk and dangerous, and threatening to massacre everyone in it if I did not agree to their demands. I remained calm, bowed to their wishes, and restored the constitution of 1812, which is what they wanted. When news of their treacherous but successful bullying reached the capital, the chief *moderado* ministers—who had drafted the new constitution—knew that they must flee for their lives."

"Some were later captured," Grimaldi growled, "their heads, ears, and hands cut off and publicly displayed in Madrid."

I shuddered at the vision conjured—and the ears in the box.

Cristina continued, "Then I made my mistake. There was no other strong military personage to keep the populace in check the way he could, so I appointed Espartero commander in chief. Don Carlos the pretender might have won the war then if he'd made use of the opportunity all this chaos afforded, but he has always dithered; he wants to be absolute monarch or nothing. Carlos was defeated and sent into exile. But the successes went to Espartero's head. Suddenly there were many conditions he wished to impose upon me! Me!" She fluttered her fan violently, shaking her head at the mere thought. "I made him a count, I made him a duke, but I could never make him a gentleman."

"Traitor," came from Grimaldi, gloomily.

"The idea of holding the regency as a puppet of that man and the progressives was abhorrent to me. I preferred to abdicate."

"And see what a mess he has made, Your Majesty!" Grimaldi couldn't contain himself any longer. He leapt up and started hurling himself about. "He is inexperienced and markedly authoritarian! And the tutor—"

"Yes, that is the final straw." Cristina sighed and placed a hand upon the baby inside, who must have been kicking. "All of this turmoil is bad for my water." Grimaldi looked abashed and sat again but appeared to be silently imploding. "I abdicated two years ago," Cristina said, "and it is true everything has gone wrong. Even Espartero's own government disagrees with the choice of Arguëlles as tutor! What is he trying to put into my girls' heads? It is so distressing." She fanned herself and then gestured to Grimaldi. "Thankfully, Juan has been instrumental in organizing the resistance campaign from France." He seized her hand and bowed over it, as she skewered me again with her diamond gaze. "I know that he—and you—will not fail me. I have vowed ferocious commitment to the overthrow of Espartero."

She extracted her fingers from Juan's grip and began counting off on them. "So, little accomplice, what we need from you. Number one, the tutor, Arguëlles; you know what to do with him, and please do it thoroughly. Number two, aiding my *moderados* in Madrid, as and when they make themselves known to you. Number three, eligible suitors for my sweet Isabel. You must report back about them as soon as possible."

"Is this wise, Your Majesty?" Grimaldi began, but she stopped him with an imperious finger (the one representing the suitors).

"At this stage there are four candidates." She began on the other hand. "Two Spanish, one French, and one German. Don Carlos's son is my first choice, though he *is* Bella's first cousin and they say that can cause problems. However, it would settle the unrest and that's what's important. The other Spanish one is also a first cousin, same style of merchandise, not very interesting. The son of Louis-Philippe the First, who is my uncle, is the French possibility. I don't know about him, and I need to know." I was feeling increasingly shocked: They're all rogering their relatives, I thought, with each others' blessing! "Leopold of Saxe-Coburg, a cousin of your Queen Victoria's Prince Consort, is the German. They will all be milling about at court, no doubt, and—with Isabel's courses set to start at any time," she placed all ten fingers upon my arm, "you must be there to smell them out."

Oh lord. Smelling out newly pubescent royalty and its hangers-on? But on the other hand, why not? Bright side, I reminded myself: get out from under the Grimaldi thumbscrews, get to Spain at last. Seduce this radical tutor, and after that's accomplished and he's in disgrace, I can flit home with my success in *La pata da cabra* as a calling card. Mulling these contradictory things, I was suddenly woozy again.

Cristina made a kissing face at Grimaldi. "This one is just right, Juan—smoky eyes, a whiff of innocence masking youthful greed and hope. You know how to make them jump for the grapes."

What had she said?

She reached for a small bell that sat upon the table to her left and rang it vigorously. "We must ensure, Juan, that this little mademoiselle has everything she needs. She must be seen to be an influential, well-connected young lady. What is her cover?"

"An English actress, travelling and invited to take a turn upon our stage. Her aim, the reason for her travel, is to learn traditional Spanish dance."

I was definitely feeling peculiar.

"What about her gowns? Shoes? Does she have sufficient numbers and styles, or will it become clear that she is not who she seems simply from scanning her wardrobe? There are servants in the employ of my enemies who would be able to discover such a thing at a glance."

Grimaldi frowned mightily. "Majesty, she has—"

Cristina decreed, "A new frock for each day of the week. Finest materials, spare no expense. English fabrics and designs. You may use my dressmaker, she is very fast." Grimaldi choked as she added, "This mustn't come out of her own money, mind. This must be a gift from your household. And I want her to receive a good salary at La Príncipe, Juan—none of this carping and miserliness you're famous for. My spies must cut a good figure—and you must admit, this one has the figure to do it!"

My head cleared enough to take this news in, and I rejoiced in surprise: new gowns! If I were to strive and fall into danger for my country—their country—at least I'd be gorgeous.

"What role have you in mind for her?" asked the ex-queen.

"Day Smakiña," he grumbled, decidedly put out. I recall thinking this was a very odd name for a character.

"Lovely! For the infantas! That is sure to do the trick!" Cristina clapped her hands in delight. A maidservant entered and was told, "The best port, and figs." The maid scurried off to obey as the royal personage leaned back and thrust her exquisitely clad feet out with a sigh of pleasure, her belly round as a ball and proclaiming its condition. "Oh Juan, when shall we be able to return to our kingdoms, you to your theatres, and me and mine to our rightful place in the firmament? It is too, too hard." She looked over at me and sighed, "You must do your best for us, pretty agent. Promise me."

"Oh, I do, Your Majesty," I said, smiling hard. During that afternoon's visit, I think I had begun to fall under her spell as much as any man.

The room was spinning again. I needed air, so I asked leave to take a turn round the garden. "Excellent timing," Cristina said. "Señor Grimaldi and I have a number of details we must sort out in confidence."

I bowed and exited, trying to find my way back through the labyrinthine hallways. Of course, I didn't mention to either of them one of my character weaknesses: that is, of getting myself hopelessly lost. I've always done it; I'd get into terrible trouble when young by opening doors in places where I was never expected: barrack dormitories (naked soldiers), water closets (go away, girlie!), my parents' bedroom (once, very young, I ran screaming for my ayah, convinced that my stepfather was killing my mother). I was lost on the Sylhet frontier with my pony for hours one day and a search party was sent out. The only reason I didn't succumb to heat and thirst was that I finally let the pony have his head and he immediately turned around and galloped home. When I go into a building and then come out again, anyone who knows me well knows that, should I turn to go left upon exiting, we should inevitably turn right instead and by so doing, find our true path. So it is not surprising that I found myself wandering—at first happily, then with increasing vexation—around the entire ground floor of the rue de Courcelles mansion. I could look out the windows and see the garden, but could not for the life of me find a doorway by which to enter it.

Just as I was about to try to retrace my steps (also usually a mistake), I heard a catlike mewing coming from a room off to my left. I stopped and listened for a moment: more mewing. I ventured closer, thinking that perhaps a kitten had become trapped inside, but that wasn't it, for the door was ajar. Then I heard Concepción's unmistakable whisper.

"No, Fernando. No, I tell you."

A rumble from the guardsman: "Please, it's been too long."

My jaw popped open like a marionette's. Could it be? I mustn't let them find me listening but I just couldn't help myself. I inched my way closer, trying to peer through the crack of the door and trying not to breathe.

His deep growl: "She is too uncomfortable, won't let me near her."

"Well, of course. You must be patient; she has other things on her mind."

"I am in agony."

A few more catlike mews from her, and then, "I daren't. There are other ways."

"I will be in your debt."

I could see shapes, and those shapes were fastened together. Muñoz was kissing her throat like a man about to take a voracious bite. He had rucked up her skirts and one hand was thrust inside, moving rhythmically; Concepción flung her head back and emitted a hot groan, which made him engulf her chin with his open mouth. She would have whisker burn from that one, if I knew anything! Meanwhile, her hand at his waistband was moving purposefully lower, inside his trousers, and she was murmuring encouragingly. He grunted and moaned, mouth still clamped to her chin. His legs became wobbly, he leaned heavily against her, and then—almost before I could believe it—he groaned a mighty groan and she placed her other hand over his mouth. "*Silencio,*" she whispered urgently. Then: "Did you hear something?"

Merde! I backed away swiftly and, I hoped, silently. Turning the corner, I sprinted for the stairs, galloping up them at full speed. I could hear Concepción in the hallway, but if she'd seen me I know she would have cried out and called me back, brazened it out. The ability to barefacedly throw an accusation back at your accuser seems a necessary skill for the Spanish of either sex. If you're good enough at it, you can make the other forget what the initial injury or accusation was in sheer dumbfoundedness at your yapping, arrogant tenacity.

I was hurtling along on the upper floor now, going fast to keep pace with my thoughts: How could I use this information? For a brief and dangerous moment, I imagined myself blurting—but no, heavens not. Who knew when I might need to barter with such powerful secret knowledge?

Then bam! A face-first crash into the piratical bodyguard's rock-hard chest, bruising myself on what I realized must be a concealed, but very large, weapon.

"Sssss!" It was like the sound of a surprised snake, and his sinewy right hand shot out, grasped my waist, and hoisted me into the air. "¡*Atento!*" He glared at me with his one good eye, the glass eye focused elsewhere. This was only the second time I'd heard the man's voice—the first was in the shooting gallery that very first day, after the bullet had thumped into the back wall. Then it had been a stream of excitable Spanish before Juan had sworn at him and whisked me away. But there, in the rue de Courcelles mansion, the rumble from the man's throat was like a close and violent thunderstorm. And how could his one hand almost encircle my waist? I held my rampant fear in check long enough to gasp, "Let me down, oaf!"

A grunt. I dropped—and ran.

I encountered another staircase and took it down. There, I discovered myself to be outside the very room Cristina and Juan still occupied. Should I seek protection from them? But wait, what were *these* two up to?

"He was like a son," Grimaldi was sighing.

"We will make them pay, Juan; it is almost within our grasp. They shall eat their own livers." She squeezed his fingers. "Do not become attached to this one, I pray you."

"She is a woman," he replied. "It is not the same."

I backed away again. They were discussing me as if I were a bullock or prize pig heading to market, of use only as the means to an end. Of course I'd guessed that's what I was to them; I'd have been a fool to think otherwise. But it is very different to *think* something that you suspect than to *hear* it, out loud and in the open. My ears *were* in danger, and my little daughter's as well. Heavily armed bodyguards skulking in hallways, nameless glass-eyed desperadoes providing henchman services for Juan. And this royal beauty never called me by my name, only my function: "little spy," "pretty agent." She distanced on purpose; she'd been born to it. I was expendable. How could I fight for them, I wondered, if I was constantly checking my back in case my comrades were about to do me in? I must be terribly careful—for Emma's sake as well as my own.

※ ※ ※

All the way home in the carriage, Concepción berated Grimaldi at fever pitch in such hasty, dialect-driven Spanish that I was hard-pressed to follow. I understood enough to know she was furious over Cristina's command that I be given a new wardrobe at their expense. They were also concerned that this dressmaking order would delay matters and that the Jesuit would be chagrined—"The father is a diligent, impatient, and holy man"—to which she added, "The rehearsals in Madrid will have to be put back by a week." At this, Juan reminded her that Day Smakiña (that odd character of mine) could be learned in one's sleep "so long as one possesses a stomach of iron." Oh, I trusted them not a jot, not any of them, including the one-eyed pirate with the long, strong hands, now riding with the driver. As soon as we'd returned to the Grimaldi home, I excused myself and tumbled into bed, curled up, and shivered profoundly. I longed to get away to Spain, the sooner the better, though the prospect of travelling under the eagle eye of that priest with the hollow cheeks was also unappealing. What would happen if I gave them all the slip, I wondered, as I slid uneasily towards sleep. Then I remembered Emma's dear ears, whimpered, and tried to keep my aching head very still.

Over the next few days I began to recover fully. Each morning, off I'd go to the dressmaker, Concepción in furious attendance. A small army of women were assisting and the gowns were shaping up swiftly. Perhaps I enjoyed the Grimaldis' chagrin over the rising costs. Each time Concepción would huff, "Finally! It's over!" the dressmaker would say softly, "*Mais non*, Her Majesty suggests . . ." and the description of another marvelous concoction would ensue. I calculated that at the rate we were going, I would need a coach or mule wagon to carry my new habiliments alone.

Concepción arrived in my room one afternoon following the third of these sessions, with Clotilde and the maid in tow. She began ripping through the contents of the wardrobe (the two trunksful provided so beneficently by my earl), flinging garments onto the bed, the blue velvet pouffe, the dressing table. "This mademoiselle is putting us into the poor house," she told her daughter, "so you might as well benefit."

Clotilde gave me a haughty smile and turned to survey the wreckage. Although at least six inches shorter than me, she was approximately the same circumference and of similar colouring. "Ah!" she squealed, pouncing upon the pink one with all the frills and furbelows.

"That one is trashy," her mother said with a lip curled.

"No, *Mamí*, the colour is perfect for my skin. It will look much better on me than on her, you will see."

"Very well, try it on," said the mother. As Clotilde slid into the dress, the hem puddled round her feet. Concepción helped her daughter pin the dark ringlets up off her neck; they peeked into the mirror, nodded, then turned again. "And what else?"

The maid's eyes lit up too as the carnage continued, the Spanish women moving from frocks to hats to boots and shoes, until almost everything had been spoken for. Francine's hands remained folded obediently before her, fingers twitching only slightly. I couldn't help myself: "Francine, choose one," I said magnanimously. But the doña shook her head sternly.

"Not for her. Take the rest away and burn it."

The waste, I couldn't believe it! I'd hardly worn the dove gray one! The Spanish seem far too enamoured of sending inconvenient objects and people into the flames.

I insisted on retaining my favourite tartan and stripes, along with the sky blue, at least until all of my queen-ordered finery arrived. Besides, the tartan was the hiding place of my earl's bank draft, and I was not about to go anywhere without that. Though I tried to think of somewhere else to hide it, I knew there was very little that mother and daughter would not paw through with impunity. So I'd keep it close, upon my back. No surprises, no parting me from my escape route. My life might very well depend upon it.

Concepción stalked out, Francine following with a mountain of fabric in her arms. As Clotilde made to follow, I stopped her.

"Tell me, do you know your father's play, *La pata de cabra*? Do you know my character, Day Smakiña?"

At this, the girl let out a sharp bark of laughter. "That's not a name, *bobo*, it's the function you fulfill! A deus ex machina."

"A what?" I decided to ignore her impudence in calling me stupid. I needed the information too much.

She rolled her eyes. "An unexpected, often supernatural force, that flies down out of the sky to save the hero at the last possible moment."

I was confused. "Out of the sky?"

"You're suspended high up in the flys—up where the ropes and roof are—for the whole performance, and they let you down for your one big scene."

This didn't sound as wonderful as I'd hoped. Up in the roof? It was likely hot, dusty, and dirty way up there.

"But don't worry, you get a nice costume. Probably." With another, mocking little laugh, she stalked off, a shorter version of her imperious mother.

※ ※ ※

My final session in the shooting gallery with Grimaldi was intense. I shot like a madwoman, demolishing an entire target, and I believe we were both proud of my newfound skill. As we rested, sweat running down our brows, I practiced reloading the little pistols with the messy powder and he gave me information about my travelling companion-to-be, the hollow-cheeked Father Miguel de la Vega. The family was ancient and aristocratic; they had tentacles in many lucrative businesses, though chiefly in sherry. There had been three sons: The first inherited the businesses, the second went into the church (this was Father Miguel), and the third was allowed to do what he liked. This third son was one of the young playwrights Juan had been supporting in Madrid when he'd run the Príncipe and the Cruz; his name was Ventura de la Vega. When the Grimaldis left Spain for France, Ventura had convinced Juan to utilize the skills of his priestly brother, and Juan trusted the Jesuit completely. "He is a godly man, Rosana. Like me, an agent of the Spanish royalty, totally dedicated to the Cristinos cause."

Although all this did not endear the good father to me in any way, I became resigned to travelling with him, for Juan also made me understand I would need help from someone who knew the hardships: first by coach to Peripignan, then through the Pyrenean passes (which were high altitudes and could be very cold even in September), down through Catalonia (Carlist territory, and the most dangerous leg of the journey), and on to Madrid. Travel through Spain was never easy but to be a woman increased the strangeness and risk.

"Very well," I said. "But in Madrid, after I seduce the princesses' tutor, what is to prevent me from being blamed and tortured or killed or otherwise treated badly?" My teeth began to chatter, softly, like distant drumming.

"The infantas will."

"But they are only ten and twelve years old. I can't see—"

"Isabel is turning thirteen. She will soon be a woman, please God hear our prayers. Also, there are other operators. They will take you to a safe house should there be any danger. But there will be no danger. The princesses will love you—you must make sure of that."

"And the names of these other operators?"

"Father de la Vega, of course. Also two of the rebel generals, de la Concha and de León. Be advised not to fall in love with them."

I retorted, with dignity, "I would not. I have the heart of a tiger; I am quite fearless—" I was exaggerating shamelessly "—and I am steadfastly on the side of the Cristinos, which is the side of justice." That sounded brave. "And what of my dancing?"

"You will dance, never fear." This sounded ominous and must have showed in my face. He added quickly, "You are going to have a splendid success in my play. Come, once more."

We took aim and fired again—two bulls-eyes!—then bowed formally to each other, pistols smoking.

"Very well, Rosana. With this extra week's enforced practice, I now believe you are the quick study you claim to be. And, since you also claim to be a tiger, I will choose to believe that as well."

Compliments indeed. I felt very proud.

"You leave in two days' time."

As I walked into my bedroom in the Grimaldi house late that afternoon, I saw that my new wardrobe had been delivered. And there, in her underclothes, stood Clotilde with her arms in the air while Concepción dropped the finest of the court-style gowns over the little jade's head and began to lace her up.

"Why are you in my room?"

"*Your* room? That's a fine thing!" the *madre* retorted, going immediately and shrilly on the defensive. "We wanted to make sure the gowns fit correctly, of course."

"Whatever do you mean?"

Concepción tossed her head. "If you do not come back, for some . . . *unlikely* . . . reason, Father Miguel has promised to accompany the return of your trunks. Since we have been impelled to spend a fortune on you, I think you will agree that if *you* are no longer able to benefit from them, Clotilde should."

What indeed could you say to such people? I lay down upon the bed and placed my forearm across my eyes, but they were not deterred: They were not English. As if my action gave them further right to carry on, they proceeded noisily with their inventory. At some point, I must have fallen asleep; I awoke with a start, alone, having dreamt of gowns and avid fingers grabbing, which had transformed into the folded hands and muttered prayers of the half-starved priest, whose tonsure had grown into pointed, black, furry ears on the top of his head.

After our supper, it was dark outside and quite warm. Like many Spanish families, the Grimaldis often took a turn through the streets at this time, about eleven o'clock, to cool their blood and aid digestion. The children usually came along, since the Spanish are much more lenient about their offspring's bedtimes than English parents. I asked to accompany them, and Clotilde decided to come as well, something she didn't usually do.

"But fetch me a shawl, will you?"

I felt magnanimous; I was about to leave them, so why not? I located a soft pink one to match the furbelowed gown she was wearing, and a blue shade for me. When I clattered back downstairs, Clotilde had just finished pinning up her hair to get it off her neck (as had I, on such a warm night), but there was my favourite comb holding it all in place! She'd obviously removed the comb from my room, along with the earl's dresses. The sauce of the girl!

We set out after the strolling family. The Grimaldi residence was finely situated in that it was only two or three blocks from the Seine, which is where the family decided to wend. A gorgeous night it was, one of those fine, full-mooned Parisian nocturnes in mid-change from summer to autumn; lovely, soft air that slips across your skin like cool silk. The streets were empty except for us. The lamps were lit and glowing at every corner but seemed almost unnecessary since the moon's face illuminated everything so enchantingly.

Clotilde and I followed along at a leisurely pace. I could hear one of the little girls piping up shrilly and the deep rumble of Juan's reply. I was stretching myself to meet the adventure ahead, my mind whirling with the hunger of anticipation, the expectation of youth. We reached the Seine, and I wanted to linger. "Let's not catch up with them just yet, Clotilde. I never wish to set foot inside a building again!"

She, of course, took me at face value. "But," brow furrowed like her father, "why would you want to be outside all the time?"

"Oh you goose!" I laughed. "I don't really mean it, it's a wish. A projection of fantasy, *bobo*," and I poked her, to get back at her a little, and she shrugged. "Oh."

For some reason, I felt strangely nostalgic, singularly sad. "I'm about to leave Paris, Clotilde, and I wish to remember this moment, this evening." I let go of her elbow to lean on the railing and gaze into the water swirling past.

At that instant, Clotilde's neck was clamped from behind by a large, strong hand, and her body lifted by the neck, up and over the railing! A tall, hooded figure in loose workman's clothing went with her over the railing, as if in flight. It happened all in total silence and at frightening speed! I could barely register what had just occurred; when I did, I regained my mind and voice enough to let out an unholy shriek, then yanked up my skirt and vaulted after them—not thinking, just reacting.

The *thing* was propelling her, dragging her, along the narrow bank, still by the throat, as I scrambled after them, howling—howling to attract attention, howling to frighten or distract this monster. The girl was writhing, her hair loose and waving over her face, as she tried to pull at the hand gripping her so mercilessly. Finally catching up with them, I reached up to yank back the obscuring hood. But the creature's other hand shot out like a piston and connected—a blow to my sternum, knocking the wind out of me, though never once did it turn its dark features in my direction. It didn't seem human; its strength was immense! I got in close again, grabbing its coat, and began to kick. I connected. Was it a shin? Get it in the balls, I told myself, kicking higher. You son-of-a-bitch! Somewhere there were voices, yelling.

All through this punching and thrashing there was not a sound from *it* of any kind, no grunts or curses, nothing. Clotilde suddenly went limp, as if she was already finished, though I could see wide, terrified eyes and her nostrils dilating in and out. That strong hand clamped on her pale neck, long fingers and sinewy wrists—I needed to break its hold! I darted in, but the free hand swung around again and delivered a crashing blow to my head. I couldn't help it, I lost hold of the coat. Then, Clotilde's neck still in its grip, the engaged hand and its powerful arm cast her into the river—and didn't let go! *It* was gone with her!

The first sound from the conjoined, silent figures was the splash as they hit the water and went under together. I scrabbled to my knees and stared, gasping for breath. At first, nothing. Then the pink gown, just below the surface, gleaming in the sparkling moonlight. It was rising like a carp coming up to take air. And I began shrieking again—help us, someone, anyone! The water broke over Clotilde's white face, still clenched by fingers that appeared to be crushing her chin; her dark eyes were open. Then the Seine itself seemed to thrash and move; the creature could swim like a river rat. Propelling the girl's body—pink dress wavering, glimmering—pushing her through the water with that hand on her throat, as close to her side as a maggot. Her white face sliding like a small ship with a wake, turned to the indifferent moon. I couldn't stand it! I leapt after them, and the water closed around my head with shocking cold.

All of these events must have taken only a minute, perhaps two. The Grimaldis had heard my banshee cries and rushed back. At the river bank, Concepción pinned the children to her side and told them not to look. Juan began yelling for the police, hoping that one or a pair of gendarmes might be within earshot—and they were. Two came running. By that time, the hooded head, moving at incredible speed, was out in the middle of the channel. In the water, my skirts were heavy, impeding my progress; out there, the pink gown must have been pulling her down as it became more and more saturated, as he impelled her small self, with such murderous determination, through the cold and unforgiving element. White forehead, nose and chin rising sometimes, going under at others; how long could a body live, swallowing water, gulping for air? Drowning, lungs filling slowly, is a fearsome death. Never let some cruel, deluded soul who drowns kittens in a sack tell you otherwise.

A gendarme swam out to help, reaching me just before I went under from the weight of my skirts. Juan was knee-deep in the Seine as we drew in to the bank, and when he saw me rise to my feet, he cried out sharply in agony, sobbing and moaning and beating his chest.

"I thought you were Clotilde—I thought it was you out there!" And he plunged in, swimming desperately after the hideous creature who had his beloved daughter. Concepción wailed in the background, cradling the children. The pink shawl lay, trodden, by the railing. The second gendarme had hastened off for reinforcements and a boat and was back very swiftly. Juan was picked up in the middle of the Seine and stayed with the officers all night, combing the river. Other boats and more men were dispatched; up and down they plied the water, but . . . nothing.

I was helped back to the house by the wet gendarme; Concepción took the children into her bedchamber without a word to me, her features shattered.

Clotilde's body was found in the morning on the other bank, covered in mud. Lungs full of brackish water, lips and eyelids and cheeks blue, dark ringlets lank. Everything else, dead white. Except the dress—pink now smirched with mud and oil and weed.

The funeral preparations were feverish and full of a kind of delirium. It was August; speed was a necessity, along with flowers of the highest scent. They cascaded everywhere, from the casket to the pews that were filled to capacity. *Tout le monde de théâtre de Paris* was assembled in the cathedral, as well as the entire Spanish contingent now in exile in the capital. Every face was tearful, every body was embraced, every voice listened to with compassion. Horrified speculation was rife about the killer, but no clues had been found. I felt completely numb throughout. My head and ribs ached from the pounding I'd taken, though I barely noticed; I couldn't believe what had happened, the swiftness of the tragedy. In my mind, all I could see was that hooded head swimming savagely away, dragging its prey. The Grimaldis wouldn't look at me or speak to me, not even the littlest, Josep, who turned his face and buried it in his nurse's black-draped shoulder.

Between the morning his daughter was found dead and the funeral, Juan had rushed everywhere, questioned everyone. He'd slammed about, berating me, as I'd sobbed and cried that I knew nothing, how could I?

I pitied the man's torment, it was so deep. He blamed himself for being enmeshed in politics. Was it an act of vengeance against his family?

"Could someone have been after *me*?" I asked, hesitantly.

"No, that's not possible," he replied tersely. "Why would anyone target you in particular? Or," he mused unhappily, "my daughter, in particular?"

By the day of the funeral he had exhausted the theory of a political motive and had come to believe it was a random act, foully perpetrated. All that the Grimaldis wanted now was for this to be over; the only other thing they wanted was for me to be out of their lives and gone. I was bad luck, and a reminder of all they had lost. As for me, I didn't know what to believe.

As the service went on, the smell of incense grew stronger and the emotions as well. I caught sight of crowlike Father Miguel de la Vega seated behind the gorgeously attired grieving family; I was supposed to travel with this stranger? I should get away from them, I remember thinking: go back to England, call it all off. The thoughts tumbled and jangled inside my brain. I tried to think, to plan—as soon as we leave the church, as soon as night falls, as soon as . . . All a muddle.

Dumas *père* and Ida Ferrier were in attendance several rows back. Dumas seemed in foul humour and had begun muttering despite his wife's embarrassed entreaties. The Grimaldi family also became aware of the dark energy from Dumas's pew, and I could tell that Concepción and Juan were equally offended. As we all rose to follow the casket from the cathedral, I saw Dumas push Ida away with a muted roar, then heard her apologetically telling others, "There is a new young collaborator who has not met a deadline. It maddens him."

I was in a strange, altered mood, dangerously stimulated by horror and the gravity of ritualized grief. And sometimes, truth is, I have no idea what comes over me. There are times when it feels as though I'm suddenly inhabited by a gust of wind, then a storm full of thunder and lightning or an earthquake rises up from my guts, and I cannot stop the momentum any more than one can stop the cataclysmic ferocity of the elements: I am inside the eye of the hurricane—no, I *become* the eye of the hurricane—and the explosion erupts with a swiftness that surprises everyone around me as much as it astonishes myself.

People were moving slowly into the aisles. Dumas and his wife were passing, the writer's small eyes looking me up and down. "You again," he said. "Weren't you the one—?"

"At the Café de Paris. Was, and still am."

He grunted dismissively.

"Shame on you for your bad mood, monsieur," I said. "This day is not about you."

"Brainless slut," he declaimed, and then moved away down the aisle.

My brain, my circulatory system, simply imploded—I saw explosions and flashes of red before my eyes, sizzling through me in a hot, fiery gush.

I leapt into the aisle and shouted after him, "Alexandre Dumas, I challenge you! Tomorrow morning at six, in the Bois de Boulogne! Pistols!" My fingers were clenching and unclenching as if already gripping my weapon and happily directing its contents into his head. There were cries of dismay from all around. He staggered with surprise and turned to look, but suddenly I was being dragged backwards and away, bundled along down a different aisle away from the crowd, then slung over a shoulder and carried at a run.

Outside in bright sunshine, several men were clustered and gusts of Spanish filled the air. I was set on my feet, then something dark went over my head. Who are these men, I wondered in terrible alarm. Why hasn't someone stopped them? A hand was startlingly at my throat—that strong, sinewy hand! Oh dear God, I thought, Clotilde's murderer? How can this be? I bucked and twisted, but my mouth was clamped shut, forcing me to swallow my screams.

"*¡Cállate!*" I heard, and other oaths. I recognized the threatening rumble of the piratical bodyguard with the wandering glass eye who'd lifted me in Cristina's palace—it must be he! I could hear shouting and the footsteps of other men too, as I was hustled along some cobbles, stumbling and almost falling. Where were they taking me? I could hardly breathe, for by then the man's stinking paw was covering my nose as well as my mouth. The stench and taste of some potent tobacco filled my senses. Before the reek had time to make me physically ill, I bared my teeth and clamped down upon a noxious finger. I heard a human roar, felt a sudden explosion of pain—and then a fall down a long, dark tunnel.

INTERLUDE: THE DEAD OF NIGHT

I AWAKE WITH A start, having slipped off the settee and hit my head on the floor. *Merde!* I remember where I am: the empty room near the theatre. The last candle is burning now and it too is nearly spent, beginning to gutter. The place feels slippery with blackness, with the possibility of movement in the corners, at the edges of my panic.

Also, I am aghast to discover, there is the sound of footsteps. I scramble up and put myself behind one of the tapestries, press myself against the paneling. A key clanks in the lock. The door opens slowly, and light spills into the room. The Cockney enters carrying a candelabra with three tapers in one hand and in the other a glass carafe and a covered dish.

When he doesn't immediately see me, he puts everything down with an oath, spilling wax all over the dish, and comes at the tapestries with both arms flailing. *¡Jesu!* He will flatten me or knock me senseless. I step out; what else can I do?

"I'm here."

I must have something to drink before I expire.

His shadow billows above me and onto the ceiling as he comes to a sudden halt. "Christ, woman. Scared me shitless."

I point at the carafe, trying for imperiousness. "Is that for me?"

"Thirsty? Tho't you'd be. Not just yet though, not allowed."

Dog.

And the big man laughs at me. "Won't let us get ya, eh? But you will, you'll come round. You'll 'ave to." He yanks one of the wooden chairs to the centre of the room, places the candelabra upon it, then pulls over the other chair and sits himself down, arms crossed, legs spread. I smell a delicious aroma coming from the covered dish and wonder what it can be. Something with meat, and sauce . . . or gravy . . .

I move away to the edge of the room, use my haughtiest Spanish inflections. "Where is your friend, or should I say, associate? Your employer? What is he?"

He sits there, following my movements with his eyes. I don't like this, not one bit.

"I want to know who you are," I say. Where has it come from, this defiance? I need water; I need to get out of here! But even more than that, it seems, I need to know that they are not with *him*—the fiend. Oh god in heaven, that is the terrifying thought that has been slipping around in the shadows.

"The Society of the Exterminating Angel!" I say the name loudly, eyes glued to his face, watching for something, a flicker, a withdrawal, a sense of pride, anything.

He opens his eyes wider, but I can't read them. Nothing in them of past or future, just of the moment, and the pleasure of his power.

"Please," I ask, "let me drink something."

"Come over 'ere," he says, "and I'll think abou' it."

This disgusts me. "No."

I see swift anger mount his cheeks, swell into his brow. He glances over at the door, then back at me. He has just remembered, and so have I. He hasn't locked it! I race over, grab the handle, twist and yank and I'm in a corridor. Which way to turn? Then I go down with a mountain of man on top of me, crushing the air from my ribs. He gets to his knees, breathing heavily, gives my forehead a thump on the floor, lifts me under the arms, and returns me to the paneled room. He presses me up against the door, which he has closed and locked behind us.

"I know an' you know," he says against my hair, "that I could do anythin' I want wi' you an' no one will 'ear it. An' I'd like to do a lot." I can feel his erection against my back. "My friend, as you call 'im, is makin' final enquiries. All the bits an' pieces comin' together. We'll soon 'ave ya. There's nowhere for you to go, or 'ide. You'll be found out, an' take yer punishment for all yer crimes. That I promise you. Snooty jade."

He releases me and steps away.

"I'll wait 'til you're broken. And you will be, after 'e finishes. Then I'll look like your 'ero, an' a Spanish widow loves her 'ero, isn't that what you said? And I'll 'ave ya."

He picks up the tray with the carafe and the dish, unlocks the door. "Get yer facts in order, missy."

And he's gone. The candelabra remains, one of the tapers broken and cold but two still burning. It's a good thing—the only good thing—because the last guttering candle from their first visit now expires. I am almost beyond fear. What in God's name are they after?

I must recollect everything, have it all at the ready. And land on my feet.

Remembering Spain

When I came to, it was dark and I could feel a rocking motion all around, as well as a soft, rhythmic jangling. I lay still, trying to remember what had happened and form a conjecture as to where I was. I could feel roughness, the warmth of blankets. When I heard the snap of a whip and a driver's cry, I realized I was lying across the seat of a stage coach, travelling through the night. I reached over and felt a curtain, which I opened enough to show me that it was almost dawn, the paleness growing and mist billowing in the hollows as the coach sped past. Then I heard a voice.

"You are awake?" It was the priest, leaning over me.

I let out a startled bleat that he muffled with the sleeve of his cloak, though I shoved his arm away with an instinctive jerk: memories of the bag over my head and my fear in the Paris street.

"Reveal nothing untoward," he whispered, perching back upon the seat opposite. "You must carry out our charade; it is very important."

I tried to sit up but my head began to reel, so I lay down again. "Charade? Where are we?"

"En route to Toulouse. This is a private coach, hired at great expense. We will be changing horses along the way, but I have had enormous difficulty arranging everything so quickly. You've caused no end of unnecessary trouble and pain—as I told the señor you would."

Oh God, the funeral. It came back in a rush: the crush of bodies, the smell of incense. "I was provoked," I protested. "Surely everyone could see!"

"The only things that could be seen were your enraged face and the kicks and screams filling the cathedral as you were carted off," he said. "The Grimaldis were mortified, on top of their misery and sorrow."

As I'd been learning, when in doubt, leap into the fray, don't just sit there and take it. "I can't be held accountable. It's your fault, all of you, with your scheming and plotting! Besides, what would *you* do if some vile-smelling thug began to choke the life out of you without explanation?"

"He was trying to shut your insolent, shrieking mouth!" the priest shouted back, with a spray of saliva, jumping up to give the upholstery behind my head a thump. Then he sat again and turned away, muttering under his breath like a bee in a bottle, and genuflecting, over and over, rocking back and forth. Balls! What a turd, I thought, what a gobshite! How could I be stuck with him for all this long journey? I suppose he was wondering the exact same thing.

Up above, the driver was busy slowing the horses, and soon he was hurrying to the coach door. His anxious face peered inside. "Monsieur, I heard a cry. Is the lady well? We are far from a town, I'm not certain—"

The Jesuit reached across and took my hand. I jerked it away but he glared, gave it a thwack, and clamped it between his two clammy ones. "She is feeling pains, yes, but will be fine," he replied with sudden composure. "It is not yet time. The journey can continue. *Mais, merci beaucoup.*"

The coachman tipped his hat, glanced curiously at me, then disappeared.

"Do not think I am enjoying this," de la Vega added, still clutching my struggling hands, squeezing them with a kind of nervous compulsion. "Lie down. Behave naturally, in case he returns."

In a moment, harnesses jingled and we continued on our way, both of us immediately drawing apart as far as humanly possible within the coach's confines. We stewed in silence for a time.

"It was instantly necessary to remove you from Paris," the priest said at last, his lean face scrinched with distaste. "Such a remarkably impulsive scene! It was also unfortunate that a number of gendarmes were passing at the time. The authorities were not easy to pacify." Certainly, I thought, a struggling woman with her head in a bag is not a usual sight in the middle of the afternoon, even in Paris. It was then that I noticed de la Vega was not wearing his cassock; instead, he was dressed in a dark but expensive-looking suit, a woolen cloak clasped at the neck for warmth. I glanced down at my body, supine across the seat. There was a large lump in the middle of it. Reaching under the blankets, I felt a heavy wad of material strapped to my belly and fastened behind my back.

"Señora Rodríguez's idea," the *padre* explained, "at her husband's request. It was a padded suit for a comic character. Modified quickly to suit our needs."

"It's supposed to be a pregnancy belly?" I squeaked, surprised.

He looked away, and in the dawn light I was astonished to see his cheeks flushing scarlet, all the way to his hairline and upwards to his now fully shaven dome. "For a woman. For—that time of life." He seemed hard-pressed to keep his equanimity under the added stress of describing the arrangements. "I am your husband. You have taken ill and must get to Toulouse as soon as possible, in order to deliver your baby under the care of a specialist doctor residing there. That is how we were able to secure this coach and our immediate passage. That is how we explained your restless unconsciousness."

"I've been drugged?" I cried, trying to sit up. The big belly made this a troublesome deed—that and my pounding head. Father Miguel pushed me prone again.

"You will not have to stay in this condition for long," he whispered.

"I hope not!"

"Further preparations are being readied for our next stage. We shall be required to keep up this parody—"

"Of a pregnancy?"

"Of our marriage." The words seemed to stick to his lips, so he wiped them fiercely and glared at the rising sun, winking through the passing trees.

"But," I exclaimed, suddenly appalled, "it must be a three-day trip to Toulouse!"

"We've been on the road many hours already. We travel at night as well, all night. The time will be halved. Keep your voice down."

"I've barely said anything!" Oh, I was sick of his priggish nonsense already.

"This may be the best way to leave Paris quickly, I admitted to the Grimaldis. But not pleasant for a priest—for a man of my nature."

I flopped over onto my side, away from him, and closed my eyes, trying to ease the pounding inside. My mind was racing: Where were my little muff pistols? Was my new wardrobe following? With all the grief in the family, would someone ensure the pistols were packed in my bags? Would the Grimaldis still keep their end of the bargain? I was wearing my favourite tartan and striped gown. Luckily for me, I'd worn it to the funeral, so my emergency fund was still upon me. Thank God for small mercies, I told myself firmly. Now locate the pistols, gather your resources, be ready for further surprises.

"I will tell you this once, Señora Gilbert, and not again." I bucked in my seat, startled: He was leaning over me, insistent voice buzzing in my ear. "You think you are an actress? Now is your chance to prove it. Are you listening?"

Suddenly glum, I mused that this was not the way I had hoped to be entering Spain for my big adventure—wearing a fat suit and pretending to swoon from my womanly condition or whatever other folly they'd cooked up.

"When we arrive in Toulouse tomorrow afternoon, you must step out of the coach, then say that you are faint." I knew it (I sneered to myself). "I shall be at your side the whole time, as your caring husband. Be careful to speak only in Spanish. We are from Madrid; I am in business. Then, you must act as if the pains of contraction have suddenly begun . . ." Here he hesitated, and I glanced over. Yes, the gaunt paleness was being exchanged for another bright crimson flush. "I hope you know what that state of being looks like."

"I'm sure I can fake it." Turd.

"Another, smaller coach, already hired, will be standing by," he went on. "We will step into that to be driven towards the hospital. Once away from the coaching inn and its overseers, the second carriage will take us to another destination, and our journey will continue under new conditions."

"Better ones?"

"Now be silent and let us contemplate the coming ordeal."

He leaned back, placed his head against the upholstery, and closed his eyes. I tried to relax, but my mind began racing again, flicking through all of the decisions and accidents that had led me to that point: accepting a lesson from Señor Hernandez, the "thwok" of a mystery bullet at the shooting gallery, two ears in a box, the river rat churning the Seine into a foul murder scene, my impetuous challenge to Dumas. All somehow funneling towards this cockeyed result—running away with a Jesuit priest! How my mother would have punished me: Uppity miss, spoiled little brat, you're not worthy of the good father's time nor concern. I began to feel a new, real fear for myself and my fate: dragged off, sedated, bundled into a belly and dispatched towards the border. Would anyone ever know what had become of me, should I not return? Was there anyone who would care? Really, no one in the world that I could think of. How terrible, how sad—I began to panic and thrash about, which provoked an exasperated "be still!" from my severe companion.

I took a deep breath and tried to make my mind drift. It did, but not towards happy times. A note I'd received from my mother one Christmas, when I was at boarding school, and the tiny pieces I'd torn it into: "Be good," it said, "say your prayers, and obey them." I could probably count on the fingers of both hands the number of times she'd either held me or stroked my hair. I don't think she'd intended to neglect me, it just never occurred to her that I craved her kindness. Her love, I suppose I mean to say. It was not in her nature, that's all. My mother, being a gay and pretty creature, flit from one amusement to the next in a butterfly fashion and was forgiven for it. My stepfather might have longed for children of his own; I have no idea. We'd never discussed it: forbidden by her, as was anything remotely connected with family history, aspirations for life, or any topic that might lead to emotion. Not that anyone could hate her for it, I told myself scornfully. The soul of gaiety, with a lovely high clear singing voice, she can accompany herself on the piano and place her admiring fingers just so on the arm of any gentleman at a party . . .

Then a terrible thought struck me. Wasn't that just what I had done, myself? Flit, flit? Several times? And what about baby Emma? Yes, she'd gone to the most loving of homes; she's adored by my step-aunt and uncle. When returning from India, escaping from Thomas, I had planned to stay with Aunt Catherine until I'd gotten on my feet: There I would have been able to see the little girl with my own eyes, to watch her grow, make sure she was loved and shown love. A fictitious relative, they might have said. Her step-cousin, perhaps? I could have been a surreptitious guardian checking in on her well-being, even if only for a short time. But what did I do instead? Fell in lust with George Lennox, ran away from Aunt Catherine at the pier, and rogered myself silly with him at the Star and Garter Inn! I abandoned my baby as surely as my mother had me!

Oh, thinking this, I rolled around and moaned some more, hashing out all the complicated recriminations I could think of for myself, until Father de la Vega thrust his lean head forwards and hissed, "Don't overdo it, you idiotic woman! Anyone would think you're having the child right now!"

After that, I did calm down. What good were thoughts like that? There I was, halfway to Toulouse, with a priest in charade as my husband. There was nothing for it but to go on, to go ahead with the plan, harebrained though it seemed. I was in too deep to back out. The drug they'd given me must have still had some effect as well, for after my internal tirade I was exhausted, sleeping most of that morning and afternoon, awaking ravenous, and descending (carefully and pregnantly, good actress that I am) to eat at an inn near Limoges, where we changed horses.

That second night's travel seemed interminable. We did not light the lamps inside, preferring not to see one another. I had to school myself not to flinch every time I imagined the pious stranger sitting across from me. I lay down again just to be able to turn my back, but my spine tingled whenever I heard him shift or sigh. Breaking our fast at seven-thirty in the morning, I was informed that we should be arriving by mid-afternoon. Finally, as predicted, Toulouse appeared; my limbs by then twitching with restlessness and the tension of suppressing it for all those horrid hours.

We arrived with a clatter at our final coaching inn. There was great bustling and excitement from the porters and horseboys, who had been apprised of "the Spanish lady's" delicate condition. I did my melodramatic best, allowing myself to cry actual tears and utter the odd real piercing scream, which galvanized the poor porters like nobody's business. Soon enough I was grasping the *padre*'s arm (reinventing the devastating pinch-twist combination I used to use on my fellow boarding school inmates, just to pay him back a bit) and clambering, clutching my big belly, into the waiting second carriage. The new horses were whipped up, the inn personnel bowed and scraped and called their best wishes to my beleaguered husband, and off we flew across the cobblestones.

After ten minutes or so, Father Miguel pounded at the carriage ceiling with his stick and shouted up, "How far is it?"

The new driver called down, "Maybe twenty minutes travel, monsieur."

We duly came to a detached house with a neat garden, and the driver helped my priestly husband get me in the front door, which a young woman, with every show of love and concern, had opened at our arrival. I was gently deposited in a chair in the front room, the driver bowed and retreated (with a healthy tip), and the door was closed upon him.

I was famished, bruised, and thoroughly cranky, so I was in no mood as the next part of the plan was revealed: This woman, Matilde, would accompany Father Miguel and I into Spain as our wet nurse. "What?" I cried. "We don't remotely need a wet nurse; I am not having a baby!" I thought they'd lost their collective minds. The Jesuit reminded me, getting into and out of Spain was a complicated business in the war's aftermath. Identities were checked, passports were required. Personal histories were often followed up.

"Understand me," he said sternly, "We are husband and wife, named Antonio and Patrizia Olivares." I was interested to see that, in front of Matilde, he was not blushing over this pronouncement. Instead, he was enjoying his power and authority—a trait I was beginning to recognize as particularly Jesuitical. "You have just had a baby, a little girl—"

"Her name is Matilde also," the woman added, at which point I thought she must be completely deranged as well as highly unoriginal.

"—and Matilde is coming with us to feed the infant," the priest concluded.

At that moment, a loud wailing came from another room. She hurried off and returned with a newborn. I thought, My God, now we're kidnaping children! Then the woman explained with a shrug, "She is mine. One week ago on Friday."

This is it, I thought. Forget being an actress; I'm with an escaped circus, some sort of wandering bedlam. I'm in the middle of a nightmare. "Help me out of this wretched belly, will you, Matilde?" I sighed.

✣ ✣ ✣

Antonio and Patrizia Olivares were, at least, a well-to-do couple. I was delighted and relieved when my royally commissioned wardrobe caught up with us the following morning as we prepared to depart. Sure enough, its transportation required a mule with a small wagon and driver, so they were added to our menagerie. We human travelers had our own carriage, in which we travelled facing forwards and Matilde, carrying her namesake, sat facing us. I had also been immensely relieved to discover that my miniature pistols, along with powder and caps, were packed in their faux book in a portmanteau. I transferred the book to my reticule, just in case. Although this made it bulge, I decided I'd prefer to be taken for a bookworm than be taken by surprise.

In the light of morning as we bowled south towards the border, my stomach now full and head no longer aching, with birds singing and the fields around waving with wheat, I found it hard to believe in the necessity of our scheming. "Are there really such people as *bandoleros?*" I asked the *padre*, who sat sunk in misery or some other bleak emotion. "I mean, now that the war is over, it seems silly to—"

"In the north, war is never over," Matilde answered. "I doubt it ever will be. And the *bandoleros* are alive and well."

Father Miguel narrowed his eyes and shot me a glance at this.

It turned out that Matilde was originally from Figueres and the hope was that her knowledge of the Spanish north, its peoples and dialects, would help deflect any—"unlikely" said the Jesuit—difficulties we might encounter. By now I didn't trust that word "unlikely" at all. I remembered Concepción and Clotilde using it to describe their greedy exploration of my new finery, in the "unlikely" event that I might not return. My Irish heritage began to assert itself: Every time anyone said such-and-so was "unlikely," my fingers would jerk with the desire to cross myself, out of superstition more than anything, since I'm not a devout Catholic in any sense of the word.

The routes through the mountains had been established by pilgrims bound for Santiago de Compostela, a holy city at the extreme western edge of northern Spain. We were headed for the southeastern pass, the one hugging the coast. This restless journeying had begun after the Crusades, when the Christian soldiers had returned from Jerusalem and no longer knew what to do with themselves when they weren't killing and maiming infidels. From what I gathered, this coastal route was the easiest, most well travelled, and least likely to harbour pockets of ruthless *bandoleros* ready to slit pilgrims' throats for a few coins and a scallop shell.

From Toulouse, the three-day route took us to Carcassonne, then to the coast city of Narbonne and south to Perpignan, where we took on some provisions before heading for the border, a few miles north of Figueres.

The weather did indeed change as we moved into the coastal foothills of the Pyrenees. All of us had been perspiring and fanning ourselves in the heat as we crossed the flat fields around Carcassonne, but now we pulled cloaks and hoods from our baggage and sat back in the coach with its windows half-closed. We passed through lush forests of holm oak and tall coney pines, and a fine wet mist in the mornings floated along the rolling, rocky hills. Greens of all hues, from chartreuse and lime to silvery olives, punctuated by an almost black conifer shade.

A little town, just a hamlet whose name I can't recall, was the border point. Before reaching it, Father Miguel had gone into a kind of stupor of concentration—perhaps he was praying, I didn't know, but it made me very anxious.

"Is our crossing all that dangerous?" I asked.

"We shall see."

Very comforting. My heart began to thump against my bodice.

Matilde leaned forwards to hand me the baby, plunking her into my arms as if she were a parcel of laundry, then sat back with her hands folded in her lap and her eyes on the passing scenery. Looking down into the infant's tiny face, all sleepy and peaceful, my nervous palms sweating onto her blanket, I wished I could recapture such innocence and lack of dread. What did I think was going to happen? I'm just a quiet young mother, I told myself, testing it out. No one will hurt such a creature. Not these lovers of Madonna, not these good Catholic men. Calm. Calm and peace.

The border patrol was very thorough. They were small, tough, dark people with snapping black eyes and wiry frames. They wore soldier-like uniforms and carried several weapons—rifles as well as pistols in holsters. Numerous other small groups of travelers stood or sat about, looking confused and in some cases, weeping. The *padre* (my husband Antonio) handed over our visas with a manly growl, and we were told to step aside while they searched our belongings. One of the young guards was looking me up and down with a rather frightening intensity, especially fixing upon the baby at my breast. I jiggled her in what I hoped was an adoring way and kept my eyes on the ground. Our luggage was pawed through. I was particularly distressed at the way my new wardrobe was being handled, but there was nothing I could do. I was glad I had the pistols with me; I kept my reticule tucked against my skirt, half hidden by the folds of material. After a few minutes of intense questioning, the priest seemed to pass the gauntlet of scrutiny; it was fascinating to hear his usually deep and ghostlike voice transform into that of a harried Spaniard on his way to Madrid, but with a modicum of respect for the northerners' cause. Very layered performance, and though I hated to admit it, impressive.

After that, our drivers were questioned. Next, Matilde; she charmed the guards, with her local dialect and the few sweet but saucy jokes they exchanged. And then it was my turn. The guards came close and surrounded me (I nearly let out a frightened squawk at the proximity of their guns and leather boots, especially remembering the muff pistols bulging in my reticule) but they all, as one, bent their heads to look at little Matilde. As she waved a fist, they began to coo in their gruff voices. Father Miguel's (husband Antonio's!) eyes were fixed on me warningly; I summoned up thoughts of all the paintings of Madonnas I'd seen in my lifetime and attempted to copy that look, but as the gravelly cooing went on, and as one bolder young man with a large hooked nose and greasy mustache put his face even closer, I caught his eye not upon the baby's face but upon my bosom (which, it is true, was heaving a bit in trepidation), and I couldn't help but murmur, "I hope you enjoy what you see." As soon as it slipped out, I realized it was a foolish remark to make, but I was so nervous. His eyes flicked up to mine and his brow wrinkled. I smiled very sweetly and fastened my eyes back to the baby (now beginning to wriggle and fuss under such acute scrutiny), hoping that the guard hadn't really heard what I'd said or had misunderstood it. He glanced at his companions, then over at Father Miguel. I decided to speak up. "Husband?" I said. "Antonio dearest, may I ask these kind gentlemen if they have finished questioning me? I am most tired." All of the guards, except the hook-nosed one, jostled each other and moved back hurriedly at my request, with a few abashed chuckles, a slap to each other's shoulders, and a muttering of "*bebé bonita,* little innocent . . ."

Hook-nose had a quick whisper with the senior guardsman. After a moment, "Your papers are in order, Señor Olivares, and extremely thorough," the older man said, looking ferocious. "Otherwise we would have had no choice but to detain you overnight while we ascertained the veracity of your visas. However," and he looked at his younger compatriot who was still openly examining me (I could tell, because I could feel the burning gaze through my clothing), "you must have friends in powerful places. In the south. Your business must be great."

"It is," the priest said, "so if there is nothing further . . ."

"The south always gets what it wants. While we pick up the pieces, isolated and neglected."

Hook-nose had his hand on his holster, for some horrible reason. Now our interlocutor did as well. It seemed everything was about to go badly awry, all because the ferocious one had remembered his feudal chagrin at being given orders from the rich centre, and Hook-nose was nursing a different, long-held grudge. But Matilde suddenly stepped forwards, holding her arms out to me for the baby, saying, "Señora, forgive me, it is time that the infant be fed." With a modest little curtsy to the weapon-laden crew, she took baby Matilde and returned to the carriage, where her bodice was loosened and the feeding begun. They couldn't see any of this, but the suggestion was there, hanging in the air. I could see it transforming the faces of even the two who stood bristling before us. They knew what was happening just out of sight; they couldn't help it, their inner vision turned to the peace and joy of their earliest memories, their first happiness. Amazing, really, what the state of new motherhood (and two lovely, heavy breasts) will do to grown men. Before we knew it, we were back in our carriage and galloping down the road.

I collapsed with relief and then had an attack of hilarity, laughing until I'd given myself hiccups. Father de la Vega seemed disgusted at this unstoppable display, though Matilde (burping her baby) smiled and patted my knee. My first encounter with northern desperadoes, and a dreadfully temperamental lot they were, with their hair-trigger reactions and twitchy fingers.

"Don't you think that hook-nosed one looked a lot like Juan's henchman, except shorter?" I gabbled, still catching my breath. "You must know who I mean. The dark fellow in Paris, glass eye, tall, looks like a pirate—"

"Pedro Coria."

Matilde looked over at us, eyes suddenly sharp and curious.

"Is that his name?" I asked, hoping to learn more.

"I know him well," de la Vega muttered. "He is not a henchman, as you ignorantly put it, he is an associate. Coria is a northerner, but he's joined the Cristinos."

"Well, whatever he is, he could be cousins with those ones!" Still laughing, I lifted the reticule onto my lap, produced the faux book, and opened it with a flourish. "Just imagine if they'd seen me with these!"

Father Miguel moved swiftly to grasp my wrist. His face had gone even whiter than usual. "You idiotic woman, they would have murdered us if they had found you concealing those." Matilde was also regarding me grimly.

I gave my arm a tug, hoping to get him to release me.

"Put them away! This cannot be borne!" He shoved me, covered his eyes with a hand, and closed us out. Mutterings and prayers followed, for a good long time, while Matilde and the baby both kept their eyes upon me. It seemed my nervous jag was well and truly over, dashed against three stern countenances.

We travelled on towards Madrid, a trip of a fortnight's length. During the day, I was stimulated by the sights and sounds that greeted us as we galloped along, and as we proceeded south the weather again grew hot, which I adore. But the Jesuit was right, the situation *was* impossible, it couldn't be borne: When we pulled up at the first hotel, the *padre* and I (to keep up the charade) had perforce to share a room. They insisted upon giving us the best matrimonial suite, and the owner was proud to point out their superior linens (by lifting and caressing a corner between his fingers), after which he cocked an eyebrow and waggled it, man to man, at Father Miguel. My faux husband went rigid with displeasure and blushed from his toes to his shaved crown, while I made some modest sort of comment, thanking the owner for his kindness and escorting him to the door. Matilde bustled about, helping us get settled and establishing herself publicly as our baby's nurse, though I do believe she found it quite amusing to observe the Jesuit's unease at domestic confinement.

Unpacking my portmanteau, Matilde pulled out from its hiding place amongst a number of soft articles a small, decorated box lined with satin.

"What is this, señora?" Matilde asked, looking inside.

There was nothing in it. Nothing visible, anyway.

"A reminder," I told her, feeling suddenly ill. In the swirl of travel, I'd almost forgotten, but the Grimaldis meant business and I must render. A pair of small ears depended upon me. How much time would they give me before . . . ? I said a prayer and sent it winging to the little girl with black hair and sea-dark eyes.

Matilde gave me a nod, then took her baby off into their own little room where they seemed very happy with each other.

Unlike the rest of the travelling party.

The Jesuit and I tried to be civil at dinner, for the sake of appearances. He did not approve of my rubbing my hands together as we sat down at table. I was absolutely ravenous and anticipating the lovely regional food with glee. I told him that on the following evening I wished to wear one of my new gowns instead of going back and forth between the two I'd brought with me, but he wouldn't allow it.

"Save the gowns for the palace."

"I won't spill food on them, if that's what you think," I teased, but the joking fell on deaf ears. When I kept on about it, he intoned patronizingly, "We'll see," as if I were a spoiled, naughty child.

"We'll see *you*," I muttered, wishing him to the devil. After the first course, I'd had enough.

"No wine," he told the waiter piously, his hand covering the glass.

"I'll have some," I said, pointing. "In fact, I'll have that carafe."

If anyone had been listening in on our conversation (such as it was), they must surely have wondered at the state of the newly married couple and guessed it would be a miracle for us to produce another child who was as happy and content as baby Matilde.

The dreaded moment could not be put off forever: retiring to the bedchamber. Up we went, the priest leading the way. Inside the room, Father Miguel de la Vega, with a very bad grace, lay a dark, musty blanket out on the floor and wrapped himself in it like a bat in its wings. The floor was very hard and the father very bony, so this must not have been pleasant—but then, when did the Jesuit ever desire pleasant? He lay as still as a post as I swiftly undressed and climbed into my sheets. I, in turn, lay still in the bed, listening suspiciously until he finally fell into an unhappy slumber. This I could tell from the sound of his breathing. Once he had dropped off, I began to relax and then fell asleep.

The next problem was that I have always enjoyed inventive dreaming, and my dreams are merry. I always have a starring role, am usually saving people from bad things or themselves, and often end up in a sumptuously appointed bed with a handsome young blade, as a thank-you for my bravery. When that happens, I've been told that my dreams become quite boisterous. It's all a wonderful diversion and at times—when life has been difficult or I'm in trouble of one sort or another—I can take to my bed and sleep and sleep, just to escape the traumas of the current situation.

On that night I woke with a yell to find the Jesuit standing over my bed, a lit candle in his hand, and his eyes wild. "Stop it!" he cried, "Stop it I tell you or I shall go mad!"

I sat up in bed, clutching the blankets. "I'm not doing anything! I'm sleeping!"

"You're . . . talking! It's . . . I'm . . . aargh!"

In my half-awake state I struggled to understand. "I woke you up? I'm sorry, I didn't mean to."

"I can't sleep when you—when I am forced to . . . For the love of God, be quiet!"

"But you were sleeping, Father. I could hear you. Are you in pain? The floor is too hard? Perhaps we could trade places—"

"No, no," he moaned. "You're a woman. I cannot." And he began pacing back and forth in front of the window, the flame from the candle billowing and sputtering, hot wax running down his hand and falling in drops on the floor. Now, I know he was a man, and I know about most men, but this tortured priest? I suddenly realized that he must dislike me, for some reason, with every ounce of his bony being. Once upon a time I would have blamed myself, I would have hoped desperately to change his mind. I would have tried to do what he wished, or in other words, be meek and silent and afraid. But, well, I knew that was a waste of time, and frankly I had other things I wanted to prepare for: my début in *La pata da cabra*, meeting the Spanish princesses, being introduced to the tutor and fulfilling my assignment so that I could go home with my loot and my newly acquired skills. Father Miguel simply never entered into it; this journey and the charade were just an annoying interlude. So eventually I lay down again, rolled over, and tried to sleep. He fell into a chair by the window, staring through the darkness at me, and groaned, "Stop talking. *Nom de Dieu.*"

And this went on, night after night, as we made our slow way south. One night I couldn't stand it. I sat up and said, "Oh for heaven's sake! I'm not talking, I'm dreaming, and as far as I know there is no law or decree against that. I'm young and I won't be bullied into doom and gloom. Goodnight, *padre*."

Not a sound from him.

Such odd, rather eerie nocturnal exchanges. Ridiculous, I thought.

※ ※ ※

At last, one day towards the third week of September, the outline of the city appeared—Madrid! During that whole day's travel, we watched it come closer. The Jesuit remonstrated with me for leaning out the window, letting in dust and collecting stares. I tried to quell my leg-jigging impatience by telling myself that soon I would be released from proximity with this melancholic, distracting myself further by wondering where I would be living, what my new acquaintances in the theatre would be like, and what the excesses and splendours of the Spanish court would reveal. Everything would fall into place, I knew it.

Sure enough, I was established in small but sufficient rooms near the Catedral San Isidro, not far from the theatre district. Matilde and the baby stayed with me the first night, then we all gathered the next morning to see her away. Father de la Vega passed over a pouch full of coins and gave her a blessing; I said goodbye with my grateful thanks. I had no idea where mother and child were going now, whether returning to France or staying in the capital, but I assumed that the Grimaldis had taken care of this detail as well as everything else. Then she was gone.

The Jesuit turned to me, bowed formally, placed his chilly hands in his (reinstated) cassock sleeves and said, "Today you are to meet my brother, Ventura, who will help you learn your duties at the Príncipe. The days will go quickly and very soon the princesses will come to the performance. You must be ready."

"Never fear," I told him curtly. "I can't wait to get started."

"My eyes will be upon you," he said, "where you least expect it."

So Jesuitical! I turned away to roll my own eyes and cross my fingers. At least I have a private room, I told myself; a bed without the dark shape of the bat lurking at the foot of it. And my own role in one of Spain's most talked-about and lucrative productions of all times!

He walked me to the theatre later that morning, sourly answering my questions about the production. *La pata da cabra* did not enjoy the father's approval. It was too frivolous. He gave me a little lecture on the *La pata* phenomenon: Apparently, the late King Ferdinand had made it difficult for theatres to function by bogging them down in bureaucracy, so canny impresarios (of whom Grimaldi was one) had experimented, importing translations of popular French plays, then eventually operas from Italy, complete with Italian tenors and sopranos. The repressed Madrileños had gone crazy, scrambling for opera tickets, imitating the songs, gestures, hairstyles, and dress of the Italians. Grimaldi then wrote his own clever adaptation of a once-popular French *comedia de magia*, calling it *La pata de cabra*. He designed it to have everything—magical effects, disappearances, comedy, colossal costumes, lavish sets and set-changes—to satisfy the populace's craving for excess. *La pata de cabra* had been in revival for over a decade; it was known in theatrical circles as the "golden calf." Father Miguel finished the lesson by sniffing, "It is unfortunate that my associate should have sullied himself with such slop, though it is the main source of his wealth and enables his patronage of our cause."

He left me at the stage door when his brother came to greet us. They bowed rather formally to each other, I thought, and the priest slipped away. Ventura de la Vega was a short, strong-looking man with dark skin and sleepy eyes, who seemed bone weary. He apologized for not meeting me the day before, but his wife had just had their third child and they were kept busy with its arrival. I was amazed at the difference in appearance between the two men; I would never in a million years have believed they were related. Ventura's appearance told of his love for the good things in life—wine, women, and the arts—although I soon came to know that he worked like a dog to keep his household afloat. His fingertips were black with the ink stains of his writing.

"We were only made aware of your impending arrival yesterday," he told me. "Of course we'd known you were on your way, but not exactly when to expect you. When the message came . . . It was slightly awkward, but we managed it." How mysterious. What did he mean? Manage what? He was whisking me along the corridors, saying that everyone was exhausted; they hadn't had a break from the show for several weeks because ticket sales had been so good. No one was pleased to have had to gather for a morning to meet the new *deus ex machina*. I told him I was determined to be fleet and fiery (my heart in my throat, courage high, and my best walking boots on). We passed the dressing rooms and finally emerged onto the stage itself where the actors waited. A quick glance around showed me that the theatre was a long and narrow rectangle, with seating below and three tiers of balconies surrounding the three sides above. On the stage was a permanent facade consisting of a two-story house, with openings for entrances and exits on both floors.

"Company, here she is."

One by one I was told their names and roles. The young leading man and woman were sweet, both from the provinces (Seville and Granada) and obviously excited to have been invited to join the Príncipe, in the capital, for this latest revival. I was introduced to the great Antonio Guzmán, who had originated and maintained the virtuoso role of Don Simplicio. There were many other characters, played by men and woman who changed roles numerous times throughout the performance—and costumes as well, I was to discover, in an absorbed frenzy, while swearing at top volume. Introductions blurred past, I bowed and smiled, pretending to understand who, what, and where everything was but not understanding anything. Then Ventura turned to Guzmán and said, "She's all yours."

Señor Guzmán, chivalrously requesting that I call him Antonio, was directing operations for the day. The others smoked and waited, not so patiently, while he explained. "Señor de Grimaldi has ascertained that you are unafraid of heights?" he began.

"Um, heights? Yes, of course."

How high, I wondered, just as he directed my eyes upwards. "The fly tower," he explained. It seemed abnormally vaulted. I gulped, then met his amused gaze.

"That's lucky," he said softly. "Our last one had a bad fear of it. Probably what caused the problem in the first place."

"Problem?"

"He'd grown too fat, even for a stock Cupid. The fly men were complaining. We had to hire extras, one each side, and even then it was difficult. And he kept missing the platform, very distracting."

"Wait. You said Cupid?"

"That is the character you are playing. Not many lines, but a great deal of business." His eyes watched me kindly, his sensitive face alive to what was going on inside of me—nervousness, surprise, disappointment.

"I was told *deus ex machina*. I'm the divine intervention?"

A hand on my shoulder, he began to walk me around the stage, to ensure that we were out of earshot. "Yes, Cupid is who he meant. My dear, I am not quite sure why Señor de Grimaldi has decided on this change of gender for our Cupid. Audiences are accustomed to chubby *putto* in the role, not slender slips of girls. But, Grimaldi usually knows best, and," his eyes crinkling, "I have no doubt you will manage to sell even more tickets once the audience gets a look at you. We will practice your stunts together, by ourselves, this afternoon."

He wheeled me around again and we came to a halt in front of the lounging, yawning actors. "Let me be clear, señoras y señores. We have been joined by Señorita Gilbert, who will be our new Cupid. She will be with us in performance tonight, so please unite with me in welcoming her."

Tonight! My inner alarm bell clanged.

"What about Emilio?" someone called.

"Emilio is in no danger. He is in hospital but will recover; it's only a broken leg." Antonio shrugged and held up a finger. "It was an accident last night. That is all. He was careless."

"No accident," someone else muttered.

"How did we manage to get another Cupid so fast—and a woman? Why wasn't it one of us, moved up from the *duennas*?" This came from an aggressive-looking female standing at the back with her arms folded.

"*Silencio, por favor,*" Antonio told her mildly. "Señor de Grimaldi's orders. He knows what he is doing. Until tonight, then, friends."

Tonight! Another clang. Dear God, I'd have other things to worry about, *pronto*, never mind a discontented actress from the chorus.

Dismissed, the company trailed off, clouds of cigarillo smoke in their wake. Ventura heaved a table from the wings onto the front of the stage, Antonio brought chairs, and the three of us sat down around it on the apron. I learned terminology from them that day: wings, fly tower, apron, thrust, down stage, up stage, stage right and left. These words and their meanings are life-threateningly important when you are about to do what I was about to do. I was introduced to the trapdoors in the stage floor and the reveals, which were small cupboard-like openings in the walls that actors could lean out of, like windows. Because the stage facade was permanent to the theatre and not specific to *La pata*, I was told that spoken cues were used by the actors to establish the where and when of the play's settings.

The two men then talked me through the action: what happened from scene to scene, as well as my cues. Luckily, considering that I was to début that evening (*ye gods!*), I didn't have many lines. The business was tricky enough both to understand and to execute. During the play, the necessary changes were accomplished by complicated machinery as well as people, so I also needed to know where to be to get out of the way. The production required forty-eight stage hands just to do the shifting and coordinate the flying (most of them standing about leering at the actresses, I was to discover, when they weren't being required to use their muscles).

The plot to *La pata de cabra* goes something like this: Young hero Don Juan is about to commit suicide, despairing that he cannot marry his sweetheart, Leonor. Just as he is about to pull the trigger, the pistols fly out of his hands into the air and I step out of a tree trunk (my first appearance!) with a talisman, a goat's foot (hence the play's title). I promise the lovers eventual happiness and exit. Complicated set change number one, with things coming in and going out in front of the fixed facade, then enter Don Simplicio, the bumbling villain—a big entrance for Antonio, much applause as he does a full circle of the set, acknowledging it, then the action begins again.

Next scene: The earth opens up, Simplicio is befuddled and amazed, the young hero hides in his love's bedroom by way of a trick mirror, some of the *duennas* transform into nymphs—I was foolish enough at this point to ask, but why? Finally the lovers are locked up in separate upper story rooms: Cue me! I fly by in an elegant carriage and rescue them! End of Act I. Most of Act II, I have a little rest while Simplicio tries to recapture the lovers and all sorts of other stage tricks and machinery are put to use. The most amazing piece of business: Antonio's cap inflates like a hot-air balloon and he flies up into the stage tower at top speed. Cue me: I rescue the lovers again. The third act has more flights, levitations (I have to levitate!), and changes of furniture and properties, ending finally with the lovers being allowed to marry, Simplicio declaring, "Love conquers all," and buckets of applause.

I felt rapturous and terrified at the end of this recital. Antonio patted my hand reassuringly as Ventura added, "The fly men arrive in twenty minutes to put you through your paces."

A woman came out with a number of tapas and I ate quite a few with nervous alacrity before wondering whether that had been such a good idea if I was soon to be hoisted aloft. The men disappeared backstage and I wandered around, murmuring my lines to myself. How would I keep everything straight? Would my voice be loud enough? Fanny Kelly's words returned to haunt me: "No amplification whatsoever apparent."

A crew of burly men arrived and stationed themselves at their posts in the fly gallery. For my second entrance, I was to be backstage right, up on a platform and seated in my carriage (really just a rickety wooden box with painted scenery attached to the front of it). At the requisite cue, I was to hold on tight and the fly men would whisk me across the stage to the lovers' second floor tower—a platform behind the facade—and the actor and actress would climb into the box with me and back we'd go, flying across the stage again. We tried it a few times, and it seemed to go smoothly. Next piece of business: Ventura helped me strap myself into an ingenious sort of harness. It went on over my day clothes at this point, but during the performance would be under my costume, only the connecting hooks visible and easy to reach. When I was required to levitate, I'd be using this harness and a small one buckled around my left ankle. Practicing, I discovered that it requires a great deal more muscle control to keep your body straight and horizontal while trying to appear Cupid-like, even *with* a harness, than it seems. I was thankful to be in good condition and wondered how a fat Cupid could possibly have done it without sagging in the middle.

The final big stunt I had to accomplish was similar to Don Simplicio's: Cupid flew up and away at the end of the play. Just prior to attempting this one for the first time, Antonio gave me a fatherly hug. "Breathe deeply, just before you're lifted. I find it helps," he counseled. And I don't know exactly what happened, but as the head fly man gave me the cue ("*un, dos, tres, ya!*"), I was seized with a little frisson of panic and must have clenched my muscles, and the fly men—accustomed as they were to a much stouter Cupid—heaved with a force greater than necessary for my size. I flew up into the air with an involuntary holler, my head got wobbly, my stomach lurched, and Antonio yelled, "Slow! Slow! Are you crazy men, let her down!" They did, apologizing profusely; as I touched the floor, I kept on going, and collapsed in a heap. Ventura rushed over, very contrite but, well, it's odd but nevertheless true, I looked up, ecstatic, and cried, "Let me try it again!"

I was an actress in a play! I was about to appear before an audience!

After the practice, I was fitted into my costume, which they'd been forced to throw together at short notice. The wardrobe mistress, pins sticking out all around her mouth and a frown between her eyes, kept shaking her head and grumbling, despite Ventura's soothing comments. Finally they deemed me presentable, and from a distance it looked quite grand, all in gold and pale blue. The problem was that it smelled a bit—no, a lot. It had seen better days and a great deal of use. Someone's, or many people's, stale perspiration, revitalized by the warmth of my body, was brought to life again in all its complicated piquancy. Night after night in this, I thought? *Mon dieu.* And *dios mio.*

Once released from the costume, there was an hour or so before Ventura was to take me for a meal, prior to the evening's performance. I wandered around, accustoming myself to the world I had entered. In truth, I was disappointed by the shabbiness. I'd had no idea. The

Príncipe was one of Madrid's national theatres, and yet I could see that working conditions were appalling. No wonder actors were often sick—though the show would still go on with them in it, they'd be coughing or puking severely backstage, then launching out from the wings into their scenes full of verve. They had to, or they wouldn't eat. On that afternoon though, I tried not to see the stains and the rips. I substituted the mystique, the audience-to-come, and the coiled energy of the building, until dirt, dust, and suspect smells disappeared. That's how it is when you are about to enter your dream.

At the *restaurante*, Ventura was good-hearted about my increasing nerves and burbling questions: "Yes, you will have a big success, and no, you will not fall, not a chance of it."

"I'm glad to hear it. Has Señor de Grimaldi informed you—"

"He's told me everything, but we won't tell the rest of the company. It will be our secret. Your cover is that you are learning traditional dance, yes? I have someone in mind. And we shall put your lessons to use. Grimaldi wishes you to dance a short fandango before your ascent to the roof."

"And the princesses?"

"Early next week is my hope. We will be arranging a royal invitation." He smiled across the table at me. "What did you make of my brother? Never mind, I can see. He and I are very different, perhaps you've noticed. He resents me, thinks my whole life is a game: third son, writes for the theatre, not a care in the world. He lives a sheltered life, my brother. Sometimes I worry about him."

I immediately warmed to this de la Vega. He was easy with women because he worked with them as equals. They were part of his enterprise; he admired and appreciated them for the many skills they possessed. So unlike prissy Father Miguel.

"Have you finished? Then come along, Cupid."

That night, giddy-headed from the mad butterflies inside, I stepped out from the tree trunk with the goat's foot in my trembling hand. I smelled the hot lights, the stale costumes, the audience's good will. I said my lines in the correct order and without a stumble, and exited. True, I tripped and fell down backstage after that first exit, but no one important saw me, just a few stagehands. The play seemed to be rushing by—soon I was clambering into my painted box-carriage and winging across the stage, heads in the audience turning to watch me go. From the wings, I devoured Antonio's performance, holding my sides with laughter, shivering with joy. Again I climbed into my carriage and flew across the stage, and then the dreaded Act III. Onstage, I managed to get the tricky harnesses attached to my back and my foot, and levitated with all my might, skirt showing perhaps a bit more leg than had been intended—but the more the merrier, I thought, for then the audience might remember me. Finally, hook the connecting buckles to the flying harness with swift, trembling fingers and—oh gods!—my trajectory into the fly tower. Up I went, up and up in a moment's breath! I landed on the uppermost platform, high in the very roof! Steadied by the fly man I then wobbled carefully all the way down the long perpendicular iron ladder (clamped to the backstage wall) to join the company in final bows. And that's when I felt it, *really* felt it, and I *knew*, standing there on the dusty, dirty stage of the Príncipe Theatre in Madrid, Spain, soaking in the applause, the warm sound of a large number of living, breathing people putting their hands together and shouting "¡bravo!" This was what my heart and soul had craved all my life. Now I understood Concepción's tension, her frustration at having to give it up. This was her core. This was where she lived. And I fell, like a stone, into knowledge. Into the deep pool of longing and desire, the stone sinking further and further: I *must have* this. There is no going back.

When I returned, triumphantly, to my rooms, I wrote a brief note to the earl of Malmesbury letting him know of my wonderful evening. I told him I was safe and with good people. I was cocky and full of the exultation the evening had given me—nothing seemed too difficult for Señorita Gilbert, royal spy and actress extraordinaire! I sealed the note with a kiss, then fell into a heavy sleep on top of it for the rest of the night.

When I woke, the small decorated box Grimaldi had included in my luggage to remind me of my purpose had fallen off the night table and was lying on its side, broken. With shaking hands, I tried to put it back together. From a distance, it may have fooled others, but I knew. It was no longer whole. Oh, I'm a superstitious creature. Juan had gauged me correctly. Thrill or not, having found my vocation or not, that mishap jarred me into remembering that I must fulfill my mission.

The theatre is an enclosed circle, a serpent swallowing its own tail. A bit like moving to a small village; you may reside there for twenty years, but if you're not one of them, you will remain the outsider, catch the sideways glance, the eyebrow twitch. In those first weeks I ignored the twitches, the sneers—or maybe I didn't yet see them.

On the nights following my opening, my skirts (somehow) rode up during my levitations, revealing quite a bit more leg. Now my final whoosh up into the fly tower received a round of applause, which was intoxicating, although Ventura reprimanded me sternly. Antonio gave a little smile and said nothing; he understood the crucial desire to be noticed. How else, in this business, to get ahead?

My role in *La pata*—as I drank up applause—also helped channel my vigorous appetite. I'd written to the earl because I missed him. I missed him in bed; I missed our funny dalliances. I was itchy and hungry for love, and I suppose others in the company sensed it. A spirited young woman acts as a kind of lightning rod. Women don't like her, or they attempt to belittle her; that was happening with some of the *duennas* in the chorus, though I tried to ignore it. With a few of the men, there were disturbances: One older actor became infuriated with me for some small slight (he thought I'd tittered at his loud ritual of gargling before performances). Then he turned thickheadedly possessive, as if he owned me or something. I had to quash that ridiculousness *tout suite*. One silly ninny simply fell apart, becoming tongue-tied and half-witted every time I passed him backstage. Meanwhile I went about my business, ever my own person, oblivious to the raging emotions around about me because I never intended to arouse them. I had an arousal of my own that was consuming me: a newly discovered joy in exercising my young passions, my young body, and that was what was driving me. That autumn in Madrid, I reached the full prime of my being. I was a nectar-filled flower with its petals open to the sun and the bees. And that, I was to realize, can be fatal.

True to his word, soon after my arrival Ventura introduced me to a dancer from the Italian opera company. Her name was Donatella and she excelled in traditional dances from the Mediterranean. "All sorts," she explained. "From Greece and Turkey, Italy, of course, to Spain, and a tiny bit from Morocco." How had she learned all this? She laughed with her head thrown back. "My father came from Greece and his father was Turkish. My mother's from the south, near Naples, *her* mother is from Andalucia. And the Moroccan? A man who came through my life. Like a swallow to a pool—a few playful dips, a gleeful cry, and then gone." She smiled ruefully and added, "Just thinking about him makes me talk like he did: words of love and no substance." She shrugged, "I am a mixed bag. We'll concentrate on the Spanish. That's what you want, *sí*?"

For several afternoons over several weeks, I spent time with Donatella, practicing in a large empty room close by the Cruz, where her company was performing. She was an excellent teacher, and her disciplined, flexible splendour as a dancer filled me with despair. I felt as if my feet became hooves in her presence. Hooves filled with lead. But I persevered. One day she mentioned the tarantella, asked me if I knew anything about it. "Though it's from Italy, of course, not Spain. From the town of Taranto, south of Naples."

"What is it like?"

"A folk dance. But exciting. I notice you like to move your body, and you have a strange natural rhythm. This might suit you. It's like a trance. Of course, the real thing *is* a trance, but we dancers, we can recreate such things and not go crazy ourselves." She threw back her head and laughed again, and I laughed with her. The dance sounded peculiar and therefore worth seeing.

She began it almost flamenco style, heels clicking and vibrating as she circled the floor. Very quick, light steps and a teasing kind of swaying, like a woman flirting with a man, then becoming faster, larger. I could see that the steps themselves, the repetition of them, brought on a kind of inebriation, and Donatella kept it up for a very long time, finally bringing the dance to a halt with a little cry of fatigue. I was extremely taken with it, the notion of tiring oneself out in such an arrestingly sensual way, which Donatella said was indeed the case. She fanned herself mightily, declaring we must go for a half carafe of wine or she would not be able to live.

Over a glass, she told me what she knew of the origins of the dance. Two hundred years ago, Taranto had been the seat of a strange affliction: Some inhabitants believed they had been bitten by a tarantula, and the only way they could cure themselves was by sweating the deadly poison out through frenzied dancing. The fear caught on and spread through the town, so all the townspeople danced until they dropped down insensible or maybe half dead, and then their bodies' extreme fatigue (or the remnants of the poison) caused them to writhe and shake on the ground. For some reason, this annual madness reoccurred year after year—a spooky transference of soul, a manic joy. Over time, the frenzy had dissipated, became mythic and celebrated, and evolved into this tarantella. "Isn't that fascinating?"

In the meantime, Ventura began organizing a masked ball to be held in opulent, rented rooms on a date to be decided, but not long after Christmas, to coincide with the pre-Lenten season when the theatres were closed. This had been another moneymaking scheme of Grimaldi's, and Ventura, strapped for *reales*, was hoping to cash in again. Grimaldi's balls had attracted up to two thousand disguised souls at a time, and while they were chaotic and a nightmare to organize, all of Madrid lusted for tickets and spent a great deal to obtain them. "I think, also," Ventura told me quietly, "that the event will serve our needs." I had no idea what that meant, but nodded anyway. A masked ball sounded wonderful. What costume should I come up with?

All the while, I kept looking around for Ventura's Jesuit brother, who'd warned me his eyes would be everywhere. On the contrary, he was never anywhere (*¡gracias a dios!*), and little by little I began to forget about him.

※ ※ ※

And then, about a fortnight after my arrival at the Príncipe, the night arrived for which my associates and I had been waiting and planning: the night the princesses came to see *La pata de cabra*. A night like no other.

I was nervous, standing backstage: I had to steal their young hearts. If I didn't, our plan would go awry before it had even begun. Ventura was sure that Luisa Fernanda, the littlest one, would be captivated. Her love for any magical creature, and particularly fairies, was well known, so we'd sewn sparkles on my stinking costume, added antennae to my hair, and heightened the makeup around my eyes so that the whites would catch the footlights.

The play began. I peeked through a small hole in the stage-left curtain to glimpse the infantas in their box. The elder, Isabel, the almost queen, was eating chocolates. Luisa Fernanda was playing with her hair, a very pale blonde; she looked like her mother, Cristina. Isabel seemed darker, her features coarser; but then, she had her hands to her mouth the whole time so I couldn't be sure. I awaited my entrance. It came, I swished out, and I managed to steal a tiny glance over at the royal box. The youngest saw my dancing steps and twinkling antennae and leaned forward, arms on the rail.

By the time I flew to the young lovers in my faux carriage, I could tell that Luisa Fernanda was entranced. My athletic levitation in Act III caused her to jump up and down in her chair, until a royally appointed adult at her side remonstrated with her. As I danced my little fandango and then swooped up into the fly tower just before final curtain, I saw her clapping deliriously and felt very pleased. She would ask to meet me afterwards; everything we hoped for would come to pass, I knew it.

The ropes hurtled me skywards, accompanied by the usual gasps from the audience and sounds of appreciative applause. The roof of the stage house approached at speed, dark and shadowy, full of dust and the smell of hemp, and the human sounds faded away. My feet reached for and landed on the platform high above the stage. Below me, the action continued: actors moving to and fro, lit from beneath, colours flickering in and out of the footlights. I sensed the fly man, just a shadow in the darkness off to my right, as I reached up to unhook the harness, still recovering my equilibrium and catching my breath. I was about to move to the ladder in order to descend when I smelled something odd, and that shadowy figure reached out, grabbed my arm, twisted it painfully behind my back, then gave my body a mighty shove! I had no time to even make a sound; the propulsion whirled me around and I lost my balance, cascading over the edge of the platform! Cast off into black spinning space!

From sheer instinct I flailed out and grabbed at something, anything! A rope—it burned through my palm, but I hung on and grabbed at it again with the other hand and broke my descent. I was dizzy, disoriented, not knowing if I was right side up or upside down. Somehow, against all odds, I'd stopped my fall and—again, instinctively—I kicked my legs frantically, entwining myself in a second bewildering rope that descended, snakelike, through the blackness towards the far away stage, where the actors carried on, oblivious.

At the very same instant that all of this was happening, a large, heavy object flew off the platform above, barely missing my head, and after an interval of some fraught, silent seconds, crashed onto the stage floor below. Screams and scurrying—chaos! People fleeing in every direction! Dangling there in the ropes, high above, I realized: The fallen object, now splattered and broken, was me. Could, by a whisker, have been me. A vision of Clotilde flashed before my mind's eye: In *that* horrific moment, too, there had been no sound. Just a whoosh of displacement, a sinister double splash, then her small head, propelled by the chin, towed into the channel to certain death. No mercy. And no warning.

Far below me, the object lay. It was one of the sandbags from the fly tower's platform. My limbs began to shake and lose all strength as I clung to the ropes between my legs and my juddering, bleeding hands, remembering again the sudden grip on my arm, up on the platform. Remembering the sinewy hand on Clotilde's throat and the stinking one that had grasped my neck and then covered my mouth in the Paris streets. I hadn't seen the hand that had just sent me cascading off the platform, nor its owner—but its fingers were hard and bony and long. They were . . . oh *merde*, oh dammit. Were they the same? They looked and felt—and smelled!—the same. Pedro Coria, the glass-eyed bodyguard? As I hung there, twisting, in the ropes, the possibility hit me: Had he followed me, for some reason? Was he insane? I peered into the darkness above. How long a span of time had passed? How many eternities? Was he up there—the *it*, the fiend, whatever such a brute can be called—cutting at the ropes, sawing away? If he was, as they frayed and split and finally snapped, I would fall.

And then I saw that three of the fly men were leaning down, arms held out to me, their eyes popping in desperation. "Señorita, *por favor!*" I was dangling several feet below their reach. They wanted me to reach for their hands. But I could not! How could I trust them? What if *it* was one of them?

Then, from the corner of my eye I glimpsed a long shape, slithering down the iron ladder with horrible speed and agility. I couldn't see the face as it scurried, like a spider, into the darkness below and thence to the stage floor. "There, look!" I managed in a croak. "The ladder, quickly!" but they were uncomprehending, their entire focus intent upon lifting me up, to them, to safety. Dimly, I heard the orchestra strike up again— the play was going on, the actors were back in formation, summoning up the denouement, the happy ending. My head began to spin; I was losing strength, beginning to slip, and my mind couldn't fathom my body's betrayal!

One of the men from above had the good thought of pulling the rope my hands were still clutching, which raised me slightly and allowed the others (a fourth shocked fly man had appeared from somewhere) to get a grip of my arms. They hauled me aloft. I lay there between them, on my back on the platform, their hands patting my hair, my skirt. They were trembling also. "Did you see him?" I groaned, and they looked confused. "Who was that, up here?" I tried again, my throat dry and voice cracking. They didn't know what I meant. They saw nothing but the result of my fall. A girl in the ropes. They're glad they were not responsible for a death; their voices were still shaking slightly, as they patted me. "We must get you down, señorita. Have you the ability?" They deployed themselves: two to remain for the final curtain drop and raise, and two to help me.

I wasn't sure I could keep myself on the ladder for all those many, dizzy steps down, even though there was an anxious man below me and one above. The combination of fear, lightheadedness, and the shakes, while trying to descend a tiny iron ladder sixty feet above a stage floor, in virtual darkness, convinced that a clawlike, powerful hand will somehow grab your ankle and rip you off at any moment—well, it was one of the bravest things I've ever done. By the time I tottered onto the boards backstage, I thought I would throw up. I put my hands on my knees and breathed deeply. One of the fly men said, "*Brava, señorita.* And you're even in time—curtain's coming, look." The cast was onstage, the curtain down and then raising again (unevenly, as the two remaining fly men toiled away), and the bowing began. Where was the monster? Was it still down here, waiting?

Ventura, in the wings, came dashing over. "Where in hell were you?"

"I . . . up there . . . I almost—"

"Get on, get on! Stay out of Antonio's light, but get on! Let the infantas see you!"

I staggered out and away from the darkness and took my place. I curtsied and smiled in the direction of the royal box. I could see the youngest was standing to clap. Could this possibly still be the princesses' night? I had lived and died a hundred years. Isabel's hands were still in the chocolate box. I curtsied again. The curtsies made me feel better, made me remember that I was onstage, doing what I loved, drinking in the sound and the smells, living and breathing (*¡gracias á dios!*) my dream.

When the curtain came down for the final time with a dusty thump, I wobbled over to Ventura. The fly men were clustered around him.

He turned to me with angry eyes. "You knocked the sandbag. It could have killed someone."

"I was pushed up there, Ventura! I nearly fell!" And in that moment, even more than when I was dangling high above the stage, I knew that if I had fallen I would have broken every bone in my body. And if I had somehow lived, I would have wished I hadn't.

He took my chin, looking into my eyes. "My God, is that so?" And to the men, "Why wasn't it secured as it should have been? If I find you've been careless—"

"No." Now I was furious. "You're not listening. There was a man, I'm sure of it. He ran down the ladder and he's gone. No one else saw anything. He really meant it, Ventura, he wanted me to die."

"We'll get to the bottom of this," he said, and hugged me. The other actors were chattering and gesticulating, still animated from the mishap. "Come, Rosana," Ventura went on, "you must change and be ready. We've sent an invitation to the royal box, inviting them backstage. Quickly, quickly. We'll deal with this later, I swear it."

My fingers shook as I flew through my preparations; the dresser had to slap my hands away because they were bleeding from the ropes. I was bandaged, my hands slipped into gloves, then I was laced into my finest new court gown, breasts high and saucy, ready for my official audience with the young Bourbon-Two Sicilies. As I gingerly removed my stage makeup, a rotund, anxious-looking man with a cast on his leg entered the dressing room. There were happy screams: "Emilio! Darling, how are you?" He'd been in the audience that night; he'd seen my performance. Emilio had a cast on his leg. He couldn't possibly have beetled down that ladder with such speed and dexterity. But wait, I thought, could he have arranged it? Could he hate me that much for usurping his role? I told myself not to be foolish. But as I watched my fellow artists and felt them excluding me, quite deliberately, I knew that to them, I had not earned my way. And that is a cardinal sin in the theatre.

Just then, the infantas arrived with their chaperones and guards. The dressing room had that afternoon been hurriedly filled with flowers, after the official royal consent to attend had been received, and now became the scene of much bowing and scraping. The little girls took this in their stride; the youngest, Luisa Fernanda, offered her small hand many times, and everyone bent over it with soft words of fealty. It was obvious that Isabel, the thirteen-year-old, disliked this ritual. She nodded her head and bestowed stiff smiles instead. She was an unprepossessing looking person: fat as a little porker stuffed into her gown, with a raw, red face and hands, and an extremely turned up nose, which unfortunately did not mitigate her porcine impression.

Suddenly the youngest spotted me and rushed over, her young face gleaming with pleasure. "Cupid!" she cried, "I love you!" Ventura bowed himself into a fever at this, others in the company looked sour, and Emilio's pudgy face seemed about to shatter.

The sweet little one reached up on her tiptoes to kiss my cheek. "I think you are beautiful," she said, taking my hand in hers. "I hope you will come to stay with us."

I could hear an audible gasp of joy and surprise from Ventura, behind me.

"Majesty," I murmured, "I would be most grateful. An honour."

"No. I hope it will be fun," she said.

So there it was. I had done it, against the odds. Courageously, strongly! The Príncipe, its tattered company, unsafe conditions and even its treacherous make-believe fly man could go hang: I'd shown them! I'd done it! Part one, accomplished. Part two, about to commence.

⁂ ⁂ ⁂

Life changed quickly after my introduction to royalty. I moved out of my rooms near the theatre district and into the royal palace, into the most glamourous bedchamber I had ever seen. More people to look me up and down with disdain, thinking I hadn't earned it: lady's maids and tiring women, Spanish grandees with pencil-thin mustaches, skinny calves, and leathery skin. Pooh on them all! I felt like a conqueror. Waking late in the morning, after my performance had tired me out the night before. Being served breakfast in bed, whatever I wanted, by a maid who was told to ensure I was happy, even if she disapproved of me with every ounce of her tight-lipped being. "More coffee," I'd say, holding my cup out just to annoy her, "black as the ace of spades, *por favor*." Once I was up, I'd wander down insanely majestic hallways and peek around imperial doorways, openmouthed at the opulence. The littlest princess had told me proudly, "There are twenty-eight hundred rooms in the palace," so I was trying very hard not to get lost! Once I'd found the princesses each morning, I'd lounge about with them, doing what they did: going for drives in coaches-and-six, playing games in a variety of incredible gardens connected to the palace, swanning up and down during lengthy and tedious appearances before their courtiers (what *do* all these overdressed people hang around for, anyway?), and sitting in the background, out of the way, while they were receiving their education from the tutor.

Yes, the tutor. There he was at last: Arguëlles, focus of my main assignment. Cristina and Grimaldi had made me fear him as some sort of radical, cerebral giant; they professed themselves terrified of the unsettling effect he was having upon the girls. From what I could see, the infantas carried on blithely being the rather spoiled children they were. The man certainly worked hard at changing their compass, and he *was* full of frighteningly extremist ideas (from a monarchist point of view). But the most dire problem was one they hadn't warned me about: Arguëlles was one of the ugliest men I had ever set eyes on, and the thought of having to seduce him was abhorrent.

With one glance, the task had taken on Herculean proportions. Large, pendulous lips that flung spittle around when he grew animated, which was often. Breath that would stun a boar at ten paces. Thin, greasy hair sitting on top of the largest, roundest head I could imagine. Making up for the hair he lacked on his head, he had meaty hands with dark fur around the knuckles, fur which extended all the way up the backs of his hands, fluffing out around his cuffs, and no doubt getting thicker and hairier all the way up (and down, *¡mierda!*). A barrel chest with a globular stomach. No ass—completely flat. And thin shanks which he (for some reason) loved to display, thinking as he did that they were his finest feature. Big paddle feet joined to these desiccated shanks—truly a work of art. Coupled with his appearance, he possessed an unlikable personality of immense aggrandizement. He was intelligent, this is true. From a poor peasant family (as most of these Spanish up-and-comers seemed to be), he had trained under the Jesuits and, through their teachings, developed his mind and political acumen. He was ambitious and ingratiating. Delicate work. Almost as delicate as the work I'd been commissioned to accomplish. We were like two agents on opposite sides, tunneling away to destroy the other's side.

Wait, we were not *like* that, silly me! That is *exactly* what we were.

On the first morning, I sat in the schoolroom observing him from the corners of my eyes. How could such an uncouthly put together bundle of manhood be feared as a radical of the first degree? As if conscious of being the centre of my thought, his glance slid up and slithered over me, point by point. I felt contaminated. I had never gone to bed with a man who did not attract me, to put it mildly. More truthfully? Who viscerally repulsed me. However would I get through this ordeal?

I schooled my lips to smile serenely. His voice droned on and on, spittle flew, and I felt ill.

After the lesson, the infantas trailed off to their next engagement: Luisa Fernanda with enthusiastic glee and Isabel in plodding resignation. Shite and double *merde*.

"It seems likely we shall be spending many hours in the same room, señor," I ventured, fluttering my lashes.

"Perhaps you will learn something," he muttered in his unpleasant, nasal voice, gathering together his papers and books.

"Oh, doubtless," I trilled, and moved closer. Ye gads, he was repulsive. He had such a dank, sour smell. "I am always intrigued by a man with abundant knowledge." I put my little hand upon his own.

His eyes flew up and pierced mine before he snatched his furry paw away and shook it, as if ridding it of fleas. Oh good God. Did Grimaldi have any idea what he was asking me to accomplish?

I tried again. "Señor Arguëlles, I would be most grateful if you would occasionally give *me* a small, intellectual chore. I am not wealthy . . ." I paused and looked down, becomingly, "but perhaps there are other ways in which I might—"

His head reared back and he peered at me sternly. "What on earth are you talking about? And why are you here in the first place? I heard you are some sort of," his voice became ironic and huffy, "thespian. Not at all the kind of person the future queen should have near her."

"You have very elegant legs and ankles," I said foolishly, not being able to think of anything else in this world which might interest him so much.

He paused, and he did look down for an instant, at himself, and I could see his ecumenical mind ticking away, acknowledging that I was indeed correct in this matter. Then he made a wet, snorting sound through his nose as if highly desirous of swallowing as much snot as was humanly possible. "Good day to you," he said, and flung himself out of the room.

After such a wretched beginning, I was more than ever concerned about the aftermath of this undertaking. I was in so deep. I had evaded a murderous demon in the theatre and nobody seemed to care, and now this? No one had convinced me that I would be safe, should I manage to seduce the brute. Arguëlles had friends in high places; why would they dismiss *him*, and not *me?* I would simply be considered some theatrical slut who had tried to get above herself, who'd tried to sleep her way into favour. Too cruel, too disgusting—I was going to fail. It was not possible. But then images of my darling Emma's ears . . . Oh, my confidence had received a rough shake, indeed.

Turmoil boiled through me as I sat in the schoolroom day after day, observing the tutor's furtive narcissism. After my compliment about his legs, I could see he believed he was impressing me; his chest puffed out even further and he kept slicking the few hairs on his head back into place. Ugh. He was coming around to the idea, I thought morosely. Men almost always do, being such prisoners to their pricks. Days, then a week ticked by while I delayed my odious undertaking; Ventura was sending me angry notes, backstage, on a regular basis: "What is happening? Has he disgraced himself yet?" Meanwhile, Arguëlles ate raw onions as a kind of mid-morning tonic; we all turned our faces away, then spontaneously fled. Could he not tell? Did he not care?

On a happier note, in the afternoons the girls and I spent hours with the croquet mallets outside the palace, cracking wooden balls through hoops, with fallen leaves rustling underfoot. Luisa Fernanda and I were both terrible cheats. Though at first we denied it, I could tell she thought it wonderful that I cheated in the same way she did: urging my ball ahead with an expert kick while Isabel wasn't looking. After a while, Luisa Fernanda and I openly cheated, snickering at each other as we did so, then lounging on the grass while we watched and waited for the almost-queen to catch up.

Poor Isabel. I say poor, but of course that's not remotely the right word. Rich as stink the girl was, and about to rule one of the world's powers (though all that marrying of first cousins couldn't be good for it). Her mind had room in it for only three things, I discovered: food, her impending sovereignty, and sex. But the biggest undoubted handicap to Isabel's wanton desires (after all, a Spanish aristocrat in search of safe haven will marry anything) was the state of her epidermis. The package she came wrapped in was that of a lizard. Apparently, *mamá* Cristina had spent a fortune on cures, but nothing ever helped on a permanent basis. Isabel had a disease called ichthyosis, causing her head, face, and entire body to be covered with a dry, scaly skin. Thermal baths, spas, sea baths: All gave only temporary alleviation. A day or two later it was back with a vengeance. When the girl wasn't eating, she was scratching. The raw redness of her face was made odder by the redness of her eyes, which protruded. Hence, poor girl. I really meant it.

"Baby Luisa," Isabel called, as she stood swinging her mallet, looking about with a halfhearted squint, "have you seen my ball?"

"Right behind you," Luisa Fernanda trilled, leaping up with a skip and a hop, "but Rosana and I are winning again."

"Bother. This is a dumb game."

Isabel was always alone, even when surrounded by people. It was like an inherited flaw; as her father had apparently done, the scaly-skinned infanta repelled sympathy without noticing that she was doing so. Watching her totter around on her court shoes, I thanked my stars that I was not born into such an elevated station. The littlest one had a much luckier life ahead, as far as I could tell.

When it was time for siesta, Luisa Fernanda would invite me into her bedchamber to lie down with her and play. The royal rooms were gorgeously outfitted, of course, but also strewn with toys and other small girl objects, I was glad to see. At least she was allowed to be herself in her own private space. Her women were upset about being turned out, but Nanda was determined. "Rosana's fun, and I want to talk with her. Now go." People who are not Spanish (especially the English) have a strange revulsion towards the noble tradition of siesta: They can't believe that the population of entire countries lays down their work in the middle of the day in order to eat, sleep, and indulge themselves with a lover for hours at a time in the afternoon sunshine. I can't think of anything nicer. Of course, the latter was not happening at this juncture. I was being very good, playing innocently with children.

The youngest infanta's favourite way to play during siesta was to tell stories. She loved hearing mine (I grew quite skilled at making them up or remembering Celtic and Indian tales I'd been told), and she loved to tell them herself. The subject of her stories was her own family history. In fact, except for my first lesson (also in bed) from the earl of Malmesbury, and some brief but vivid sketches from Grimaldi, most of what I know about Spanish royalty and vengeance came from the fair-faced princess—no doubt distorted and embellished through a ten-year-old's perspective.

The facts I eventually distilled go something like this: At Isabel's birth, the high dignitaries of the Catholic church, the apostolics, rejoiced that King Ferdinand had fathered a girl. They hated him, for he'd leeched away all of their lands and riches. Although his new wife Cristina and her termagant sister Carlota had convinced the king to sanction the baby's reign, whatever sex it might be, the apostolics believed that eventually the old rule of male successor to the throne must be upheld—which meant Ferdinand's brother, Don Carlos. The apostolics were also angry at Ferdinand's lack of enthusiasm for the Holy Inquisition, which pious Don Carlos had sworn to bring back. The country's loose morals and religious and political backsliding needed cleaning up, according to the churchmen, who vowed to place Carlos on the throne by force of arms if necessary. But then the unthinkable happened: Ferdinand died, the Pragmatic Sanction somehow passed into law, the queen regent and her now *two* female children ascended, and the people rejoiced. An apostolic call went out for "Religion, King, Inquisition" and madmen of all stripes leapt on to it with conviction. This had been followed by full-fledged war.

Don Carlos, meanwhile, had continually refused to take an oath of allegiance to his niece—unlike the third brother, Don Francisco, who was married to Carlota. The rest of the world then stuck their oars in: England supported Cristina and the rights of a woman to rule (we'd had a remarkable queen once, after all, one the Spanish remembered well). France backed the women reluctantly, partly because they were all related by their Bourbon blood. Portugal was involved in its own civil war over the rights of a pretender, so they were not to be trusted. The old Holy Alliance of Austria, Prussia, and Russia refused to recognize Isabel for the usual reason of her sex, and because they feared the rise of liberal principles which had begun to percolate all over Europe. Austria's gouty old Metternich had described Isabel at age three as "revolution incarnate in its most dangerous form." Luisa Fernanda told me this story with a wicked giggle, proud of her sister's reputation.

"*Papí* had three wives before *Mamí*, but hadn't got any children from them, and he was getting old and sick. *Tía* Carlota says he'd been," here the little girl put on a raspy, world-weary tone, "'too busy with women other than the queens to have managed to officially replicate himself.'"

That made me laugh.

"*Mamí* changed all that," Nanda went on. "She made him get down to business, because she wanted to see us as soon as possible."

"That's one way of looking at it," I murmured sleepily. It was beginning to strike me that all this war, death, hate, and destruction had been caused by one thing: emphatic denunciation of the rights of a woman to rule.

"We have lots of half brothers and sisters now, but we never see them. They live in France." The girl's voice was a little sad. "*Mamí* fell in love again too fast. But she'd never really been in love anyway. Not to *Papí*. He was too mean and grumpy. I understand that; do you?"

"Oh yes."

"Anyway, everyone knows she and Muñoz are married now. But they were married even when she was queen regent. They got married secretly, with the help of the Papal nuncio."

The pope had approved? But—? Oh never mind.

Nanda had her white stocking-clad legs in the air at this point, admiring her feet as they twirled in one direction and then the other. "I don't mind him, and I do like their babies. Though they're dark like Muñoz and they're only half royal, so they don't really count." I remembered Concepción's whispered relieving of the big man's itch and wondered how many others he might have been fathering on the side when circumstances lent themselves to full dalliance. "He's rich now," the cherubic princess added innocently, "because when they were living here, he got stock tips from different finance ministers. And I heard him tell some of his friends." Interesting. Could that possibly have included the Grimaldis? Was that why

Concepción had been so accommodating? I filed the Infanta's gossip for future reference; you never know when you might need some scuttlebutt to save your own, I thought. Then we fell asleep in the afternoon sunshine.

※ ※ ※

Back to Isabel. Her importance can't be forgotten, though she herself often was. Isabel—and sex. It was on everyone's mind, not only Isabel's.

The truth cannot be shirked: The chubby infanta was embarrassingly randy. When she sat at her desk, chewing her pencil and trying to conjugate French verbs, she would rhythmically rock back and forth on her chair. Under the table, she would rub at herself; Arguëlles, noticing, would make his violent snorty-snot sound. Nanda had told me that political as well as royal fingers had been crossed on Isabel's birthday, hoping it would herald the arrival of her courses, too long delayed. But so far, nothing. What could be keeping the girl from becoming a woman?

"What about him?" Isabel would whisper to her sister during their interminable courtly audiences. "Look, he smiled at me."

"Too far below you," was the reply. "And he's ancient."

"What do you think it will be like to fuck?"

My ears burned! The fat girl was incorrigible.

"Don't call it that," Nanda scolded. "That's rude! *Mamí* would say you sound like Tia Lota."

I was beginning to understand Cristina's anxiety for speed as far as selecting a potential suitor was concerned. One day I overheard the British ambassador telling a visiting English dignitary, "She must be married somehow and to someone *immediately*," as they watched the princess licking a sweet on a stick with more than usual gusto. The ambassador went on, with a grimace, "As the Spanish would say, if we don't make haste, at this rate the heir will arrive before the bridegroom."

Arguëlles himself seemed to be settling into a horrible charade of courtliness towards the chubby one. In the schoolroom, he'd pull out her chair and help arrange her skirts once she was in it. He started sharpening quills for her and other small gestures of devotion. He was filling the girl's head with strange ideas.

"Your Majesty, never mind recent history. Leave the skirmishes of the battlefield for the men who understand them."

"But I should take an interest, that was *Mamá*'s war," Isabel said, scratching her cheek, then her wrist, then her torso.

"The prime minister knows what is best. That's why your mother left him in charge. In charge of Spain, our beloved country, and of you, Your Majesty, and your dear sister." His voice slippery and persuasive. "What Spain requires now is more young people—more babies, in fact. You will make a supremely fit mother, Your Majesty. You will set the standard for mothers."

"Do you think so?" she asked. I nearly gagged at the tutor's blatant foolishness, but he was much smarter than I could bear to think him. He played to her weaknesses.

"Yes, Highness. A beautiful bride, and a tender young mother."

And tears actually came into her red, raw eyes at the image of herself, breast-feeding and enjoying the nightly rumpy-pumpy that she craved.

Luisa Fernanda, at least, didn't take the tutor's fawning hypocrisy lying down. *She* could see clearly, her head not yet clouded by burgeoning lust and an unappeasable stomach.

"I don't like these lessons," Nanda told him. "I don't think *Mamá* wants us to be told such things. Right now we need to know about the *Cortes* and why the war happened." She flung her pencil down and walked out.

Arguëlles looked over to Isabel, who was digging out a sweet. As long as the soon-to-be-queen was still in the room, he was content. He was Espartero's minion, the fat girl had no time for me, and there didn't seem much that I could do about it.

And still every night, coded, impatient notes from Ventura were being left for me at the theatre: "Time is wasting," followed by "Do not fear, but do not wait," and then the more forthright, "Soon it will be spring, so make winter come soon!" I was in an agony. I *had* to make my move!

The moment finally came three days later. The lesson had been a particularly nasty one: Spanish history, spiced with gristly battles and descriptions of obedient royals who'd heard the word of God as delivered through His earthly messengers, the apostolics. Then, just as the three of us thought he was winding down, Arguëlles suddenly wound himself up again. The glories of the Holy Inquisition really made the spittle fly. I watched with horror as his enthusiasm rose, informing us of some of the more intricate forms and devices of torture devised to winkle out heretics. Isabel seemed quite taken with it, but poor Nanda placed her little hands over her ears. When I saw tears trickling from the corners of her eyes, I spoke up.

"Please, señor, that is enough for today. Their Royal Highnesses are fatigued and must retire. It is past the usual time."

He dug into a pocket to retrieve a large, wrinkled handkerchief with which he wiped his perspiring face. Then he rose and bowed. The girls scurried away.

The day had been as long as the lesson, and now the swift autumn dusk had fallen. Though servants had come to light the lamps, the room was still quite dimly lit—luckily, I thought. The less I could see of Arguëlles, the better. I summoned all my courage for an assault at the malodorous, arrogant carcass.

"Dear señor," I breathed, moving gracefully towards him, in the kind of S-curve motion that Fanny Kelly would have appreciated, "I cannot help myself any longer. I cannot bear to be in this room with you any longer—" Oh, what was I saying? Turn that around "—without delivering myself of my deepest emotions."

"What's that?" he huffed, wrinkling his bulbous brow as if the sound of my voice caused him pain.

"I am saying I must tell you, señor, that your, your—" ('Struth, I told myself, spit it out!) "—your *ankles* have driven me to distraction. They are beautiful. They are . . . manly!" The idiot actually looked down and pointed his toe so that he could glimpse the marvel to which I was referring! Are all Spanish men in love with their lower limbs? I stuttered onward, "I have fallen, Señor Arguëlles. I am . . . speechless." I was running out of ammunition. My brain was starved for inspiration, and the man just stood there, one toe pointed, the rest of him looking for all the world like a great, hairy-bodied, bald-headed brown bear with constipation. What could I do? I threw myself at him. I clutched his coat and then plunged my hands inside and around his waistcoat as far as my arms could reach—which wasn't far. I clung like a limpet.

"What? What is—? Señorita, cease this silliness!" Luckily I was looking at a waistcoat button, so the shower of spittle wetted my hair, not my face.

"I can wait no longer," I managed, face pressed against his buttons and out of range (I hoped) of that fearsome breath. What I would do about full frontal avoidance, in what I earnestly hoped would be only a few minutes of intense dalliance, I wasn't quite sure but—sound the charge! "I *must* give in to my impulses, señor, though I have no idea what may happen now . . ." I let my voice quaver, hoping to sound like an innocent, overcome for the first time by newly awakened lust, while removing one hand from his ponderous belly and inching it lower and lower in the usual way, tickling and fondling to stir the juices. Face pressed to his sour torso, I couldn't see his expression, but hoped for the best. "Oh, I admire your intellect, your knowledge of the past—"

"The ingenuity," he croaked suddenly, "the pain intensifies . . ."

What was this? Hurry on, Rosana, what was the man muttering? My nimble fingers roved, the palm of my hand connected with a soft roundness. I gave a sensual squeeze. I'll be honest, I was expecting the man to have a set the size of a walnut but—*¡Hijo de puta!* And son of a bitch again! It was huge! His balls were enormous and hard, like a melon. I scrabbled about, at a bit of a loss. Where was his prick? Ah, there it was, but! It was soft as an earthworm!

His eyes were squeezed shut, and his lips were babbling: "Sacred duty . . . Sorrowful agony . . ." What in God's name? I was trying to instill life into a bean-sized cadaver, and what was he going on about? Then it struck me, as his tiny prick finally began to stir and stiffen: He was imagining the instruments of torture he'd just been describing to Nanda and Isabel!

With a sudden bellow he pulled away and shoved me backwards into a desk with painful force, his face a blotchy patchwork of red and white. We stared at each other, both in our own ways completely appalled.

"I am not remotely interested in you, you actress," he finally uttered, showing yellow teeth like a rodent's. "How dare you presume. How *dare* you harbour hopes of intimacy with a man such as myself."

"Not intimacy, then," I countered bravely, "but—"

"No. Never. You! Do not exist in my universe." And the great ape turned on his elegantly shod heel and lumbered from the room, carrying his indignation like a banner before him.

The man dreamed of torture! His own, or someone else's, I wasn't quite sure—but I had to flee the room and wash my hands over and over to rid myself of the taint of his *partes íntimos*. And then I was in a complete mess: What would I tell Ventura? How would I be able to insinuate myself back into the degenerate tutor's trust (not that I'd ever had it)? Visions of sweet Emma's ears haunted me. How much time did I have left? Why had I been squandering it, diddling about and putting off the inevitable?

That night, in my opulent room at the palace, stormy raging and pacing filled the hours. Was I about to fail in my mission? And then the most terrible thought yet: Had the demon from the fly tower actually been sent by Grimaldi? *Dios mio,* how could I be such an innocent? Such a *bobo*? Why hadn't I understood the danger I was in? And then I realized, no, that's absurd. That is far too nefarious. Why would Grimaldi send his bodyguard to watch me? No, no! I'll just tell Ventura the truth, that the plan cannot work, the tutor cannot be seduced by any means, and we'll come up with an alternate plan.

But the lingering fear remained, no matter how logical I told myself to be. Was I about to be removed?

During the weeks leading up to Christmas, I looked for Ventura at the theatre, startling at shadows and turning in jittery circles to check behind me. I could never find him. Back at the palace, I began to observe various aristocratic men, surrounded by their supporters, being put up to the mark: sidling towards Isabel's throne, bowing themselves into contortions of grandiosity, then backing away from the girl's charmless presence. Their eyes, having also flicked over to the adorable white-blonde sister, would fill with woeful remorse. Luisa Fernanda found the endless parade hilarious and was kind enough not to point out the men's reactions to her obtuse sibling.

Then the redoubtable Tia Lota and her husband Don Francisco arrived from La Granja, the royal summer residence where they'd been lingering, the autumn having stayed so mild. They brought their two sons with them: Francisco, Duke of Cadiz, was the eldest, a scrawny, epicene sort of young man, and Enrique, Duke of Seville, who was much handsomer. The servants lived in mortal fear of Carlota: Carlota, Cristina's older sister, who had been in the Spanish royal family for decades and had seen Ferdinand's other queens come and go (meaning, dead). Carlota from Naples. As I came to understand, *the* Carlota.

What a woman! She was about forty years old, living at full throttle and grown to fit her power. She breezed into the palace like a ship in full sail, her attractive but meek husband Don Francisco bobbing along in her wake. "Darling, precious!" she cried as she folded Luisa Fernanda in her arms. "Son of a whore, but it's hot out there! I told your uncle, no, it is Christmas. We must go and keep an eye on the girls!" She released Nanda and swept up Isabel, ignoring the almost-queen's struggles to get free. "You're about to become a woman, Bella." Taking hold of the girl's chubby chin, she whispered, "Anything yet?"

"No, Tia Carlota."

"Pity. You must try some medicines, physical exertions, get it flowing."

"Yes, Tia Carlota."

"Let me see you." She held the girl at arm's length and made tutting sounds. "Good Christ. Don't eat so much, how many times must I say it?" Then she turned and gave me the benefit of her blazing, turquoise eyes. "Who are you?" One look from those eyes and I was bewitched. These daughters of the king of Naples are fatally attractive: tall, blonde, full of grandeur. And this one even more so. I immediately knew that I wanted to be exactly like her and exist in such a gloriously individual way.

I curtsied and answered, "Eliza Rosana Gilbert, Your Majesty. I'm at the Príncipe, with the company of *La pata de cabra*—"

"Ah. That screwball play."

"—and the infanta invited—"

"I understand." Placing a hand on my arm, she whispered, "You met my sister. I know about you: Give nothing away. Son of a bitch, I need a drink."

She headed off, courtiers all around bowing and scraping and scampering out of her way, followed by Don Francisco and the rest of their retinue. Nanda grinned over at me and said, "Isn't she wonderful?" I couldn't have agreed more.

I lost no time, after this potent reminder, in drafting a polite little letter to Cristina, in Paris, to say that her sister had arrived, that a number of potential suitors had been received during audiences with the infantas, and that I hoped to have more complete news soon. With deepest respect, etc., etc.

I was in above my head, and no mistake!

⁂ ⁂ ⁂

Meanwhile, I was still meeting with Donatella and pursuing my dancing lessons—one of the most enjoyable portions of my week. I carried on energetically in my role as Cupid, burning the midnight oil in true Spanish style. Spaniards, I've come to understand, are tempestuously exhausting, and usually exhausted. That is why they need siesta; after sexual satisfaction comes the only hour or two they're truly asleep. I was at the palace all day, I danced in the late afternoon, performed all evening, didn't eat until midnight, and my night was still going strong at two or three in the morning as I tried to slow down enough to be able to sleep. The only thing missing was the sex, alas.

Not everything was rosy at the theatre. It was Christmas; the audiences seemed in raucous moods prior to the closing of the season. I did finally track Ventura down; he'd been organizing the impending masked ball in a different venue and was pulling his hair out over it. "It's our best opportunity, Rosana. I'm receiving updates from Grimaldi daily."

My stomach lurched. "And is he pleased with our progress? I mean, with mine? We must speak about the tutor, Ventura. It's damnably difficult, the man is so—"

The playwright looked up from his desk. "What?"

I blinked rapidly and tried to stay calm. "He is corrupt, but in this matter I believe he is incorruptible. We need to come up with an alternate plan concerning the tutor."

He looked down at his papers and pursed his lips. My heart lurched in my chest. Why was he not saying anything?

"That matter of the fly tower," I said. "Did you ever discover—?"

"Nothing."

"There was a man in Paris. Your brother said he knows him as an associate. Pedro Coria? Has a glass eye; tall, mad bugger? Is there a chance that he—"

"We don't know who it was," he said, returning to his paperwork and ending our discussion, "but it will never happen again."

Oh, I was sure of that too, because I'd decided to take my safety into my own hands. Every night now, I flew with one of the little pistols tucked into my costume, powder tamped and little metal cap secured over my left nipple, ready to place in the loaded barrel at a moment's notice. I kept the second pistol hidden in its faux book in my dressing room; they returned with me to the palace at night. I was taking no more chances. Now, when I landed on the platform (like a tiger on a roof) after my flight upwards, one hand was at my waist, ready for the return of that shadowy demon.

Desire to remain sharp also led me to ask Luisa Fernanda whether I could set up a target in one of the palace gardens and be allowed to shoot. This request thrilled her and, being the curious child that she was, she even managed to pry out of me a bit of the story behind the request. I told her the theatre was dangerous sometimes and that there had almost been an accident. With a cry of triumph, she grabbed my hand and ran me over to the captain of her guard. "Rosana requires a bodyguard every night," she trilled, "beginning tonight. To accompany her to the theatre and back."

And so it was. This extra attention (and another lumbering male backstage) did nothing to endear me to the cast, but made me feel safer, somewhat. The bodyguard seemed to annoy Ventura, which I regretted. "We may be coming to the end of this stage," he told me curtly. "Be prepared to move on."

"What do you mean?"

"Changes are coming—plans, decisions. I'm run off my feet."

"What is happening?"

"You'll know soon enough."

I kept up my target practice.

And then. On one of the following evenings, a few days after Christmas, I went to the theatre as usual to begin my preparations. Marietta, the nastiest of the chorus *duennas*, was looking particularly smug, which made me wonder what had happened. "You'll find out," was all she'd say. Well, that, and "*puta coño*" under her breath.

Five minutes before curtain, Ventura came hurtling backstage and pulled me aside. "This is your last performance as Cupid," he said.

"What! But why?" I was shocked.

"Change of plans. Marietta is taking over until we close for the season, and when we reopen Emilio returns." And he strode off the way he'd come.

Marietta. Now I understood. The curtain went up, and we were off—my final Cupid. I hadn't even had time to prepare myself to say goodbye to the role I now realized I had come to love. The whole performance I kept my tears in check, but they were at the ready. It was only at curtain call that I sobbed in real grief, listening to the roar, slaking my thirst at the magical pool one final time before silence descended. Antonio gave me a heartfelt hug as the curtain thumped onto the stage. "You've done a good job, little one," he said. "No one can take that away. Lock it up in your chest, this feeling. You'll find your audience, I have no doubts."

Everyone seemed to know. The dresser was kinder than usual and left me, at my own pace, to change out of my costume, the smelly thing that I had grown dependent upon. The others seemed to hasten into their street clothes and depart for the café with jubilant cries. They were free of me. The circle was complete again, tail in the jaw, no outsider allowed.

And then another nasty shock: Stooping to do up my boots, I noticed the hem of my tartan gown had a four inch tear in it. I grabbed it up and examined it with horror: Someone had sliced the material with a knife! My weekly salary as Cupid had just come to an abrupt end, and now my earl's bank draft—my emergency fund!—was gone. My first confused thought was Marietta, then Emilio—then a worse, but perhaps more accurate possibility entered my head. Could it be the would-be assassin, determined to cut off my escape route? What was I to do now?

Just as I was about to fall into a fresh bout of nerves and dismay, a knock sounded at the door. "Come in," I said, thinking it would be Ventura, ready to unveil Grimaldi's latest anxiety-inducing scheme. Instead, the door burst open and a small, muscular military man stood in the frame, outlined from behind by the candelabra illuminating the hallway.

"Señorita Cupid?" he said. "May I enter?"

Jésu, who was this? He was armed! Was there anyone else left in the theatre? A quick squirt of fear flashed through me and I leaned forwards, camouflaging my hand as it reached for my pistol. "Do I have a choice?"

He grinned as if he knew what I was doing and stepped into the room. As he moved into the increased light I noticed the man had the most decadent, glistening mustache I have ever seen, which also served to underscore both the whiteness of his teeth and the syrupy brown of his long-lashed eyes. "No need for that, I am not dangerous. Not yet, or not at this particular moment."

"Who are you?" My tiny pistol was now in my hand and I brought it quietly into my lap.

"Ventura told me I would find you here."

Did he now?

"My name is General Diego de León. Perhaps you've heard of me?"

My mind flipped rapidly through the many Spanish names I had heard over the past months, and then I had it. Grimaldi's voice, informing me of some of the secret Cristino operators I might be meeting: "Also two of the rebel generals, de la Concha and de León. Be advised not to fall in love with them."

I looked this general up and down, and this made him smile even more broadly. He snapped his teeth together twice, looking me up and down as well, obviously appreciating what he was seeing. These

Spaniards, either they were lamenting and cursing their lot, or their minds were hot in pursuit of the next conquest.

"What is it you need to say to me?" I demanded.

"Ah, señorita, you were so beautiful tonight, so delicate," and his eyes sparkled as he added, "So athletic."

"You were there?" I was slightly mollified by his words. "And you thought I was good?"

"Indeed, the best. Most impressive. May I?" And he indicated his hat, which was part of his uniform—a large, barrel-shaped one with a peak over the brow and an enormous plume extending beyond the top of it. I inclined my head, then he removed it with a low bow and a smart click of the heels.

When he straightened again, having revealed a crown of thick, curly black hair, I saw that he was really quite short, at least two inches shorter than me. Still, there was quite a lot of man in that uniform. "Sit then," I conceded.

"You can take your hand away from your pistol, señorita," he said.

"I'll decide that," I answered.

"Ah."

We sat there in silence for a moment, de León still smiling and holding his ridiculously large hat in his lap. He sighed, as the silence continued, and began to play with the plume.

"Is Ventura coming? Is that why we're waiting?" I asked.

"When?"

"Now."

"I don't believe so."

"For heaven's sake," I fumed, standing suddenly with pistol in hand, "tell me what you've come to say and let me get about my business. I have finished here for the evening—and not only for the evening, but for good! Forever! And I have no way home!" To my horror, tears suddenly sprang to my eyes.

"Oh, lady. Oh *dios mio*, don't cry." He gently slipped the pistol from me and placed it on the table. "You'll go on to other triumphs, this is only the beginning." And the mustache was against my upper lip and his mouth was kissing me. I'd had no idea that a mustache could be so soft, like a kitten, when—

"How dare you!" A resounding slap, his cheek flared crimson, and I had done it.

"Whoa!" He rubbed his face, syrupy eyes now suffering. "*Madonna*. What was that for?"

"You know what for. You took advantage."

"Never. You were sad, I was trying to improve your condition."

"Stand away from me. I don't trust you."

He backed up, retrieved his hat from the chair, and sat down again. There was a welt on his cheek. "*Dios*, you pack a wallop. Very athletic indeed."

Now I felt contrite. "Very sorry, I'm sure. And I didn't mean to cry. Too stupid and female of me. Tell me how you and Ventura are connected."

He stroked his mustache thoughtfully, that kittenlike softness rasping as his fingers moved through it. The ends were twisted and curled upwards, again like a cat—the smile of a cat when it is pleased with itself for a belly full of milk or for finding a warm place in the sun to while away an afternoon. His white teeth gleamed, an occasional sparkle between his lips, his finger twisted and rasped. Like a siesta . . . Oh, what was wrong with me? I picked up a fan and flapped it vigorously. How absurd. It was the middle of the night, I was alone in the theatre, the theatre where someone had tried to kill me and almost succeeded. There was a possible assassin, one or more, out to get me. I'd just lost my job and had no idea what was ahead except the ongoing hideousness of trying to seduce an ugly tutor whose fantasies consisted of torture. The soft rasping suddenly stopped.

"Señorita Cupid," he said.

"My name is Eliza Rosana Gilbert."

"I know it is. You wish us to remain on a professional footing. I respect that, so let me tell you how I fit into the puzzle." I put on a haughty glare as he continued, "I'm not sure Ventura de la Vega would agree, but I believe it best for you to know what is about to happen, not just your own role in it. There is a difference of opinion between Ventura and myself in this regard." He grinned again with those strong, white teeth, and his finger returned to the mustache with a raspy twiddle and a twist. It was very distracting. "Please, may I?" he asked, indicating the door.

He wanted it closed. But, despite the charm, how was I to know he was not the shadowy demon who wanted me dead? Or if not, then in league with glass-eyed Pedro Coria, if it *was* Pedro Coria, up in the flies?

"Leave it," I commanded, snatching up my pistol again and waving it.

He put the hat upon the floor, raised both hands in a placatory manner, and came towards me. "I must speak softly, then, as no one must hear. Our lives may depend on it. Please sit, and I'll draw closer."

Diablo, that hadn't been my intention.

"You know that Don Juan de Grimaldi and I are associates?"

"So you say."

He brought the chair up close, indicating that I sit upon the settee. I did so, and he sat knee to knee with me. His knees were hot.

"You also know that de la Vega has been organizing a masked ball?" I nodded.

"It is to happen in four weeks' time. The princesses have been invited, along with the other important people at court. If all goes well, there will be an enormous crowd, all disguised and enjoying themselves."

"Ventura has told me he needs me for this event, yes," I said. "More than that I don't yet know." I was holding on to my dignity with all my might.

"You are very close to the princesses now, I believe?"

"I like to think so. They are sweet girls, like any children. Why is Ventura not telling me all this himself?"

"He's occupied tonight."

My finger twitched on the pistol. Ventura was a cad. I'd have to be careful.

"Señorita, you'd best be careful," he said, as if reading my mind, then glanced at the weapon. "We wouldn't want it to go off unexpectedly."

"I'll be the judge of that," I retorted, but realized something else. The metal cap, required for firing, was still on the end of my left nipple. Damnation. I removed my finger reluctantly from the trigger.

Diego de León leaned forwards from the waist, and now his sleepy-lidded eyes were only inches away, their irises boring into my own. "Dear Señorita Cupid, it is all very fine, this dance of ours, but we don't have time to be coy. Listen to me carefully. You can trust me with your life. In fact, you must. Ventura de la Vega and I are avowed Cristinos, as is Don Juan de Grimaldi, who sent you. One other associate, General Manuel Gutérrez de la Concha e Irigoyen, is also deeply involved in the plan. He is known as to his friends as Concha. You will meet him shortly." He placed a brown hand upon my knee and squeezed. "Everything depends upon the next few weeks. You must be strong, and brave, as you demonstrated tonight that you can be. And quick."

And with that he seized the pistol in my lap and placed it behind himself on the floor. As I reacted and tried to jump up, his grip on my knee tightened. "Shh!" I could hear nothing, but he twirled, scooped up the pistol again, and, crouching, ran to the dressing room door. He certainly was lithe, like a small black cat, sure of its agility. He peered either way down the corridor, then turned back to me. "This time I must protest. Let me close this. Let me lock it?"

"Very well. For a minute or two." Then, oh fool! I thought. He has your pistol!

He threw the bolt, returned swiftly to the chair, and sat, knees again touching mine. He kept hold of the pistol. My knees began to tremble. "Two things more. First . . ." He blinked, and those eyes again turned syrupy, dreamy. "*Madonna*, they never told me you were so beautiful. What is a man supposed to do—"

"Who do you think is out there?" I asked, terrified, and hoping to break the lock of his eyes upon mine—to no avail.

"Shadows. They're everywhere. Trust no one." His other hand came up and began rasping through the mustache again, twirling, twiddling. "I've become jumpy as a cat these last few months. Forgive me, beautiful Cupid . . ."

We were both puffing up at shadows. What was the plan? Was he about to kill me? Why had I ever let go of my pistol?

"You were saying?"

"*Sí.*" He became brisk again, but his voice remained low. "First, there has been a change of plan. We shall be relying upon your intimate knowledge of the royal household. You must try to learn more about the palace guards, who and what they are, how they function. Where they are stationed, at all hours, how they are deployed within the palace itself, as well as when they are out in public, accompanying the royal family."

"I know one of them; he's undoubtedly waiting for me right now. He's been assigned to look after me."

De León looked alarmed. "Outside, here?"

"As usual, I'm sure." How could I have forgotten? I wondered whether I should scream for him, shout for help.

"Then we must hurry." De León leaned even closer, moving his body forwards to the edge of the seat, his knees pressing at my own. The man exuded heat; I needed to fan myself desperately. How could such a small body be so crammed with muscle and energy? "The night of the ball is the night it shall happen. Nothing must be allowed to go wrong. Everything depends upon timing, cooperation, and luck."

"And what exactly is supposed to happen?" I was getting lost in the cryptic murmurings and his alarming temperature. Or was it my own? His finger rasped on in his mustache, twisting, twiddling. The mustache was bewitching . . .

"My dear señorita. You breathtaking woman . . ." One knee was suddenly between mine, the other pressing the outside of my skirt. "The mission has changed. Señor de Grimaldi has affirmed, and now everything is moving, with the seal of approval from María Cristina of Bourbon-Two Sicilies, and—"

The pistol was on the floor again. How had that happened? The other hand now left his upper lip and was travelling south.

"And?" I whispered, blinking and breathing rapidly, a she fox cornered by a pack of hounds.

"In the excitement of the evening, taking advantage of the disguises and all of the comings and goings, under cover of that—" his face was so close I could feel the heat of it. "We will kidnap the princesses."

I gasped and fell back upon the settee. Kidnap the princesses?

"And second, Señorita Cupid . . ." His breath at my ear was sweet and as hot as the rest of him. This was impossible, I couldn't take it in; that hand, where had it gone? Then I knew. I could feel heat upon my knee, then moving stealthily up my bare thigh. It was under my skirts . . . how—? His voice murmured softly, "There is no longer any necessity for you to seduce the tutor."

Oh! I understood that, and gave a cry of delight. "Oh *dios mio*! Oh, I'm so happy!" and I kissed him, his mustache at that moment the most compelling and amazing thing I had ever seen in the world, and it simply had to be experienced again. "The man is so obscene," I gasped between explorations. "I had no idea how I could ever—"

"Shh, Cupid . . ." He kissed me silent. Somehow he had vacated the chair, which had fallen over with an unnoticed clatter. Our tongues were mingling; I was all of a melt. "No necessity to seduce Arguëlles. The plans have changed." They certainly had, and I no longer cared that the door was locked, that the palace guard was waiting and likely wondering where I was, that any moment he might come looking. This stealthy, lithe cat of a man, this mustache-twirling dynamo, had captured all my attention.

De León had one finger up me when he added, "You must seduce General Espartero, the prime minister."

❧ ❧ ❧

Oh I was caught in a desperate whirlpool of events, good and proper. I could barely react to these alarming words and the intention behind them—being so completely distracted by what was going on inside—when suddenly there was a violent pounding on the door and the bodyguard's deep voice called, "Señorita Gilbert? We must return to the palace. The entire theatre is closed. Señorita?"

Attempting to disentangle myself, I called shakily, "I am just coming!" (Oh, and I was!) "Not now, I must . . . Stop that this second," I panted, and then could say nothing more, the black cat having placed a velvet paw upon my mouth and muffled my abrupt, ecstatic moan. A little death. Oh my god, this man was good.

"Remember, señorita," he whispered into my ear as I shuddered and shook in the aftermath of such abrupt and surprising pleasure, "not a word about all this. It will happen on the night of the ball; you must be ready." He kissed me again. "Are you listening? Say nothing to anyone, particularly not to the Infanta Carlota of Naples, who I hear has arrived from La Granja."

I leaned away from him, and then walloped him across the cheek, the one I hadn't walloped the first time. "*Diablo!*" he cursed, and tried to restrain me, but I clambered off his lap, picked up my makeup bag and dark wool cloak, and rushed to the door.

"Cupid," de León called softly. I turned back to look at him: A red welt was appearing, and two perpendicular fingers were held to his lips. "*Me llamo* Diego. I will be in touch again. Very soon." And he plunged the fingers into his mouth.

I unlocked the door and fled into the night.

✤ ✤ ✤

I tossed and turned in my bed until dawn. I was appalled, and thrilled, at the man I'd just met, couldn't get him out of my head. I wanted him badly and was angry at myself for having allowed this to happen. I'm not a stupid, wanton girl with no experience, I chided myself. Have a care, he could be dangerous. No, I'm *sure* he's dangerous, dangerous to my health! No matter, I still craved him, lay awake, wet, for him. Damnation! And this new, extreme plan of kidnapping the princesses? It seemed so radical, so madcap! Must we go so far to keep them safe? How did I know that it was Grimaldi who was directing operations? Was Diego to be trusted? No one was what he seemed to be in this place. Warned to say nothing to Carlota? But how could I ensure that I was in fact following Cristina's orders? If not, and if I was to get into trouble, how much more deadly would be the trouble I'd be in if the object of my mission was a prime minister rather than a royal tutor! And my missing emergency fund—a disaster! What was I to do?

Cautiously, I went to Ventura the next morning for advice. He was harried, sitting at a desk on the stage itself, surrounded by papers and diagrams.

"Ah, Rosana, we must sit down, but not yet."

"I am desperate for information, Ventura. Diego de León—"

"Good man, good man. He's filled you in on the change of plan?"

"Well, that's exactly what I need to know. He gave me the outline, not fully, just sketchy. It sounds half mad. What does Grimaldi say, when—?"

From the shadows of the theatre, a figure stepped forwards. "We meet again, señora." It was the Jesuit, Father Miguel de la Vega, his tonsured hair grown in again, wearing his black attire. He looked even thinner, if that was possible. Positively concave.

"You remember my brother?" Ventura asked, as if I could forget. "Miguel, perhaps you can help her."

The black eyes glittered in that way I remembered. "What is your question, señora?"

Always he had to remind me of my married state. I despised the man. I hid it nobly and said, "Is Diego de León to be trusted? How am I to know that what he tells me comes from Grimaldi, and therefore from Queen María Cristina of Bourbon Two-Sicilies?"

"*Former* Queen Cristina," he answered, and then, "alas."

The man was so pompous, so correct in his . . . everything! Had to be just so, had to be phrased in such and such a way! Had to show himself up as perfect in every particle! So *Jesuitical*! I took a deep breath. "Could you tell me, please?"

"General Diego de León," the priest said slowly. "What do *you* think of him?"

His question took me aback. Unfortunately, I also felt an immediate blush suffusing my cheeks. "I have no thoughts one way or the other." A vision leapt into my head: the man sucking his fingers with a lecherous grin. "I am . . . trying to follow orders," I went on, "in a chaos of—. I am trying to return home safely as soon as possible. Surely you understand that, Father."

"Oh, I understand," the devout ass intoned. He surveyed me with his mouth like a sucked lemon and folded his attenuated hands. "Yes, de León is a man of the Cristinos. Undoubtedly."

He continued to look at me but said nothing further. Ventura took my hand, patted it, and said, "There you are then, fears abated. Forgive me for having been so distracted, Rosana. Now, think about a costume, if you have any suggestions. Money not an object, brand new, for your figure. You must dazzle them."

This was exciting. My mind raced in all directions. By the time it had returned to earth, only a few seconds later, I'm sure, the Jesuit was gone.

Ventura saw my reaction and chuckled. "Never mind, *cariña*. My brother has always been odd, even when we were boys. He never seemed to live in the same world that we did."

I couldn't imagine such a spooky close relative. "What made him this way?"

"God only knows—and I say that with piety," Ventura answered with a shrug. He went on to tell me that their eldest brother was a model son who never rebelled, that he himself was the baby and a dreamer, his mother's pride and joy, and that perhaps Miguel, the middle child, had felt left out, neither parents' favourite. In any case, when Miguel was a young man, he left home. He set out one day; they didn't know where. When he returned a year later, he wouldn't tell them much except that he'd decided to be a priest. Over time, through things he let slip, the family discovered he'd been following Father Merino, the warrior priest. This priest had been on the wrong side, an early Carlist. A Castilian. A ferocious old War of Independence soldier whose heroism was legendary, so he attracted followers like moths to a flame.

"I swear," Ventura said, "*that* war was what made the men ruling us now so bloodthirsty. They can't get enough, just have to keep starting it over and over again. They need blood to feel alive. Blood of men, of women and children . . ." He shook his head and continued. "Volunteers joined this Father Merino as he made his way north. Almost ten years ago, Rosana, in '33. Hotheads were everywhere, men on the move. Miguel would have been twenty-five, restless, looking for a cause. Father Merino's example was austere: He didn't smoke or drink. His followers believed he never slept. Miguel liked that."

I'll bet he did, I thought, remembering the man wrapped like a bat at the foot of my bed, wishing bad dreams upon me.

"I don't exactly know what changed, but after his march north with Merino, Miguel broke away again and came south, joined a seminary, and began his studies. So you see, although he may have considered joining the Carlists in the very early part of the war, he came to his senses and found his vocation. *And* his cause. Make no mistake, he is every inch a Cristino; he fights for the monarchy, for moderate liberalism. He fights the good fight."

Ventura was nodding to himself. He seemed more than usually troubled.

"Is something wrong?" I asked.

"This damned masquerade." Running his hand across his eyes, he began rubbing them. "But it's also . . . he's been bothering my wife, who is so very tired these days with the new baby. He wants her to be more modest. He's such an ascetic, unused to women. Anyway, he's staying at the seminary now; it's where he's most at home. Things should be better."

I felt for her, this beloved wife. One man so tender; this other, though of the same blood, so rigid. Blood can be a frightening bond; one can look into the face of brothers or sisters and recognize the same features repeating themselves with small variations, yet inside that outer mask of similarity beats an entirely different soul. It is very strange.

"I nearly forgot," Ventura went on. "I've changed my base. I'm over at the Teatro de Oriente, where the ball will be held. So when you come looking for me, you won't have to be reminded. I know you're still sad about leaving the play."

"That's true," I admitted, looking around at the familiar backdrops and props, but shivering a bit as I glanced up into the flies. "I have a worrying problem," I faltered, venturing at last into my pressing private concern. "I don't know how to tell you, but I must. I had an emergency fund of my own, tucked away—quite a large one—and it was stolen, here at the theatre. It's all gone. I have nothing now, and I must know I can leave, that I'm not completely dependent—"

His look was almost ferocious. "I'll give you whatever you require, on behalf of Grimaldi. But you cannot leave, Rosana, you have a crucial role to play in this next venture. We expect your full attention."

"And you have it! But really, Ventura, you mustn't keep me in the dark. I've been going mad with worry."

"Trust de León. We're in good hands, we'll succeed beyond our wildest dreams. Believe me."

And I could get nothing further from him.

The date of the ball was set for the last Saturday in January. At the Oriente, Ventura whirled like a dervish, directing operations. The enormous room he'd chosen for the event was designed for painting curtains and sets, but in the pre-Lenten season the space was not required for its usual function. He could do what he wished with it.

Men carrying rugs, hundreds of candelabra, thousands of candles, dozens of huge gilded mirrors and other decorative luxuries were being set in place. Musicians wandered around, investigating the acoustics; they were members of the full orchestra which had been hired for the evening. Ventura was organizing all of the tables, chairs, silverware, glassware, and linens required, as well as hiring the best chefs in Madrid to create delectable concoctions for the hungry crowd of exuberant, disguised guests. He was also negotiating as good a price as possible for the necessary costs of policing by the national guard (as few as possible) while attempting to keep the barrage of free tickets the military officials were demanding (as they usually did) to a minimum. These events, it appeared, were feared by the authorities because they were considered a licence for disobedience and possible anarchy. The ticket price was another hurdle: Too steep a charge would keep people away, but at the same time it was important to discourage the riffraff, especially if very important and wealthy people such as the royal family (particularly) and the politicians (a necessary evil in the royals' wake) were to be persuaded to come. "A masked ball without the confusion, shoving, and shriek of a crowd is worthless to us," Ventura said. "The mayhem is its heart and soul."

I love fancy-dress turbulence. I'd experienced some of it in India, on the arm of Thomas, but now I was free of jealous, grabby husbands, free to be my own spirited self! Great fun! And I'd decided on a costume. The ball had a theme, which Ventura advertised in the city's papers: the Four Elements. He believed this gave great leeway for costumes of all styles and centuries.

"I want to be the Cloud with the Silver Lining," I told him triumphantly.

He cocked an eyebrow, smiled. "Then let's get to work. By the way," and he took me rather sternly by the arm, "you must do something for us in the next few days."

"What is that?"

"Diego mentioned it to you: security at the palace. Find out how many, where they're placed, anything you can. Don't dally. But be discreet."

A skilled dressmaker had been hired to provide the costumes for all of us connected with the organization. And as the dress took shape over the next few weeks, I must say I was almost more pleased with it than with any other garment I've ever worn. It was all my own design: a huge froth of soft grey and white on the billowing, layered skirts, undercut with a cunning, shiny silver taffeta which peeked through occasionally when I moved, or when I danced—which I was intending to do, oh yes! There was silver undercutting the bodice, which was tight (of course) and very low (extremely becoming). My breasts sat as high as crisp apples on a tree. Or angels on a cloud—what you will. You couldn't miss them even if you wanted to, which I couldn't imagine anyone wishing to do—other than Father Miguel de la Vega, of course, should we be unlucky enough to have to endure his attendance at such an ungodly event.

While all of the fittings and so on were happening, the rest of the world didn't stay in one place. I was still living at the palace, where I continued to avidly observe the magnificent Tia Lota and her indolent family, and smugly ignore the now-forgettable toad, Arguëlles. Spending siesta hours with Luisa Fernanda, I questioned her about the guards and their functions: "How many are there? What kinds of things do they do? Are they all extremely muscular, or crack shots with pistols and bayonets?" She looked at me strangely, until I turned my questions into a fanciful story about a clash between commoners and a fairy kingdom.

One afternoon I sidled up to Javier, the bodyguard who had accompanied me all of those nights to the theatre.

"What is it like to be a royal guard?" I asked in a small voice. "I mean, it seems confusing to me. Are you in the employ of royalty, or the government? Who are you guarding them from? Forgive me for my stupidity, I'm just curious."

He frowned and rubbed his big head. "Don't worry yourself about that, señorita," was his answer, after a long pause. And after another long pause, "You're safe enough, if that's what's on your mind."

"Ah, thank you, Javier. Now I feel better." I tried again. "No, but, I mean—if for example the prime minister were staying here one night and a fire broke out, would you rush first to save him, or to save, say, Princess Carlota of Naples?" I fluttered my eyelashes.

"Uh . . ."

I stopped fluttering, as it was distracting him, and I wanted an answer.

"There'd be more than one of us," he finally said, "so of course we'd save both. We're bodyguards. That's what we do." His eyebrows came together again, and he looked rather grumpy.

"Yes, I see that." Another approach: "But in the household, are there some who are specifically delegated to one person or another?"

"Of course."

Good, I was getting somewhere. "So, are there groups, who are on different sides?" Was that a hint of suspicion on his face? How to be less complicated? "Oh piddle, I'll just come out and ask it, my question. And remember, I know nothing about politics, I'm just a flighty Irish girl and you'll forgive me for that, won't you?"

His smile was shy and very charming. "Of course I will."

"Is there anyone here who is on the queen regent's side? I mean, the princesses' mother, María Cristina? On her side?"

There was a long pause as he looked over my head and into the distance at some unknown thing. His face became impassive. "Not here, not anymore. They've all been executed."

Diablo. I think I had my answer.

✣ ✣ ✣

The royal family announced they would attend the masquerade. The entire palace was sent into a frenzy of motion, with the family itself as its calm centre. Relatively speaking.

"Son of a bitch, this bodice is too tight! What do you want me to do, keel over dead?" Carlota was berating the royal seamstress who had been sweating and slaving, night after night, over the most flamboyant costume I had ever seen. The royal galleon had decided to go as the Fires of Hell, and I'd been aghast and thrilled at the copious wired layers, the bright yellows, oranges, and reds, and the enormous, Gorgon-like headpiece she had dreamed up and which the seamstress (a worker of miracles) had been steadily turning into reality.

Carlota twisted and preened before the mirror while I was privileged to watch. The young princesses were in their own rooms, being fitted as a mermaid (Isabel) and a fairy (Luisa Fernanda, of course).

"You have to admit my parents married right, with an eye to appearance," Carlota exclaimed, adjusting her splendid breasts inside the bodice. "We all benefitted—amongst the squat and hairy Neapolitans, particularly. We stand out, we're majestic." No shortage of self-assurance, either, I thought. "Now we're being reduced to leftovers; getting shorter, darker. We have squints—just look at Isabel, fat as butter and scratching as if she's infested with fleas. But what could you expect, the king was ugly as sin. We're going down the drain! Oh, hell's bells, woman, this fucking headdress is cutting into my neck!" she barked at the seamstress, who was down on her knees amongst the many dancing flames. "Let go of me for a minute." As Carlota flounced towards the mirror, one of the points of the flames caught the poor woman in the eye, but she simply followed the infanta on her knees, apologizing and trying to keep up.

"My son's no better," Carlota sighed, staring moodily at her reflection and smoothing an eyebrow with a wetted finger. "Cadiz and Seville I call them, to keep them straight. Cadiz looks better in velvet than *I* do, it's a disgrace! He wants to go to the masquerade as a water sprite! I ask you! He'll look as blowsy as a slut's nipples." Seeing something she didn't like, "Here, fix this," she cried, flinging the complicated headdress to the floor.

At this moment, the younger infantas entered, screeching in delighted, shrill voices about their costumes. "Look, Tia Lota, isn't it lovely?" This from Nanda, as she twirled in circles, wearing a gorgeous, expensively silked confection of a gown in forest colours, with gossamer wings. The seamstress, her wounded eye still streaming tears, seemed pleased and apprehensive at the same time, looking to the imposing elder infanta for approval.

"Nimble. Nubile. Very pretty, *flor*." Carlota's Medusa eye swiveled to the almost-queen, who tried to pirouette and nearly fell down. "Good Christ, girl, what the hell are you supposed to be? You look as if you've been pickled in brine! What is she, besides hopeless? Besides obscene? Not you, Bella, the costume. Do it again!" This to the now-cowering, hand clasping seamstress.

This really wasn't fair. Isabel's costume was intricate, made of the finest materials, many real seed pearls hand sewn onto it, representing long hours of eye-popping labour. The skirt was the tail of the mermaid, narrowly open at the feet for her to be able to walk—but this was the problem. Pulled tightly onto Isabel's growing corpulence, the tail made her look as if she were stuffed into a glistening barrel, and because it was tight, she couldn't walk normally but had to take tiny steps—which she was unaccustomed to do, couldn't get the knack of, and hence kept tipping over.

"Come on, Bella, I'll help you out of it," said Luisa Fernanda to her now pouting sister. They went off again.

Carlota's bad mood seemed to have been heightened by the mermaid affair. "Shit on a stick," she began to mutter. "Cadiz, Cadiz, my scrawny son. Too enamoured of fripperies, little splat of acidic vomit . . ." I wondered if she even remembered that I was there. Her eyes were fixed upon her own in the mirror. "Isabel and Cadiz. Hate each other mutually. And we have to think of the future." Casting my mind back to Cristina's discussion of suitors (there had been four serious contenders, one French, one English-German, two Spanish), I recalled that one was the son of Don Carlos, a first cousin. And the other, another first cousin—good Lord, Carlota's son, the epicene youth, Cadiz! And Cristina herself was dead King Ferdinand's (her husband's, and Isabel's father's) own niece, I'd heard somewhere. So if Isabel married her aunt's first son . . . *dios mio*. Carlota was right, the royal line *was* in deep shit.

"*¡Jesu!*" the majestic Carlota cried out suddenly, clutching her stomach and doubling over. I rushed to her side, but she waved me off. "No, no, ignore it, it goes away in a moment." Her beautiful face had gone green and now broke into a sweat. The seamstress, distraught, was trying to fan her. "Leave it, damn it," Carlota panted, then, "Go away now, all of you. Rosana, bring me water?"

We hastened to obey. Once she'd drunk down the full pitcher, Carlota began to look a bit better. "Unlace me, will you, *querida*? Get this fucking thing off me."

I went around behind and began gently loosening the stays. From there I could admire her immensely thick blonde hair, coiled up off her neck, strands of the honey-coloured stuff coming loose, her back muscles strong and toned. She was resplendent, even with the faint tinge of sweat from her mysterious pain still lingering. Perhaps because of it. She was so alive, so volatile.

Eyes closed and breathing deeply, she said softly, "I think we must send you back, Rosana, after the ball. Back to your own. Not good for the girls to have too many toys or pets, or people on whom they depend. Must grow up sparely, to be safe. You understand, don't you?"

She turned her head to look at me, a flash from those wild blue eyes, and I nodded. "So that's that." I continued unlacing, and after a moment she added, "But we'll enjoy you 'til then."

Luisa Fernanda rushed back into the room, still in her fairy costume. She was stamping her feet and then started jumping up and down in one place.

"What's that, *pequeña flor*?" Carlota inquired.

"The tarantella, Tia Lota, look. *Mamá* used to do it."

"Not like that, surely."

"I've changed it, watch!" The little fairy girl began to run around the room, back and forth, then gave a small gasp as if she'd seen something frightening. She ran towards the spot and stamped upon it furiously many times. Then it was as if something had run up her leg and into her dress, and she started shaking her skirts and shrieking.

"Shh, shh!" Carlota cried. "You'll take my head off. Oh, the shrillness of little girls!"

But I was fascinated. Luisa Fernanda began leaping into the air, twirling, shaking her skirts with abandon. And then she did something even more interesting. She crouched, legs bent, hands touching the floor, and began to hop, to skitter, to crawl—and I understood her game. She was miming, at first a girl who'd stamped on a spider's nest, and then she was the spider itself, galloping about on all fours. I was laughing and clapping, and Carlota was too, as Luisa Fernanda's spins reached a crescendo and she collapsed upon the floor, very pleased with herself.

"That's my version," she panted. "I'm the tarantula. Did you understand, Tia Lota? Wasn't it funny?"

"Wonderful, *flor*. You're a devil. Look, you've ripped your dress."

It was true, she had shredded the lovely thing. The poor seamstress.

"That's not the way I remember the dance, sweetheart. But the delirium, you captured that well." Carlota added, to me, "A dance from our country."

"I know it a little," I said.

"Crazy peasants—get an idea in their heads, you can't shake it. Now they're proud of it." The unlacing finished, I helped her step out of the Fires of Hell. She stood, breasts firm and stomach flat, staring at herself again. Her eyes seemed sadder, and she dismissed me.

※ ※ ※

I was at the Oriente, passing a second message on for Ventura to post with my impressions of the suitor situation: "Put this straight into the hands of María Cristina, post-haste!" I also informed him that I'd be needing my old rooms again, or somewhere else to live, since Carlota had told me that I must be ready to leave the palace right after the ball—was that when I could assume that I'd be able to leave, to go back home, with my reward? Wherever home was, I thought with a sudden pang.

In the middle of these unanswered questions, in he came, swaggering in his uniform, boots polished to a high gloss, mustache twirled and cocky, thin cigar trailing an ephemeral wisp. Diego de León.

"Señorita Gilbert," he said with a bow, "I am most pleased to see you again."

"Thank you, General," I responded, and left it at that.

He'd come to deliver a number of items for the ball; Ventura and he went away together while I wandered around, examining everything new that had arrived since my last visit. I was beginning to see what the room was to suggest: a Venetian scene, complete with an impending canal, which was being constructed across the far right corner.

Before I knew it, Ventura had suggested that General de León escort me to my old rooms to see if they were still available. De León gave a chivalrous bow and ushered me ahead of him. We left the theatre and turned to the right. True, I am hopeless at navigation, but as we walked along even I began to realize that this was not the usual route I would take to reach the Oriente, from anywhere that I knew. Most of the buildings we were passing I had never seen before. "Not much further," de León said, "I promise you." Two or three blocks later, we turned in to a large building with a fine garden at its front and began to walk up the steps to the front door.

"Just a moment," I told him. "This isn't it."

"This is better."

"You've already found rooms for me? That's impossible."

"Come and see."

Did I guess? I was nervous and all aflutter at the same time. He looked sumptuous in the daylight, packed into that uniform, which he filled in all the right places, a broad sword swinging against one hip, a pistol on the other one. We proceeded up a wide, curving stairway and came to a door, which he opened with a key tucked in his trousers. I went in, he closed the door behind us demurely—and then swept me up in his arms, ran with me across the large, sparely furnished outer room and into a bedroom with a huge bed. He threw me across it and flung himself down after me: *¡Hola!* Our mouths came together like the Red Sea crushing the Eygptians, a voracious ocean in between that carried us away and drowned us, all afternoon.

In that first rush of exhilaration, we had no time to remove more than a hint of clothing—just the bits and pieces that were in the way. I was panting and laughing as he pushed up my skirts and wrestled with the waistband of his breeches, and he was laughing too. The madness of passion is a hilarious state, even while you're in the throes of it; at least, the sort of passion that leads to intense pleasure lends itself to that deliriousness. Wild kisses, hands everywhere, everything fast and deep and gorgeously full of sensation, that first time. Almost too fast. We rolled away from each other, out of breath, feeling completely undone and yet still not satisfied. We lay on our backs, then Diego leaned up on one elbow to gaze at me and to gently circle his finger around my breast; we said sweet things, whatever came into our heads, to show our joy. After a short time, we were ready for more, and this time was slower; removing clothing, observing each other's bodies avidly, reaching out to touch and familiarize ourselves with the unknown terrain. He preferred to keep his boots on, I learned, which caused great hilarity when he and his trousers become entangled by them—but we swiftly managed.

Oh God, Diego de León could make a stone cry out! He had obviously acquired skills through a great deal of practice, but oh my, how he enjoyed himself. He was not one of those men who are absorbed with their own pleasure; no, it had to be mutual. His small, compact body was nimble and flexible and could contort like a cat's. I've mentioned his fingers, but what that man could do with a tongue! And with the correct positioning of a number of pillows, well! Once I'd recovered from my shock and delight (and from my third little death), I got down to the business of discovering what Diego's favourite dalliances were. And that's when I realized why he'd complimented me, as Cupid, for my athleticism. For that is where Diego's heart lay—or perhaps I mean other parts than his heart: *Action* was his meat and drink.

Like all Spanish men, he was in love with his uniform, so that garment featured strongly in many of our first (and ongoing) escapades. Spurs, too, were on the menu. He'd wear his boots (and nothing else), while I'd don his spurs. He loved a little pain; some men are like this. I think he fancied himself as a horse, in his most secret fantasies. Who knows what men are thinking as they are coming? I certainly wouldn't tell anyone what *I* am thinking in the same, private moments. Why should we? That is for our own soul; it feeds us and fills us with pleasures both describable and inexpressible—and then we return and thank God for each other, for the fulfillment and satisfaction that swells our hearts and blood vessels in the moments after. In the arms of a good lover, the world is made right.

He adored his mustache, and played with it constantly. He was rude, and made me laugh, when he'd say he could taste me on it for hours afterwards. He was proud of his manhood—well, what man isn't?—referring to them as his "crown jewels." As for me? Well, with Diego I understood why it is called a little death. Under his skillful touch, I could imagine myself as the hand inside a glove, and then the way that hand feels as the glove is swiftly slipped off: naked and free, for uncharted moments, shorn of everything but sensation. Such bliss . . .

☙ ☙ ☙

I moved in with him, not caring whether Ventura approved nor whether Grimaldi would be angry from afar. I was angry with them, I thought defiantly, and anyway, Diego promised to smooth things with the playwright. Luisa Fernanda was sad that I was leaving, but she was young and her world constantly revolved, accommodating aristocratic relatives, royal functions, kittens and puppies, and her mother's absence. I promised we would dance together at the ball. "Very well," she said, "I will anticipate that with pleasure." Already more distant, already moving into her destiny. Already I felt like a traitor to her.

Isabel didn't notice my departure, but that was nothing new.

Carlota and I met briefly—she came to my room as the last of my trunks were being carried out. "I didn't mean that you must leave us immediately, dear. But perhaps it's for the best." I almost told her then; I came so close to blurting it out. We're going to kidnap the princesses, by direct order of Cristina! Do you approve, do you know this is about to happen?

She must have sensed my turmoil, as she pushed a strand of hair back from my forehead and said in her matter-of-fact way, "You're lovely. I don't need to know, but be careful. Choose your friends wisely. Listen to your heart." The servants bowed as they left the room for the final time. She turned to look about, checking their work. "We will be off, too, after the ball. Cadiz and Seville are restless; their father as well." She moved to the window and gazed down into the courtyard below. "I feel a heaviness . . ." It was true, she appeared tired, those splendid features rather drawn. I didn't know what to say to her, her presence made me tongue-tied with admiration—the only woman I've ever met to cause such anxious yearning in my heart.

"Damn," she suddenly cried. "Those shitheads have brought my favourite stallion out for Cadiz!" She yanked open the window and shouted, "Not on your life, boy! Get your turd-filled boots off that stirrup! You'll ruin his mouth!" She ran from the room, calling back, "I'll see you at the ball—as the Fires of Hell!" And she was gone.

Those next few weeks—waiting, and living with Diego—were some of the most whirlwind of my life. I had called him a dynamo and that is surely what he was. He went about his military business during the mornings; he was a general, after all, and highly regarded. The populace loved him for his bravery and swashbuckling charm. He'd fought heroically and gallantly in the Carlist battles, earning the loyalty of the people as well as the title of Count of Belascoain, a thank you from Cristina.

One morning, as the church bells struck noon, he arrived with his comrade, General Manuel Gutérrez de la Concha e Irigoyen, another handsome, uniformed fellow, but taller and thinner—the other general Grimaldi had mentioned. Diego filled us in on the plan as he knew it.

"We are to kidnap the infantas on the evening of the ball, deliver them to the fastest coach we can muster, and head for the border. We need you, Rosana, to keep Espartero amused, distracted, while we get them away. At first he won't know what is happening—his office is only a few streets from the Oriente, and that is where you must get him to take you. By the time reports have come in and they've found him to tell him, it will be too late. We know a secret route over the border. We'll disappear."

"But the girls will be frightened!" I protested.

"There's a woman coming with us. She'll be good with them, never fear."

"They know me, they trust me. I should go with them."

"Too obvious."

A pang of jealousy shot through me. "May I see Grimaldi's instructions?"

"You don't doubt me, surely?" Diego grinned, then frowned.

"Of course not. But it seems dangerous."

"It *is* dangerous!" He snapped his teeth and rolled his eyes at de la Concha, as if to say, "Women . . ."

This made me angry. Did he think me afraid? I was determined to be as brave and as reckless as my athletic lover. Why shouldn't I be? Did he think I couldn't do it? Concha added a few soothing words: "The princesses will be safe, not frightened at all." But neither of them would part with any further details.

This was the only wrinkle in an otherwise rhapsodic interlude of days and nights. Diego made love like a man dying of thirst. I realized he must have other women elsewhere; he was just built that way. But during this time he was almost constantly with me—and I didn't care, anyway. His spurs strapped to my ankles, digging into his sides, made him bleed: The crazy man shouted for more! When I'd pull them off and kiss his wounds with sorrow, he would roll me off the bed and then under it, amongst dustballs and centipedes, until I'd crawl out gasping and running for the other room, with him in aroused pursuit.

He took me to a yard where dozens of exquisite horses were being paraded up and down, all up for sale from a distinguished horse-breeding establishment in the Sierra de Guadarrama, northeast of Madrid. Diego's taste in horseflesh was as discriminating as his taste for the other pleasures; he knew exactly what he wanted. He settled on a sleek, black, three-year-old gelding with a white star on the brow and a white left foreleg. As we led the beauty through the frosty streets, I kept looking up at his large brown eyes (the horse's, not Diego's), listening to the soft breath through his nose. "Oh, he is gorgeous," I said, taking the hand of the fine military man at my side. Diego stopped, grabbed my waist and hauled me to him, kissed me fiercely, and whispered, "He's yours."

We stabled the gelding in the place where Diego kept his favourite stallion, Conquistador; a spacious, clean stall for each horse, fresh straw, sweet water, and only good feed to eat. Diego spared no expenses for "the most gracious and noble animals in the world." Seeing the horse settled, he said, "At three, he's old enough to have experienced a few things, good and bad, and young enough still to be keen to learn. The act of gelding is barbaric, yes, but he won't be distracted. Conquistador is a terror sometimes."

"Just like you," I said into Diego's ear.

He stroked my black horse's neck, rearranging the thick mane with tenderness. "This horse loves to run, you can see it in his lines. He'll run until he drops if he's asked to. He's gentle, he's loyal; he'll keep you safe."

"He is the most wonderful gift I have ever had, Diego." And I meant it—even jewels, even diamonds, in that moment, could not hold a candle to the splendour of that living, breathing, beautiful beast.

"Call him Lindo."

"I will."

"For his calm, and his good nature. I can trust you with him. And he'll be right here for you, in case you need him."

This seemed to be important, since he was very serious when he said it, and Diego did not allow himself often to be serious. I tried to question him further, but he shook his head. "That's enough about it. I'm glad you like him."

This worried me, yes, and it also made me curious. But I was trying to live in the moment with this marvellous man, and so I told myself that the gift of Lindo, from one horse lover to another, was a pledge. And it was.

We rode together frequently in the days following, as I acquainted myself with the particular singularities of Lindo and improved my riding ability. I've always loved it; I have a good seat and am quite unafraid, though riding with Diego made me realize how much I still had to discover. One morning, after it had snowed prettily, inducing a frisson of celebration in the city, we headed out together to a flat field where the military men trained. Diego began galloping, creating circles in the fresh snow, Conquistador's hooves flashing as they kicked it up. "Watch this," he called, and flung down the cap he was wearing. I pulled Lindo to a halt and rode off to the side. Diego was urging the stallion to go faster and faster, then finally he turned him swiftly and rode full tilt at the cap sitting small in the whiteness of the snow. Just as I thought the horse was sure to gallop over it, Diego swirled his body to the side—I thought he was falling, going under the animal's belly—and in a seemingly impossible move, he reached, plucked up the cap, and righted himself all in one smooth action. He gave a loud whoop, Conquistador laid his ears back against his head, and they dashed off in a riveting charge to the edges of the field, racing nobody but themselves, the day, the hour, and their own might. I laughed when Lindo raised his head in the air and whinnied.

"What were you doing?" I called as they whirled to a halt beside us.

"I met a Cossack four years ago," Diego grinned. "He'd left Russia and come south for the warmth, but he missed his savage sports. He used to practice this endlessly on a field near where he lived. I learned it from him."

"And where is he now?"

"Oh, he's dead."

"From doing this, no doubt."

"No, they thought he was a Carlist. He was executed. Because of the Carlist leader who pretended to be a Cossack. Those were jumpy times, Rosana."

"Well, they were mad, and he was a madman! And so are you!"

"I know!" he shouted with a happy laugh and kicked Conquistador into motion again. This time I raced after him, Lindo straining at the bit to be given his head and catch up with the bolt of lightning streaking before us, plumes of snow billowing up from his hooves.

At some point during that lovely, cold, kiss-drenched day, I remember asking Diego about the rebels. "Did you go to the north? The mountain bandits, I hear they're difficult to fight because they know their mountains so well. Anyone not from there is sure to be outdone."

"Not quite true," he answered, "but almost. They are ruthless, yes. But to look at it from their side, they've been wronged and abandoned for so long. Each time they are roped in to fight, in their minds they are fighting not for the centrist government nor for a king they never see, but for their *fuegos*, their traditional rights. That crucial element is forgotten at peril. It makes them cagey, because they are always being used. Mountain people see different things—not so far, perhaps, but deeper."

This made sense. I nodded thoughtfully, reminded of the border patrol who had almost intercepted Matilde, Father Miguel, and me. And of the only other Spanish northerner I'd met: Pedro Coria.

"Afraid of bandits, my darling?" Diego smiled. "I'll protect you."

"I'm afraid of nothing," I said with a toss of my head, "not even you." And to prove it—though I'd been about to—I didn't even tell him about my near accident in the theatre fly tower, nor my worries about the shadowy figure who'd attempted to kill me.

"Ah," he whisked his mustache across my fingers, which he'd raised to his lips, "*la bandita*. That's who you are!"

He loved this sobriquet and used it often afterwards, particularly in the throes of passion, with my spurs laid on hard. He adored word games and naming things he cared for, as I was to discover.

The night before the fateful ball, Diego introduced me to a different love: He was a gambler, particularly cards. Of course, being in the army and often needing to while away the time, either between nerve-wracking bouts of fighting or idle, weary waiting, cards and dice had a long history with the men. But Diego took it beyond such a mundane occupation: He was crazy about it. I was sleepy and sated, trying to relax before our big event, but he glowed with energy. In his hands, the deck of cards flashed and spun; I could barely see how they came together in new configurations. His sweet-smelling little cigar was clenched between white teeth.

"I've always been lucky at cards—*ventiuna*, *écarte*, any kind. The higher the stakes, the better I'm pleased."

"I find it unnerving," I yawned.

"I could teach you."

"I like to dice?" I offered.

"Dice takes no skill," he responded. "No, in cards, it's all about equal conditions. Establishing them, keeping them. If your opponent is belligerent or overconfident, you must be so in return. You must keep control of the crowd, manipulate the outcome, so he doesn't gain advantage. And plan your ambush."

"Ambush? Sounds like the bandits."

"*Sí, Bandita,* now you're understanding. Dice is open, blind fate; you simply wait for disaster. Cards are concealed. That's the only advantage you can count on: your own skill and daring, all other conditions being equal."

I rolled towards him and stroked his thigh, but he wouldn't rise. Or, he rose, but ignored it. This had become more important for some reason. He lay out a hand, showing all four suits.

"Concealment is an advantage?" I tried to follow.

"*Sí*. Like breaking in a wild horse. If you fall you get right back on, show no fear, or it will gallop away and never come back." The cards whirled in a new dance.

I'd lost him. "And we're talking about . . . ? Love?"

"How to win, *Bandita*. Listen to me again: The fundamental principle is equal conditions. If your opponent is more powerful, or unscrupulous, prone to violence or clamourous distraction, if he's deceitful, can disturb your concentration by making you afraid or angry, if he can turn the crowd against you—then he means to destroy you, forever."

I sat up then, since his words were frightening me. "You can't be talking about cards anymore, Diego."

"In my opinion, it applies to everything," he whispered, happy now that he had my full attention, and ready to tickle me again with his mustache. "Life *is* gambling. *Never* let them see your hand." He reached across me with a muscled arm and picked up the candle, then blew it out. I felt him putting it back down again by the side of the bed, able only to see his shape in outline from the tapers burning in the other room. "Do you understand now, *Bandita*?" He could feel my hair and then my lips against his arm, where I'd turned to kiss it. "You must keep your head, trust your skill and your daring, and play hard, without fear. This is what I have learned, and what I believe." He bent his head and kissed me. "All our lives depend upon it. Now, if we understand each other?" He leapt up and we were at it again.

By dawn, we lay in each other's arms, past sleep, the disquiet of impending action affecting us both.

"Have you killed many men?" I asked.

"Yes, I've killed. Only bad people, ones who were on the wrong side. By the way, I've seen your Cloud with the Silver Lining—enchanting. Espartero will be yours for the night, I guarantee. I'll try not to be jealous, for the cause." One hand was on my breast, warm and heavy. I didn't want to think of the man I had to seduce but rather concentrate on the one I was seduced by. Perhaps he guessed it. "Be brave, sweetheart . . . One night is not so long." He sighed into my hair, then asked, "What are you going to do when you get out of this?"

"Be a dancer, and be famous," I said pertly, then faltered. I wanted to be truthful with him; I loved the courage he gave me to be true. "Well, that's what I'd like. What are you going to do?"

"Leave the army. Settle down with a wonderful woman and have twelve children."

I laughed and said, "I don't see myself with many children. So it won't be me then."

"I think we both know that, *Bandita*."

That made me suddenly sad. And regretful. So I told him about the little girl I'd once had, my fears for her, and my hopes. Why I'd given her up. How lonely I'd been, and then how angry. About my mother's ways, and how I couldn't bear the idea of being anything like her. Even Grimaldi's threat of blackmail and the decorated box and how it applied to my daughter—I actually said the words, and they thrilled and frightened me: my daughter. I felt absolutely safe in the warmth of Diego's arms, speaking of love and true, honest things, no need for prevarications or lies. He was a man who would take me as I was. I was so happy.

"Truthfully," he said when I'd finished my story, "I can't see you settling for any one man. Perhaps as truthfully as I can't see myself with any one woman. But I think I should try."

We both laughed at that one, and let it pass. Diego's cries of ecstasy often included prayers in favour of his seed, or of women about to go into labour—a bit strange or religious, but somehow endearing. Spaniards take their faith seriously, all aspects of it, like medicine.

He returned to business. "I warned you to say nothing to the Infanta Carlota of Naples."

"I remember. And I haven't."

"She's too impetuous, always has been. Thinks she can solve everything herself if she just behaves arrogantly enough. Cristina expressly forbid her sister from knowing the plan for that reason. They had a falling out."

"Really? Why?"

"Carlota thinks Cristina's a silly cow for actually falling in love after the king's death. Visibly pregnant much too soon. The people were screaming, 'Death to the whore!'"

This chilled me then, and chills me now. Why are women always made to pay for their passion? And it reminded me again of the princesses.

"Diego," and I propped myself up on one elbow to look him in the eye, helped by the sun beginning to peek through the curtains. "You need to assure me that the infantas, Luisa Fernanda and Isabel, will be in no danger. That they will be absolutely safe on their journey to Paris. Do you promise me?"

"As much as I can promise anything, *Bandita*. Even I am not in the know about the full repercussions. Other moves are in the works, apparently. General Narváez, who had to flee Spain when Espartero took over the government, has been living in Paris. He is greatly admired by María Cristina. She's advocating a movement to get Espartero out of office and Narváez into it. Again, I know no more than this—and even this I shouldn't have told you." He kissed the hollow at the base of my throat. "Life is gambling. A new hand, a new chance—throw it up in the air, see where it lands."

I thought about this for a moment, and when I looked over, he was asleep.

✥ ✥ ✥

Ventura's hopes had come true: People had gone mad for tickets and the event was sold out. Cunningly, these masked balls are reviewed, exactly like a theatrical production: Attendees are commented upon in the papers, and this whips ticket holders into a frenzy of competition over costumes and masks.

The entire ballroom now resembled the Piazza San Marco in Venice, tricked out for a public, midnight event, as if taking place during that watery city's *carnivale*. I stood with Ventura, our arms linked, wondering what the night would bring.

"Madrileños dread the abstentions of Lent. It's perfect timing," Ventura said proudly. "We're setting up the conditions for *carnivale* behaviour, Rosana. Bent on pleasure, excited revellers believe anything can happen—murder, mayhem, even revolution!"

"And then it will," I added softly, and with new dread.

"I didn't hear that," he said and pulled his arm away. Like all of us, he was nervous. It had come down to this: He had his role and I had mine, and we must go ahead and play them without further distractions.

Diego had kissed me as I'd been about to leave that morning, with warm lips and sleepy eyes. "I will see you tonight in your finery. And then, who knows when?"

"I'm nervous, Diego. What if the prime minister doesn't—?"

"Have no fear on that score. Don't think of us for a second while you're with him. Concentrate all your forces."

"I will, of course." I felt foolish, but said it anyway. "Will you be jealous?"

"No. But I will find you; I will make sure nothing bad happens to you, *Bandita*. Believe me."

"I love you." The words fell out before I realized they were true. "Be careful."

"Always."

Then, just as suddenly, it was upon us.

※ ※ ※

I'd hired a clever woman to do my coiffure. My black hair, washed in rosewater the night before, was piled with elaborate abandon on the top of my head. I had the seed pearls that had popped off Isabel's mermaid costume; dozens of the beautiful things hadn't even been missed. I'd gathered them up and now had the hairdresser distribute these tiny pearls amongst my tresses, with ingenious little pins. The effect was gorgeous.

My makeup I effected myself. At twenty-two, not much can go wrong. All you need do is highlight what's there; the stage of covering and concealing has not yet arrived. I thought about this while darkening my brows with a pencil and outlining my lips. Diego's words about life as a gamble were haunting me; I'd never really thought of it that way. He was in his thirties, he was used to making tactical decisions; I was young and had always been rash. Maybe he was right: You had to play the game with skill, not just luck. Not just beauty and youth. Not even fueled only by anger or the need to "show them." I looked myself in the eye, pencil in abeyance. Beneath these more sober, mature reflections, I was also excited with that shivery joy of performance ahead. I wanted to shine, to prove my skill, to have Diego take me in his arms afterwards, ride each other all night, and make him shout that he loved me. But I told myself I would be careful, too.

In my Cloud with the Silver Lining gown, I surveyed the final result. Weeks of strenuous lovemaking had given me a high colour, along with increased strength and confidence. What I saw gave me hope that all would go well. Cristina would award me with a pile of money for my role in her drama—why not?—perhaps also a title. Countess? Who knew? Diego and I would buy a castle, live happily ever after . . .

The clock struck and broke the spell.

I was ready too early. It was not supposed to get under way until eleven o'clock and would carry on until dawn. I had a small glass of wine to steady my nerves. And then another. Finally I could stand the waiting no longer and had Diego's manservant summon a carriage. I climbed in, mask in hand and my legs trembling. And then after all I was not too early, because of the unexpected crush of horses, carriages, and other vehicles in the streets. It was like nothing I'd ever experienced before. Drivers yelling; nervous animals nipping at each others' flanks, sometimes causing one to squeal and lash out with its hooves. Costumed merrymakers leaning out of the windows, castigating the drivers and laughing at the same time, bottles in their hands. Torches carried along the streets, heat and smoke trailing up into the cold, night sky. It was like a scene out of Dante's Inferno, but all for joy and excitement rather than despair.

A troop of mounted policemen moved through, blowing whistles and brandishing bludgeons; the royal carriages were coming, so the rest of us had to make way. I caught a glimpse of Luisa Fernanda's small hand at the window before someone yanked down the blind. The second carriage held Carlota and her family, seated across from each other and looking severe. Perhaps, even for royalty, a crush such as this was unnerving. Who knew what might happen? Soberly I thought, I do.

The third and final carriage in the wake of the policemen was that of the prime minister, Baldomero Espartero. Blimey, criminy, there he was! Accompanied by several of his ministers, silent in their costumed frippery; a glimpse of the amphibious tutor as well. I studied Espartero as he went past, unmasked, glaring around with a stern expression, without fear. About fifty years of age, I guessed, with a thick silver head of hair. I wondered what he was thinking about. Were these excitable functions ones he enjoyed or hated? Did he love the power he now wielded? His posture was very straight, that of a military man who has always been fit but who has thickened into vigorous middle age. Did he ever soften? How could I get him to notice me if he was so cautious and grave? My stomach gave a skittery lurch.

Once the carriages of the important personages had passed, the crowd began to surge and curse with renewed energy. I wished I could just get down and walk, but decided against it. The streets were muddy, full of horse dung and bits of straw. My dress was too fine to ruin in such a manner.

At last I arrived and was swept into the Teatro de Oriente on a tide of masked humanity. Mayhem was ensuing inside; our cloaks were taken away with no clear tickets of repossession. I was forced onward by the crush, managing to work my way to the wall so that I could don my mask. I was thrilled with this, too; it had been made by the maskmaker who worked at the Príncipe. The colours matched those of my gown to perfection: wispy mare's tails of clouds above my forehead, heading up into soft peaks. The eye holes were large; I could see well through them, and the wearing of the mask was easy, light on the face. The cheeks were painted to resemble fluffy, pink clouds with the hint of a storm gathering, in ominous silver, where the mask ended just below my cheekbones. My mouth was free, to speak, to eat and drink—and whatever else might be called for.

Fully disguised, I entered the ballroom and began to circulate.

It took at least half an hour to get to the other side, where I had agreed to meet Ventura and receive final instructions. Eagerly taking in all of the costumes as I moved along, I tried to recognize my important cast of characters: There was Espartero, now masked, but recognizable by his silver hair. He was dressed as Neptune and carried a large, wicked-looking trident. I sincerely hoped he wasn't planning to use it. His henchmen were supporting roles as mermen or some such—odd little gills at the sides of their necks, and fish faces. Arguëlles, the tutor, wore the mask of a deep-sea fish with bony red spikes and bulgy eyes; he needn't have bothered, for it was surprisingly similar to his own blotched visage. The maskmaker's little joke, no doubt.

A man brushed past me, very close, and I felt my bottom being pinched, hard. I gave a stifled shriek before realizing that the grin beneath the dark mask, now disappearing, was Diego's. What on earth was his disguise? He called back, "a thunder clap," and I found this hilarious. Why then, were my teeth chattering as I laughed and kept going, following in his wake? He soon disappeared, and I was alone again in the heaving, writhing, yelling sea.

There were the royals, standing on their own dais, surveying the crowd, Carlota with her enormous fiery headdress towering above the others. She had a flute of champagne in one hand and was gesturing extravagantly with the other. Her husband, Don Francisco, was dressed soberly but imaginatively as a devil, no doubt to complement his wife's concoction. The two sons were there—Cadiz, the eldest, dressed as a sprite. Has ever a water sprite worn so much lace? I caught a glimpse of Isabel sourly surveying her cousin and understood her consternation: In his costume, Cadiz was far prettier than she. It looked as if she had fattened up even more in the few weeks since I'd seen her; she was packed into her fishtail like sardines in a can. How would it hold up as she was bundled into a carriage to be whisked off to Paris? I hoped someone had thought to bring a change of clothing for the girls, something warm. It was maddening, being one small cog in this mysterious wheel. So much could go wrong!

Beside Isabel stood Luisa Fernanda, the most enchanting fairy I have ever laid eyes on. She seemed entirely joyful with the excitement of being in disguise, of staying up late and partaking in fully adult pleasures. Never mind the aristocratic trappings: At heart, Nanda was an innocent, uncontaminated little girl. *Dios mio*, I realized as I looked at the enraptured young countenance: Emma has turned eight. How could this be? Her birthday had passed and I hadn't remembered it, shame on me. But my daughter was safe, she was in good caring hands. Who would be looking after this little fairy all the way to Paris? My concern was mounting.

I made my way to the royal party, curtsied, and greeted them. The princes looked down at me in their young male way, cool and distant, though I did see Seville glance admiringly at my breasts. Luisa Fernanda was gratifyingly happy to see me again and had to tell me all about the chaotic goings-on since we'd last been together.

"Tia Lota," I could hear Isabel whining, "you will let me dance with some of the four elements, won't you?"

"We don't know who they are, Bella. I'll have to vet them first, look under their masks." Carlota called Javier, the bodyguard, over. "Keep a close eye on the infantas, especially the fishy one." He bowed low, and backed away again. "You'll be dancing, darling, I promise," she consoled Isabel, "but why don't you start with your cousin? You're both representing the same element, after all."

Cadiz and Isabel flicked glances at each other. Isabel wrinkled her raw, red nose.

"The other one, then. Keep it in the family." Carlota sounded bored already. "For Christ's sake, girl, you're a princess, don't forget it again or I'll skin you!" She said to me, with a look of disgust, "Can you believe, I caught her playing hide-and-seek in the palace with one of Espartero's ministers—like a five-year-old! God *knows* what she was getting up to, never mind what *he* thought he was doing. Idiot child!"

Hide-and-seek, or something more grown up? Maybe this was why Cristina had ordered the kidnapping of the infantas: The thirteen-year-old's lust and gullibility was poised to create an international scandal!

"You look good, very perky," Carlota told me, finally noticing. "What is it you're supposed to be?"

"The Cloud with the Silver Lining, Your Majesty."

She stared at me for a moment, and then threw her head back and let out one of her big laughs. "I like it, it suits you. Lovely cleavage. Enjoy yourself."

As the orchestra began another overture, I curtsied again and backed away from the royals' dais. Carlota had grabbed another glass of champagne and was surveying the crowd, swaying in her Fires of Hell gown to the strains of the music—what could be heard of it over the shrieks and bellows of the mob. Don Francisco appeared to be reading a book: a mild-mannered, bright red devil with a monocle and studious expression.

At that moment, a voice in my ear, deep and hoarse, said, "I must speak with you urgently." I turned, and faced a man's chest. A tall, dark-featured figure stood beside me, partially raising his black half-mask so that I could see his face. I looked up, and nearly fainted—it was glass-eyed, mustachioed Pedro Coria! He *was* here; he *had* followed me! The man who had dragged me from the cathedral in Paris, and perhaps—most probably!—had murdered Clotilde! The demon from the flies!

"Get away from me or I'll scream," I said, taking a breath to do so.

"You must listen, I am warning you—"

I dashed away into the throng, and after strenuous maneuvers over and across like a ship under sail, was able to single Ventura out in his station as the centre of a maelstrom of organizational activities, and costumed as a whirlwind.

"Ventura!" I shouted, trying to make him understand who I'd just seen and what it must mean. I pointed across the room, but of course we could only see the surging mob, not make out individual participants. "The man from the flies—the assassin! Pedro Coria, the northerner!"

He tried to soothe me, smoothing his hands down my arms like stroking a cat. "Coria? I don't know him, but perhaps. We have agents everywhere; I'll let them know. They'll keep a watch out, don't worry." Once I seemed calmer, he pushed the rope mask up to the top of his head, wiping sweat from around his cheeks, and whispered urgently, "It's past midnight. *Your* mission must get underway immediately. Go, Espartero's there—good luck." And he turned away.

Unbelievable! Diego pinching me and dashing off, Ventura's bossiness: little boys playing, spying away, being the *hombre importante!* Off you go, pretty thing, seduce the prime minister, that's what *you're* good for, nothing to it. Our jobs are *so* much more crucial! But I'd just been boldly warned, by a man who had already tried to murder me!

I was just about to give Ventura a blast when I glimpsed a figure moving swiftly towards us, all in black, wearing the mask of a wolf with a white, bristly muzzle. He raised the mask for a moment and I saw who it was.

"Father Miguel," I said, trying to stop my lip from curling. "What are you, may I ask?"

His voice as supercilious as ever, "The North Wind."

"Why does the North Wind have a wolf's head?"

The eyes glittered from behind the mask. "Why not?"

Ventura put a hand on his brother's shoulder. "I'm worried about the palace bodyguards, Miguel."

"Don't be," the Jesuit answered. "Quiet now," with a little cock of the head towards me—one man of the world to another, in front of a brainless female. Ventura didn't even mention my sighting of the northerner to the priest; he'd forgotten already.

I saw red, my brain started to fizz. Where had that bottom-pinching Thunder Clap got to? I wanted to give him a good piece of my mind, too! And I couldn't *abide* the sight of that wolf in wolf's clothing; I'd no idea *he* was intimately involved in this event! How could they trust him with such delicate work? There were children involved! Balls to them all, I fumed, turning and launching myself savagely back into the mob. When I set my mind to something, I told myself hotly, I go ahead and do it. I don't just give orders, dress up in costumes, and race about like a delinquent gone wild—no! I accomplish things!

There he was, the prime minister, straight ahead. As far as I could tell, he wasn't accompanied by his heiress wife; all the better for our plan. The orchestra had begun a lively, traditional air, one to which my little fandango could be matched. Or—? Damn it, why not?

I began the other steps I had learned with Donatella: the tarantella, but slow and graceful, as the music demanded. People nearby began to make room for me to move more freely; several men stopped dead in their tracks and could not be budged by their wives. I twirled closer to my prey. Someone began to clap to the rhythm of the music, and at the sound, Espartero glanced up, eyes cold and hard behind the sea-green Neptune mask. The conductor, sensing something new was happening, also looked over and saw me. After a moment, he picked up the idea and turned back to his musicians, increasing the pace. I began to move faster, feet flying and fingers snapping, and the crowd clapped to the rhythm. I hardly knew what I was doing, so driven was I by frustration at the little-boy-men, by fear, due to the glass-eyed pirate's reappearance, and—at the same time!—by fierce pleasure and acknowledgment of the appreciative audience. When I finally brought the dance to an end, the clapping turned into enthusiastic applause and I drank it in, curtsying before Espartero.

Behind the mask of the water-god, I could see that he was mine. He couldn't see me, not the real me, just the body in the costume. And he wanted it.

The crowd had come together again and moved on, an ocean wave constantly in motion. Arguëlles the Odious was evaluating me with his filthy stare. I could tell he had no idea who I was, and I was not about to enlighten him. Please, prime minister, I prayed, please step forwards. Follow your impulse. Do it now.

And he did. He passed the trident to one of his gilled cronies and came up to me, then bowed. "Enchanting, señorita," he breathed, kissing my hand. "May *I* be so bold as to request this dance?" Bingo. "Though I assure you, I am not so beautiful nor elegant as you."

I curtsied again.

The orchestra had taken up a waltz, so I was in luck. Off we swirled, and he was very good. His hand at my back was steady; he led well. But now I was nervous.

"May I ask," he murmured, "with whom I have the pleasure of dancing?"

"I'm afraid not," I answered. "It's a masquerade, isn't it? We are under the spell of the evening and cannot break it. I, too, cannot ask your name, I shall just have to wonder."

He let out the briefest honk of a laugh at this. As I waltzed with the prime minister, I realized that the man who'd begun the applause had, of course, been my Thunder Clap, and I surreptitiously looked around for him now, but he'd disappeared. In my gown, my breasts sat very high, nipples tucked just inside the top of the bodice. Espartero's eyes smouldered behind the mask; I felt quite naked under his scrutiny. Calm down, I told myself, everything is going well. And that is when a minor little accident befell me.

The prime minister was very strong. At one point, we turned sharply (having come to the end of the room), he dipped me, and what should happen? My left breast popped right out of my dress! I was aghast and wondering horridly what to do, when my partner, with the coolness of a Sierra Madres mountain breeze, reached over, took hold lightly but firmly, and thrust it back inside my bodice. I blinked several times and opened my eyes wide as we took another few turns around the room. I could feel myself flushing up to the eyebrows, although it might not have shown under the mask. An appalled giggle fell out, however. "¡Santa cielo!" I sputtered.

"I fancy no one noticed, señorita," the prime minister whispered, "except, I beg your pardon, for myself."

At these gallant words, I bit my lip and tried not to guffaw, then whispered back, "Do you know the poem, you probably don't, it's a ridiculous Anglo Indian one: 'But Qui Hi, disregarding care, fell headlong on a prickly pear.' That's how I feel!" Espartero's hand at my back whirled me around again as he said, "Not at all. Never seen finer." By the time the dance ended, we were both half choked with trying not to giggle, belly laugh, or snort. Then he bowed, kissed my hand again, and seriousness was restored. The twinkle in his calculating eye now also heralded the possibility of a crucial proposition.

I shouldn't have said that about an English poem, of course; I kicked myself for it. Don't be distracted, I then thought: Focus on the man and his desire. And it came.

"Señorita, I suspect that you are feeling the heat. Would you care to step away from the ball for a half hour? I could walk with you, only a block or two, in the night air. My offices . . . if you become tired . . ."

"Wonderful idea," said I, and gingerly took his arm. Now that it had come, stories of Espartero's brutal retaliations during the war were flying through my head like bats. This was a man who killed, no question.

Killed for country, killed for profit. Killed for self-interest. And without remorse. He made even the threat of Coria seem remote.

Above the crowd, Carlota's headdress still bowed and wove, flames licking the embers of a dying fire. There seemed to be many others on the dais now with the royals; courtiers and grandees, having toadied and groveled their way onto the platform at last, sweaty in actual masks rather than the merely facial ones they usually wore.

"Let me find your cloak," Espartero offered.

"It is quite a tangle in there," I answered. "Let me retrieve it and I'll meet you outside."

"I'll be smoking, then. The finest cigar money can buy; you'll recognize the scent."

Not as sweet as the ones Diego smokes, I wagered to myself. Likely large and thick, the more to impress.

"Very soon, señorita?"

I assured him, and we parted. Out of the frying pan and into the fire good and proper, I shivered, contemplating fleeing the scene altogether. Then I thought of Diego's faith in me, and carried on.

It was extremely hot in the ballroom, made hotter by the streams of molten wax that had begun flowing from the candelabras onto the wigs, hats, and clothing of the crowd; you had to keep your head down so that you weren't hit in the face by droplets or rivulets of the stuff. Squeezing my way to the cloakroom, flinching and ducking, I almost missed but then suddenly saw a tall, dark shape pass with a small figure in tow. Heading towards the door to the backstage corridors, clutching the hand of a struggling child. There were gossamer wings, half hidden under a dark cape—Luisa Fernanda! With this person I didn't recognize? Was this what was supposed to happen?

I heard a high-pitched scream of fear, quickly muffled, as the figures struggled on. Matching fear squirted through my guts: the vision of a muddy river bank, a helpless girl. Nanda's pale, beautiful face in an aureole of silver blonde hair. Carlota's words ringing in my ears: Listen to your heart. What if this was *my* little girl? Hearing that frightened scream, it was impossible to do anything but what I did. I didn't think, just leapt towards them, grabbed the arm of the figure and wrenched it around—black wolf with dark eye holes, looking down at me! The priest!

I was confused, but still followed my instinct; I ducked low and whispered hard in the princess' ear, "Run to Carlota! Now!" She yanked her hand free of the man and darted off like a deer.

"*Mujer estúpida*, do you never *think*!"

"Stupid? Worse than stupid. ¡*Bobo!* You've ruined months of planning, wasted thousands upon thousands of *reales*—"

"Enough!" from Diego.

The following morning, sitting (or pacing) amongst the wreckage of the ball, the group of conspirators met to berate (me!) and blame (me). Concha was livid. Ventura sat tearing at his hair. I could almost *see* it thinning; his fingers were covered with it and he kept shaking them off, then starting in again. The woman who was to have accompanied the princesses in the coach to Paris was the same Matilde who had guided the Jesuit and me through the mountains—she too was there, a Grimaldi conspirator now deprived of her task. She too sat in the wreckage and looked glum, the cherubic baby at her breast. Father Miguel lurked like a bad spirit in the background, once again robed in his cassock, the North Wind wolf mask thrown away.

De la Concha, vicious with rage, his lean limbs flinging themselves into arabesques as he remembered fresh injuries, continued the cursing. "They get a scare and what does royalty do? It flees, bodyguards before and aft, swords drawn and revelers injured! All our plans, all this time wasted! What will Cristina think of us? She should have us taken out and shot! Especially *that* one!" and he pointed at me.

"Hush." Diego was pacing like a caged animal, kicking his way through the rubble that littered the floor.

"María Cristina is waiting in Paris! Longing to see her children! Like any mother, what is she to think? She'll be frantic when she hears!" From Concha's frenzied despair, I could tell that he too was smitten by the fair former queen regent. He continued muttering incriminations as Diego turned to me.

"Rosana, what happened, again. Never mind the General here, we're overwrought from lack of sleep and frustrated energy. Tell us everything."

I looked over at the priest. He was staring back with a horrible intensity, but what could I do but tell the truth as I knew it? "I saw Father Miguel leading Infanta Luisa Fernanda by the hand towards the door behind the canal construction. I've told you this."

"It's a lie!" From the Jesuit, a man who'd surely been trained never to lie. "As you know, generals, that was not my assignment. I was stationed where I had been posted—the southwest corner—waiting for you both to apprehend the infantas and to give you cover until the carriage was away. I was fully armed and ready. Do not allow this . . . woman! This liar! . . ."

I knew what I saw. "The man was dragging the princess by the arm, and she was screaming. He was wearing a wolf mask," I argued.

Father Miguel almost pounced upon me, his fingers taut as talons. "So were dozens of men!"

Was that true? "I saw no others," I snapped back. "No, it was you; I'm sure it was. We looked each other in the eye."

There was a lull in de la Concha's cursing as I said this, and everyone suddenly turned to the Jesuit.

"The canal exit was not the plan," Diego murmured, half to himself, "it leads to a completely different part of the building. Into the bowels of it, with no real way out. Father Miguel? Could you explain this for us?"

I'd never seen the priest look so ashen. I was going to best him! I was going to expose him for the sanctimonious ass he was—and perhaps for treachery, too! Oh, that would be sweet! So I added, triumphantly, "And there I was worrying about the reappearance of Pedro Coria, when all along we should have been worried about *you*."

The priest's face changed as fast as a spring dirk on a pistol. "Coria? You saw him where?"

Ventura answered, "At the ball. She told me so."

"Yes," the priest said, nodding. "He was one of the other men wearing a wolf mask, and I'd been aware of his movements the entire evening. I don't know why Coria is here. He *is* very dangerous, and ruthless, I know this. He would be a bad enemy to have. My guess is that he may have turned sides, become a double agent. Now. At the moment in question . . ." He seemed rattled, I thought, but was speaking calmly.

"My attention had been caught by Espartero's exiting the ballroom, and I decided to see where he was going. Perhaps it is true I abandoned my post, momentarily. But I quickly returned. So this . . . woman," as he shot me a look, "in mistaking me for Coria, may have done us a favour after all. Perhaps Coria was dragging the infanta off for some reason of his own. Some counterplot?"

I was confused. Had he just turned what I'd said around?

"*Diablo!*" Concha swore and cracked his knuckles. "This is a mess."

"I've never seen those bodyguards move so swiftly," Diego added. "We've underestimated them. It could be that even if our plan had gone smoothly, they'd have been on to us and cut us down before we could get to the coach."

Matilde rocked the baby back and forth, eyes on the ground. De la Concha was still stamping back and forth, but slowly now, considering Diego's words.

"Perhaps it wasn't such a foolproof plan for getting the princesses away." Diego rubbed the bristles on his chin, then his curly hair. I sat stock still; the Jesuit had manipulated the accusation away from himself. Is that what had just happened?

"Just a minute," I said. "Can we—?"

"Let's think this through," Diego went on, preventing Concha from cutting in with a hand on his arm, and giving me a swift, reassuring smile. "We must not alarm Grimaldi, that is very important. Ventura, you'll send a message today—fastest rider, spare no expense—letting them know that we had to abort, but that another plan is forming which is safer, which can be implemented within a week or two. *No* word about what went wrong, nor why. Do you understand me?"

The playwright looked sullen.

"There's another little girl's life involved, Ventura, in another country. An innocent little girl. You of all people should understand that." I was taken by surprise. He had remembered my baby with the sea-dark eyes. Diego, bless you. He lit a cigar, puffed away for a moment, frowning like the thunder clap he'd been at the ball, then, "It won't be long. Let it all go. Let everyone calm themselves, let them relax their vigilance after this sudden shock. I will think of a better way."

Matilde glanced up quickly at this, and down again. In a flash of clarity, I saw: She's worried for him!

"Don't let *that* prize idiot have anything to do with it, León," Concha snarled, jabbing a finger towards me again. "She botched it. I don't trust her. Stop wasting your time bouncing the silly jade every two seconds; we have more important things to be thinking about!"

Matilde rocked, head bent over the infant, not looking at the men.

"Jealous?" Diego punched his fellow general in the arm. "Shut up about it now and let's think. We need Rosana; she'll be brilliant, she just lost her nerve."

I know he was trying to defend me, but suddenly I'd had enough. "Stop talking about me as if I'm not here!" I snapped. "Of course wrong things will happen if you lie and get cocky, if you keep changing who's supposed to do what!" Everyone stared, with varying shades of surprise, hatred, and—in Matilde's case—an enigmatic interest.

"What do you mean, lie?" Diego looked curious. "At this stage, if you're taken, it's better if you only know your own task in the venture."

"Why?" I persisted.

"If you're tortured you'll give us all away, of course," Concha sneered. "Though in your case, you blabbermouth, that's a given anyway."

Diego punched him again, swiftly, and leaned in to his face. "Sabres! Dawn, tomorrow morning."

"Stop it!" Matilde suddenly screamed, "Stop it this minute! All of you!"

There was a pause, then Diego told Concha, "She's right, forget about it." He faced the other conspirators and gave each a task to perform over the next week: Mine was to return to the palace, to discover everything possible about the regular movements of the guards within the vast building, and to ascertain the layout of the private rooms that no one but the family used.

The meeting broke shortly thereafter. "Just look at this mess," Ventura sighed, and placed his head in his hands. Discarded masks and frippery, bits of lace, broken glasses and plates, chunks of food, the odd undergarment—the entire floor was inches deep in the stuff.

"But you made money?" Diego asked.

"Oh yes, lots of it."

"Then celebrate that! Go out and get drunk. Life's short, start living it, man."

And he took me home.

✠ ✠ ✠

Equal conditions. I couldn't get the idea of it out of my head. I'd been beaten in that round by Father Miguel, I just couldn't work out how. That night, I told Diego everything I knew about Pedro Coria and urged him to follow up on this knowledge. Was the priest right? Coria, a double agent? Sent to do what? That was horrifying too, if true.

And of course I worried myself sick about my lover's bravado. This glorious man I'd come to care about so deeply was playing dangerous games for the sake of a blonde, exiled princess who kept producing babies with her guardsman. Diego honestly didn't seem to care about the dangers involved; the more there were, the better he liked it. How could my bravery compare with that? I was bested there, too. "Remember the little princesses, and remember yourself," I'd tell him; he'd nod absently, stroking his mustache, working out his new, foolproof plan. I lashed out angrily, "At least give me some money then, in case I need to flee!" to which he responded, "I have plenty of money. You know I'll give you whatever you need." And he told me where he kept it.

I began my new task by asking to meet with Infanta Carlota. I had a great deal of trouble convincing the front line that she might wish to see me. Finally, after a wait of two hours, I was summoned to an inner room. "I haven't got long," she said, sitting at a writing desk in a voluminous gold-threaded gown, "but I advise you to stop whatever it is Cristina has put in motion."

I tried to conceal a gasp of surprise. Is that why I'd come, to tell her? I hardly knew, myself, I was so overstrung. But I managed to say nothing.

"I don't even want to know—no, *don't* tell me!" She waved an imperious hand in my direction. "Espartero has had the wind put up him and he's not a man to be trifled with, I warn you." She was looking exhausted, dark shadows etched under her fine eyes. "Confusion prevails in the *Cortes*, even before this latest scare. Espartero was a powerful man in the battlefield, but he has no idea how to command a country except through bullying and terror." I didn't like those words. I liked, even less, to see Carlota glance over her shoulder and lower her voice. "He prefers to spend whole evenings with us, drinking chocolate. He's mad for the stuff. Nobody commands and nobody obeys, in his government; it's a Tower of Babel. He's taken over a wing in the palace—to keep a better eye on things, he says. There's no hope for any of us until he's deposed."

She looked at me searchingly for a moment, then took my hand and sat me down beside her. "I know you haven't the benefit of my blood nor my wealth, but I have some advice, Rosana Gilbert. Do not let yourself be the pawn of wealthy, powerful men. You must find a way to prevent this. And it will, of necessity, be your *own* way. Find it, follow it, hold steadfastly to it. Or you'll be swept aside in the tide of events, as all women are." This last point filled her with melancholy, I could see.

"We're returning to our home in Cadiz, leaving tomorrow," she continued. "I can't abide Madrid with that man in it. And I need rest—my *bastardo* doctor will make me take some terrible muck. Damn it all to hell . . ." She waved her hand again, dismissing me. When I reached the door, she looked at me one last time with those blazing blue eyes. "You have a good heart. Go now."

I went to find little Luisa Fernanda.

I've never forgotten Carlota's words, and never will. I vow, if I get out of this mess—and I will, I must—I'll set my star by them. No man's pawn, ever again. Find my own way. To America, the land of the free.

Can I bring myself, now, to this final, terrifying place? I must, get it clear in my head, relive it all. To survive.

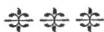

Diego's plan was ready. It had taken two weeks, and it made me very nervous, but he was convinced that this was the way. Working on many different fronts, the conspirators (including myself, from an inspired storytelling session I'd had with Infanta Nanda) had discovered four important facts: First, that Espartero had moved his offices into the palace, the scare at the ball providing a good excuse to muscle into the royal's private life. Second, that the royal family had stepped up the security of their forces and there was only one time weekly when the entire regiment of guards was changed. Third, the exact location of the infantas' bedrooms within the enormous palace configuration. And finally, that there was a secret passageway (a priest's hole, Nanda had called it, excitedly) that could be accessed from the paneling on the right hand side of the bottom of the stupendous main staircase.

It was news of the secret passageway that had particularly pleased Diego.

"And where does it come out?"

I told him how Nanda had led me through it, chattering, candle in hand, her wide skirts brushing the narrow sides of the stone walls, collecting dust and cobwebs all over the magnificent silk, which I'd taken pains to clean off before the mess could be noted by a snoopy someone. "The southwest side of the palace, in the oleander garden." I'd taken particular note of the direction Nanda told me, had scratched it into my palm—SW—to be certain I would not forget or get muddled.

Gathered together as a group, Diego outlined the plan for us: During the hour of the changing of the guard, at midnight, Concha and Diego would enter the palace. As the newly arrived and departing men exchange words and any orders in the regimental office, the infantas would be taken from their bedrooms, down the main staircase, and into the secret passageway, to be met with a carriage waiting at the oleander garden and then swiftly away!

"Shall I go with the princesses? They know me," I urged, again.

The Jesuit was sneering in the background. I ignored him.

"No, Rosana. I need you to stick with the original task: Take up with Espartero exactly where you left off at the ball. He's at the palace now; he needs to be dealt with, distracted."

Tears of shock and dismay filled my eyes. The planning continued, buzzing around my ears, as I tried to make sense of Diego's words.

Privately, back in our bedroom, my lover tried to underline his reasoning, but I hit him hard in the chest.

"Why must I do this? Shouldn't I do something else, something more useful? Distracting the guards, or—"

"No, *Bandita*. That would be extremely dangerous. You've asked enough questions on that front. We can't rouse suspicions; you've been very successful and very persistent. Don't you see, you must let that lie now for your own safety. Please believe me." We hugged each other, hard, and I began to cry against his chest. "As you know, *querida*, what you are to do will be desperate enough. You must bed him, keep him occupied, and then you must flee. As quickly as possible, but not before a certain time has passed." He kissed my palms, one after the other, and looked into my eyes. "I know it's very difficult, and I'm truly sorry. Try to make yourself look different, another disguise. He's never seen you unmasked?"

"No." I was shaking.

"You don't want him to recognize you later. Crucial. Keep focused on this, and all will be well. But do not underestimate his ferocity when he finds he's been duped. You must be far away by then."

I was to approach Espartero in his temporary office at the palace in the late afternoon of February 16. Two days hence.

"We will say a prayer."

I will do more than that, I thought, but said no more; it was no use trying to stop the behemoth now. Behind the conspirators' haste, I knew, was always the thought—particularly driving Concha—of Cristina, awaiting her children, cursing her loyal and brave men for their delay.

The next day, Saint Valentine's, was my birthday. Diego was with me, and we made love the whole day. And then, for a change of scene, we took a blanket, basket of food, and several bottles of wine and repaired to the stable, to Lindo's stall, freshly strewn with new straw and full of the smells of horse and hay.

Lying together, legs entwined, we smoked one of his thin, sweet South American cigars. I asked him about Matilde. I couldn't help myself.

"She was Concha's woman for several years. I consoled her, one time."

"And baby Matilde? Is she yours?"

"I think not. Otherwise I'd sense it, I'm sure." He pushed my hair away from my face, looked into my eyes. "One time, Rosana. She was not the one for me."

I asked again about the war, how he'd survived it. There had been frightening times, and Diego had gone into hiding for several weeks at one point. He stared into space, then heaved a sigh. "The war is over but not won. I'm a military man, but I never fought so that an arrogant fanatic like Espartero should rule. I believe in kings and queens; I want stability in our country and history on our side. The Infanta Isabel is the rightful heir and she should rule as her family always has—humanely, justly, with God behind her. We must make that possible."

"Grimaldi spoke about torture." I faltered. "Would there really—?"

"There is no brutality like that left in us; we are all full of remorse. It will never happen again. Spanish men are gentlemen."

He rolled over, lifted himself onto his elbows, and kissed me tenderly. "I understand nerves, *Bandita*. Don't punish yourself for the ball. This new way is better, you'll see." Then he grinned. "Because *I* thought of it."

We made love again, removing items of clothing slowly, bit by bit, tickling and biting each newly revealed piece of skin. Lindo observed, occasionally snorting and shaking his head up and down, spraying us with bits of fresh, or half-chewed, hay—which made us laugh.

Oh God. That night in the stable—so much laughter and life. Panting, laughing into each other's faces, now fully naked, myself astride Diego's hips, and Lindo's big nose coming between, with gusts of grassy breath. Afterwards, stroking the man's wet thigh and the white star on the horse's brow, both at the same time, thinking, "This is heaven; this is everything. Make it stop right here, right now. Just stay . . ."

"Breathe into his nostrils," Diego told me. "He'll learn to love you this way. He'll learn you belong together, that you're his, as much as the other way around." And so I did, breathing softly into the large, velvet nostrils with soft, antennae-like hairs surrounding them. Lindo taking it in, eyes liquid and alert. And the horse breathing back, straight into mine with summer-soft breath, like warm wind in a ripening field. A message from the gods, that's what it felt like. A communion, an agreement.

I cried with happiness that night, as Diego held me. I'd never done that before, and it took me completely by surprise. We rocked back and forth in each other's arms, heads on each other's shoulders, not saying anything. Did he feel it too? He didn't say so, but he didn't deny it either. He just held me.

That moment passed too, as all moments do—good, bad, and terrible. Somehow they pass. We lay in the straw again, the blanket still beneath us, drinking the second bottle of wine. Lindo dozing on his feet, only occasionally switching his tail and shifting his weight from one foot to another.

"Ah, *Bandita*," my lover whispered. "I am done for. I am no more."

Stroking the hairs on Diego's chest and hoping what he had said wasn't true because on this night I wasn't in the least bit tired, I asked, "If I were Spanish, what would my name be?"

"Mm, let me think." His hand came up to his mustache, always the indicator of deep thought or growing lustfulness. "Dolores," he said finally.

"Why that?"

"My mother's name."

I hit him.

"No, really. It's a beautiful name. Lola for short."

"Oh!" I sat up. "That I like. Lola . . ." I tried it on for size.

"Also Maria," he added, "because every woman must have the name Maria, to keep her safe and bring her luck—the Madonna's blessing."

"Is that why? I always wondered. And last name?"

"What about Contreras?" I shook my head. "Cantero?" Another shake. "Why not?"

"Doesn't feel right."

He rhymed off a dozen or so other surnames, but none of them spoke to me.

"Lola," I repeated. And then I really sat up straight, taking a large swig from the bottle as the idea hit me. "I want to change my name for good, Diego! I've always hated the name I was given. Eliza, that is *my* mother's name. Eliza Gilbert. Listen to it, so flat, so—"

"It doesn't suit you, I'll agree."

"You do?"

"Yes."

Oh, I loved him even more at that moment! He understood! He could see that I was held back from my real potential because I hadn't stepped into my true identity! More surnames flashed past our lips, we grew carried away and lusty again with the sheer pleasure of it all. We woke Lindo up; he swung his big head around to look at us and we laughed some more, before he turned back to stare at his hay, his wall—his head sagged, his eyelashes drooped, and he was asleep again.

"This time I truly am destroyed," Diego murmured against my hair as we lay again staring up at the stable's beams. "Ah, wait, what about this? An old aristocratic family name, fallen into disuse because of the wars. All the young men are dead."

"What is it?"

"Montez."

I remember lying there in his arms, the smell of us all around me, on my lips and hair and skin, as it sank in. Lola Montez. My limbs relaxed; my eyes closed.

After a sleep we awoke, surprisingly ready for more, so it seemed that, in celebration, the name also needed more. Ornaments, he called them. Embellishments, I averred. The crazier the better, until I was hooting with delight. "No, no! I have it, *Bandita*, the ultimate: ¡*Devoradora de hombres!*"

"Devourer of men?" I screamed with hilarity, "Is that what you think of me?"

"Well, what else would you call what you've just been doing with me? You beauty, you bewitching one!"

"La Lola!" I cried out, jubilant, and riding him again. I had found me!

※ ※ ※

Two evenings later, I made my way to the office of Prime Minister Baldomero Espartero at the royal palace. Having observed the man's schedule of duties and attendances since the night of the ball, we knew that Espartero always worked on his own for several hours in the late evening, and that this was when he was at his most relaxed.

I had attempted to alter my appearance as much as possible, as Diego suggested: I'd gone to Ventura, and we visited the backrooms of the Príncipe. He knew where to lay his hands on a pale golden wig, able to be fastened to the head with realistic grip, expensively constructed from real hair.

"But I was wearing my own hair at the ball."

"You think he noticed your hair?" Ventura countered. "Anyway, just tell him *that* was a wig, if he asks. Which he won't."

He also helped me with makeup, painting my face a more olive complexion, with lips fuller and eyes outlined. "A golden Cleopatra," he muttered, as he finished. "Now you resemble his wife when he married her, twenty years ago. When he fell for her money. Now he'll fall for you. He'd better."

"He will." The others still didn't trust me. Shaky but brave, I was determined to prove them wrong. I put everything but my task aside, everything that they were about to do had to go on without me—concentrate, and succeed!

At Espartero's office, the men in the outer chambers looked surprised to see a woman enter on such a blustery night. When I asked for the prime minister on a personal matter, their eyes swung towards each other and little smirks appeared at the corners of their mouths. How I hated that. I knew what they thought of me but consoled myself with the fact that they saw only the outside, and only I knew what was about to transpire. The last laugh would be on them, I hoped. I passed them a card with my particulars printed upon it: Patrizia Olivares, Actress. (Might as well put her to use, I'd thought, sans *padre* husband.)

I'd carried a fur muff with one of my little pistols and the mask from the ball hidden inside, and I waited, staring out at the frozen grounds. After about fifteen minutes, I could hear a firm, heavy tread approaching, and the silver-maned tyrant entered.

"Señorita? You wish to see me?" There was no recognition in his steely eyes.

I pulled one hand out of my muff, revealing my Cloud with the Silver Lining mask. Shyly, I held it up against my face.

"You?" he said.

"It is I."

He ushered me ahead of him to a more secluded corner, the men in the room turning their heads to watch.

"I smoked three cigars, waiting for you."

"I lost my nerve." My heart was genuinely pounding with fear. "I'd guessed who you were," I added, suddenly inspired.

He liked that and chuckled. "I suspected as much. Come. Come inside, my dear." He glanced at the doorman, who immediately swung the door to an inner chamber open while staring rigidly ahead. "Tell everyone," Espartero called in a commanding voice, "I am not to be disturbed under *any* circumstances!" We passed through and the door clicked shut again, smartly, behind us. I imagined all the henchmen rushing to the door in a clump, shoving at each other, trying to hear.

Now I'm in the lion's den and no mistake, I thought.

He took my hand and led me through this first palatial space—his newly transformed public office, where he'd hold meetings, draft new constitutions and regulations, and petrify his minions. It was appointed in dark wood and leather so that even with a gallery of windows along the side, the room felt sombre, masculine, threatening. Looking at it all, it began to make sense to me that he'd relocated here: Having entered their private domain, he was infiltrating even their sacred spaces, letting them know that he would continue to reduce their power and influence, piece by piece.

Moving to the back of this room, Espartero ushered me through a further door, and here were his new private chambers. *Dios mio*, I prayed, let me come out of this safely.

He closed and locked the door behind us, and then, God help me, fell on me like the lion I'd pictured. His hands were heavy, full of force. His lips, open and wet, devoured my face—*merde*, I squeaked inwardly, don't let him chew off my new complexion! Or, even worse, dislodge the wig! "Señor," I panted, pushing at his chest, "please!"

He came to, and stared at me, blinking. "Señorita Olivares, forgive me. I've been dreaming of you, and your breasts . . ." Oh dear. "Let me see them?" This man had no time for niceties.

I hadn't anticipated this voraciousness. He was, after all, at least fifty. I wished I hadn't worn such a low-cut gown; it would set him off like a steam engine as soon as I removed my cloak. And how would I keep him occupied through the rest of the evening? I sensed that this man, with his haste and heavy responsibilities, would be good for one round and that would be that. Foolishly, I'd assumed the chase and the flirtation, begun at the ball, would take a few hours at least to reach fruition. Timing was crucial, Diego had cautioned me, and I now realized this would be my biggest challenge. How to keep him on the boil, but not turn vicious? Suddenly remembering something Carlota had said, I fanned myself and whispered in a tiny voice, "First, might you indulge me? I wandered around outside for several hours, trying to work up my courage. It is such a cold evening, would you perhaps . . . have any chocolate? As a warmer?"

"Of course! Of course, my dear," he blustered. "Forgive me for not thinking of that myself." He yanked a bell pull near at hand; I could hear the jangling somewhere far off in the building's depths. "It should only take a moment."

"Please," I said, "let us take as long as we can. I am a modest sort of woman, even though I'm an actress." My hands were still engulfed in my muff.

"Of course you are. Mm, mm." He was nodding in a soothing sort of way, his eyes on my demurely shrouded chest.

"I cannot believe that I have come here." I made a move as if to leave. "I am ashamed, señor."

"No, no!"

A rap at the door, and a young man in livery stepped inside. "Your Honour?"

"A jug of chocolate. Immediately."

The livery retreated. Espartero was wiggling his fingers, as if longing to fondle the merchandise, so close and yet so far. Ye gads, this would be funny if it weren't so scary. I truly hoped I wouldn't end up black and blue. Or worse. With such a man, used to power and force, you could never tell. I vowed to myself that I would never, *never*, allow myself to be manipulated into such a position again. Oh, how many times must a young woman make that vow? It was frightening and yes, shaming, but I was doing it for Diego. Not Grimaldi or the Cristino cause. For Diego, because he needed me, and I would not fail him this time.

In due course, the chocolate arrived. The young man who brought it kept stealing glances over to where I sat wrapped in my cloak. "Fine, now get out," Espartero growled, wanting to have me all to himself, "I have no more need of you."

"Your Excellency," the man bowed, and slipped away. My last chance to do the same. Be stoic, get through it. Survive.

"Are you warm yet?" Espartero urged me, as soon as the cup touched my lips.

"Not quite."

He jumped up and strode around, gnawing at his fingertips, filling me with dread. What else would he be gnawing on in only a very few minutes? My nipples tingled with alarm. And then I remembered: I had placed one of the firing caps for my pistol on the end of my left nipple, as usual, for safety. Oh no.

He came back, loomed over me. "May I remove your cloak now? I could massage your fingers, if that might help." He reached for my muff, to take it.

Good lord. I'd have to let it go. Where would he put it? Would he find the pistol? Would we end up in a bed, would he fall asleep afterwards, and for how long? Would it be over in a moment, or go on and on and on, requiring groans and screams of feigned ecstasy? Perhaps he preferred real fear—well, that I could supply. No, I told myself firmly, no. Be a *bandita*. Be Lola. Be what you need to be, for Diego.

I placed the muff on the floor, out of his way. The cloak eventually came off, and as he'd promised, he rubbed my fingers—and warmed them further in his wide, hot mouth. I convinced him to drink some of the chocolate, hoping that this favourite of his would distract him, but no. His eyes slid again and again to my breasts; he was obsessed. It was all because of my Cloud with the Silver Lining gown and its cleavage! Finally, I turned my back, retrieved the firing cap deftly, dropped it surreptitiously to the floor and kicked it away. In hopes of surviving the attack, I turned back with a smile and permitted him to touch the objects he desired. With large fingers, he stroked them devoutly; this is fine, I thought, holding my breath. Then he leaned his silver head in and licked the curve of them, as they lay revealed in my bodice—strange, but gentle. I could see my heart beating swiftly against the white skin. And then he had them both out of the bodice and up around my collarbone; he was very rough and I cried out. He apologized profusely, eyes still fixed upon them. What is it with men and breasts? Men and bottoms? Men and feet? Men and *parts*! Why not the *whole*!

Oh I can't bear to remember this. This, and the horror that was to come. But I must go on, must think it through, unearth all the details that may possibly save me.

I fulfilled my mission. And then awoke with a start and a rush of fear in the dark.

※ ※ ※

There was noise in a corridor, the sound of male voices, yelling, and then in the antechamber, the pounding of feet running closer. I was in Espartero's bed, in the small private room where we'd ended up. The evening had continued with bursts of voraciousness and then contrition on his part. Perhaps that was his amorous style. If so, it left a lot to be desired. He'd removed me from my gown with hard, impatient fingers; my breasts were raw from his teeth and beard stubble. My insides, too, felt raw and hot, and not from the overactive pleasure that I'd often felt with Diego after many languid or joyous comings-together over a short space of time. No. On that night, from a hurried, repetitive banging against my flesh, while propping himself above me and appearing to be suffering some form of protracted rictus. It reminded me of Thomas, my estranged husband. How could these men believe they enjoyed sex when they suffered so much from it, like a guilty, narcissistic, contorted form of torture? Going deep inside their heads and staying there, the whole time, while their bodies struggle on to bring them the release they long for yet fear intensely. I blame religion, any religion that celebrates guilt and pain—and in the conquering world, is there any that doesn't?

At any rate, all the striving and excruciation had finally resulted in some sort of spasm, and he'd rolled off me like a man who'd been felled by a plank. Immediately asleep, *gracias á dios*. I pushed him further off and used his sheet to wipe between my legs, wipe him away. Then I said a little prayer for Diego, sent it winging through the night. Be safe, be well, my darling, somewhere in this enormous palace with its thousands of rooms. Before Espartero had blown out the lamp, I'd tried to ascertain the whereabouts of all my belongings and memorize them. I'd resolved to wait until he was deeply asleep, then creep away. Unfortunately, what with the anxiety and fatigue of the endless banging, I too had fallen asleep.

So there I was, bolt upright at the sound of the shouting voices, pounding feet, and now pounding hands on the door. "Prime minister! It is urgent that we speak with you! Prime Minister Espartero, Your Excellency!"

The silver-maned lion beside me awoke, growling loudly, "What do you want? I told you not to disturb me!"

"We must speak with you; it is of very great importance!"

"One moment!" he roared, and rolled over with a groan, heaving himself to his feet. He stalked to the wardrobe, pulled out a robe, threw it about his body, and went to the door. I knew this only from the sounds. It was so dark I couldn't see a thing, but he knew where he was and could navigate unerringly. He flung open the door. Outside in the anteroom a dozen men were congregated, carrying torches. I cowered into the covers, peeking out at the sudden light and noise and glancing frantically around for my muff with its hidden pistol.

"An incident, prime minister," one man said, stepping forwards. "We must have your advice." My mouth fell open. Surely I recognized—? It was Javier, the bodyguard, the man who'd guarded me at the theatre, night after night. The one I'd questioned in the garden, with the shy smile. He did not look shy at the moment, but flushed with excitement and haste.

"Tell me." Espartero looked fully in charge once again, even half naked—legs braced, shoulders squared, running a hand through his silver mane.

"We've come directly to you, now that the scene has been secured," Javier continued. "The men were all coming on duty, two dozen of us positioning ourselves throughout the building. Shortly after midnight, I heard a commotion on the stairway. I called up as many as were within earshot and we raced in that direction."

Oh God, I thought, trembling. I don't know what has happened. But I know we are undone.

"Two men were running down the staircase with the infantas in their arms. Infanta Isabel was screaming, Infanta Luisa Fernanda still sleeping, and these men would almost have escaped but for the quickness of the guards bringing up the rear."

"And the infanta, Isabel, where is she?"

"Safe, Your Honour."

I had crept out of the bed during this exchange, fumbling for my clothing, trying to sense what was what in the darkness of the shadowy room. My hands were shaking so badly I could barely manage, but I persevered.

"There was bloodshed—not the princesses'—but several guardsmen were wounded," Javier went on. "The two men had set the princesses down in a corner and began to fight back. One cried out, 'We're on the queen's business! Make way!' Infanta Isabel ran screaming down the hallway towards her bedchamber, but Infanta Luisa Fernanda remained, now awake. We were all terrified for her, that she would be hurt."

"And was she?" Espartero barked impatiently.

"No, prime minister."

"And the result of all this, man? Get to the point!"

"We have apprehended two men. They are General Manuel de la Concha and General Diego de León. We have them in irons."

I died. My knees buckled beneath me, and I fell to the floor.

"We await your instructions, Your Honour." And Javier bowed.

I was whimpering with fear and clasped a hand across my mouth to stop myself from howling.

"Bastards! Those bastards!" Espartero began to bellow. "Traitors! Intriguers and conspirators!"

I had crawled into the wardrobe, curled up and trembling amongst his boots and whips. I could hear other men outside beginning to add their impressions to the mix, angrily but admiringly: "They fought like tigers," "We were sure we would all be killed!" "But when reinforcements arrived—we have them heavily guarded. They won't get away."

"I fought with those *cabróns* in the war!" Espartero was yelling, "I am their commanding officer! And moreover, their ruler!" He was in a towering rage, and now he was charging back into the room. I barely had enough time to uncurl with a frightened gasp, scramble across the tiled floor, and roll under the bed, pulling the hem of my gown and my boots in after me.

Espartero flung off his robe, hurled himself into riding breeches, and ripped his boots out of the wardrobe. Stamping into them, he asked in a brutal voice, "What is the time?"

"Two in the morning, Your Honour."

Espartero then shouted, "Death by firing squad! At dawn!"

I clapped my hand over my mouth again to prevent the scream that tore through my heart.

There was a startled murmur of dismay from all of the men still gathered in the anteroom. Javier, too, sounded shaken as he replied, "But Your Excellency, no trial? I mean, this excessive speed. What will the people say?"

"I don't care!" Espartero snapped, pulling on his shirt and grabbing up the uniform jacket. "Do the unexpected. It's the only way to govern, the way to keep control. That'll teach the bastards to intrigue against *me*!" I could see the hard, shining boots striding out of the room, a horsewhip flicking against them as he went. "Let me see them! Let me show them! I'll eat their hearts!" The men swirled around him and they were gone, out past the antechamber and on.

My God, get moving! How could I have fallen asleep? Idiot! I rolled back out from under the bed, scrabbling about in the dark, and finally lay my hands on the muff. But as for the firing cap, it was lost and gone. Where are your equal conditions now, Diego? My teeth chattering like a gibbering monkey, my fingers felt as if they were cooked pasta, unable to grasp and lace and button. Somehow I managed most of it and staggered to my feet. He means to destroy them! Where to go, what to do? Where were they? Oh my life, my heart of gold, how to save you!

Somewhere, out there, the sound of gunfire, two or three shots in swift succession. God, no! Now what?

I ran towards the inner office and fumbled around. The torches having gone with the men, it was pitch black again, I could only feel my way and pray that I was moving in the remembered direction. But they were out there; I heard vague rumbles and the occasional raised voice. Had something just happened? Why were they lingering? I couldn't go that way, not with them still gathered in the outer rooms. Was there another door? I fumbled on, gabbling now a nonsensical language that transformed itself into a children's rhyme, one I'd hated as a child and now couldn't get out of my head: "Round and round the mulberry bush, the monkey chased the weasel . . ."

Merde, they were right there in the next room! Javier's voice continuing stoically, "That's what I'm trying to tell you, Your Honour. I don't know who that man is, but I was first alerted to the possibility of unusual activity by questions from an actress I was guarding nightly at the Príncipe." I stopped breathing, eyes popping in the darkness.

"An actress?"

"Yes, she was asking about how our shifts were organized, whether each of us guarded particular personages, and who was employing us. I was suspicious then."

You sly bastard, I gulped.

"Then came the attempted kidnapping of the Infanta Luisa Fernanda at the masked ball, and I knew something was wrong. The actress was intimate with the princess, and she'd continued to ask questions. Another guardsman reported a conversation she'd initiated with him, just last week. I presented this information to my senior officer, and as of tonight, we'd posted extra guards, employing emergency caution during our—"

Espartero's grating voice: "Stop," and he returned to the previous point. "Actress, you say. Named Patrizia Olivares? Blonde?"

Oh *Jésu*!

"No, Rosana Gilbert, also known as Eliza. Dark."

Triple *merde*! My hands were fumbling again, arms out in front of me like a despairing blind man about to fall from a cliff. I banged painfully into something hard and barely felt it. *Merde*, oh *fuck!* Yipping with panic, and then! A doorknob! Oh *God*, don't be locked! I grabbed and twisted, and it opened! A corridor stretched before me. The voices were off to my left. I flung myself down the hall, to my right, running for my life—running where, I had no idea.

I was looking back over my shoulder, fleeing with my skirts yanked up around my thighs and bootlaces trailing dangerously, so I didn't see him. I crashed into him with full force and went sprawling onto the stone floor, the wind knocked from me. Then I hit my head, hard, and went out like a light.

※ ※ ※

Pounding, hammering. Splitting pain. And yet, soft underneath. A tickling sensation—Diego? I could feel myself smile, oh thanks be to merciful God and sweet baby Jesus it was all a bad dream. Kiss me again, and again, make this pain go away. I opened my eyes; the ceiling spun and then slowed, and there was a young stranger staring down at me, stroking my hair.

I was up again, crouching, like a spitting cat about to tear his face off, when he held up a hand, "No, no, señorita, it's me!"

The young man in livery who'd delivered the chocolate. "Do you know the way out?" I gasped, my head on fire and the room spinning sickeningly. I fell over and must have blacked out once more. After an unknown amount of time, I could feel him again solicitously cradling my throbbing orb in his lap. "Will you help me?" I whimpered, eyes closed.

"Of course I will. I would *kill* to help you," he said in a passionate voice.
"Stop speaking of killing!" How much time had I lost? "I must sit up." He assisted, and again I thought I would heave out my insides before calmness prevailed and objects stood still. "How long have we been here? Where is this? I must get away!"

"Perhaps an hour? Or slightly more. My sleeping quarters."

"Oh no, an *hour*? Not so long, please, oh please!" Reaching up, pulling out as many of the pins as I could find, I yanked off the wig, taking some clumps of my own hair with it.

The young man looked astounded and his eyes bulged. "I thought it was your own." He seemed disappointed. "I brought you in here, out of the corridor, and lucky I did. Two guardsmen ran past, searching for you, only moments later."

Oh *merde* and triple fuck! "Where can I get rid of this so it will never be discovered?" I begged, giving the wig a shake.

"I will be honoured to take it." And the poor fool, kneeling beside me on his bed, held out his hand with a gentlemanly gesture.

"I can't do that, you'd be in terrible danger! If it was ever found on you—well, let's not think of the consequences!"

"The danger would be worth it if just once a woman as beautiful as *you* came looking for *me*," the silly boob uttered, eyes uplifted with the rapture of a martyr. What *is* it with Spanish men and danger?

My head was clearing. I was thinking swiftly. "Why are you willing to help me?" I asked.

"These days, no one is who they seem, señorita. We all have our eyes in different directions."

Fair enough. I thrust the wig at him and he secreted it inside the breast of his liveried uniform. "Lead me out?" I whispered, getting to my feet with only a small wobble of nausea, then retrieving my muff, which had been lying with me on the bed.

He knelt at my feet, gestured for me to raise my skirts. Oh for the love of God! Then I realized and raised them while he did up my bootlaces, so I wouldn't be as likely to break my neck. A practical young man. Now at least I was clothed and decent, I could hopefully pass unnoticed into the streets. Just get me out.

"There was a man," he said. "You tripped on him. He's lying dead."
"What! My God!" I shook him by his liveried shoulders. "Show me!"

He took my hand, peered round the door out into the corridor, and we began to run, back to the hallway where I must have fallen. There, lying in a pool of his own blood, now congealing, lay dark, strong Pedro Coria. Unmistakably. Long hands upturned and grasping the air, mustache bristling. Glass eye still open, staring at nothing. What was he doing here? Always, wherever I turn, there is Coria. Now, no more Coria.

"Go, go!" I urged the youth.

We ran on, down a set of stairs. My head was beating a staccato of questions: Diego, my reckless stallion, my beloved, where are you, what's happening to you? Out through an enormous, shadowy kitchen to a darkened back door. The boy found the key, turned it in the lock, and swung the door open. The night beckoned, full of menace. I could see the hulking presence of the royal palace, huge in its aloof grandeur, looming above us. No one in sight. I turned back and gave the young man a kiss on the cheek. "*Gracias por tutto*. Get rid of the wig—burn it immediately!"

"I will do what I need to do, you can be sure, dear señorita."

A thought struck me and I stared at him, horrified. "You'll keep it as evidence! You're going to give me away!"

"Never! I would never do such a thing." He looked appalled at the thought. "It's just that . . . I wanted to keep it. To remember you by."

I grabbed his shoulder and hissed into his face, "Don't you dare, you stupid boy. Remember this, instead." And I kissed him on the lips, with full force and grateful thanks. "Burn it!" My last image was of the dazed look in his eyes. A conspirator in training, happy to sacrifice his life for a kiss. I ran.

⁂ ⁂ ⁂

Light was beginning to leak into the sky as I fled down the street outside the palace, clutching the pistol concealed in the muff. I tried to be as inconspicuous as a woman could be while running, panting, and holding a stitch in her side. I fixed a smile on my face as if everything's fine, I'm just in a bit of a hurry, children to feed, husbands to placate. When really the terrified refrain pounded on: What to do? Where to go? What's the time, if light is appearing? Not yet dawn, the sun's not up, therefore surely not yet! Death at dawn! How can this be prevented? I started gibbering again, brain banging around inside my poor half-fractured skull.

Rounding the corner onto the Plaza de Palacio, I came up short. People were milling everywhere; a huge crowd had gathered. What were they looking for? What had they heard? I immediately feared the worst—was this a military contingent? Sent to quell the populace? Rifles, bayonets? Desperate men?

I grabbed the shoulder of the nearest person and asked, "What is happening?"

"I don't know, doña. Someone said conspiracy. The army is out, be careful for yourself."

"If there were to be reprisals, executions . . . ?"

He turned appalled eyes to mine. "Such things will never happen again. And never here."

"Then where?"

"Somewhere else!" He rushed away. I asked others, weeping and trying to dash the tears from my eyes, but they shook their heads or shook me off with brusque voices: "Not here, doña!" and "We don't know anything."

"Then why are you all standing around! What are you expecting?" I shrieked, and they ran away from me, covering their heads and faces in fear of being recognized.

I didn't know what else to do, so I ran the few blocks to the Príncipe—perhaps Ventura was there. Maybe he'd know where the prime minister would have taken the prisoners. But surely, I tried to reassure myself, Espartero would *surely* have reconsidered, after the heat of the moment. He couldn't possibly go ahead and shoot the generals in cold blood, with no questions asked—no trial, no possibility of reclamation. It wasn't human! Then I remembered the rictus-distorted face above me, only hours before. I grabbed up my skirts and ran on, panting and sobbing.

The stage doorman stormed from his booth and attempted to stop me, but I hurtled past, not listening. "Ventura!" I called, "Ventura, are you here? Please! Help me!"

In the principal dressing room, I found him. And his brother. The playwright was sitting, head bowed. Father Miguel stood, as usual, in the shadows.

"Do you know what has happened?" I cried. "Get up, you must help me, we have to go—"

"The military have just been here," the Jesuit said, severely. "They were looking for a certain Patrizia Olivares, actress. Always you involve us, always you say too much. We told them we have never heard of her, but my brother has now come under suspicion."

"Oh my God, oh Ventura—"

"Don't torture her, Miguel." Ventura looked up with red-rimmed eyes. "It's over. They're dead."

I sank to the floor. I was too late. And it swept over me with the force of an ocean: My love, my gorgeous Diego, was no longer in the world. The world was emptied, barren and bleak. There was nothing in it.

"We should never have trusted a woman like you," Father Miguel was saying, the words stinging with a fearsome rasp. "I tried to warn Grimaldi. Adding insult to injury, only yesterday news of your divorce arrived from Hernandez. It was heard in court, just before Christmas. It is done; you are free." Something in his hateful tone now made me look up, miserably. "Free, that is, as a woman such as yourself understands it. Shamelessly."

"Miguel, stop. It's neither the time nor the place."

"She must understand her guilt in this matter!" the Jesuit screamed at his brother, before spraying me again with his vitriol. "Distractions! Seductions! Women like you are poison to men of integrity and resolution. You suck the marrow from us; you make us weak!"

Ventura was looking at me with clouded eyes. He hadn't the strength to stop his brother's tirade, and I could barely decipher the words, demolished as I was by grief and remorse.

"The military also asked about a traitor they shot dead late last night. They believe you to be connected. I suspect it was Coria, was it not?"

The Jesuit was almost prancing with malice. "I've revised my opinion, Ventura. This female and he were in league together! They've been spying upon *us*, for their own treacherous purposes!"

I leapt to my feet and would have torn the beard from his abominable cheeks, if Ventura hadn't jumped between us and pushed us apart with a roar. "Have some respect! Our brothers are dead!"

Father Miguel turned away in disgust, and I again sank to the floor. My head was throbbing and I thought I'd be sick: Someone please wake me from this horror. Round and round the mulberry bush—

"*¡Puta!*" the *padre* spat.

—pop goes the weasel. It didn't matter; none of it mattered. I put my head down on the floor and wept. And sobbed. What did I care what either of them thought? My stallion, dead? My heart cracked in half.

Ventura was saying, "This operation has been a disaster from the beginning. Her Majesty María Cristina blows hot and cold, and we ride the storms." Then, perhaps to himself, "All we can hope is that Grimaldi will return to Spain. We need him. Maybe he will come back—by invitation, now. Return as a statesman."

I stood up, took two steps towards him, and slapped Ventura's face, hard. Then I turned on my heels and, once again, I ran.

✤ ✤ ✤

This time, my feet knew where I needed to go before I did. It was difficult to breathe with the conflicting emotions reverberating through me: load my pistols and go back to his offices, shoot the white-haired fiend? Return to the theatre, shoot Father Miguel at point-blank range in the head? Such mad thoughts. I stood gasping outside Diego's home, asking myself what he would have wanted me to do. Then I rushed inside, crying out to his manservant that we were all undone, that his master was dead: "Executed without mercy, along with General de la Concha. Tell the others, and look out for yourselves!" His frightened eyes told me all I needed to know: He, and the rest of the household, would be gone within the hour.

I hurried into our bedchamber, not looking anywhere but at the wardrobe, where I yanked out a pair of Diego's everyday trousers and a loose white shirt. I pulled them on, then stuffed the toes of a pair of his boots and jammed my feet in. I knotted my hair up on top of my head, crying and muttering desperately to myself, ransacking his things—that smelled of him, that remembered his shape!—until I discovered a soft felt hat, which I rammed on my head. Grabbed his favourite dark cloak and tied it on, for the cold. Then I pulled the faux book from the drawer where it lay, with the second pistol inside, took the first one out of the muff and placed it with the other. Ensured that the powder bag was full, found several other caps and loader, closed up the faux book and put it into a leather bag with a strap. Rifling through another drawer where Diego kept a stash of money, I threw everything that was there into the bag. From a drawer where I kept my jewels, I hesitated briefly, then pulled out my favourite peridot earbobs and stuffed them into one pocket, the diamond necklace from the earl in the other—to trade for cash, should I run short. By the window was a pitcher and basin; I washed my face, scrubbing off the remains of the evening's makeup with a shudder of revulsion. Then I ran out of the room, down to the kitchen, grabbed a loaf of bread. Go, *bandita*. Don't look back.

I set off down the street, consciously lengthening my stride and trying to keep grief from consuming me. Not far now, only a few long blocks: Look normal, like an ordinary young man going about his business. I could still hear the noise of a crowd towards the palace, near the plaza. What is happening, I wondered, and then thought, it doesn't matter, because I can't prevent it. I can't stop the world's ending. Diego is gone.

Dashing the last few yards, I hurled myself through the doorway, closing it behind me with gratitude and unbearable anguish: the scent of horses and grass, forever connected now with him. One of them whickered softly, anticipating oats. As my eyes adjusted to the dim light seeping through wooden slats, I saw Lindo throw his head over the side of his stall. The sight of his large, black eyes gleaming was enough to set me going again.

"Stop, or I'll shoot you!" a woman's voice called, high with fear.

I threw my hands in the air. "I've come for my horse. Please. I'll be gone in a moment."

A head peeped around the edge of Conquistador's stall—Matilde. Though I'd tried to disguise my voice, she'd obviously recognized it. The baby lay in a sling round her neck, and when she saw it was indeed me, she slumped back against a bale of hay, cradling the child and keening. So she knew.

"Matilde, how can we bear it? It has all gone so wrong." I knelt down beside her. The infant's face was unbelievably peaceful, not yet privy to all the world's woes.

"My cousin." I could barely hear her, the voice coming deep and thick. "He's in the army. That's how I got myself into this mess—with him. It seemed like a good idea, a way to escape poverty in Figueres. What a fool."

"Your cousin?" I couldn't follow where her thoughts were taking her.

"That is the horror of it. He is lying on my bed, totally destroyed, vomiting his guts out. Soon he'll have to return to duty, as if nothing has happened. That bastard, that despot! To do such a thing! Monster!" Hunched in a fierce and protective ball around the child, her face was contorted with hate.

"Espartero?"

"Of course!"

I asked her to tell me everything. It came out in a torrent.

"My cousin was woken in the middle of the night, told to join his regiment, and from there, straws were drawn. They didn't know what they were supposed to do, but from the rank smell in the air from the higher-ups' sweat, it seemed it was a terrible task. Ladrón drew a short straw. He and eleven others, muskets loaded, marched to the square in the middle of the military headquarters, the high-walled one. Two men were being dragged out, hands in irons behind their backs. Nobody knew what they had done. And then Ladrón recognized them."

"Diego and Manuel."

Matilde covered her eyes. After a moment, I reached out and held her. At first she tried to push me away, then she sagged into my arms and held on tight, the baby cuddled between us, rocked back and forth in a sea of grief.

After a long silence, she continued, her voice a steady monotone of heartache. "Ladrón said he could see their faces clearly, see them shift from confusion to disbelief when they realized what an armed guard of twelve must mean for them. The square where they were standing had two thick posts towards one side, where they were to be tied. As the guards who had charge of them tried to shove them along, Diego broke free and called, 'You know us, brothers. You can't do this thing; we haven't been tried!' The guard smashed him in the face with his rifle."

"Oh God," I moaned.

"Manuel appealed to them too. 'The prime minister doesn't want anyone to know of his vicious retaliation, but you must tell them! If this is to happen, you must not keep it quiet!' He was beaten as well. Ladrón and the others were completely dismayed—de León and de la Concha were their comrades in arms, their superior officers. You can imagine their horror. They began to mutter, and several, to cry."

Baby Matilde's eyes fluttered open and looked up at us with an innocent trust. Tears were falling on her upturned cheeks like warm rain.

"The commanding officer in charge of the firing squad furiously called them to order. Just then, Diego, blood streaming from his face, told his guards to give them a moment, as gentlemen. He told them that he and Concha could now see no respite would come, but that the soldiers must not suffer the guilt that should be reserved for the prime minister. 'Let me speak with them for a moment, to reassure them,' that's what he said." Matilde's voice grew slower and heavier with each phrase. "So Diego's guard stepped back, rifle aimed to kill. Ladrón says Diego walked steadily over to the twelve soldiers, asking the first one to reach inside his uniform jacket and pull out a box. He told the man to open it, and inside were a dozen of the smallest, finest cigars, the ones he orders direct from South America. The sweet-smelling ones."

We were nodding, heads together, eyes closed. Her voice went on.

"He walked with that first man down the line of men, with individual words and a cigar for each. To all he said, 'These were for the celebration, afterwards. But now they're for you, brothers. Just do us a favour, don't miss.' And he grinned. Manuel bowed to them, adding, 'Do your job, but don't believe the propaganda that will cover this up.

Be swift, if you love us.' The commanding officer yelled for order, and the two were yanked back towards the thick posts and tied there. Each man on the firing squad placed the cigar he was given against his heart; each man was peering through tears and pain. No one understood why this order had been given, no one would tell them—not their job to know, just to obey. The order was given, they shot in unison, six to each prisoner. And they were dead."

I tried to imagine the cousin's sick terror, to take my mind from the images that were flooding my brain. The philosophy behind a squad of men is that no one man will suffer full responsibility. But in a case like this? Where they *know*, and admire, the men they are killing? I was sick too with my own understanding that, thanks to my continued questioning, the bodyguard Javier had reported his uneasiness, which led them to step up their watch. Therefore they were ready for the generals when they came.

"You know Manuel was rich? He was an aristocrat," Matilde was whispering. "That is why he couldn't acknowledge me as his wife, why we never married." Oh, the loneliness in her voice. Though Concha had abandoned her, she would never besmirch her memory of him, not even to herself. "But how he was longing for . . . He was about to step into his title, Marqués del Duero. I can't bear, for his sake, that he never will . . ."

And Diego, the astounding, piratical hellion. That charisma, all the bunched sinew and brawn, that grin, gone? How to believe it. How to face a monstrosity. To know a man so intimately, to have his flesh under your fingers, feel his warm muscles under the skin, cooling after your pleasure—only moments ago! His heart thumping under your ear, its pulse beating in his throat, and to think of that heart with six bullets through it, stopped at the whim of some terrible old man. Oh, no, it was not to be borne!

At that moment, the baby reached up her fat hand and patted my cheek. It was the softest, sweetest thing I have ever felt in my life. I thought of all the children Diego had dreamed of, never to be born. A soft life in the country, his army days behind him. It was inconceivable to think of moving on, moving past this. But for the three of us crouched in the stable, the present and future were pressing hard. We would have to go; we had to get moving. Impossible, unimaginable. Somewhere that adored body lay (crumpled, bloody), and it would not be treated with reverence, with esteem. But it was only a body now. (I wanted to howl! It was *his* body!) The essential Diego would never return, light a cigar, then flash his saucy grin, strip off his trousers, and throw me on the bed . . .

We *have* to go.

How quickly we switch from being all present and future—to all past. And how cruelly life kicks us back into action, those of us left standing. It is brutal and I've never understood it, how we keep going.

Matilde's thoughts were echoing mine. "We must leave here; they'll come looking, the army. How did you get away?"

"I heard Espartero's orders, and I ran. A young man hid me. They came searching for me—or for the actress who'd been in his bed."

"So they've traced you to Diego? They know of our hand in the plot?"

"Not yet, I don't think so."

"They will." She jumped to her feet with desperate energy. "We must split up. I must steal one of these horses—"

I grabbed her arm and turned her to face me. "Matilde, no. Please. We can go together, do a reverse of the way we entered the country. I'll be your husband."

She looked me up and down at this and gave a snort. "No one will believe for an instant that you are a man." She pointed at my heaving chest, then at the breeches I was wearing. "Breasts you cannot hide. Hips of a woman. Swaying walk, pretty face. It's out of the question."

"Matilde, I beg you," and I truly was. "Without you, I'm lost. I can't find my way out of a hatbox. You are the most skillful guide I've ever met. You're heading north?"

She nodded reluctantly.

"I need to get back to Paris as soon as possible, and then London."

"I'll go only as far as Figueres," she said. "I want to disappear."

"Not through the mountains? If I had the money to pay you?"

She shook her head, then added disbelievingly, "You're going to face Grimaldi? After everything that's happened?"

"I have no choice. I need to assure myself that he has released me. My little one's life depends upon it." I cradled baby Matilde's head for a moment, and this she understood.

"So Diego said, I remember." She asked no more questions, but added quietly, "Then hurry. We can't take Conquistador, he will be recognized."

"We *have* to take him. Diego loved him," I argued. "Espartero is crazy enough to kill even the horse of the man he has murdered. His blood lust is up, and nothing belonging to Diego or Concha is safe this day."

Lips between her teeth at the thought, Matilde nodded again and said, "Then cut the mane, the tail. Disguise him as much as we can." I could hear Lindo moving uneasily in his stall. Among the tackle hanging on hooks we found shears, and by luck they were very sharp. Quieting the stallion, trying to keep our nervous energy from infecting the horses any more than it had, I stroked the glorious chestnut neck and spoke to him softly. Matilde clipped and then clipped even shorter the entire mane and forelock, until none was left. Then with one motion of the shears, the stallion's fine tail, which Diego had groomed daily with almost erotic pleasure. A tail which swept the ground, thick and russet in colour, now only as long as the tailbone. A swishy stub of its former self. The horse looked around as if he too was surprised. "Put it all in here," I said, holding out the leather bag with my pistols, the money and the bread. "If we leave it behind, they'll know." The mound of coarse hair filled the bag.

"You'll ride Conquistador, then?" she asked. "He's jumpy, and with the baby—"

"*Sí*. Take Lindo."

We saddled and bridled the horses without further discussion. Round and round the mulberry bush, beating its refrain in my half-broken head, inside my cracked heart. Once everything was ready, Matilde told me to pull off my shirt. Confused, I did so; she untied a scarf she had at her waist and bound my breasts with it. It was unexpectedly painful, but I could see that it helped. I drew the shirt back on and left it untucked.

She reached up and shoved the hat further down on my head, then made sure the infant was securely fastened in the sling round her body. We led Lindo and Conquistador outside, swung up onto the saddles, and galloped away.

We rode as swiftly as we could out of the city without breaking into anything more than a sedate canter in the few stretches where there was no carriage traffic. Conquistador *was* skittish and required all my concentration to keep him from shying, rearing, and snorting at various surprises along the way: a baker moving his cart, a yapping dog called to heel by its young mistress, a loud drunk being chivvied from his pavement bed by the boot of a merchant. Lindo cantered sedately alongside, steady and true; he was the kind of horse who could maintain a comfortable, easy canter at a slow pace while Conquistador minced about between trots, side-steps, and a bone-crunching stiff-legged gallop, seemingly at his own whim. My mind, meanwhile, was playing out all sorts of scenarios: Espartero was, at this moment, squeezing the truth out of Ventura—or, more likely, his slimy priest brother, who would happily squeal my involvement with Diego. The prime minister's men would be sent immediately to Diego's home and to the stable. Or perhaps Espartero would march there himself, blazing with fury and desire for further revenge. Did they kill women with the same unseemly haste? What the *hell* had the devil Coria been doing in the government offices—following me again? At least he was dead; I had nothing further to fear on that score. Did we leave anything behind to call attention to our departure, besides, of course, the missing horses? Oh God, Lindo, could he be traced to me? Don't think about it, *no importa*, keep riding. My head had begun pounding again and occasionally I'd be overcome with dizziness, swaying alarmingly in the saddle.

"Hold on," Matilde warned, "don't fall, or we'll be found out."

Grimly, I obeyed, willing the muscular stallion to calm himself, which of course did not help: He was his own creature, and Diego's, used to bravura behaviour and delighting the multitudes. How does a horse know that he is beautiful? Somehow he does, and, like humans, it goes to his head.

What with increased mercantile traffic in the later hours of the morning, it took us until the sun was nearly at its height to reach the outskirts of Madrid. Luckily, it was a mild and sunny day; we both had cloaks for the coldness of the night slung across the back of the saddles. I stopped to buy the horses oats, and Matilde and I ate the loaf of bread. A drink at the trough for them, sips from the tap for us, and a quick feed for the baby, then we were off again.

On the main road now, we made up for lost time. The horses were fresh and eager to run, and we let them. I don't know how many miles we rode that day, but there must have been many. We passed through Guadalajara in mid-afternoon. All of us were exhausted by the time we entered a final village, purchased feed and human supplies, and found our way to an out-of-the-way farm building as the sun was setting. We settled the horses in a large pen—no need for hobbles tonight—and lay out our cloaks on old straw nearby. For myself, I was feeling somewhat more hopeful. Now, with the miles between us, I couldn't believe that Espartero would waste his time searching for the girl in his bed. I tried not to remember his towering pride, which might be enough to prompt such a thing. Men such as he hate to be outwitted—and by a mere woman. Perhaps if he knew now that I had been with Diego, he could satisfy himself that my grief would be enough of a revenge. Matilde did not have the same optimism in our escape; she was very Spanish in this, full of melancholy and deep, deep woe.

"If Manuel isn't in the world," she mourned, folded up on her side, cloak tucked around, with little Matilde against the hollow of her belly, "even if he no longer loved me . . . just to know he was there, to aspire to his approval . . . I have nothing to live for."

"Don't say that! You have Matilde." I was fiercer than I'd meant to be, hearing her speak like that.

She said nothing else, and I regretted my words. We all mourn in our own way. And who was I to say anything; I who had a lost child, and now a lost darling, a murdered love. I, who could keep nobody safe.

I lay awake a long time, remembering Diego's acrobatic lovemaking, his decadent mustache and virtuoso fingers. A dark, dreadful night.

When we rose at dawn, we had an unpleasant and mysterious surprise. Conquistador was circling fretfully in the stall; Lindo looked over with what appeared to be reproach. "What is it?" I said, stepping inside to stroke his nose and exchange breaths. And then I saw.

"Matilde, come here, quickly."

She turned from what she was doing and joined me. We looked at each other, stunned. The bottom half of Lindo's mane had been sheared roughly. Some of it now stood up straight, from halfway down the neck to the withers.

"How could—?" I was stroking the horse's neck, trying to reassure myself. "If someone came in here—? Wouldn't they have whinnied, or—?"

"*Dios santo*," Matilde prayed, crossing herself.

We saddled up as quickly as possible and hurried away, only stopping to feed and water the horses once we'd put an hour or two between us and the barn.

"If Espartero's men are following—"

"Hush," Matilde told me. "Don't speak of it, you'll bring us bad luck."

I thought this was palpably silly, but I bit my tongue.

"Tonight we must seek out company," she continued. "We'll stop before dark, as we see shelter. There is more safety in numbers."

Who on earth would be travelling at our pace, I wondered, but then tried to relax and put myself in her hands. After all, this was why I was with her. She knew the country. She was once again my guide, and if need be I knew she'd suggest that we leave the main road and gallop up into the hills. This I dreaded, however, because of my fear of the northerners, the *bandoleros*. We weren't in the north yet, but getting close. Our goal was to be past the Castilian border by nightfall.

We rode like a gale the entire day. The horses were still up for it, the road flat and well maintained, certainly until we began to see the hills of the Serrania de Cuenca beginning to rear up and away on our right-hand side. Late in the afternoon, as we passed through a town on an elevated height of land, I thought I wouldn't be able to stay upright a moment longer, but somehow we went on, back down to the plains, now searching for companions to share the coming darkness. Matilde's plan made me very nervous.

"How am I supposed to maintain my disguise?" I asked. "They'll know, won't they, and then when the military follow, asking questions, we'll be remembered."

"We'll tell them. We'll pay them to keep quiet."

Oh brilliant, I thought. First of all, I needed Diego's money to stretch as far as possible, and at this rate Matilde would run through it all before I even reached France! Secondly, who were these so-called companions going to be that they should be trusted with our secret? More than likely they'd be a group of men—with two young women, strangers at that? It would mean trouble.

Exhausted, we came into and passed through another small town, where the road branched. We kept to the northern road. Zaragoza, a big city into which we could vanish for a day or two to rest the horses, was no more than a two-day ride. The provincial border being only a few miles farther, we pressed on.

"Stop," she called, for I'd been galloping ahead, fretting and stewing, and hadn't noticed a purposeful group moving off to the left, on the plain, surrounded by sheep. She'd found our companions: three shepherds with a converged flock, heading at a leisurely pace for their spring upland fields in the Sierra Ministra. They eyed us suspiciously, but the youngest quickly seemed interested in sharing our company. We dismounted and began our negotiations; these men were the sort who spent months at a time saying very little, so Matilde was having some trouble making herself understood. Their dialect was thick, but she smiled winningly and held out the baby for admiration, and as explanation. Their leader was a dark-faced greybeard who kept gesturing towards me with a frown, shaking his head. Finally, Matilde whispered, "Don't flinch," just as the old man reached across, touched my breast, and gave it a quick squeeze as if testing an orange. His face underwent a transformation. Suddenly everything seemed to be possible, everyone (except me) gave a laugh of delight and understanding, and Matilde told me, "We're safe for tonight. They'll let us stay." I was not very sanguine about the idea of bedding down near this ripe-smelling old billy goat—God save me, another Espartero with a fixation on breasts? But I was wrong; the men were very sweet and gentle. They had only wished to be sure that what Matilde had told them was the truth: that we were women on the run from a bad man and we needed both their protection and their silence. These they promised to give, and Matilde made me sweeten it with a handful of *reales*.

We walked along together for perhaps another mile until we reached a shepherd's hut. The men whistled at their dogs, which ran around the flocks, herding and barking, until the sheep seemed to understand that this was a stopping point and they all lay down. We five humans shared what food we had, the horses ate oats, and before long we were all rolled up in our cloaks or blankets, hobbled and shifting from hoof to hoof, or panting on the ground in a heap of fleece—succumbing, in our various ways, to sleep. It was incredibly dark and silent there on the plain, even though there were many of us, breathing, resting. I lay awake a long time, and then finally weariness overtook me.

In the middle of the night, I awoke suddenly to hear a dog barking and to smell smoke. I sat up, instinctively crying, "¡*Fuego!*" and then I could see it, a flame licking at a corner of the roof of the hut. The shepherds leapt to their feet, and in what seemed to be no time at all the youngest had clambered up the outside wall to the thatch, beaten at the flames, and then smothered them with his blanket while the others beat out stray sparks that flared and fizzled along the ground. The dogs were snapping at the heels of the sheep which were rushing about in a panic. By the time this commotion had calmed down, I could see quite well by the light of the three-quarter moon, and what I saw filled me with terror. Perhaps a hundred feet away, a figure was mounted on a horse—and as I realized what was happening, it dug its heels into the animal's side. The horse reared, neighing and pawing the air, then tore off into the darkness.

I rushed after it, scattering sheep. Still hobbled, another horse's shadowy shape was nearby, snorting quietly. It was Lindo. Conquistador was gone, stolen out from under us. A horse thief, in the middle of nowhere, in February? Or an ominous shadow I suddenly suspected had been following us from Madrid—the one Matilde didn't wish me to speak about, in case of bad luck.

Well, bad luck was certainly what we were experiencing now, and everyone knows that bad luck spawns itself. In the morning, the shepherds wished us good speed, but it was clear they did not welcome any more of our company. As we saddled Lindo, as I swung up and took the baby, as Matilde swung up behind and settled the little one in her sling—during all these preparations I could see the men surreptitiously crossing themselves.

My pistols were loaded with black powder, the necessary caps for firing in the usual place, ready at a moment's notice to be placed in the firing chamber. For security, I'd been using the saddlebag as my pillow, and we were not yet short of money. But we needed provisions, and we needed a plan. Lindo was now carrying double the weight; we couldn't go as quickly. And the dark figure, the *pursuer*, now had a fleet, edgy stallion to ride. Lindo knew Conquistador, and would likely welcome his reappearance rather than warn us at his approach. Watch for friendly whickering or pointing and swiveling of ears, I told myself. If I was aware, Lindo would still alert me—and this time, I had the pistols in my belt and vowed I wouldn't hesitate to shoot first and ask later.

"Come on, sweetheart," I whispered into the gelding's hairy ear, "carry us bravely."

And he did. Oh, that horse, that calm and lovely animal. With his steady, mile-eating canter, the morning and then the afternoon wore away. He kept it up, but I could tell he was tiring. The breath came snorting through his nostrils now, his sides were lathered. For his sake I wanted to stop. For all of us, I didn't dare.

What was most unnerving of all on this day was Matilde's dispirited silence.

"Perhaps we're safe now," I told her at one of our longer stops. I watched Lindo eating oats from the ground, velvet lips seeking and finding the grains, large jaw flexing with each hungry chew. "Perhaps whoever it was really *was* a thief, following because he could see that Conquistador's such a fine horse. And now he has what he wanted, he'll leave us alone." Did I believe it? I can't remember. Nothing seemed like a comfortable answer: If it were true, the horse would be sold, and then who would use and abuse Diego's darling? If not, why would someone, anyone, be following us in order to frighten but not apprehend us? Pedro Coria was dead, for God's sake, I'd seen it with my own eyes! I also realized this couldn't be Espartero's man—such a one would take me prisoner and haul me back or do away with me there and then, under orders, not play these wicked games. He wouldn't steal the stallion, or hack off half of Lindo's mane. *This* pursuer's purpose was to instill fear. And then what?

Somehow the valiant Lindo had carried us as far as the borders of Aragon. In a village there I spent quite a few of Diego's *reales* to stable the gelding and ensure he had a good feed and watering, as well as secure a room for Matilde and the baby, and get a hot meal for us in the village's one hotel. "I'm sleeping with Lindo," I told Matilde. "We can't afford to lose him too." Though extremely nervous—alone in the stall with the horse, other horses all around—I was glad to be there, and the night passed with no mishaps. Matilde and the baby also had a peaceful night, the rest she'd needed, a good wash in the basin (to which I also availed myself gratefully), and we enjoyed a breakfast of meat and eggs.

That morning, I could see that Lindo's eyes were brighter and his step was jaunty again. I vowed not to overtax him, and in honour of that, spent another chunk of money purchasing a second horse. This one was not nearly the animal Conquistador was, but she would have to do: a slightly spavined pale brown mare, the only one on offer. We set out again.

"From Zaragoza," I called, as Matilde cantered alongside on the mare, "we go east to Lérida, then towards Barcelona? How many more days?"

"Four or five at least, maybe a week. Once we turn north, in Catalonia, it is mountainous, slower."

"Absurd! Why don't you have any good roads in this country?" I retorted, with heat. In my fear and longing to be safe in England, Spain seemed to me now so backwards and barbarous. I tried not to think ahead too much, as it all seemed so impossibly slow. I still believed I'd be able to talk Matilde into guiding me over the Pyrenees to France, where I'd take the fastest coach to Paris, do my business with Grimaldi, and flee home to London. By then I'd decided I would have to leave the horses with her. Lindo, darling; how could I part with him? I'd have to face it somehow. And I thought that was the worst thing I would still have to face.

When we stopped at midday, Matilde was surprisingly loquacious. I think now she'd been silent in mourning; suddenly it all poured forth. With the infant at her breast, stroking dark hair away from the child's starry eyes, she told me, "She could be Manuel's, or she could be Diego's. Who do you think she resembles?" Gathering my wits, I was about to make some kind of reply, but she didn't need one. "I loved Manuel with my whole heart, and when he would not accept me any longer, because I am not of good blood, because I am a peasant, I was shattered but still his. All of me." That man needed a good kick up the backside, I thought, for his supercilious ways—but then of course I remembered, and felt ashamed. "I hope you do not hate me," Matilde continued, with a shy sideways glance at me, "because I also was bedded by Diego." Quaint way to put it. "I was very happy that night, just one night. He could make you feel so beautiful."

Oh, yes.

I can't bear this, can't bear remembering. But it's part of the whole and I cannot stop now. But swift, swift and fast, it's the only way.

We rode on until the early afternoon, when the mare suddenly went lame. We'd reached a town called de Doña something, a good twenty miles or so short of Zaragoza. I cursed and swore, but there was no help for it. The horse would have to rest, have her hoof looked at by a farrier. We found one; he promised to treat it and stable her overnight, then take another look in the morning. Would I have to leave her where she was and buy another? I counted the cash that was left. How would I ever keep enough to pay my fare home? When would I escape this diabolical nightmare of fleeing?

"No!" I shouted at Matilde when she suggested another hotel was the best idea. "We haven't the money!" In a temper, I led Lindo ahead, searching for a deserted outbuilding or somewhere to shelter from the rain that had started and seemed likely to continue. I was cold and miserable, just as she was, but I didn't know what else to do. I will *not* be stuck in some Spanish hellhole in the middle of nowhere, I told myself, seething. I will *not* run quivering at every noise and shadow. This time, I'll have my pistol in hand and I'll shoot to kill.

There was a small barn beside an abandoned tiny farmhouse. It was perfect: There was a little haymow above, with dry hay from several seasons ago. There was hay on the stone floor, enough to sleep on. A stall for Lindo.

"Tomorrow," I told Matilde, "once we get to Zaragoza, I will be calm. It's a city; I understand cities." I was loading black powder into the chambers of the two little pistols, to be on the safe side. One I kept with me, the other was placed back in the book and into the leather bag.

"And money? Cities cost more money."

I waved this aside. "Tomorrow. It will seem easier in the morning."

The sound of the rain eventually lulled me to sleep, and I must have been exhausted and more demoralized, too, than I'd realized. At one point, in the middle of the night, I woke with a start and called, "Matilde? Is that you?" There was no answer, but I reached to where she lay sleeping, two feet away, and touched her hand. Lindo snorted and shifted his weight. I relaxed again, still clutching my pistol, and fell asleep.

Dawn came. A beam of weak sunlight found its way between two boards, touching my cheek and then my eyelid. Light woke me. I turned my head and saw the most terrible thing I have ever seen.

Matilde lay shrouded in blood. There wasn't a pool of it because it had seeped away into the hay, but it was all around her—and me. A huge pucker of skin marred her throat—unnatural, hideous—which I suddenly recognized as a violent knife slash, from ear to ear, nearly taking her head off. A rush of vomit came up from my stomach and out, but turning my eyes away from the very dead woman, I saw something worse. The baby, Matilde, pale and white and equally dead. Serenely smothered. Splashed with her mother's gore.

Lindo's head came up and over the side of the stall. His eyes were wide; I could see their whites. He was frightened, could smell the blood.

"God," I moaned and tried to stand. And then a whoosh, a black shape out of the corner of my eye, and down from the haymow flew the ungodly, the hell figure, the shadow. All in black, landing on its feet. Father Miguel de la Vega, of course.

The man was mad. This much was certain, where everything else was in flux. Before I could move or scream or anything else, he had twisted my hands behind my back and tied them painfully together. Then he scooped up my pistol, lying in the straw where I'd dropped it to vomit. Why had he saved me for the end, why had he waited for my eyes to open? Meeting his fearsome gaze, I understood: He needed a witness to sate his corruption. To my shame, I fell down again, knees shaking with terror, into the hay that was saturated with Matilde's cold and congealing blood. I prayed for a speedy death—I could foresee nothing else at the end of this minute, or hour, or day.

He was speaking, no, screaming. His thin lips quickly became coated with white spittle and saliva. I made out about two words in ten, but together they painted a portrait of diseased ambition. He raved about the praise he was sure to reap from his society, for having rid the world of two more whores—for whores they surely were, mother and child. How the society would adulate him for bringing to them a living witch, and what pleasure they would jointly take in dispatching this third whore. He yanked my hair and forced my head up, as he cried, "I am speaking, of course, as a member of the apostolic party's terrorist wing: the Society of the Exterminating Angel!" There was more, much more, but my heart had quailed; I was busy surviving and it all swept over me, then, in a wave of undifferentiated hatred.

He ordered me outside, and we left the scene of death. What would happen to their bodies—one small, and one tiny? Who would stumble upon this scene of horror? Then I was up on Lindo, shoved and poked with the barrel of my tiny pistol, my hands now tied in front and under the saddle; he had readied the horse while I was still sleeping. If I were to faint or fall, bound in such a way, I would surely be trampled;

neither Lindo nor I could get free. The Jesuit swung himself onto Conquistador, tethered to a tree nearby. He was taking me to these people, this society, he said; we would ride fast, he would not spare the horses. The stallion was acting badly, spooked and nervy; it was obvious the man had abused him in the time since the theft. As we rode, and as he raved, the priest applied the whip indiscriminately to the animal's most sensitive area, between the ears, and he could not see that it was this that was making the horse ungovernable and, in his view, needful of ever more constant beatings.

We took another road, not the main one, but one that headed off at a completely different angle, through flat plains where wheat ripened on hot summer days. Now, flat nothing. Cold, dry wind. Nobody about, no one to call to for help—if they had dared. Simple country people, seeing a frantic, bound woman in blood-soaked trousers with a man of the cloth? Who were they to intervene?

As the initial shock wore off, perhaps, and the body's instinct for preservation kicked in, I began to understand more of what the maniac was muttering, or shouting, as the spirit moved him: "A disgrace! Soon to be rectified once and for all. Church wealth was raided, given away! By that monkey of a king! Soon we will get it back, make them all pay! Return to the throne a king who properly fears God, who will reinstate the sacred Inquisition to rid the world of its rising impurities! And I will be part of that great whip of wickedness!" I desperately tried to put these words into some sort of perspective. King Ferdinand had siphoned off church monies and lands, but that was years ago and now the pretender, Don Carlos, was happily exiled in France. And terrorist wing of the apostolic party? What in God's name was he talking about? Who and what was the Jesuit following?

We rode all day, the priest whipping Conquistador continually; both horses were labouring, their breath rasping painfully. He did not stop to rest them or water them. We did not stop to eat. I had no idea where we were, but he had begun to talk about Pamplona, the society's base in the north, "near Logroño, site of Father Merino's valiant campaign." His voice took on a silky nostalgia as he said this. Racking my brain for the name, I finally recalled Ventura speaking about his brother before he'd found his vocation: young Miguel, following a warrior priest who'd gone north to join the Carlists, the veteran priest who so impressed his men because he neither slept nor ate. And here the former young man was, retracing those footsteps, neither eating nor sleeping. Heading for the lair of a fearsome, secret society, where I could expect a nest of others just as mad as he, perhaps only one day's ride away.

Finally he called a halt, when the night was pitch black and Conquistador had stumbled so badly onto the road that the flesh over his right knee joint was torn and bleeding. The Jesuit untied my hands (numb, raw), pulled me out of the saddle, and flung me onto the ground. With my pistol, he gestured for me to lie still where I was. He hobbled the horses—no food, no water, still sweating in their skins! Conquistador's leg was a bloody mess! They would be ill; horses can't be treated so. Then he retied my hands and threw himself onto the ground, pistol at my temple. I had no idea whether he'd found one of the spare caps, kept in the faux book; as far as I knew, the others were still on me, in their intimate place on the ends of my nipples. Did he now know there was a second pistol, and black powder, in the book? If the pistol he had in his hand was primed, with the cap ready and waiting in the barrel, any slight jiggle could fire it straight into my brain.

"The day is nearly here," he began to mutter, like a nasty schoolboy recounting the pleasures of pulling the wings from flies, "the day for which the Society of the Exterminating Angel has been working, in secret and in perpetuity. We will close the universities. We will curb the press. No more liberal backsliding. No more Neapolitan jezebels to waggle their white asses and claim to rule us." He clarified himself with rabid asides. "Secret marriage, to a guardsman? With the aid of a corrupt papal nuncio? Armageddon! Death to the whores!" And there was a frightening crack as he fired the pistol—at first, I thought I had been shot, that I was dying, and then I feared for the horses, but no. He'd fired into the air, apparently, in excitement and anticipation. His words were thrilling to him. And it must mean he knew about the other pistol and the powder. Sweet baby Jesus. At that moment I wished I *had* died so I wouldn't have to endure whatever it was that he was hideously planning, with me as main course, to be shared with a roomful of like-minded zealots.

Just as I'd thought he had finished his ravings for the night, he sidled his attenuated body closer and began to whisper. "When you had the temerity to ask if you should trust General de León? Do you remember this? I could smell him all over you! When you were asking if you should trust him—ha! You already had." Oh my God, I cringed, he was going to list my faults; he had them all catalogued in his perverted mind. Another shriek: "Whore of Babylon!"

Then the priest laughed, an oily sound that a snake might make if a snake had lips. "And there you were, busy seducing our prime minister. Such a meddling little slut." His body squirmed even closer; I could smell the putridity of his starvation breath and something else, some other scent that made alarm bells ring in my head, though I couldn't then place it. "Princess Luisa Fernanda was almost mine, you *puta*, but you made me lose her. She could have helped pay for the sins of her mother. Too pretty, too beautiful, too pampered and spoiled. The pretty one first, *because* she is pretty—slit her throat and leave her to be found in the bowels of the Oriente. Then later the fat one . . . You ruined it. But she won't escape me. I'll go back for her. Another generation of whore. Must not be allowed to breed."

He had waited a long time for the satisfaction of these disclosures. His joy was obscene.

Oh, how could I have so grossly underestimated the fanaticism of the man? I'd despised him, found him abhorrent, and so I'd ignored him, at my peril. It all seemed so clear. *He* was the double agent, infiltrating the Cristino conspiracies; he feared beauty, he feared women. How could I not have known?

He giggled and wriggled again. "I killed Tristany. Sent his ears in the box, just as I was leaving Spain to come to Grimaldi's aid. We arrived almost at the same time, which I found very satisfying." His voice was becoming sleepy, like a snake digesting. "You should know, too, I made good use of the earl of Malmesbury's bank draft, *puta*. Sent it to my society. They purchased many rifles, and other implements of justice. Of course I knew you had something valuable hidden—fingering your hem all the way south in the coach, such a vain and puerile female." He gingered himself up again with a hiss and gave me a painful poke in the throat with my little pistol. "I tried to hurl you from the top of the theatre, spawn of Satan! Showing your legs, with pride, to the audience! Lifting your skirts for anyone to see!" The scent, the stench, was in the air, and my senses suddenly placed it: the long paws of Pedro Coria, covering my mouth in the Paris street, the hand at Clotilde's throat, propelling her over the rail. I glanced down at the priest's hands, just visible in starlight: one clutching my pistol, the other clenching and unclenching. Abnormally long yellow-white fingers, like spiders at the ends of his arms. Long, strong, cruel fingers, fastened around Clotilde's neck, and then it became real: not Coria! It was the priest, all along!

"That pink dress," he whispered then, as if following my thoughts, "the one I'd seen *you* in, the day Grimaldi introduced you to me—pink, decadent, like female flesh with all the extras adhering. I was going to stop you before you began. But you gave it to her, and so she died. I mistook her for you. But, no regret, she was a vain little bauble, perfectly dispensable. Grimaldi is a sentimental fool."

He was scrabbling, one-handed, in a pouch he kept at his waist, and pulled forth a long thin *cigarillo*. Once he'd lit it, I understood even more: the scent on his hands, on those of Coria, the potent insistent smell. I recognized it from India, from our native porters and gardeners: It was ganja. Strong ganja.

"Pedro Coria," I faltered. "You knew him; you told me so."

"The Society of the Exterminating Angel will exult when it hears!" Oh God, then I wished I'd said nothing, for he was immediately frothing again, claiming that Coria the northerner was a turncoat, worked for a foreign organization, but the Society of the Exterminating Angel could never glean from him which one. Coria would smoke with the priest, they both had the compulsion, but Coria had never relaxed his guard— de la Vega could get nothing from him. "Foreign devil! Expunged!"

Then there was a horrible silence while he smoked and dreamed. Then he leaned even closer to whisper directly into my ear, in breath suffused with the scent of the drug. "That reminds me—Lola Montez. Your new persona?" I could hear his lips on his teeth, in what for the priest constituted a smile, and I closed my eyes, shuddering violently:

There was only one place and only one time when he could have learned this. In the stable, with Diego. In the heat of our passion and joy. "Lola Montez will not be your shield," the Jesuit promised, and then, "I wish I'd seen you fall from the fly tower. But if I had, I wouldn't have this day of glory, in front of my society, to anticipate." An unholy snigger came from his throat, followed by, "I warrant you're sorry now that I had to endure your lecherous dream sounds, night after night. Aren't you?"

"Yes." I gave him what he wanted to hear. And it was the truth.

✥ ✥ ✥

When morning came, Conquistador's leg was crusted with blood and mud, and he had a bad limp. The Jesuit was in a foul temper over it.

"Let me free for a minute. Let me look at it and tend it," I begged, almost beyond hope for myself, trying to focus my attention upon a tangible goal. "If you don't, he'll be no good to you. It's the waste of a beautiful horse."

"What do I care about beautiful horses?" the man snarled, but he eventually relented. He untied my hands and kept the pistol trained at my head while I led the horse to a stream. The stallion drank and drank, then began ripping hungrily at the grass while I bathed the leg and tried to clean it. I reached to tear the hem of my shirt—no longer white, but one of the only parts of me not spattered with Matilde's blood.

"What are you doing?" the Jesuit cried, with real horror.

"The leg should be bound."

"Leave your clothing alone! Succubus! You will do anything to corrupt me!"

I closed my eyes, let go of the shirt. If I looked at him, if I acknowledged his evil, my quailing heart told me, I wouldn't survive another second. Eyes still closed, I went on, "Please. Please let me take the other horse to the stream. He's so thirsty and hungry. They can't go on."

It angered him to listen to me, but he must have realized the truth of what I was saying. Carefully, I tethered the stallion, then went to Lindo and removed the hobbles. His eyes, dark and huge, regarded me, then

I led him to the water. All the time, as I stroked the horse's skin and his throat worked, drinking, my mind raced: These are my only chances. When my hands are free. How am I to get away? De la Vega will kill me the instant I make a move. He will kill Lindo. At the end of today, I may be in the clutches of the society. And then I *will* die.

But Pamplona is a city, and it is easier to hide in a city than on a flat plain. How to ensure he unties me again, long enough to—do what? Something, anything. No way to ensure a thing. But seize the opportunity. Is it now?

Too late. I suddenly felt the cold steel of the pistol against the back of my neck. "Time to go, whore." I could smell the scent from his hands, again pungent and thick. Where was the powder bag and the other pistol?

Again, we rode. Conquistador's leg began bleeding again almost immediately. It was sickening to see how gallantly the horse carried on, how he tried to obey the brutal human who kept torturing him with blows to the flanks, blows between the ears. I've never known such hatred—in the priest, but also growing within myself. Every time he struck a blow, my fury grew and my focus narrowed. My hands, again tied, began to go numb, but all that morning I concentrated on flexing and moving them, determined to seize it—whatever *it* was—at the next possible moment.

We rode past a group of field workers with hoes and spades over their shoulders. Feverishly, I debated whether to call out to them. That moment, too, passed. He turned back and smiled a yellow smile. "Good choice. We're in the Navarre and you're a Cristino—I will inform them. These people have long memories."

"They're human beings."

"Unlike myself, do you infer? Oh no no. I am a Jesuit priest. The Navarre is the home of the sainted founder of our order. They are deeply religious. Why would anything that I do be under suspicion?" He was in that odd, exalted mood again, and I understood—it was the ganja. His only indulgence, but my, how he was indulging now.

Hour after hour we rode. As far as I knew, he had not eaten anything at all since flying down from the haymow to the bloody mess below.

I certainly had not. I began to fear faintness, while trying to remain steeled for action. Such a state is exhausting, on no food or water, and for hours on end. Was it hopeless? Not quite yet. Or so I vowed.

Late afternoon, de la Vega's energy again began to escalate, his mind to wander to the coming exhilaration. I sensed we were not as near the city as he'd hoped because of the stallion's injured leg, and this was increasing the man's agitation. He gave the horse another blow. Conquistador squealed and reared, and the priest nearly fell. He cursed, yanked at the reins, and flung himself to the ground. "Enough! This horse is useless!" and he dragged out my pistol, opened it, messily poured in the black powder, then flung the leather bag down from behind the saddle, searching for a cap to complete the loading—all the while dragging on the reins and causing the stallion to rear and startle.

"No!" I was screaming, "What are you doing? Let me ride him!" Then I thought of something. "If you kill him," I said quickly, "there will only be one. You don't want to ride on the same horse with me." Just thinking of such proximity made me shudder. But, as I'd hoped, it made the priest shudder more.

He cursed again, dropped the stallion's reins and came towards me. Conquistador danced and snorted at the sudden movement, then lifted his trembling leg and lowered his head. Stay there, I prayed. Remember your training, my beauty, just a little longer: When the reins are on the ground, you stay where you are. The Jesuit approached me with distaste, reaching up to untie my hands. To do so, he placed the pistol at his feet. Lindo, unusually, danced sideways, perhaps trying to get further from the noxious presence. "Calm, Lindo," I told him. My hands were free. The priest bent immediately and retrieved the pistol, stuck it aggressively against my ribs as I was dismounting, poked me with it as I moved towards the stallion. And then—how it happened, why it happened, I have no idea, but it is true—I heard a loud squeal behind me, a grunt, and a thud. I wheeled around, and de la Vega lay sprawled on the ground, pistol in the dirt six feet from him. Lindo's ears were flat to his head: He had reared, striking the priest and knocking him down. Conquistador, galvanized, galloped stiffly off down the road, reins trailing. *Carpe diem!* I pounced on the pistol, then trained it on the priest, while with the other hand I gathered Lindo's reins. That's all I'd need, having both horses desert me. *Dios*, I prayed, please give me strength.

De la Vega sneered, looking at the pistol, and said, "You wouldn't dare. And it's not fully loaded." He sat up, and I waggled the weapon at him threateningly. This gave him pause, at least. Then, at top speed, I reached inside my bodice, pulled out the cap that was waiting there, broke open the gun, slipped the cap into the chamber, and snapped it together. How glad I was that I'd practiced so assiduously! Appalled to see my hand at my breast, he'd started frothing and cursing, but when he realized what I was up to, he lunged. I jumped back and shot, startling Lindo. It was a bad shot because I'd been taken by surprise, but there was a grunt, and blood began to spurt from his thigh, followed by a high thin whine of pain and disbelief. We stared, each perhaps waiting for the other to make the first move. Then I moved, fast, leaping towards the saddlebag, scrabbling with the faux book and yanking out the second pistol—still there, *gracias à dios!* But still loaded with powder? I had no idea. Blessings on Lindo, he'd circled around with me and was standing, ears cocked. The priest was writhing around and bleeding profusely as I pulled the other cap from my bodice and began the speedy ritual again—the second pistol *was* loaded with powder, thank all the saints and their mothers.

"I must kill you," I said, completing the action with a snap, and pointing the second pistol at his head. I couldn't believe what I'd just uttered, but it had to be done. "I do it for Matilde, and her baby." I took a deep breath—a shaking hand, needing to steady my aim, another cautious step closer to ensure it was fatal—"And for Diego." I'll never forget the look on the priest's face. He was about to meet his maker, sins unshriven; other atrocities for which he'd require atonement, not possible now, perhaps passing before his eyes. Go straight to hell, *fanático*, and good riddance, I thought. I pulled the trigger and . . . nothing. A feeble click.

"Shit, *merde!*" I grabbed the saddlebag, shoved my foot in the stirrup, and swung up onto Lindo. I whispered into the stiff, hairy tube of his ear: "Run, Lindo! Save us!" Leaving the clearing only half in the saddle, I righted myself as the horse tore off down the road, hooves flying. My heart was in a frenzy of haste and fear. Still alive! Oh fuckity fuck! Streaking along, clinging like a limpet, as I'd often been known to do at age six, in India, racing my pony across the plains, but this time for real, and the treasure is my life! Fly!

I should have smashed him with a rock, bashed his brains in, I babbled away into Lindo's ear. But what rock, and how? He's a fearsome assassin; he would have grabbed you and beaten you to death instead. Sacred Mary, Mother of God! What is he doing at this moment, crawling and cursing? Dragging himself to the road? Is he bleeding enough to make him pass out? Is the road well travelled; will he be found very quickly? Of course they will help him; he's a man of God. He'll tell his tale, then a posse of men will be rounded up, ready to search out the treacherous woman who could have done such a thing to a son of St. Francis Xavier, saint of the Navarre.

Such were my frantic speculations, clinging to Lindo's back, listening to his laboured breath and pounding hooves—as if the horse understood the gravity of the situation, the requirement of speed, and needed no urging. Diego had been right, Lindo ran like the wind, neck outstretched, legs reaching, heart pumping energy into his exhausted, hungry limbs.

We must have galloped several miles when off to the left I caught a glimpse of dark copper between the bare branches of a grove of trees. I reined Lindo in and circled back. It was Conquistador, with his head down, wheezing. As we approached, the stallion flung his head up again, ready to bolt away. Lindo whickered, and perhaps this was calming. I dismounted carefully, held my hand out in what I hoped was a soothing manner, murmuring words of encouragement. One moment I thought all was lost, when the stallion again threw up his head and snorted violently. He'd been so hurt, a proud horse who had trusted and had the trust beaten out of him, but then I took hold of the one unbroken rein still trailing, and he stood for me.

I gibbered away to them both—what to do, what to do—while I stroked Conquistador's neck and then Lindo's. One thing was certain: The most dangerous man in the world was too close, and we couldn't linger. I shoved the second pistol into the saddlebag with the first: a quick look, and yes, the faux book and the powder bag were still there, along with whatever remained of Diego's money. Thank God. The priest's dark black cloak was also tied across the back of the saddle. It would be warmer than mine, but I'd have to remove the insignia, and how could I bear the smell of him? I could bear it, because I needed it, half frozen as I was. But then the worries began again: how to ride fast while leading the stallion? Doesn't matter, just get going, somehow a way will be found. Sling on the cloak, fasten it at the neck, and ignore the reek.

We set off. Soon I could see that Conquistador was in a very bad way, that travelling far would not even be possible, no matter how slowly we went. At this realization I began to cry. Fear and anguish came tumbling out, but were quickly suppressed because it would do no good. We'd have to leave the road and try to find a path through the hills where we could hide, at least for a few days. But where were we going? How could I escape the gang of searchers I was now convinced would be set to find me when I didn't even know where I was? The only sure thing was that I was in the middle of uncompromising Carlist territory. This was the land in which the insurgency was bred, a hard land full of hard men who wouldn't understand or sympathize with a foreign woman and her desperation to get home.

We turned up towards the hills and carried on for perhaps another hour. The trees on either side became more numerous, and I followed what appeared to be a track, perhaps for cows, as I guessed from its meandering. Was the ground hard enough not to reveal the hoofprints? Two horses, travelling together . . . Stop thinking.

We came upon a small house surrounded by a large garden. A woman was working in it, bent down to peer at new plants beginning to push through the winter soil. I tried to turn the horses and disappear, but she saw us and called out.

"Are you looking to see me?" She was not young. There was something in her voice, an authority . . .

"I need help," I said. Then, "Please, can you help me?"

She pushed hair away from her eyes, came towards us. "That is what I do. I can certainly try."

✢ ✢ ✢

Her name was Juliana de Porris. She'd lived in these hills to the east of Olite her entire life, all fifty-some years of it. Her property was well tended, everything made to serve one and often several purposes. Its situation was secluded and very beautiful. From the house, the Rio Aragon could be seen curling through the valley. She lived alone—a husband had died, but many years before. She had a son, Paulos, grown and married, living several miles away due north. Juliana was a herbalist, a healer.

"I've been a midwife, but these have been hard times," she said, leading Lindo towards the stable. I followed with the limping stallion. "When men go through adversity, they distrust everything. I don't fancy being burned or dismembered. That's not to say the women I help would give me away, but . . . Sometimes men are difficult to turn from a path they are on. Is this the kind of aid you require, on top, of course, of hoping to heal that beautiful creature?"

"No," I told her. "I'm not with child; I have no husband."

She tethered Lindo to a stall, then turned to look at Conquistador. "When did this happen?"

"Two nights ago."

"These horses look winded."

"They're more than that," I answered. "They spent a night in the cold after being ridden hard all day. They're hungry, haven't eaten—" and now I had to work hard to keep despair from taking hold. I longed to let down my guard, fall into her seemingly capable hands, give myself over, but did not yet dare. "I'm being pursued," I said.

"By what?"

Her question, the way she'd worded it, made me trust her instinctively. And even if my instinct had been faulty, what else could I do?

While she measured out a scoop of oats and emptied it before each horse, while she bent and peered at Conquistador's injured knee, I told her the rest. Then I helped her. We warmed water, washed the wound, she applied a salve and then bandaged it lightly, the whole time saying nothing. I had no idea what she thought. Did she suspect that I was lying? That I had stolen the horses, made up some tale? Finally, she straightened, touched me on the shoulder, and said, "Come with me."

"Will his leg be all right? Will he heal?" I asked, following.

"The bone has a chip. He may be lucky. I see no infection, but horses and legs . . . Difficult. A front leg is slightly easier. We'll have to see."

My heart sank.

The house was immaculate. One side of the big room was given over to herbs and salves, large worktables, mortars and pestles, open rafters for drying plants in hanging bundles.

We sat at two chairs at the front window. "And you, have you eaten?" she asked me.

In a small voice, "No."

Again she said nothing, simply watching as I devoured what she put before me. Bread, cheese, winter apples, fresh goat's milk. Slices of lamb. When I'd finished I looked up; she stood, arms folded, looking down.

"I believe you," she said gently.

And then I did give way. I sobbed as if my heart would break, and in fact I know that it was broken. Diego, Matilde, the baby. Diego's comrade, Manuel de la Concha. Espartero, and the black wolf from hell. I'd been attempting to displace my terror and despair by transferring it to the horses, my last link with a gorgeous, virile man cut down in his prime, lost to the world, while men like the Jesuit lived on to kill and maim in his own reptilian way. Who could not be killed like the snake he was; I'd missed the chance, and he'd slithered away. How would I ever forgive myself?

When I was calm again, she sat down beside me. "You must leave tomorrow," she said, "you cannot risk any more time. I have an idea, though. I think you should give yourself into the care of the brothers of the l'Abbaye de Leyre, through the mountains, no further than a morning's ride from here."

"Brothers?" I cried, "A religious order? No!"

"They are Cistercians. I do a great deal of business with them. They too are good with herbs, but not as good as I am, and they know it. They are trustworthy, peaceful men."

"No," I said again. I was so afraid.

"Listen to what I am thinking first," she said, and went on. "Their abbey is at a crossroad. It is one of the least-travelled routes through the Pyrenees for pilgrims. It is spring; there will be some pilgrims returning by now."

"Returning?"

She told me that the majority of pilgrims make their way to Santiago de Compostela, to worship at the shrine of St. James, in the fall, when the heat is not so intense. Then they have to return, of course, and many of them do so in early spring. The Cistercian brothers offered refuge for pilgrims who chose the less-travelled way, which cut north just beyond their abbey. Further west, one of the four main routes was lower, the passes not so high, but Juliana said that way was too far for me to reach safely. The one north of Leyre would be my best chance.

It all seemed too difficult. My nerve was failing.

"I will ask my son to take you to the brothers. We'll let it be known that you are my niece, that you are going to France, to Toulouse, to join a convent there."

"Me? A convent?"

"You are also mute." There was a sudden twinkle in her eye: How much did she guess of my usual character? "This may keep you from revealing too much. In any case, it will be safer." She reached across the space between us and took my hand. "I will look after the stallion; if anyone can heal him, I can. You must leave him with me. I promise him a good life. I have a mare; she's just had a foal. He can join them. The other horse may recover, if you don't push him too hard. And you'll need him."

So that is what happened. Juliana rode off on the mare later that afternoon to tell her son, and the whole time she was away, I was sure I would be discovered. That somehow Father Miguel was whole and sound and on my trail, scouring the land, full of vengeance. He knew I would have killed him like a rat; he'd seen it in my eyes. As Diego would have said, this had upped the ante, and nowhere was safe. But Juliana returned, we fed and watered the horses, I washed in water warmed by the fire, we ate and went to bed. I lay awake a long time, haunted by my lost friends, trying not to make a sound. Diego, my love . . . Haunted by my refusal to take a hotel that last night with Matilde—if we had, perhaps she and her baby wouldn't be dead. But he would have swooped upon our little party at some point, and nothing would appease him except death or torture. Haunted . . .

In the morning, Paulos arrived. Juliana had helped me remove the Jesuitical insignia on the priest's cloak, so I wrapped myself in that. She had also given me a simple, warm woolen dress, shoes that fit, wool stockings, and a wool cap. I left behind Diego's filthy, torn shirt and trousers, but removed from one pocket the diamond necklace the earl had given me, so many months before. I tried to give it to Juliana.

"No," she said, "I have no need. Give it to the brothers, for their church."

From the other pocket I took my peridot earbobs and wore them. My last vain, beloved possession.

Lindo looked well, and I was relieved. In my saddlebag were the pistols and powder, the rest of the money. I took a moment to say farewell to Conquistador, and a prayer for Diego's darling. "If you have the stallion," I said, realizing, "you may be in danger too."

"Nonsense," Juliana responded. "If anyone has the presumption to ask, I'll say he was bartered to me by a stranger in return for aid. In a way it's the truth."

"You must let me know that you are fine," I told her, and thought quickly. Then I had it: the earl of Malmesbury, at the Houses of Parliament. "You must write," and I put down the address. Juliana nodded philosophically. "Say you will."

"I'll write." She patted my cheek. "Now, think of yourself, and go. Paulos has my letter of introduction to give to the brothers. Remember, you are mute."

I swung up onto Lindo.

"Go in peace."

We rode for several hours through some high, wooded hills. By noon we came down out of the hills and joined a larger road, where others were also coming and going with carts, or flocks of sheep, or on horseback. I kept my head down, cap pulled low. I'd been wearing a shawl over the cloak, which I pulled up to cover my head as well. My legs turned to water. I needed to get my courage back, that was certain. I spoke sternly to myself, and as we rode on without incident, little by little I began to look ahead, be more like myself. I've never been one to dwell on the dark side—though it was no wonder, at that point in time. But the way we survive is through hope. For future happiness. That is life; that's its strength. What else is there?

The Cistercian brothers of l'Abbaye de Leyre were everything Juliana had promised: kind, helpful, concerned. There were a group of a dozen or so pilgrims staying with them at that time, so the abbot spoke on my behalf and it was agreed that I should travel with the pilgrims through the pass and on to Pau. From there I would need to make my own way to my convent in Toulouse. Did I have resources? Could they help me with that? I shook my head, smiled. Would I be ready to travel on the morrow? I nodded. That night, in a tiny narrow cot, I slept like a rock.

I sought out paper the next morning, and left a note on the pillow: "For your church, with grateful thanks." The diamond necklace lay underneath it. And that was the first and only time I will give to a religious institution.

My sojourn with the pilgrims was slow; some walked. Everyone had scallop shells, a tradition of the pilgrimage, and each night we pushed on towards the next hostel on the route, using the shells as proof of our purpose. The mountains were very cold, especially when the wind, called the *cierzo*, blew, as it does at that time of year. Some of them told me, though, that the *cierzo* was much worse on the plains, when it could be so strong that you'd be knocked off your feet. One of the days was terrible, at the top of the pass. Although not long in miles, it was steep and frightening, and that morning the mist rolled in so that we could barely see the road: hairpin bends, steep drops to unseen rocks and scree below. I kept imagining the rabid priest emerging from the mist with a straight razor raised high, the shadows of fifty mounted Exterminating

Angels massed behind him. What would a dozen assorted pilgrims and one frightened woman be to them, besides glory? I calmed myself with difficulty, placing my hands against the gelding's withers for warmth and leaning over his neck to whisper words of encouragement.

It was that day that hurt Lindo, in his already weakened state. By nightfall we were on the other side—we were in France—and descending quite quickly through foothills towards rolling countryside. But the horse was ill. I brushed him, fed him carefully, walked him. He was wheezing, and so tired. These large, peaceful creatures we use and depend upon, they're hostages of fortune through no fault of their own. I put the cloak over him, but he shivered all night, as I sat up watching and speaking to him. His calm eyes showed suffering. By morning, he was lying on the ground, his eyes dull, and I was beyond consolation. One of the pilgrims, a monk from the Gironde, told me he would do it.

Big heart, best friend... He'd saved my life, and I could not save him.

Now, even if Juliana's note had not made me mute, I would have been. I was numb; I didn't care what happened to me. I dared not look back for I would have stayed, keening by the side of the dead black gelding. Someone let me ride behind them. Days passed, but I hardly knew. We reached Pau, and I left their group and made my way to the coaching station. I bought a ticket to Toulouse. Now I could have spoken, but to say what? There was nothing to say. Somehow by then I'd conflated everything that had happened, and considered Father Miguel responsible for Diego's execution as well. For all I knew, he was. I kept the pistols both loaded, one tucked into my shawl, and waited, almost hoping to see him so that I could kill him. Lindo's death had brought my courage back—but it was a twisted, flat courage, one that desired revenge.

The rolling, swaying motion of a coach travelling at speed became my only sensation. From Toulouse, I purchased a seat on another for Paris. That was nearly the end of Diego's money. I ate as little as I could to conserve the rest, but eventually that too ran out. Several men in the coach to Toulouse had signaled with glad eyes and I'd glared back, repelled them ferociously. But now? It was a simple matter to smile at one of my travelling companions to Paris—a smile that reached the teeth and nothing else. The man was travelling to England on business, and before we parted, I made him promise to take a letter for me and mail it, fastest post, once he reached English soil. I would not go along with him, even if he was offering to pay. I had one final piece of business to fulfill in Paris.

My cryptic but crucial note was addressed to the 3rd Earl of Malmesbury, care of his parliamentary office: "Returning England. Desperate need of friend. Write immediately to Doña Lola Montez, Spanish consulate office in Southampton. ERG."

Paris, Again

AND SO I GOT out of Spain with the clothes on my back and my peridot earbobs.

I hailed a hansom cab and directed the driver to the Grimaldi residence. Juan was at home, and so was Concepción, both in mourning attire. The manservant admitted me to their drawing room; from my precipitous flight across Spain I'd become quite thin, and it was some moments before they recognized me. Once they had, I told them everything that had happened, particularly dwelling upon the perils inherent in trusting a Jesuit: "*He* killed your agent, Tristany; he told me so himself! *And* sent the ears! Your most trusted agent is a double agent—and a serial killer! And not only that, Prime Minister Espartero executed the generals without a trial! Diego de León and Manuel de la Concha!" The whole time, Juan frowned and looked dubious, while Concepción vibrated with anger. I cried at last, "Do you not believe me?"

"We do," Juan murmured. "We believe you have made a mess of things, Miss Gilbert. You must have said too much, as you always do."

I was furious and indignant, but gathered myself and said what I had come to say. First, that they must swear to leave my daughter alone, forever. Second, that they must release me from their service then and there, with no further association of any kind. If they refused, I said, I would be forced to go to my consulate.

"Breathe one word of all this and you're dead," Juan said.

There was no emotion in either his face or his voice. Completely terrifying.

"I need funds to get home," I told him, my heart in my throat. "Just enough to take me to London."

"You are on your own," he replied. "We will have nothing further to do with your bungling ineptitude."

"Nor with whatever danger you think you have unleashed upon yourself," said Concepción. She rang a little bell, and the manservant opened the door. "Show this person out."

I hesitated, then thought of Diego, of equal conditions—life *is* gambling, *Bandita*.

"There is one final thing you should know that I know," I said, ignoring the waiting manservant and braving both Grimaldis. "I have ascertained the source of your wealth. Muñoz had stock tips from the Spanish finance ministers, and he told a few friends." Their eyes met and Concepción's widened, so I pressed on: "That's corruption. And so is what I saw your good wife doing with that same former guardsman, now royal stud at María Cristina's mansion on the rue de Courcelles. But perhaps that, too, is simply part of your grateful thanks? Release me, and my daughter."

Before I quite knew what had happened, I was facing the front door from the outside. My final glimpse: Grimaldi's formidable eyebrows raised to his hairline, his nostrils flaring and large hand lifted as if to be used in some violent way, Concepción launching into a shrill defensive action with lavish gushings of tears, then silence.

So this was how they repaid their spies! Reptiles, the pair of them.

I needed money. That afternoon I found a likely someone and talked myself into a new frock, ditching Juliana's hot woolen one. My new companion bought me a one-way ticket in return for overnight favours. The coach and four left at eight o'clock in the morning. The entire way to the northern coast, I kept my eyes closed, rehearsing what I was about to do. In England, my first stop would be the Southampton consulate, hopefully to hear something from Malmesbury. I'd take the title of widow—after all, who else had such right to the claim?

On April 14, in driving rain, I boarded the ship for the first channel crossing of the day.

❈ ❈ ❈

Oh, remembering this, and all that came before . . . I'm so cold, and so very, very hungry. All of the candles have burned out now; it's been dark in here forever. Will they leave me in this room to die, the mysterious European and his Cockney thug? Is that the real plan? Am I am too tired to care?

Finish what I started. Not too much further, and then?

I no longer know.

Return to London

When I stepped ashore, something in me couldn't believe that I was back in England, nor the relief that I felt: another country between me and the black dog nemesis with the hopefully septic thigh—may he rot in hell. All I could think of was safety, how to acquire it, how to salvage some part of a life. Be busy, keep moving, put away sorrow until it could be digested and somehow overcome. Or at least subdued.

It was mid-afternoon as I hastened to the Spanish consul's office, fingers crossed that the man himself would be there and ready to listen to a woman in distress. He was. I spent several minutes finding out whatever I could about him; before long, he had revealed that he was a Cristino supporter and had been throughout the war. So I knew how to pitch it. I used my most elegant Spanish.

"Señor, I throw myself upon your mercy. I am the widow of General Diego de León, recently executed in Madrid. Do you know about this tragic event?"

His face blanched and he nodded, told me the news had come through that week.

"I am destitute and have fled our country," I said, holding back tears. I told him that before my marriage I had been a principal dancer from Seville, often playing in the capital. In order to support myself in my tragic widowhood, I would therefore once again take up my stage name, Lola Montez, and resume my work. "Will you help me?"

"Señora, I will."

I was uncertain here, and murmured, "Has a letter arrived for me, by chance? I am expecting to hear from a very kind English gentleman, a member of their parliament, who knew my husband. The 3rd Earl of Malmesbury?"

There *was* a letter. I ripped it open with trepidation: "Travelling from country seat, arrive 9 am April 15, to greet Señora Montez. *Saludos cordiales*. Malmesbury."

Thank Christ. My sweet chubby earl to the rescue.

※ ※ ※

James Howard Harris was in fine form when he met me the following morning. He bustled in, gave me a quick wink from the side of his face not facing the consul, and pumped the man's hand up and down in an enthusiastic greeting. Then he bowed over my outstretched, gloved one and kissed it delicately. "I shall be delighted to offer protection and aid with all matters necessitated by your arrival, dear señora," he said in halting but exquisite Spanish. "My wife has extended an invitation for you to recover from your journey at Heron Court, my country seat in Hampshire. If you are ready to depart?"

I nodded and rose, thanked the consul for his understanding and solicitude—and for the swanky meal and hotel room I'd enjoyed, presumably compliments of Spain—and then left with the busy, important member of Parliament. As soon as we were jouncing along in a cab, Howard peeled off my glove and clasped my hand. "*¿Cómo te va?*" He kissed me fervently with a lot of tongue and begged to hear everything. After holding myself together for so long, I admit that I fell apart a bit with the dear earl's arms around me. I even told him about my love affair with Diego, I couldn't help myself, and that my lover was dead. He was very understanding, and the story cooled his ardor enough for him to be able to be more comforting than raptorial.

At Heron Court I met his aristocratic wife, who looked remarkably like a greyhound. They were a strange couple: he so round and jolly; she very long and lean. She was civil enough, and I was grateful to her for the invitation. At first I was sure she had no idea that the Spanish widow upon whom the earl had taken pity was in fact one of his former dalliances in the city. For several days, I simply slept, alone. I was so exhausted. For a few more days after that, I tried to be a better guest and give something back for the hospitality I was enjoying. Howard arranged a benefit concert for me at Heron Court, where I performed a dance to a number of Spanish ballads and sold several Spanish veils and fans to his rich opera-loving friends, wives, and daughters. (The fans were actually the earl's, collected many years earlier on his travels—from whom, I wondered with an inward smile.) I was the grieving widow all that week—the earl kept himself in check with some difficulty, but was also enjoying his own rising excitation—and then I accompanied him by train to London. By that time his wife was anxious to see the back of me—women always know when something is off—and she made it clear that Howard must return swiftly, with an unsullied bankbook. He informed me that she was keeping a close eye, now, on his expenditures.

So, after two secretive nights of nocturnal reacquaintance in his small Parliamentary apartment—which I found quite difficult, at first, and then a kind of sorrowful consolation—and having listened carefully to the rest of my fearful adventures, Howard began to muse with me on a plan.

"Her Majesty's Theatre is London's most prestigious stage, and I know the impresario, Benjamin Lumley, rather well," he said. "How *is* your dancing coming along now, Eliza—or shall I say, Doña Lola?"

I told him about my newly invented dance, based on the tarantella and, joy of joys, he announced that he had the score of the original folk dance, a souvenir of his travels.

"I will speak with Lumley. I'm sure he'll consent to meet with you. And after that, he won't be able to resist you. We must get you working—you must set yourself up. I am sorry for that, but . . . Do you mind, my dear?"

I remembered Carlota's words, that I should waste no time in finding my own way. "No, I don't mind. I wish it." And I really did.

A few days later, I met with the impresario. My raven hair, dark blue eyes, and long, shapely legs made a favourable impression, so Howard reported later.

"He said you had something piquant and provocative about you, and so he will allow himself to be 'taken in'—something I must let you know he very rarely does. He keeps rooms for dancers from out of town, and he'll find a place for you there. Of course Lumley realizes that you are a complete novice—"

"I am not!"

"—as a dancer, but it doesn't matter. You have something, and that something can bring in money. That's what counts."

The earl rubbed his hands together energetically and beat a happy tattoo upon his thighs. "He is scheduling your stage début for the third of June, when you will dance between the acts of a gala performance of *The Barber of Seville*. Is that not fitting? The queen's uncle, the ancient king of Hanover, will be there; London's bejeweled elite are expected to attend. The tickets are rushing out the door. It will be stunning, Lola Montez! *You* will be stunning."

I screamed and ran around, jumping up and down.

So, it was done, I had an engagement. It was to happen.

Now I had to dance. And that's when I realized: I'd spent so little time actually learning the basics, learning the techniques! Should I find another instructor? No, I decided, I would simply have to capitalize upon my innate enthusiasms and acrobatic body and continue to refine the dance through which I had seduced the Spanish prime minister. I called it *El Oleano,* a nod to the pretty, scented flowers which proliferate on the hardy oleander bush, flourishing in flinty, barren, unwelcoming ground. As I vowed to do.

Lumley found an empty studio for me, and I began to practice in front of the enormous mirror leaning against one of the end walls. Then I hired a rehearsal pianist from the money the impresario advanced me, and began my experiments in earnest. I added embellishments, thanks to the little princess, Luisa Fernanda. Tell a story. A young girl, a nest of spiders, a frenzy . . .

During the following weeks, word of the executions of the Spanish generals filtered into London and hit the newspapers. In my little room, I read them avidly, soaking the pages with my tears. The people had begun to turn Diego into a folk hero. His uniform—the one he and I had put to such delicious and unofficial use, now with six blood-stained bullet holes across the chest—was becoming a symbol of the government's corruption, and some were talking of putting it on display in protest. The cigars he'd handed out to the firing squad were to be added to the display—they hadn't been smoked; the soldiers honoured his gesture too much. Little by little, it seemed that public outrage was growing and spreading—Diego's final political act.

Shockingly, I also read that Grimaldi and his family were about to return to Spain so that he could take a position as statesman. Espartero's government had toppled, partly due to the people's disgust at the summary executions of de León and de la Concha. General Narváez, Cristina's choice, had now taken the reins, and she'd be returning to Madrid in triumph any day now. So I risked my neck, and Diego and Manuel lost their lives, for nothing, really. For a nervous mother's whim. A rich, powerful, twitchy mother's whim.

This is the way the world wags.

I thought often of Juliana de Porris during these weeks, and badgered the earl to write to her on official parliamentary stationary, but nothing came. It was her succour, above all, which saved my life when I was most in danger of losing it, and I pray she has not been made to pay for that generosity. I have added her name to my chosen one, proudly borne: Doña Maria Dolores de Porris y Montez!

As I rehearsed, *El Oleano* became an outlet for my fears and furies. The young girl enters, as if dancing gaily across a meadow of flowers, bending to sniff, and pick, and smile at the blossoms. This dance of joy section takes about five minutes, give or take my enthusiasm for the pastoral on any given day. Then, the girl discovers that she has stepped upon a spider's nest. There are little spiders everywhere, and not only are they little spiders, but they are little tarantula spiders! The sting of a tarantula, as everyone knows, can cause spasms, convulsions, and death. And think how many have leapt up her skirts! She grabs the ends of her skirt, whirling, shakes it up and down vigorously—thus revealing more and sometimes *more* of her legs, though she is moving so fast that naturally it is never a lewd or scandalous display. Besides which, she is a young girl, and every honorable man knows it is morally depraved to slaver over innocent children. Just as it seems that the poor young thing is about to succumb to poisonous convulsions, the little spiders run down her legs, off into the meadow. The girl, exhausted, breathless, spies the parental spider, standing hairily on the nest. The girl rushes over to it, begins stamping—take that! And that! It is the very poetry of avenging contempt.

And very curative.

I think my pianist wondered what on earth he'd gotten himself in to. But then Howard would come to watch, sitting with aristocratic hands braced on his spread knees, laughing uproariously, clapping immoderately, and the musical crosspatch would shrug to himself: whatever pays the rent.

Lumley cranked his publicity machine into action on my behalf. Malmesbury also did everything in his power: His circle of opera friends were all enjoined to purchase seats and bring others along. These friends were rich, and many of them were minor European royalty: Germans, various Saxons and Teutons, plus assorted former-barbarian toadies. One afternoon, about three weeks before the date of my début, Lumley sent along a friend of his own to watch my rehearsal. This friend was a critic from the *Morning Post*, who was to write me an advance piece. He was, therefore, a Very Important Person. I chatted him up, made him laugh a few times (cocking my head at the pianist to warn him to keep his eyes in his head thank you very much), and once the critic was sufficiently buttered, I danced for him.

When Lumley arrived a few days later to see the dance for himself, he reported his press friend's reaction: "He found you a sparklingly brilliant creature, Señora Montez, his very words. His advice, however, is that we must discourage viewers from comparing you with the classically trained French-Italian ballerinas; rather, we must insist that you are in a class by yourself, you are something that the English public has never yet seen: a bona-fide, purely Spanish, danseuse. Now let me see what we have."

I danced. Lumley was astonished, and went away, I think, happy.

The next day, the earl also brought along a pal to see the rehearsal. This pal was one of the minor royalty types, a German relative of Queen Victoria's, prince of a tiny little duchy or some such called something like Lohenstein-Abershof. His risible name was Prince Heinrich the LXXII. How do you have seventy-two male scions, all called Heinrich? Like ducks in a shooting gallery! Royalty is impossible! Listening to the silly middle-aged booby gas on about his castle and about life there with the bucolic peasants, I thought the entire place sounded demented. But far be it from me to insult a man's love. He stammered and flirted like the shy, red-headed bumbler he was, ending by inviting me to visit him in Lowerstummy-Avershoof (or whatever it was) any time, to view firsthand the life of a bachelor prince. Sounds exciting, I thought. In your dreams, freckled chum. He nearly wet himself watching my rehearsal. It was somewhat embarrassing, even for Malmesbury, who usually finds great amusement in such observational moments.

Finally—just a few nights ago, unbelievable!—I was given access to the orchestra for several run-throughs of the dance. They, too, seemed thunderstruck; bodes well, I thought. I am something brand new!

Then. Two nights before the début, I awoke with a startled shriek. I'd been dreaming of Emma, seen a bloody knife held to the side of her little, dark head. After that, it was impossible to sleep; all I could do was mull over what this could mean. In the morning, I hastened to the best jeweller and purchased an elaborately decorated jewel box. I went home, pulled my beloved peridot earbobs from my ears, and placed them inside: the only things I cared about which I'd managed to bring out of danger—my little girl, keep out of danger. I sent them posthaste to Aunt Cat and Uncle Herbert's address in Durham, with Emma's name on the outside and a note on the inside: "I hope you enjoy these for many years. I am told—I believe—that they bring luck. I think of you, my dear little one, very often, and of your dear ears. Believe me, I am yours. Aunt Eliza."

And as soon as I'm out of this dusty black hole of a room, away from the Cockney and the dour little European—oh God keep me safe—I will travel to Durham to see her for myself, to hug her and hold her and become part of her life. I swear it.

It's true, that dream had me rattled. It's easy to be bold in the middle of the day, surrounded by life and activity and an approaching large event which is consuming your entire focus. But darkness is a different story. The priest, the hellhound—I could no longer force the fear down. Where was he? His wound, had it healed? Was it slowing him down or making him crazier? I'd heard him whimper. He would never forgive that, I thought. That night, two nights before my début—just two nights ago!—I locked my door carefully and placed a chair under the door handle. And I sat back down on the bed, shaking. Looking at the handle, studying it. Holding my trembling fingers still in my lap and thinking. I could almost imagine a whiff of cigar smoke and the stable, a hint of the warmth of Diego's brown skin: "The only advantage you can count on is your own skill and daring, all other conditions being equal." A twirl of the mustache. "Never let your opponent gain power, turn the crowd, cause distraction by making you angry or afraid, or he'll destroy you utterly." Oh, Diego. Let me love you again. "Keep your head, trust your skill and your daring, and play hard, without fear. Do you understand me now, *Bandita?*"

And suddenly I did. I removed the chair from under the door handle. Courage. And shuffle the cards.

※ ※ ※

And so that is that. I danced my début. In my moment of triumph, the hideous voice denounced me: "That's not Lola Montez!" That voice, that spidery, attenuated shape—I danced it out of the theatre!

Then I clambered to my feet. Backstage, a new kind of chaos was erupting. The opera singers, stagehands, all seeming not to know their next moves. The stage manager finally hustled over, grabbed me by the shoulders and hissed, "Get the bloody hell to your dressing room, young vixen. Get off my stage."

Passing into the wings, no one would look at me. A group of excitable men in evening clothes, circling someone, whispering and gesticulating fiercely—circling Lumley, the impresario. I heard: "You'll be embarrassed, no, you'll be *excoriated* for perpetrating a fraud!" "—drag members of the nobility into a much worse scandal—" "I remember this young woman, she—" "Apprehend her!"

Run, Lola! Get to your dressing room, change into street clothes, grab your pistols. I hurried down the corridor, threw myself into the room, closed and locked the door, turned—and uttered a little scream: the earl of Malmesbury, his face red and sombre.

"My dear, what have you done?" He took a long swallow from the bottle of champagne clutched in his fist.

"It's the demon, the murderous devil who—!"

"What about this apparition?" He sounded tired.

I grabbed his hand, stopped him from taking another glug. "Is *here*, in the theatre! How or why I don't know but—"

The earl sank onto the settee. "Don't be preposterous."

"Here, I tell you! Coming to kill me!"

Malmesbury put his face in his hands, murmuring, "You know and I know, Lola sweet, Eliza mine, that the whole sodding Spanish story, though entertaining, can't be true." He raised bleary eyes at me, head wobbling. "You made it up, for me, for my delight. And it *was* delightful. But it's over now. You've gone too far, dear. I'm exhausted, can't keep it up."

I was flabbergasted, horrified. He hadn't believed . . . ?

As if he'd heard my shocked thought he added, "There *are* a number of nasty gentlemen out there, and many seem determined to pull down nobility who may, somehow and unknowingly, have become amorously entangled." His eyes all bloodshot, hair a rumpled mess, he suddenly looked much older than his years. "My wife is the rich one, you know. I am the lucky beneficiary of her bounty." What in God's name was he talking about? I took a hopeful step towards him.

He raised a hand to stop me. "I think, my dear Lola, that you are on your own."

And then—it was as if a chill wind had blown down the back of my dancing gown. The beast was there. I could feel it. I knew with certainty. It was coming, smelling me out, oh *dios mio*! No time to lose, no time for niceties—I reached into my makeup table's drawer, drew out the faux book with the pistols. Fingers shaking slightly, I broke each weapon and poured in the black powder, spilling some, then tamped it down. I placed the cap directly onto the first one so that it was fully loaded and dangerous. The cap for the other I pushed into my bodice, to the usual place. The earl was shaking his head at me—or was it just a drunken, muzzy attempt to focus?

"As a last favour," I whispered hoarsely, "create a diversion. I beg you."

I opened the door, peeked out; the coast seemed clear. Malmesbury was asking, "A diversion for *whom*, my dear?" as I fled in my dancing costume and bare feet down the corridor.

Outside, the stage doorman called after me, "Mind your way now, miss, remember what I told you!" And I was off down the alley, running like a deer. And then! I don't quite remember how, I *was* apprehended. Had they been in the crowd? Or backstage? I had no idea. They brought me here. To this room. The Cockney and the small man.

What's that?

They're coming, I hear them.

And Now: The Denouement

The dapper one stands before me, candelabra in one hand, a jug and a cup in the other. He is alone.

"Where is your thug?" I ask. I'm blinking and shielding my eyes from the suddenness of light, at last. "Where are my pistols? How did you take them from me?"

He places the tapers on the floor. "You're full of questions, even after all this time. To answer one of them: He won't be returning. His intentions were not honourable."

The man pulls a small loaf of bread from a pocket and holds it out. I snatch it, then try to restrain my haste. Take small bites. I need water.

"I only now discovered that my colleague did not leave you the meal we had prepared, nor the wine," he says. "For that, you have my apologies. I have sent for more, and hope this may tide you over until it arrives." He puts the jug down in front of me.

Water, thank God. I fill the cup. Never has anything tasted so splendid.

He moves around the room as he says, "I have finally finished my investigations into your alleged movements, Lola Montez. Talk to me. Tell me the truth of your involvement in international affairs—and understand, in advance, that I have been very thorough."

What to do? On the one hand, the first pricklings of relief: the Cockney thug, banished. Perhaps I'll make it out of this alive. On the other, trepidation. I sense he is uncharmable, this man. I do not know how to deal with men like this one. But I will not let myself show fear. I am Lola Montez, danseuse, friend of royalty and widow of a rebel hero. I am carrying the name that Diego and I created together. I will move into the future, never stay in the past.

"British authorities recently became aware, and then concerned," the small man continues, "about the Spanish dancing sensation—all that advance publicity—who suddenly appeared in our capital. When someone appears out of nowhere, it's going to raise eyebrows, correct?" I take another quick nip at the bread. "So I ask myself, on behalf of our government: Who is she? Where has she come from? Who has sent you, and what are you supposed to find out? Are you a papist spy?"

I remain silent, then sip from the cup. A papist spy? How ridiculous.

He looks very thoughtful, before saying things which astonish me. "I shall begin, then. In Southampton, the Spanish consul was happy to assist. Farther back, your trail was more difficult. Finally I unearthed a pilgrimage; the presence of an unknown, beautiful, young and *sometimes* mute nun was noted amongst the pilgrims, and at the border. Farther back still? Diego de León had never been married. You are not his widow. No papers, no records anywhere. Lola Montez, apparently, did not exist until seven weeks ago. When you set foot on English soil, madam."

Damnation! I lick my lips. They are suddenly so dry.

"You're an entertainer, this much is obvious." He just goes on and on! "But a charlatan, perhaps. A chameleon, certainly. You understand our dilemma?"

I must escape this room or expire! I have reviewed it all, for hours and hours. I believe I have it ordered well—what to say and what to avoid. Bluff it out, Lola! So I begin to speak, using my best Spanish-inflected English, and I tell him the truth, or a semblance of it, about many things and many people—Grimaldi, Cristina, Diego—with numerous references to the homicidal dangerousness of the Jesuit priest, presently loose in London, but nothing about my previous incarnation as Eliza Gilbert. Of course not.

When I finish, he surveys me with unreadable eyes. "If what you've just told me is true, why are you here? In England?" We stare at each other. Blast and damn! "You arrived with nothing, according to the Spanish consul—no baggage, no possessions—claiming your widowhood, then throwing yourself upon the mercy of the earl of Malmesbury. He's a government man. You know that, don't you?" When I nod in some confusion, he adds, "And so was Pedro Coria. He worked for us, for the British government. He sent dispatches back on a regular basis . . . Miss Gilbert."

What! How did—?

"Once he realized what was happening, Coria was actually trying to look out for you, both in France and in Spain—a giddy girl who had gotten herself involved in affairs far beyond her grasp."

Wait, Pedro Coria? The glass-eyed pirate was an *English* spy? My head is reeling, and not just from hunger.

The small man looks extremely stern now. "The earl of Malmesbury is a romantic fool and has been severely reprimanded. He may lose his parliamentary position over this. He should never have put the idea of a visit to Spain into your silly head. You are fortunate to be alive."

I have to sit down, and do so.

"In conclusion, Miss Gilbert—"

I want to interject and protest at his use of this name, but he holds up a prissy hand and won't allow it.

"In conclusion, it is as I suspected. You have cost us a great deal of time and money, but you are free to go."

I stand up again, ready to berate him and his sneaky government, hotly.

"You are free to go because you're a nobody, Miss Gilbert. You have simply gotten in the way."

At this moment, there is a knock at the door and a woman enters, carrying a tray. She sets it down on the floor, gives a little curtsy, and exits.

The dapper little shit turns back to me with a brief nod. "Good day to you. I have concluded that this is a case of insignificance, of fancying yourself to be important. Now go away and try not to cause any more mischief in the future, or you may not be so lucky," and he follows the woman, leaving the door ajar behind him.

※ ※ ※

Oh! I'm so angry I could spit! You bastard! I'm not, I'm *not* a nobody! I am Lola! I will make something of myself, you wait and see! You can't stand to see anyone this full of verve! You want to smash me, crush me, stop me from taking what joy and pleasure and power I can in this world. Well, I won't let you!

I burst out onto the street, and find myself, to my amazement, still in the theatre district. There's Her Majesty's Theatre, right over there! Sod it all and bugger boots! From the light in the sky, I guess it to be early evening—but of what day? First things first. I rush to the stage door and convince Bell, the doorman, to let me in. He is trying to tell me something, yelling words after me, but I don't stop to hear them. There are only a few stagehands about as I barge past and into my dressing room. But wait, the room has been emptied of my belongings!

This is part of a plot, it must be. They are taking away my identity, bit by bit!

The stage manager thrusts his uppity head inside the door. "Bell told me you were here. You've been dismissed; your contract has been cancelled. Get out."

I rise precipitately, looking about for my pistol—and would use it too!—except that it is missing. In that second, I realize that both of my darling muff pistols must still be in the hands of the small man and his thug, and that my poor cold feet are still bare! There's a riding crop on the floor, however, so I snatch that up, then nearly fall down again from lightheadedness, having rushed from my prison room so precipitately, and bypassing the meal that had been delivered. Oh, life is too cruel!

Now the stage manager rushes in and—this cannot be believed!—grabs me bodily by the back of my dancing costume and by one flailing hand, and propels me out of the dressing room, down the corridor, and past the stage where the singers are beginning to warm up their voices. All the while, with the other hand, I am trying to land him a good wallop with the riding crop, but he's agile, as if accustomed to dealing with all manner of wild cats. Or drunken actors. Which of course, he is. His assistant is following nervously with a bundle of my possessions in his arms: cloak, hat, dressing robe, and so on. As we approach the stage door, I manage to twist about and land the stage manager a good one, a neat flick and a sting with the tip of the crop, and a vivid slash of blood spurts forth from his cheek! Huzzah!

Before I know it, I am out on the street, my things are thrown out after me, and Bell has closed the door firmly. I even hear the key turn in the lock.

Bastards, all of them! I can't believe it. I must start again, do it all over again. I have no allies, obviously. I have been used! Abominably!

And then I stop still. I cease my stamping and snarling. Something feels wrong; a heaviness, suddenly, a concentration of malevolence. From the corner of my eye, I see it—a shadow detaches itself from the wall. A long, attenuated shadow with the breath of a snake. Holy Mary, Mother of God, it's the priest, stepping out from behind a stack of crates in an evening suit, as if he has been waiting there all along, waiting for me to return! I take off like a ball from a cannon: fly!

✣ ✣ ✣

The best thing, I tell myself frantically, is to twist and turn through these narrow streets, try to lose him, then head for the Strand. But of course I can't rely on my sense of place. I'm the idiot who can't find her way out of a matchbox! Is there a police station nearby? What do I know of this section of London except the theatre building itself? Why oh why don't I keep my eyes open and actually register what I see? Alternately castigating and encouraging myself, I run like the wind. Then I step on something horribly sharp, a broken bottle. *¡Mierda!* Now limping and panting, I hear booted feet. And gasping breath, gaining on me. Oh *Jésu*! Why am I always running? Through my head, nightmare images: the black-robed wolf falling down from the sky. A slender throat slit from side to side. A smothered baby. Fleeing on horseback, crouched over Lindo's ears. I look over my shoulder, and, oh God, how I wish I hadn't! Father Miguel de la Vega is swooping after me like a death dragon, lurching unevenly from side to side but still coming fast, mouth open and breathing fire, demon eyes blazing. We charge down the narrow dirty cobbled street, high brick buildings on either side hemming the world into one long rectangular cage, where I'll die like a rat, without a soul to mourn me. Still flying pell-mell, I check again, see him draw forth a knife which he flicks open! I let out an eldritch screech, put on a burst of speed, and—

Another shrill noise cuts the air. I can't place it, high-pitched and strange. I spy a small, filthy alleyway and bolt down it, pray it's not a cul-de-sac, but he's still with me, the limp very pronounced but not slowing him down at all. God, God! I'm dead! At any second I expect to feel the hair ripped from my head, the knife flung with great force between my shoulder blades—some horrible form of painful death. Another quick frantic check, searching about for a side alley, a landmark, anything at all! And then—wham! I fall to the ground, winded; so does the immovable object I've crashed into. A very big man in a funny hat.

"My God, look out!" I scream.

The man turns to look.

With the last of my breath, I wail, "He's a killer! Oh God, he's the killer of women! He's been preying on women! But he'll kill you too!"

Then, from out of nowhere, like some glorious *deus ex machina* duo, two other burly men charge, converging upon the hurtling priest. The Jesuit snarls and lashes out, and one of the men falls to the ground, blood gushing from an arm. The first big man and the third now converge, one grabbing the priest's knife arm while the other punches him hard. The flick knife is kicked away, Miguel's arms dragged behind his back and tied, then the biggest one sits on him. The other blows his whistle repeatedly while scrambling to the aid of their fallen companion, yanking a length of clean cloth from an inner pocket and applying a tourniquet to the gushing arm.

"Are you well, miss?" the big one says gently, as if he isn't sitting upon a madman's heaving body. "Has he hurt you?"

Policemen. The shrill noise—I can place it now. Their lovely whistles.

"No. No, thank God. And thank you." *London* policemen, thank God and bless them! If I was going to keep crashing into men, let them all be policemen!

"But your foot? There's a lot of blood, miss."

My foot? I barely noticed. "Will be fine, I trust. What about your comrade?"

"Can't tell yet. You must come with us, to aid our inquiries."

I don't want to stay anywhere near that depraved Spanish lunatic, whose head is twisting and writhing, whose torso is trapped beneath the large policeman's buttocks. "Do all women a favour," I say, unable to look any longer at the devil incarnate.

"And what would that be, miss?"

"If you can't kill it, incarcerate this thing in the deepest of dungeons, and throw away the key."

"After what he's done to the officer here, that might be fairly easy. And that's the only good thing about this whole sorry business, miss." Miguel turns his loathsome head to try to speak or snarl or spit, and the officer thumps it. The priest appears to have fainted.

"Oh dear," says the policeman. "Sometimes I don't know my own strength. Shame."

Almost before he's finished speaking, a police wagon drives up at speed. The unconscious priest is loaded in unceremoniously, with several more unnecessary, but hugely satisfying, thumps. The wounded officer is helped up to sit by the driver, looking pale but strong. My large friend turns to me and says, "We need you to accompany us, miss, but, as you can see, this conveyance hasn't the room for yourself. We'll send another."

"Send it to Her Majesty's Theatre, then. It's a cold night," I tell them, thinking fast. "I need to retrieve my cloak and belongings first."

"Right you are. We'll leave Thompson as escort. These are mean streets, as you no doubt know. Another wee thing snuffed out, only yesterday evening. Though we'd like to hope we've caught the man now, a young woman can never be too safe."

"That is too true, officer."

He turns to go, then, bashfully, turns back. "So you're with the theatre?"

"I'm a dancer."

"Is that a costume, then? With no . . . shoes or . . . ?"

"It is."

The big man is flummoxed, but perennially polite. "Very good, miss. May we be permitted to offer you the assistance of a pair of our boots?" We look down at his enormous footwear, then at the shiny black appendages on the other men—possibly even more immense—and look back at each other. I shake my head.

"But I'm grateful, I assure you."

As the police turn to step up onto the wagon, I stoop and grab the Jesuit's switchblade. It's small and deadly, about four inches of razor sharp steel. I flick it closed, and slip it into my waistband.

Thompson accompanies me to the theatre to retrieve my pile of possessions. I'm thinking hard the whole way. I'm sure that de la Vega *has* killed, while waiting to find me—two more young women, snuffed out to sate his lust. If the police believe the Jesuit is the murderer of the women, will they really need my testimony? The priest has the look, the smell, the *feel* of a killer. He doesn't even look like a priest—he's wearing evening clothes, a glittering tiepin. Surely they'll manage to make a conviction stick. The last thing I want, after everything that has happened, after all the betrayals I've suffered, is to go to a police station to "aid their inquiries" and be held there myself on some trumped up charge of who knows what. Indecency? Adultery? Being a divorced woman? Sleeping with members of Parliament? Consorting with spies? Using a false name? Oh my God! Any one of these will sink me!

A hundred yards from the backstage door, I stop. Actors and singers are still entering for the evening's upcoming performance; stagehands stand about, smoking. They may recognize me and spill the beans that I've been released from my dancing engagement.

"May I ask you, officer, to kindly go around to the lobby and fetch an important envelope that is waiting for me there? Name of Lola Montez."

"But—"

"I do not wish my public to see me. It would cause too much of a stir."

He scratches his ear, no doubt thinking, Theatre people, they're a right odd lot. But he lumbers off down the alley. I can see him burling his way through the crowd on the main street, and then he's out of sight.

Mind whirling, I grab my cloak from where it lies in the street. I'm thinking: The night may be cold, but England's too hot for me. What to do, where to go. I have no home, nowhere I belong; I can't even narrow it down to one country. Nowhere. At this exact moment, outside the stage door in the dark unsafe alley, I feel more alone than I've ever been before in a lifetime of lonely wandering. I walk down the alley towards the street, look over at the glittering mob clustering at the front entrance, jostling and laughing, the mob which was mine the previous night, all mine. They'd never seen anything like me, and now? Well, it's as if they don't know, or care. I turn away, in the opposite direction, move down the street, hugging my cloak around my shoulders.

Hooves clatter by, and a carriage. I hear the clanking of bridle bit, the creak of reins. There is a face at the window as the carriage is passing. At first I think: a stranger, staring at a woman, sizing me up, wondering if I'm a lady of the night. *¡Hijo de puta!* Why must they always think this! I'm ready to spit curses when I recognize the face. "Heinrich?" I call up to it. "Heinrich the seventy-second?"

"Indeed," comes the stammered answer, then, "Stop the horses." He goggles at me, says, "I had to miss your opening last night, Señora, so I came tonight instead. I've been told you are cancelled. I was so disappointed, because I am leaving for my homeland in two days. The newspapers are stupid, *nein*? I hope you're not paying attention to what they wrote. But what are you doing out here, in the cold?"

The door is pushed open. I hesitate about three seconds. Then I hop in.

The horses are whipped up. I lean back against the cushions, let the man burble on excitedly. My mind racing in all directions: Emma, my dear little unknown girl. I made a promise to myself last night that if I got out of this safely, I would go to her. But if I go to her, I'll be Eliza Gilbert again. And then there's the madman! Will I be forced to appear, to testify against him? As Eliza Gilbert again. I'm still shuddering with fear and revulsion, the need to put distance between myself and that loathsome creature. *Significant* distance. Which leads me to another thing. I also told myself, when the Cockney and the little shit first left me in that damnable room, that if I ever got out, I would go to America, land of liberty, assertiveness, and impulsiveness! Americans are not afraid of a woman like me, with an excess of verve and a crack shot with a pistol! Lola will survive. Lola must seek fame and fortune in a new land, a bright and wild frontier! Even if she must first escape to—to the German countryside? Someplace like Lowersbum-Bovinehoof? Why not?

I close my eyes, sit very still. Emma, I'm so sorry. Some day I'll make you understand, I promise that. Your Aunt Eliza will come home, famous and rich, and whisk you up into the life of your dreams.

Think about that later. I'll just rest a minute. Just to catch my breath.

Carefully, slowly, wiggling my bare toes, curling my fingers like soft paws, Heinrich the seventy-second's reedy voice riffling along on the edges of my consciousness. England is a backwater; London a rat trap. I must seek my fame and fortune elsewhere. Leave them behind, the lot of them. They've used me, cruelly. Now I will use the world, in its freest sense.

I allow myself to be seduced, by this. By sleep.

AFTERWORD

HISTORY BOOKS AND BIOGRAPHIES are silent on the hows and whys of Lola's sudden transformation, as was she herself. This deficiency of facts, of course, gave me plenty of room to imagine something big for her to journey into and through, as fiction. Perhaps some readers will be interested in discovering which is which; if so, you might enjoy consulting the books mentioned below.

The real Lola loved to exaggerate and embellish—and with Lola the adventure comes first. In the novel, time is somewhat elastic, even altered—certain events which may factually have happened in 1841 may have ended up in 1842, so that Lola may be part of them.

I am deeply indebted to historians and biographers: To David Thatcher Gies, for his fascinating study, *Theatre and politics in nineteenth-century Spain: Juan de Grimaldi as impresario and government agent* (Cambridge University Press, 1988). I'm equally grateful to Edgar Holt for *The Carlist Wars in Spain* (Putnam and Company Ltd., 1967).

For excellent biographies of Lola Montez, I cannot speak highly enough of Bruce Seymour's *Lola Montez: A Life* (Yale University Press, 1996). His fascination and amused admiration for her is clear in every line; his research is staggering. I also consulted *Lola Montez* by Amanda Darling (Stein and Day, Incorporated, 1972), for a different perspective.

The aforementioned writers took great care to get the facts straight. A trip through Lola's world would not be complete, however, without reading her own autobiography and her lectures, always in print—a fact that, in itself, would astonish and amuse her, I'm sure (*Lectures of Lola Montez Countess of Landsfeld Including Her Autobiography*, Kessinger Publishing's Rare Reprints).

From the time of her trip to Spain until her early death in 1860, Lola whirled her way around Europe, America, and Australia, causing heads to turn and tongues to wag at her audacious exploits with lovers, whips, and pistols. She traveled almost unbelievably far and wide for a woman of that time. She danced in the Paris of Alexandre Dumas, George Sand, and Franz Liszt; she was in Bavaria on the arm of a King during the uprisings and revolutions in Europe in 1848; she followed two gold rushes, one in Australia, the other in California. The place in the world in which Lola seems to have felt most at home was America. She first arrived in 1851 and performed in Manhattan. News of the gold rush in California was beginning to stir things up, and Lola must have felt drawn to the unfolding adventure in the west. By 1853 she was settled in Grass Valley, riding horses astride, keeping up her excellent marksmanship, and playing with a pet bear. The house in which she lived is still known as Lola Montez's cottage. There is even a mountain named in her honour (Mount Lola) in Nevada County, California. She was witty as well as a true raconteuse, so a number of years later, when she began to tour America again as a lecturer, she attracted large audiences to her new venture. She spoke on topics such as *The Art of Beauty* and *Comic Aspects of Love*, and continued to dance, reviving again and again her famous *El Oleano*, or Spider Dance.

From the first moment I read about her, Lola Montez made me laugh. My biggest acknowledgement, then, is to her—a sparky woman who would not be kept down. A million thanks, Lola.

A huge hug to my wonderful partner, Andrew Willmer, for his unflagging enthusiasm over long periods of time, as well as fact checking, map reading, pushing and extending his technological frontiers on my behalf, and miscellaneous research in many crazy directions. *Ti amor!*

Many thanks to Astor + Blue Editions, particularly to my publisher, Robert Astle, who was keen on this idea from the beginning, and gave me the encouragement and the push that I needed. To Tony Viardo, thanks for welcoming me aboard. To Ali Bothwell Mancini, enthusiastic and insightful editor, *mucho gracias.*

I owe a debt of thanks to writer George MacDonald Fraser for the countless hours of reading pleasure I enjoyed—as teenager and then as adult—with his wonderful Flashman series. Inspirational fun!

Other thank yous—to Concordia University for sabbatical leave during which I had the time to research and write the first draft; the following friends and acquaintances for writing time in beautiful places: Keith and Alice Green for Fonte Pecciano in Umbria, Alan and Carole Pearson for Trullo Patrizia in Puglia, Marina Cervelli for Il Bizantino in Venice, Bruce and Kathy Willmer for their cottage in Ontario. Also, thanks to Caroline Davis and her book club in Hilo, Hawaii, for her thorough, early notes and then for their enthusiastic responses to the novel as a book club read; Frances and Michael Corbett in Gioiella, Umbria, for early exuberance; Raymond Lee in Ohio for expert advice on historical firearms—any mistakes (or exaggerations) are undoubtedly my own; Vern Thiessen, for technological advice; and to Helen Heller, for getting me up and running, a big thank you.

About the Author

KIT BRENNAN WAS BORN in Vancouver and grew up in Kingston, Ontario, Canada. She is a nationally produced, award-winning playwright, and teaches writing and storytelling at Concordia University in Montreal, Quebec. The Victorian era and its personalities have always been a big interest for Kit. Her play *Tiger's Heart* explores the life of Dr. James Barry, who was a woman who lived her life disguised as a man in order to practice medicine, which was not an option open to women at the time. Kit divides her time between the vibrant city of Montreal and the quiet wilds and beautiful lakes of Ontario, with her husband Andrew and a variety of animal friends. *Whip Smart: Lola Montez Conquers the Spaniards* is her first novel. Visit her online at www.kitbrennan.com.

Photo by Andrew Willmer.

Forthcoming from Kit Brennan and published by Astor + Blue Editions: *Lola Montez and the Poisoned Nom de Plume*.